D0922710

The Library of Scandinavian Literature

CLENG PEERSON

Volume I

ALFRED HAUGE

CLENG PEERSON

Volume I

TRANSLATED FROM THE NORWEGIAN BY
ERIK J. FRIIS

INTRODUCTION BY
KENNETH O. BJORK

LIBRARY OF SCANDINAVIAN LITERATURE

TWAYNE PUBLISHERS
A DIVISION OF G. K. HALL & CO., BOSTON

Library of Congress Cataloging in Publication Data

Hauge, Alfred.
  Cleng Peerson.

  (The Library of Scandinavian literature; v. 28
  Slightly abridged translation of the author's trilogy published
separately under titles: Cleng Peerson, hundevakt; Cleng Peerson,
landkjenning; and Cleng Peerson, ankerfeste.
    1. Peerson, Cleng, 1782-1865 — Fiction. I. Series.
PZ3.H29257C   [PT8950.H3374]   839.8'2'372   75-9740
ISBN 0-8057-8153-6

The Library of Scandinavian Literature
Erik J. Friis, *General Editor*
Volume 28
Cleng Peerson I, by Alfred Hauge
The original published and copyrighted by
Gyldendal Norsk Forlag, Oslo
Copyright © 1975, by G. K. Hall & Co.

Preface

The fact that *Cleng Peerson*, Alfred Hauge's widely admired novel, appears in an English-language edition in 1975, the year in which the Norwegian Immigration Sesquicentennial is being celebrated, is indeed a source of gratification to the author and the translator alike. We also feel deep satisfaction at the work having been selected as an Official Publication of the Sesquicentennial celebrations in the United States.

In these days of greater emphasis on and interest in one's ethnic heritage, Alfred Hauge's epic novel, which hews close to historical fact, will serve to familiarize American readers with a significant segment of pioneer history and with the influx of Norse immigrants who first settled in New York but later made the Midwest what to many seems to be their special domain. And Norwegian-American readers, many of whom may have roots in this country going back to the time of Cleng Peerson, will have their sense of the past and its continuity into the present greatly strengthened. *Cleng Peerson* is not only a fine biographical novel; it also vividly reconstructs life in Norway of the early eighteen-hundreds as well as frontier life at the time the United States was a young nation; and it is above all a hugely entertaining story. The prizes it has earned its author were indeed well deserved.

Cleng Peerson appeared in Norway in three volumes, published by Gyldendal Norsk Forlag, and immediately attracted attention on both sides of the Atlantic. Great interest was expressed from time to time in vi

the possibility of having the book translated into the language of the descendants of the Sloopers. And when I first met Alfred Hauge we immediately agreed that this might be a project on which we ought to cooperate. We felt that the work should be cut by about 10 or 15 percent and should appear in English in two volumes. Mr. Hauge did the cutting himself, and I think one can say that he has used the bluepencil very judiciously and has not infringed on the flow of the story. Those who have read the original may notice that the Thirty-third Tale in Volume One (originally the First Tale in Volume Two) now appears in a more chronological order, and certain liberties have been taken with some of the Prologues and Epilogues.

A note on the Norwegian monetary system of the time, which may be confusing to the modern reader: The basic units of currency of Norway and Denmark were the speciedaler and the rixdaler, which equaled 120 and 96 skillings respectively. The value of the dalers were the equivalent of 4.00 kroner for the speciedaler and 3.20 (2.00) kroner for the rixdaler. The real value of this currency in terms of purchasing power is of course hard to estimate. Incidentally, the krone became the sole official currency unit in 1873 and 1875.

A literary work of the magnitude of *Cleng Peerson* cannot possibly be turned into another language without the aid of various individuals and institutions. To the Norwegian Cultural Council, Oslo, go my heartfelt thanks for a grant that enabled me to translate the first two volumes of the original trilogy. Support for the work on Volume Three came from Mr. & Mrs. Orson Hill of Creston, Illinois, and it is here gratefully acknowledged. My thanks are also extended to Mr. George Strand of Fox Valley, Illinois (where so many descendants of the Sloopers live) for the great interest he has taken in the translation project. Lastly, my deep appreciation is hereby conveyed to the Norwegian Immigration Sesquicentennial Commission, Inc., New York; the Norwegian American Immigration Anniversary Commission (1825 - 1975), Chicago; and Scandinavian Airlines for materially supporting the actual publication of this translation.

ERIK J. FRIIS

Introduction

It is appropriate that in 1975, the 150th anniversary of the beginning of organized Norwegian migration to America, Alfred Hauge's fictionalized trilogy about the career of Cleng Peerson, the "father" of this migration, should appear in English in only slightly abridged form. People of Norwegian descent will welcome the opportunity to read about the eccentric Peerson, and they will now be able also to learn more about the passengers of the sloop *Restauration*, who left the homeland in 1825 and established the first Norwegian settlement in the New World. Hopefully, too, the reconsideration in 1976 of our beginnings as a nation, together with the present interest in ethnicity among all Americans, will assure the even wider reading that Hauge's work deserves.

Alfred Hauge, although well known in the Scandinavian countries, makes his first appearance in English in this publication. Born in 1915 on a farm at Sjernarøy, some thirty miles northeast of Stavanger and not far from Peerson's birthplace, Hauge knows the life of the coastal people who combine their struggle with a stubborn soil with fishing and sailing. From his mother, who told her children from memory the familiar stories from the *Arabian Nights*, Hans Christian Andersen, the novels of Dickens, and other sources, he developed an early interest in literature. From the Stavanger district, strongly influenced by piety, he inherited a feeling for religion that characterizes his writing. His ear, sensitive to the local dialect, easily mastered the New Norwegian *(nynorsk)*, which is largely based on the traditional speech of the country's western coastal districts, and he was to use this language effectively as a literary medium in later years.

Although yearning to be an author, Hauge was convinced while still very young that he must acquire an education and master a craft that would enable him to earn a sure living. He left home at the age of fifteen to attend school, and graduated in 1935 from the preparatory school *(landsgymnasium)* at Voss. It is significant that, in qualifying by examination to become a university student, he received a prize of 500 kroner for the "best artium style in Norway in New Norwegian." In 1935, he began the study of theology at the Independent Theological Seminary *(Menighetsfakultetet)* in Oslo University. Two years later he transferred to the Teachers College in Oslo and graduated from this institution in 1939.

It had been Hauge's intention to resume theological study, but since leaving the seminary he had begun a literary production that was to continue to the present and to divert him into activities other than serving parishes of the state church. He was a teacher in the Fredtun Folk High School at Stavern from 1939 to 1945, literary adviser at the Ansgar Publishing House in Oslo from 1945 to 1951, a journalist with the newspaper *Vårt Land* in the same city from 1951 to 1952, principal of the Ryfylke Folk High School at Sand from 1952 to 1953, and, finally, a distinguished journalist with the *Stavanger Aftenblad* after 1953.

Hauge's literary career began seriously in 1941 with the publication of the novel *Septemberfrost*, a veiled attack against Nazism and the German occupation of Norway. Since then he has written some thirty volumes of novels, poems, plays, children's books, travel narratives, essays, and short stories. In recognition of his work, he has been awarded the Norwegian Association of Critics' Prize in 1965 for *Cleng Peerson* and the Norwegian Cultural Council's Prize in 1967 for the novel *Mysterium*, as well as other prizes. He has also been the recipient of a variety of travel grants from such organizations as The American-Scandinavian Foundation and Nordmanns-Forbundet and also from the Norwegian government. He is a member of the leading national societies of authors, critics, and dramatists. For a couple of decades he has served as a member of committees that are working on a new Norwegian hymnbook, and he has been a member of the committee that performed the preliminary work on a new translation of the Bible. His interest in language is indicated by his membership on the

Norwegian Language Jury (Språknemnd), and in politics by his cultural services for the Liberal Party.

Hauge's major artistic activity includes arranging and writing for other media. For some time he has worked on a cycle called *Utstein Kloster* ("Utstein Cloister"). One of the novels in the cycle has been adapted to the opera *The Legend of Svein and Maria*, which had its premiere at the Norwegian Opera in 1973. *Cleng Peerson* has been dramatized, and it was presented at the Rogaland Theater in 1970. His recitation *Hafrsfjord* was written for the 1972 International Music Festival in Bergen in recognition of Norway's beginning as a united kingdom 1100 years earlier. He has also prepared prologues for a number of church and national occasions.

In 1962, Hauge made an interesting study trip following in the footsteps of Cleng Peerson and the earliest Norwegian emigrants by way of England and Madeira, across the United States — both east and west and north and south — and afterwards he wrote the book *Gå vest* ("Go West"). Similarly, in 1972 he led a company of interested persons over the same route. When not traveling, he works in his study-dwelling Sjoarbu, which he built near his birthplace at Sjernarøy. From it he frequently departs to participate in radio and television programs. He is currently working on a new long-range historical project which deals with the present century. The first volume, *Perlemorstrand*, appeared in 1974.

It is not easy to describe Hauge's *Cleng Peerson* except by saying that it is a three-volume fictionalized biography of its major character and fictionalized history of the Sloopers, as the passengers on the *Restauration* came to be called. *Hundevakt* ("Dog Watch"), the first volume, appeared in Oslo in 1961. Like the succeeding volumes, it is made up of "tales" supposedly written by Peerson from his last home in Texas to "Anne," who once called him "father," and it carries the story to Cleng's first voyage to America in 1821. Three years later appeared *Landkjenning* ("Landsighting"), which tells of the *Restauration*'s voyage in 1825, the pioneer experiences of the Sloopers in the New World, and Peerson's first trip into the Middle West. *Ankerfeste* ("Firmly Anchored"), the final volume, which was published in 1965, concentrates on Cleng's activities thereafter as a promoter of new settlements but also carries the story of the Sloopers to the Fox River Settlement in Illinois and of their subsequent experiences.

An enormous task indeed, even if it were possible adequately to document the career of Peerson. Hauge acknowledges his indebtedness to those professionals who have written the history of early Norwegian-American migration — especially Theodore C. Blegen and Ingrid Semmingsen — but above all he expresses his gratitude to J. Hart Rosdail for his book *The Sloopers: Their Ancestry and Posterity.* To a considerable extent Hauge follows historical sources; yet he does not hesitate to treat them cavalierly at times, and much of what he writes is pure fiction, although fiction largely justified by his purposes and intent as an author.

More significantly, perhaps only fiction can paint anything like a living picture of Peerson. The many informal titles that have been given to him — "the father of Norwegian immigration," "pathfinder," "advance agent," the "Peer Gynt of the prairies," "vagabond," "scoundrel," and others — suggest the interest and disagreement that attend his career in America as restless leader, promoter, and colonizer in the story of Norwegian migration to the United States. There is about him that aura of mystery and romance that leads to endless conjecture and controversy among scholars. Legend and speculation will continue to play major roles in discussions of Peerson for some time, as there is actually very little in the way of reliable documentation of his activities — the few letters that he probably wrote, the written remarks of some contemporaries, and oral stories passed on by Sloopers and others to later generations.

In evaluating Hauge's trilogy, it is perhaps most helpful to attempt to present the consensus of scholars in their interpretation of Peerson. There is general agreement that he was born in the year 1783 on the farm Hesthammer in Tysvær parish, which is in the Skjold district of Stavanger *amt* (now Rogaland *fylke*), a short distance north of the port city of Stavanger. Originally called Kleng (or Klein) Pedersen Hesthammer, he apparently traveled as a young man on the European continent. It is reasonable to suspect that as early as 1818 he had difficulties with the Lutheran state church, and it is probable that, as a young man, he married an elderly widow of considerable wealth.

In 1821, when only thirty-eight years of age, Pedersen (Peerson) journeyed to America in the company of Knud Olsen Eide, almost certainly as the agent of a small group of Quakers and other pietists who were contemplating migration to the New World for religious and economic reasons. While in America, until 1824, he and Eide suffered considerable hardship from lack of money. If we accept a story in the *New York American* of October 22, 1825, a fund raised by the Stavanger group for the exploratory journey was lost when the business of the man in whose hands it had been placed failed, and the two men were forced to work. Eide in time became sick and died. Peerson traveled about the East on foot, going as far as to western New York, studied the economy and customs of the land, and later sent a report of his discoveries to the prospective emigrants in Norway. Neither Eide nor Peerson was a Quaker and they were not agents of the Society of Friends in Stavanger, but the leader of the men they represented was Lars Larsen, who was both a formal member of the community of Friends and very active in it.

Cleng returned to Norway in 1824 and naturally reported more fully on the prospects for settlement in the United States. In the summer of that year, a number of persons with Quaker and Haugean sympathies decided to leave the homeland. Peerson, after only a short stay in Norway, returned to America, this time accompanied by Andreas Stangeland. The two men spent some days with Cleng's friends in New York City, then proceeded to Albany by steamer, and worked their way to Troy and Farmington, where Peerson also had friends. Leaving his comrade, Cleng walked to Geneva to reserve land for himself and his Norwegian associates. He secured six tracts of land on the southern shores of Lake Ontario in Kendall (now Murray) township, Orleans County, about thirty-five miles northwest of Rochester. The land transaction that he made with Joseph Fellows — a Quaker who was the agent in charge of the Pultney Land Office in Albany — was to be valid until the following fall. Writing to his family and friends in Norway in December, 1824, Peerson said he was erecting for another person a house that would be completed by New Year's, and that in the spring he would build on his own property. He already owned five acres that he intended to clear in time for planting in the spring, a cow, and some sheep. He also reported that friends in Macedon would care for his sister and others until their cabins were built. There should be little difficulty, he added, in selling a small vessel in New York; his friends there would assist the passengers in the sale.

Obviously encouraged by Peerson's optimism, the prospective emigrants in Stavanger raised a sum of 1,800 specie dollars (about $1,400) and purchased a 39-ton sloop renamed the *Restauration*. A cargo of rod iron was loaded for sale in New York. On July 4 or 5, 1825, fifty-two persons — including a crew of seven — sailed from Norway in their tiny vessel. The passengers included ten married couples with children — all but two from the countryside — an unmarried woman, and some unmarried men of varying ages. A child was born to the Lars Larsens during the voyage. Contrary to popular belief, only one of these passengers, Lars Larsen, was an actual member of the Stavanger Society of Friends, but it is believed that at least seventeen of the Sloopers were in fact Quakers in faith, if wives and children are included in the count. The others were Haugeans or sympathizers with them and the Friends.

Two historical events explain the composition of the passenger list. The first was the pietistic revival in Norway under Hans Nielsen Hauge in the late eighteenth and early nineteenth centuries. In some respects this movement resembles the Methodist revival under John Wesley in eighteenth-century England; in others it can be likened to Puritanism. While Hauge and his followers did not separate from the state church, they were denied by law the freedom of religious meetings outside the regular churches, and lay preaching was punished. Like the Puritans of England, the Haugeans were also advocates of social and economic betterment.

The Quakers — few in number, having only small societies in Stavanger and Christiania — were an interesting product of the Napoleonic wars. In the last of these, Denmark and Norway were the reluctant allies of France and both were victims of the British blockade. Captured Danish and Norwegian sailors and privateers were held captive on ships in British ports. Those at Chatham were visited by Friends and some, converted to Quakerism, later brought the religion to Norway and retained connections with fellow believers in England.

It is well to emphasize, however, that the Sloopers were also influenced by economic considerations. Their country had experienced seven years of war, during which a considerable part of the population was reduced to acute suffering and poverty, largely the products of the blockade. When peace finally came in 1814, it was followed by years of hard times and high taxes, and the heaviest burden fell on the rural population. Both the Haugeans and the Quakers were among the poorer elements of the country as well as a minority persecuted by the state for religious reasons.

The *Restauration,* after sailing through the English Channel, traveled as far south as Madeira. According to Ole Rynning, an early writer about conditions in America, the sloop drifted leaderless into harbor at Funchal, after its crew had drunk the contents of a floating cask of wine that was brought aboard. Despite the fact that their flag was not hoisted when they arrived, the passengers were well received by officials and the local inhabitants as well as by the residing

American consul. If wine was near to being their undoing in Madeira, whiskey, which they had sold illegally, had come close to creating serious problems in an English port — again if Rynning's report is to be trusted. All that we know for certain is that — after a long, trying, and circuitous journey — the *Restauration* arrived at New York on October 9. Cleng Peerson was on hand there to greet the passengers; he was not one of the Sloopers as Hauge indicates.

It is perhaps not strange that New Yorkers showed considerable interest in what one newspaper called the "novel sight" of the Sloopers, a quaintly dressed group with almost no knowledge of English, who had shown great courage in crossing the ocean in so tiny a ship. More seriously, the Norwegians soon learned that they had been grossly overcrowded, thus violating the clauses of an American law of 1819 limiting the number of passengers in Atlantic crossings on a cargo-tonnage basis. Despite a lenient interpretation of the law by officials in New York, the Sloopers were saved from a major predicament only by a pardon signed by President John Quincy Adams. They were less fortunate in the sale of the sloop, for which they received a mere $400 — a great disappointment, but a fate better than the outright confiscation permitted by law.

Cleng Peerson proved to be extremely helpful to his compatriots in this as in other situations. He secured aid for them from local Quakers and other sympathizers. Also of assistance was Fellows, the land agent, who, like Peerson, met the passengers on their arrival. Most of the immigrants left by a Hudson steamer after a week and a half in the city, and, thanks to the recently opened Erie Canal, came to their new home in early November. They were charged $5.00 an acre for their land in Orleans County, and each adult received a tract of forty acres. Payment was to be made in annual installments over a period of ten years. Obviously, neither they nor Peerson realized that there was better land, easier to clear and selling at lower prices, farther to the west. They were, in a sense, victims of the land speculation in New York stimulated by the construction of the Erie Canal.

It has been said that twenty-four Norwegian settlers at Kendall built a log house which was their only shelter during the first winter. Some found work with American neighbors, but their lot for several years was hard: they were poor, many became sick, and the language barrier was serious. Their land was heavily timbered and difficult to clear, thus delaying the day when they could raise crops to support themselves. Their friendly neighbors, themselves poor, could offer only limited help. Peerson did as much as he could during these years to secure aid from Americans elsewhere, but the results were meager. In time the lot of the settlers improved, but many remained dissatisfied.

Again it was Cleng who became their trailblazer. Never fond of heavy work, he was perhaps happy to take off in 1833 in search of desirable land to the west. Traveling on foot, he penetrated Ohio, crossed Michigan, and went through northern Indiana into Illinois. It is possible that on this journey he walked from Chicago along the western shores of Lake Michigan as far north as to the site of Milwaukee. There, from Solomon Juneau — according to legend — he was told that Wisconsin land was heavily timbered and otherwise unsuited to settlement. Peerson returned to Chicago and continued from there to the Fox River Valley in Illinois. Near Ottawa, in Mission township, La Salle County, he found a site that was to become the second Norwegian settlement in America. Peerson later told how, on first viewing the Fox River country, he was reminded of Moses and the Promised Land. Returning to Kendall, he completed a pilgrimage that had extended over two thousand miles.

The dissatisfied settlers at Kendall responded to Peerson's report of the New Canaan in Illinois. In 1834, six families moved there and established the Fox River Settlement. At the time, La Salle County and the whole Illinois River Valley was experiencing rapid occupation, and improvement schemes filled the air. A half dozen years before Peerson visited the region, a land grant had been made to aid construction of a canal from the Illinois River to Lake Michigan, and work actually began on it in 1836. Settlers assumed that the canal would connect with the river in La Salle County, not only providing an opportunity for them to work at construction but also raising land values as the Erie Canal had done in New York. When the Norwegians arrived, land along the Fox River was available for $1.25 per acre, and access to markets promised to be excellent. They took up claims in 1834, and in June of the next year Peerson and his associates from Kendall made their purchases. Other Norwegians, both from Kendall and directly from the homeland — and almost certainly influenced by Cleng — joined the first contingent to settle in the townships of Rutland and Miller as well as in Mission. This settlement was to become a vital center from which later immigrants were to proceed farther west into Wisconsin, northern Iowa, southern Minnesota, and beyond.

Thus far, Cleng Peerson's influence on Norwegian migration was unmistakable, and it has generally been conceded. Thereafter, however, with minor exceptions, his counsel was ignored by his countrymen.

Some of the earliest settlers at Fox River were disappointed in the area, and later immigrants soon found the best land taken. A group of disillusioned settlers asked Peerson in 1836 to search for a new and more promising location. Cleng, instead of traveling northwestward, as subsequent immigrants were to do, selected a place in Shelby County, in northeastern Missouri, and on his return reported an abundance of land west of the Mississippi. Trusting Peerson, a dozen or more prospective settlers left Illinois with their leader, going first to Hannibal and from there driving to a place some twenty-five miles from Shelbyville, took claims, and built cabins. Lacking money, the Missouri settlers knew very hard times. Far from village and mill, the settlement was all but isolated from the stream of life. Even so, Peerson, again in New York in 1838, was able to persuade a party of new arrivals to leave with him from Rochester to Shelby County. Other new recruits came in the same year and the next, but the project was unsuccessful and the settlement soon began to break up. Among other reasons for this was a natural desire among the Norwegians to follow the crowd into Wisconsin and their strong dislike of slavery.

Some of the dissatisfied immigrants in Missouri moved to southeastern Iowa, where they were joined by people from Fox River in the Sugar Creek Settlement, founded in Lee County in 1840. Cleng was also associated with this project, and probably was sent there by the immigrants in Missouri to hunt out a suitable location. In all probability, he also lived for a time at Sugar Creek.

The restless Peerson returned to Norway in 1842 and while there most certainly stimulated emigration. *Bergens Stiftstidende* described him as an emigration agent who had been active in Voss and Hardanger, and pictured him before a company of fascinated peasant listeners — damning Bishop Jacob Neumann, an outspoken opponent of emigration, and singing the praises of Ole Rynning, a champion of the New World. Cleng answered the paper by letter, saying that, while he was entirely in favor of America and would confirm Rynning's account of it, he was no agent and had not attempted to provoke emigration from Voss and Hardanger, which he had not visited. But he returned to America in 1843 with a party of emigrants.

In 1847, Peerson joined the Swedish communitarian colony of Bishop Hill, Henry County, Illinois, where he also married a second time, but soon returned, sick, to the Fox River Settlement — leaving his young wife. He set off for Texas in 1849, to investigate possibilities there for his countrymen, and next year was back in Illinois in an effort to interest settlers in the eastern part of that state. There, he said, his countrymen raised good crops — even though they had not selected the best land and had settled too closely together — and enjoyed a fine climate. He clearly regretted the heavy migration into the upper Mississippi Valley, which to the end he considered inferior to the South. In September he returned to Texas with a small party, which he guided to Dallas County, possibly hoping they would help him to realize a dream of a more widely dispersed settlement of Norwegians. There he lived out his days, supporting Elise Wærenskjold in her public defense of Texas. A few years later he moved to Bosque County, and there, surrounded by Norwegians, he died in December, 1865.

There naturally remain more questions than answers about a person such as Cleng. One is whether or not he could write. The evidence seems overwhelmingly in the affirmative. In addition to the letters already mentioned was a long one from his pen in *Democraten* of Racine, Wisconsin, on September 7, 1850, favorable to Texas. But it is true that he wrote very little and was most effective as a storyteller. Norwegian immigrants could think of nothing more exciting than a visit by Peerson, who held old and young alike spellbound with accounts of his travels. One wonders, therefore, why Hauge structured his book as a series of *written* — rather than *related* — tales. It is extremely doubtful that, even in his last years, Peerson would have had the patience to write the full contents of the trilogy.

Hauge raises a much more important issue: the extent to which Peerson, at least in his earlier years, sought to influence the Norwegian immigrants into living in common after the manner of the Shakers, Harmonists, and similar utopians. There is reason to believe that he made some efforts in this cause. Mario S. De Pillis maintains that he was "the father of Norwegian-American communitarianism and perhaps of Norwegian-American dissent." He quotes Ole Rynning's remark of 1838 that "Cleng Peerson's endeavor was . . . and is still, to unite all Norwegians into one community owning all its property in common." De Pillis mentions, among other things, the discovery of a letter written by Cleng on June 27, 1826, to the Harmonist (Rappite) colony of Economy (now Ambridge), near Pittsburgh, asking for a loan of $1,600 to buy 400 acres of land in the Kendall settlement by early 1828. The money, according to the letter, was essential to alleviate the sufferings of people who were "poor and penniless" and were hoping to build a sawmill. Six Kendall settlers cosigned the letter.

There is no way of knowing whether or not the loan was granted, nor is the letter in itself proof of Peerson's communitarian tendencies. De Pillis points to a possible Shaker influence on Cleng; it is interesting that the Shakers had settlements relatively close to Kendall, and headquarters near Albany. He also mentions Quaker associations with the Shakers in England, the ready response of Norwegian converts to early Mormon communitarian projects, and Peerson's residence at Bishop Hill. It is quite possible, too, that Cleng visited either Economy or Harmony, Indiana, in his wanderings, and was thus influenced by the Rappites. That communistic colonies were no strangers to the early Norwegian immigrants is further illustrated by the attempt of Nils Otto Tank in 1850 to establish one in the Moravian settlement at Ephraim, near Green Bay, Wisconsin.

The Norwegian rural population, although of a ruggedly individualistic bent, was characterized by a strong sense of community, and this spirit was naturally enhanced by the persecution experienced by Quakers and Haugeans alike. It seems unlikely, however, that the Sloopers had anything like the religious fervor and unity essential for successful utopian colonies of the kind founded by the Shakers, Harmonists, Hutterites, or even Mormons.

It remains to comment briefly on the translation of Hauge's *Cleng Peerson*. The task was fortunately undertaken by Erik J. Friis, director of publications for The American-Scandinavian Foundation and general editor of the series in which the book appears. His profound knowledge of Norwegian literature and his rich experience in the publication of English translations of Scandinavian literary works are combined with a sensitive mastery of both Norwegian and English. Hauge wrote his trilogy in *bokmål* (or traditional literary Norwegian) to capture the spirit and overtones of the "America letters" written by the immigrants. Friis had the difficult assignment of rendering the Peerson story in an English that would retain as much as possible of the character of the simple but powerful language of the original. He has succeeded remarkably well.

One of the great strengths of Hauge's work is that it gives an excellent description of the background of earliest Norwegian migration — not only the plight of the Quakers and Haugeans, but the whole structure and nature of Norwegian society — and especially the lot of the farmers and fishermen. Fortunately, most of this material is retained in the American version, volume one of the translation ending about midway through volume two of the original trilogy. The two-volume *Cleng Peerson* in English is deserving of a warm reception and will offer fascinating reading for Americans of all ethnic origins.

KENNETH O. BJORK

St. Olaf College
Northfield, Minnesota

CLENG PEERSON

Volume I

Prologue

Cleng Peerson was a wanderer, always on the move, like a drifting cloud or a ship under sail. His wanderings took him far, across distant oceans and through strange countries, and everything that he heard and learned and which he found to be of importance, he would pass on to others. When Cleng arrived at a farm, the people would stop working as if it were a Sunday evening, and old and young would gather around him to listen.

Some say that he was mostly concerned with making his stories sound interesting and that he would put little stress on their veracity; let us hope he was not indifferent to either requirement! Now he is an old man, almost seventy-six years old; his knees are bent under the weight of his body, and the hand that holds the pen is shaking. It is he himself who writes the following.

I was born on the farm Hesthammer in the parish of Tysvær, in Stavanger County in Norway, on May 17, 1782. As was the custom in those days, I added the name of the farm to my given name and my patronymic and called myself Kleng Pedersen Hesthammer. When I had lived in the United States for some time, I dropped the name of the farm and, people began to anglicize the spelling of my name. That was all right with me — I pay no great attention to such matters.

The first time I arrived in America was in 1821; the second time was three years later, and when the immigrants on the sloop *Restauration* arrived in New York harbor on October 9, 1825, I was there to bid them welcome. My sister Kari, who later called herself Carrie, was one of them.

These are the people I want to tell about: the approximately fifty souls who entrusted themselves to the Atlantic and to the Almighty; they saw nothing but ocean for more than one hundred days and nights, except when they sought shelter in the harbor of a small town on The Lizard on the south coast of England, and when their ship lay at anchor at Funchal, the capital of Madeira, for about a week.

Both before this voyage began and later on they were buffeted toward many storm-lashed coasts by the shifting winds of fate. Most of them have long since arrived in the land beyond the last horizon, and in a little while, whether it be days or years, and they can hardly be numerous, my small vessel will follow in their wake.

I will here recount what they themselves told me, and also what I have seen with my own eyes. If in the process it becomes an account of Cleng Peerson himself, then so be it! I hope it turns out to be sincere, as behooves an old man, and candid, like the speech of a man to whom the judgment of others means very little.

I am writing to you, Anne, because you called me father, and I loved you as if you were my own child, and you knew how to listen. When I close my eyes, I can still see your face before me, transformed by the flickering light of the fire, and your eyes large in wonder. Many a night we slept under the open sky, and many fires were lit during our long journey from Milwaukee to Fox River. You were a child then; now you are a wife and a mother. You must take your children in your lap and once again tell them these stories when the wind whispers in the grass on Cleng Peerson's grave.

Today is January 8, 1858.

On New Year's Eve I was visited, as so often before, by Norwegian friends from the neighboring areas; there are many of them living in Bosque County now. As was customary, they brought meat, bread, and fruit, and other good gifts, and when we had finished eating, I lay down on a bench with my knitting — you know it is a habit of mine — and I began to tell about the land that we had left; Norway is still in everyone's heart.

Then Ovee Colwick said, "Put these tales of yours down on paper! You have no worries now and plenty of time."

True enough; I turned all my worries and my lack of time over to him when I gave him my house and my property; as you know, the state of Texas presented me with 320 acres of land in appreciation for my having brought Norwegian settlers to the state.

Nevertheless, melancholy will often haunt an old man; life is on the wane and death is waiting. Perhaps it was just for that reason I replied, "Yes, I will write them down." The truth of the matter is, Anne, that in spare moments over the years I have made notes and jottings; the big drawer in my desk is half-filled with loose papers. I want to put it all together to the best of my ability and fill in wherever something is missing. Take it for what it is! I could always handle a rifle better than a pen; I have no pride to worry about as a writer, and you certainly are not a dull-witted person.

Our journey in time takes us back to Norway, to the city of Stavanger, from which the *Restauration* sailed, and the county of the same name.

The county of Stavanger no longer enjoys any status or renown worth mentioning, although it does seem to me that people in many other places live in smaller cottages and under lower roofs. But in a distant past this southwestern part of Norway was the most powerful region of the entire realm. Even before the saga age, we find that kings and chieftains made their homes here, in strongholds and on great estates. From these coasts they launched Viking expeditions to distant lands, and the men of Rogaland — Rogaland is the ancient name of the county — discovered Greenland, and later on Vinland, which is America.

But the age of greatness was followed by a period of decline. For many generations the people struggled under the sway of a foreign power, and what was left behind by famine was taken in levies by tyrannical rulers. Destitution was a frequent guest in many a home.

My own parish was reckoned to be one of the poor ones in the county. Marshes, heather-covered hills, and rocks and mountains were our heritage, and fertile soil had been meted out by nature in a niggardly manner. Our parish could be compared to a gray and hungry tongue jutting out from the blue throat of the fjord. But who doesn't hold his own home dear and deem his neighborhood to be the most beautiful? If you would ask me that question today, Anne, my answer would be: Tysvær could be compared to the Land of Goshen, more fertile than any farm in Bosque County!

The cold weather would seldom spoil the grain in our parish, but rain can also ruin a harvest, and it does happen that a cow falls down dead in the barn, and that the sea withholds from us its bounty. Then a man may be forced to chew on birchbark like a goat, uttering curses or prayers, or suffering in silence.

The farm Hesthammer is located near the southernmost point of land in the parish, on a plain facing the Bokna Fjord. A small river runs through the plain; it runs slowly, and rushes grow along its banks. The stars and clouds of the sky I have seen mirrored here; I have even seen my own face reflected in the stream, noticed it shimmer and disappear and then come back sharp and clear. In due course my childhood lay behind me, and I asked myself for the first time, "Who am I?" Later on I would ask myself that question quite often, just as people have done in all ages; but none of us has ever gotten an answer that we are fully satisfied with.

In the same way, it can be said that we ask about so many things: such as why I should become the one who led the first immigrants across the ocean to America. It seems to me that no one was less qualified, and less worthy!

In the past, the town of Stavanger too had been more resplendent than it appeared during my childhood and youth. Among its residents few were rich and many poor, in spite of the fact that a grapevine had been placed in the city's coat of arms and its ships were on the seven seas. Only the old cathedral, dedicated to St. Swithun, testified to the grandeur of the past.

Such is the character of the county: Far to the south, nature is savage, the soil barren, and mountains abound, to such an extent that a priest is said to have called it "the land that God created in His wrath." Farther to the north there is a wide and waving plain, where the horizon retreats for miles and miles, but the land is still very unlike the prairie. Rocks are strewn about everywhere; toward the west there is nothing to be seen but the ocean, and nothing but hills to the east.

A wide fjord basin, with fertile islands, cuts into the land at Stavanger. Farther inland huge rifts separate the mountain peaks from which the snow never entirely disappears.

But where the coastline and the shores of the fjord merge with the rolling hills, there lies Tysvær.

This is a region in which there are big differences as to both nature and the conditions of life enjoyed by people; I believe there is no other area of its size in all of Norway that displays such great contrasts. For many years the place seemed to me to be so distant and faraway, but when old Cleng today thinks back on his younger days, Tysvær once again appears so clearly to my mind's eye as if I were actually seeing it.

Here I spent most of my life until I turned forty; here I encountered much that was good as well as evil, and I myself was both good and evil. Here I roamed about on land and sea. But in our own hearts, too, there are seas to be sailed, there are forests to be traversed, and wastelands in which to lose one's way, and there are roads leading either to the house of the publican or to the house of God.

This is what I want to tell you about. And I say to myself: There sits Anne, on the chair by the window in the house that Ovee Colwick built for me. I know that you live thousands of miles from here; you have a husband and a child, and your hands are kept busy with tasks from dawn to dusk, and your feet are never still; but now I shall fetch you and carry you here, and you are lighter to carry than the time I found you next to your dead parents' bed in Milwaukee. They were lying in the straw, and their bodies had begun to stink; the ravages of the cholera have never been as severe among us Norwegians as that year. Do you remember that I asked you your name? "Anne," you answered. "Then you must be Norwegian!" I said. And after your parents had been buried, we set out for Fox River together.

Welcome to Bosque County, Anne. Sit down by the window, and just let your eye take in merely what is right before you, as the seasons change and my tale progresses; I won't finish very soon.

In the garden grow such plants as thrive in our southerly clime; the sunlight and the wind play hide-and-seek in the top of an old oak tree. Farther away the cotton makes the fields gleam white, and perhaps you can see the cattle lumbering over to the watering-place. Wild plums and grapes and pecan trees with juicy nuts grow along the riverbanks, and the hills in the distance are covered wtih flowers in all the colors of the rainbow. There are plenty of turkeys, ducks and pigeons, rabbits and deer in the hunting grounds, and if your husband had also been here, he would surely take off with his gun once in a while. I myself am no good at it anymore; my hands are shaking and my eyesight is failing. All I can do is to walk around on the farm, carrying a child on my back; the end of my life is being spent as a beast of burden. But never mind! Have I deserved any better? That is why I gave away the land that the Texas legislature had given me; but I am proud of the fact that the highest authorities called me "the father of immigration"; that is a name I like to be known by.

We thrive here, we Norwegians; the countryside has much in common with many places in Norway, but the plant life is more luxuriant, and the climate is warmer. Just look, Anne, the fields are green, even now, in the middle of January, even though they were white only a few days ago. But the snow disappeared in an hour when the sun and the south wind returned, and cows and sheep and goats can resume their grazing. And soon it's time to put the seed in the ground.

I have no worries that the farm work is not going to be done at the right time and in the best way; Ovee Colwick is an able farmer. But maybe I'll go out and have a look just the same. And a little boy or girl will come over and want a ride on Uncle Cleng's back; and I will lift them up — I can still manage two at a time — and I say to myself, "Soon your bones will find rest in the earth, Cleng Peerson, and you need not fear it; you have grandchildren, and the family name will go on from generation to generation."

That is the way I dream and imagine things, Anne. For you know that I have neither children nor grandchildren, even though I was married twice. Fortune never smiled on me in the matter of love and marriage.

Most of those who crossed the ocean in the summer of 1825 belonged to the Quaker persuasion even though only a few were listed as members of the Society. For this faith of theirs they had been persecuted and had suffered greatly, and when they traveled all the way to these shores it was for the purpose of maintaining inviolable freedom of the spirit and freedom of conscience. Yes, they sought freedom above all, and I was allowed to be their servant, their guide, and their pathfinder. I myself did not become like one of them; the sincerity of my heart did not suffice. But I saw that their teachings and their way of life were good and noble.

Much has been said about Cleng Peerson: Some have maintained that he was a pious man, others have called him a heathen and a freethinker, a few even claimed that he was a swindler who deserved to have been whipped and there were those who said that he was a righteous man. God help my poor soul!

But I have a few tales to tell, and you are going to hear them, Anne. We shall go back to our source, to the land where it all began.

The First Tale

The first thing I can remember is a sunrise. The sun rose up behind the mountains beyond the sea, and it seemed to be on fire and enormous.

I do not know how old I might have been then. At times it seems as if that morning belongs to another existence, before the time I was born.

It must have been many years later that I decided to journey toward the region where the sun rises; but in my memory there is no semblance of distance.

I stretched my arms out to the sun and they were reddened, and a feeling of great joy rose within me and made me cry. The only circumstance that I remember about my departure was that it was twilight and I was standing in the doorway of our boathouse at Kårstø. From within exuded a sweet and acrid smell of rotting fish and pitch-stained nets. The boat lay by the jetty. I untied it and jumped in. Perhaps the weather was windy; it drifted away from shore. Whether there were any oars in it I do not remember; I hadn't learned how to handle oars yet. I must have thought that if only I went on board and wished to get to the land of sunrise, then the boat would find its way. And it did.

When the night came, I didn't see the shore any longer. I was afraid of the dark, and even more afraid of the gleaming phosphorescence in the water. But there was one thing that made me feel safe: a bumblebee which was aimlessly roaming across the sea; quite invisible, it was buzzing all around me for a while.

Perhaps I was hungry; at any rate, I was thirsty. I lowered the bailer into the water, filled it, and drank. The taste of the water was salty and bitter and I spat it out. Later on I must have been sleeping, but the wind woke me up, aided by the rushing waves and the tossing of the boat. The clouds were hanging low, a light rain had made the thwarts and the floorboards soaking wet. I got down on my knees and licked the moist wood and my tongue no longer felt large in my mouth. It was almost daylight, but I merely saw the land as hazy, retreating outlines far away. Fear welled up in me; I felt a violent desire to step outside the gunwale and it almost overwhelmed me, as if I was convinced that I could walk on the water. I found a piece of sailcloth and put a corner of it in my mouth and bit hard, and my fear flowed out of my body through my teeth.

Later on I spread out the sailcloth between two thwarts, and crept under it, lay down, and tried to get some more sleep, but the moisture penetrated my clothes, and I was freezing. Then I suddenly discovered that a little man had joined me beneath the canvas cover. I saw him quite distinctly, even though it was dark underneath the cover.

I was neither frightened nor amazed. When he began to talk to me, his voice was friendly and subdued.

"Why are you alone out here on the ocean?" he asked. "I'm going to the sun," I replied. "It is far," he said, "and it is not certain you'll find it." "It rises right behind a mountain," I said. "Can that be so important?" he asked. "It's all dark in our house," I said, "There's no light in our parlor." "Don't you have windows?" he said. "Yes, we have a window," I replied, "but it's dark just the same, because my father's face is so black." "Is his face black?" the little man asked — I understood clearly that he didn't believe what I confided to him.

"Father just sits there, and he gives off no light," I said. "Is he supposed to give off light?" the man asked. "Almost everyone gives off light," I said, "you know that." "No, I didn't know that," the man maintained, "do I, too, give off light?" he asked. "You give off the light of night," I said, "and my mother gives off the light of day. But just because my father is dark, she doesn't give off light any longer. She carries food in to him, but he doesn't eat, and when she says anything to him, he doesn't answer." "Are you going to bring the sun back home with you?" the man asked, and I said to him, "No one can bring the sun back with him!" "What do you want, then?" he asked, and suddenly I felt perplexed, and I began to stammer, "Just to be there, just to see it."

An entire day and an entire night must have passed. The weather became misty, and the boat and the boy seemed completely alone in the world. I became terribly hungry; I chewed on the piece of canvas, and I tried to slake my thirst by licking the thwarts again and again. The little man had disappeared, and I missed him.

I slept fitfully, but when the next day dawned I was awake and saw the blue sky above me; in the direction from where the sun was to appear, the sky had already taken on a red tinge. The wind had died down, the waves had turned into a calm swell, and my boat was drifting near a rocky shore rising sharply up to form a rounded mountain top. Around the peak I saw a ring of light, and suddenly I knew it: Now I have reached it. The sun will rise right behind it.

Just then the boat touched land; a small tongue of land was jutting into the sea just at that spot. I climbed up on the gunwale and jumped, and I felt firm ground underneath my feet. The boat must have drifted away; I didn't see it, and I didn't think any more about it.

I felt neither hungry nor tired as I was crawling up the slope which gave little foothold. Sorrel and white clover were growing there, and I picked a bunch and stuck it in my mouth.

Not until I got close to the top did a feeling of weakness sweep over me, and I trembled. The luminous ring at the summit of the mountain sparkled in the brightest colors; I was staring into a scintillating void: Now it is going to happen!

What did I expect was going to happen? I do not know. What I do know is that my disappointment knew no bounds when I stood on the top of the mountain and saw the sun so infinitely far away, high above a pale-blue peak. I wanted to cry, but I couldn't, and I dropped to the ground face down. Then once again the little man was standing next to me. He said nothing, he merely looked sadly at me, and I didn't dare ask him anything. Suddenly he turned his back toward me and was gone, and since that time I've never seen him.

I saw some houses in the distance, and I thought to myself, "I must get over there!" The mountain sloped just as steeply on the land side as on the ocean side, and I climbed along escarpments and held on to grassy tufts on the very edge of dark abysses, and at last I got down without a scratch. On a low isthmus I crawled over large round boulders and then I once again reached more level ground. I discovered berries growing in among the heather, and when I picked one handful after another and had eaten for quite a while, I sat there for a long time, staring into a spiderweb that was stretched between the twigs of a little willow tree, bright with dew. The mooing of cows in the distance called me back to the present; I got up and waded on through the heather; it reached to my shoulders. At last I was standing on top of another steep slope, looking down into a long and narrow channel that separated me from the place where the houses were. I was on a small island, and I had no boat.

But there was an abundance of berries on the little island; there were bumblebees that buzzed and dragonflies with transparent wings, and rock faces upon which the sun was shining, transforming them into red portals.

My greatest need was also fulfilled in all this natural splendor: Through my half sleep I heard human voices, and when my eyes were no longer blinded by green and fluttering shadows — for I had been lying with my face turned toward the light — then I could make out human figures over on the other side of the isthmus, at the spot where I had been before: A man was mowing, a woman was raking, a boy was playing down on the beach; he was throwing white shells into the water of the inlet — on its surface there was hardly a ripple.

I ran toward them through the heather; I fell down and got up, I shouted. Out on the isthmus I slid down among the boulders and scraped the skin of my bare leg, and my wooden shoes were filled with salt water from the rising tide. Just then they caught sight of me. For a little while they stood there without moving; then the woman put down her rake and hurried down toward me.

"Where are you from?" she asked. "I don't know," I answered; "it's far away." "Did you come drifting in a boat?" "No, I wanted to come here." "Why did you want to come here?" they both asked.

Suddenly I recalled the little man who had been with me in the boat and again at the highest point of the island, and I thought to myself, "I don't dare say what I wanted to do here." "Are you hungry?" the woman asked. "Yes," I replied, and she opened a small box and a bundle, and she put some flatbread and herring on a stone, and next to it she placed a large bowl of sour milk. I ate my fill, and then I fell asleep.

When I woke up, the sun was very low in the sky, and the three others had made themselves ready to board their boat. "Where is your home?" they asked once more, and I answered, "I don't know," and I began to cry. "We'll find out," said the man, and I went along with them in the boat.

The next day every one knew that a child had been found on the little island, but no one had heard about any child that was missing.

A week or so passed. Then one day my father stood in the doorway. Was he angry or was he happy? Well, maybe both angry and happy, but that was of less importance. What was all-important was that the light was again lit within him. "Father is speaking again, Father is eating," I almost shouted for joy. I ran over to him, and he embraced me, I burrowed my head against his chest and felt him twitch as if he suffered a convulsion; I hid my face in his beard, and I heard his mouth emit a sound which was neither crying nor laughter; since then I have heard that sound a few times in my life, and I know what it means: The burden of a great sorrow is being released and recedes from the mind.

This was in the evening; early the next morning we made our departure. I had been told that the island on which I had landed, was called Finnborg. The thought has occasionally come to me that if my soul does not find rest after I am dead, I will want to return to that place and roam about among the willows and the gleaming cobwebs.

But when we were walking toward the shore, I suddenly stopped short and put my feet wide apart; I bent down and, looking back between my legs, saw the world upside down as if transfigured: The fields were greener, the air clearer, the sea was more brightly blue and glittered from the light of the sun.

And my father said, "What are you doing?"

I answered him, "I want to see everything just the way it was that morning."

"Which morning?"

"The morning I got to the island."

"What did you see?" asked my father.

"I saw everything," I replied, "just the way it is."

Through the arch of my legs I saw the world as if in a concave mirror. Thus can a child search for a lost paradise and later we continue to do so, each in our own way and along separate paths until the end of life. Who of us found what we were seeking?

There was hardly a ripple on the surface of the water when we cast off. Father was rowing, but after a while the wind rose, and father hoisted the sail. While he was busy doing that, I noticed that the palms of his hands were red like the flesh of a slaughtered animal. A feeling of tenderness welled up inside me, and I thought, "If only he keeps his hands open just a short while, if I put my face down close to them, I may touch them with my tongue, the way I licked the damp thwart when I was thirsty — ."

The years passed, and many things happened that have been forgotten during a long life. As I begin to write, the images once again rise up within me. They are dear to me, just as almost everything is dear when the distance is great, and I could tell you much, but I have other things in mind. Just a few more memories, so that you will know something about my childhood, Anne. For we change very little from childhood to old age. A little boy has always lived within me; a little boy who laughs and cries.

I roamed about in the outlying fields of our farm; it was a day in winter, without any snow, a long time after my boat trip; I was about eleven or twelve years old. Then I met a woman with a load of brushwood on her back. The load was heavy and the woman was small, but it seemed as if she could manage it. All the same, I made her put the load down, I asked her where she lived, and I carried the load to her house. I chopped all the wood for her and brought it into the woodshed, and kept it up until dark, and in the moonlight I walked home across the hills.

I had not done this for her because of any kindness on my part, but because I thought that her mouth looked like a helpless cry. If you want to find something out about a person from his appearance, Anne, then first notice his mouth, then his hands, then his eyes.

Once my father asked me to walk over into the woods and fetch a lamb. It was my lamb, and he wanted to slaughter it. We had only eaten fish for a long time, and Father would at times feel such a great urge for meat that he could barely control himself. He used to chew on pieces of tanned hide; he would walk about restlessly, saying, "If we only could have some meat!"

We owned other lambs, and we had sheep and goats, and I refused to go and get the one that belonged to me; I wanted it to live. "You go and get it!" he said and had an evil glint in his eyes. "I will not go," I said. Then he seized the poker and swung it above his head, and I thought to myself, "I will not yield in this, and I'll find a way to make him give up the idea." Since we were going to have breakfast, and Father was already seated at the table, I went to the woodshed and placed my hand on the chopping block and struck off the little finger on my left hand; I carried it in and placed it on a piece of flatbread and said, "Here's a piece of meat for you, Father."

He looked at it and then at me, and I held out my hand so that the blood was dripping down on the bread. His face became ashen like wax and his mouth looked like a narrow gray line; he got up and went out.

But my lamb was allowed to live.

As far back as I can remember, my father had from time to time been in the grip of a deep melancholy. At such times he was silent and depressed, and hardly ate or drank anything. Mother had to force him to eat, but he lost weight just the same and was at times so weak that he could scarcely stand on his feet. When he at last, once again, was at his usual place at the table, we knew that a horrible time was coming to an end. His first meal he would bolt down without any moderation; he would eat until he vomited, and if it so happened that he thought my mother had put too little food on the table, he would collect everything down at his end: porridge, herring, and whatever it might be, and we others were not allowed to touch any of it until he had pushed the leftovers away from him and told us he was full.

But when the cycle of starving himself and then overeating had come to an end, he was completely changed: he was friendly, amiable, and full of fun, at times even excessively jolly — until he once again, unexpectedly and without any good reason, shut himself in behind an invisible wall where we couldn't reach him, either through words or good deeds.

Hesthammer was a farm that originally was assigned to the pastor at Skjold, who received the profit from it as part of his salary, and Father had to account to the minister for the farm yield and the latter's rightful share of it. The minister there in those days was Ananias Dyrendahl. When he died, he left behind him the reputation of having been a man of great integrity, with a warm heart, a thorough theological education, and a wide knowledge of ancient history. The last-mentioned was very true, but he managed to hide his warm heart from us at Hesthammer, and he practiced his righteousness more by demanding his own right than by giving others their due. He saw to it that he received his full measure, even though there had been a crop failure or a bad year for the cattle or the ocean had been less bountiful.

One day in late winter — I might have been about twelve years old — the pastor's farmhand came riding over the hills with a message and a warning: Dyrendahl would show up next week and collect his share of flatbread and meat according to the lease.

It was part of the terms that Father himself was to bring the pastor's share to his house, but the harvest had been poor, and if we delivered all the flatbread we were duty-bound to give him, there would be very little left over for those who had done the actual work.

One night I overheard Father and Mother discuss this after every one had gone to bed. "We'll have to ask for an extension," Mother said. "He never grants an extension," Father said. "Like many others we'll have to be satisfied with scraping the bottom of both bins and barrels, but you know as well as I that in his own storehouse the meat is rotting and the bread gets moldy from old age." "We've never starved at

Hesthammer," Mother replied. "Are you sure you can say that?" Father said.

Finally I fell asleep, but I woke up some time during the night. I was lying in the attic underneath the slanting roof; a little bit of light came in through a crack in the timbered wall. I peeked through the crack: I saw Father standing in the middle of the large attic room, between the empty bin and the stack of flatbread. He was dressed in his Sunday best, and his hair and beard were combed as if he were to read from the book of sermons. He held a burning tallow candle in his left hand; he raised his right arm over the flatbread and cursed it: "May it burn as sulfur on the tongue of him who is going to eat it; may his belly burst and his guts rot; may his excrement be like tar, and the water he passes be blood! May his flesh rot and his bones molder! May he never in eternity eat his fill, since he robs the poor man of his bread!"

He spoke in a muted and mumbling voice, and I was seized with a great fear, for I realized that he was about to make a leap into darkness. Perhaps that was just the reason why I felt convinced that his curses actually had the power which he attached to them, and somehow I would have to save the minister in order that these terrible things should not befall him. And how could I remain silent if the curse were consummated? Would I be able to live with my secret knowledge when the agonies of the minister became evident to every one?

Father lowered his arm, he blew out the light, and I heard his shuffling footsteps across the floorboards and down the creaking stairs.

Father did not come to the table the next morning. He sat silent on a stool over by the fireplace, with his hands in his lap, staring vacantly straight ahead. Not until some time during the forenoon did he get up and go out. He started to carry stones from a rock pile located a short distance from the house, bringing the stones into the farmyard and placing them in front of the door leading down to the earth cellar. He kept on doing the same thing the next day also. At last he got so tired that he was reeling as if he were drunk; Mother had been unable to make him eat or drink; he did not answer when talked to and did not open his mouth at all.

On the third day he began to carry the stones down into the earth cellar, and when that had been done he at last walked into the kitchen and asked for some food. That made us happy, and we hoped that perhaps his mind was clearing. When Mother put some flatbread on the table, he asked if it had been taken from the large stack or from the small one. "From the small one," Mother answered. "That's good," he said, and he began to eat in a deliberate manner and with great dignity as if he were a guest at a great feast.

This was a Saturday. On Sunday morning he got up while every one else was still asleep; he filled the large kettle in the fire-house and lit a fire under it, and when the water was hot he poured it into the wooden tub. He undressed and took a bath; then he put on his best clothes, unbolted the door, and went out.

Father was a good-looking man, tall and erect, with an unusually full beard which had not yet started to turn gray. Mother was just about to go to the cow barn, and it was my day to help her with the chores; we ran into him in the middle of the farmyard.

"Have you put on your best clothes so early in the day, Father?" she asked. "Yes," he answered. "Are you going some place?" "I'm going to church," he replied. "But you won't get there in time, Father," she said. I noticed her fear, like a white flicker, in her eyes. The church in Skjold was about twenty miles away, and it was difficult to travel on that road in the winter when there was snow on the ground. To row across the fjord would take hardly less time.

"I'm not going to church today. I'm going to church tomorrow," he answered. And he looked up to the sky; it was cold and cloudy. "It's going to snow," he said.

It began to snow right after that, smoothly and evenly; the fields were covered and gleamed in the twilight when the clouds drifted away and the moon rose.

Father had read in the book of sermons as was his custom, and there was nothing about him to give cause for alarm the rest of the day. He said very little, but we were used to that. I thought to myself, "Maybe he'll be well again soon."

The pastor came on Monday afternoon. He had traveled overland, for during the night a storm had come in from the north. The snow had collected in huge drifts, but it was not so bad that one couldn't travel in a sleigh.

Father did not rise when he entered the room. The pastor flushed all the way up to the hairline, and the muscles in his cheeks were twitching. "Aren't you getting up, Peder Jansen?" "No, I'm sitting," Father replied. "How dare you show contempt for the ecclesiastical authorities?" Father answered, "I'm not remaining sitting because of any contempt, but because the pastor is subordinate to me; he is in my employment and in my pay; he is fed when I stretch out my hand and starves when I withhold from him the needs and the nourishment of the body." "I think the man is possessed!" the pastor snorted. "That time the pastor used the right word: possessed, even though he has not yet received any sign or proof of it," Father said, "but from now on it won't take long." "I'm going to take away from you your position as administrator of the Hesthammer church property," the pastor said. "That position I've already voluntarily given up," Father replied.

Then the pastor turned around and said to Mother, "Go and get me the bread."

I went with her up to the attic. We placed the large stack on a wooden tray, put a white piece of cloth over it, and carried it down.

Flatbread is thin and brittle, as you know; one cannot fasten or attach it to anything with the help of ropes or bands. For that reason I was ordered to sit behind the driver's seat and keep it in my lap so that the storm would not sweep it away.

In my distress I had thought of telling the pastor about Father's curse on the bread, but now I perceived another solution. I jumped quickly up on the driver's seat, and Mother gave me the flatbread; the stack was so large that I was just barely able to get my arms around it. The pastor placed himself on the front seat and took the reins.

The wind was blowing harder than before, strong gusts whirling the snow up into the air. While we were at the middle of the bridge, a sudden squall pounced on us very conveniently, and with a sudden flip of the hand I threw the flatbread up in the air. The wind took care of the rest. Floating through the air, the flatbread looked like a large bird with brown wings. The bread careened above the river; there was ice on the water along the banks but there was none in the middle of the river. The bread sailed along on the water like little boats before it sank to the bottom. And whatever did not land in the river was swept away by the drifting snow, crushed into crumbs, and spread all over the fields.

The pastor stopped the horse with a jerk. His face was almost blue, and he shouted, "You did that on purpose, you little devil!"

I could have answered yes, but I told him, "No sir; you must not be angry with me, for when you brandished your whip it hit me in the face, and the pain made me forget myself. Do you want me to gather all the crumbs together?"

"Let the crumbs lie there for the ravens and all the devil's ilk," the pastor said; "jump out of the sleigh and get yourself home. You'll pay for this prank! For two whole years you'll have to study with your pastor before you are accepted for confirmation! In truth, you are as stubborn as your father."

I obeyed the order; the pastor applied the whip and the horse reared and started off at a trot. I turned around and walked back to the farm.

That day also Father was dressed in his Sunday best; it was as if a cloud of solemnity and of horror surrounded him. He asked Mother to place the food on the table: "All the kinds of food we have in the house," he said.

As we were sitting at the table, Father broke the bread himself and doled it out to each one of us, like a patriarch of old, as the Saviour did on the last evening He was together with His disciples.

Father was silent for a long time, but suddenly he began to sob, and with tears streaming down his cheeks and into his full beard, he put out his hands — they were brown from the specks of grain in the flatbread, and he was sweating in every pore — his voice cracked: "I've loved you all so deeply, very deeply." And he got up and clasped Mother's head and pressed it against his chest, and from her he walked over to each one of us children, and he stroked our hair and face very gently, and to all of us he said farewell.

Mother had risen: "Where are you going, Per?" And he answered, "I told you yesterday: I'm going to church. I must do penance for the great injustice that I have done to those who are dear to me, and for the distress I have caused you all. In every way I've been a failure in life; that's why I'm leaving it now. You'll see no more of me."

"But Father, — Father!" Mother cried. "You've never been anything but good to us; we've nothing to reproach you for! Sit down, don't go! Think about what you're doing!" And she grabbed hold of him and tried to keep him back, but he forcibly tore himself loose and went out of the room, and all of us followed him. Dusk set in, the evening approached; soon the moon would rise in the sky.

Father walked over toward the earth cellar and crawled in through the narrow entrance. We remained standing directly outside. "Leave me in peace!" he begged us.

Mother brought us back to the house, and she told us, "Things are not well with Father. What shall we do?" — she directed her question toward me who was the oldest. "I'll go to Falkeid and talk to Aron," I said.

When we returned, Father had already filled in the small opening into the earth cellar with bricks. Aron Falkeid began to pull the bricks out of the opening, but Father threatened and begged from inside, "Leave me in peace: otherwise I'll have to use my weapon," he said. "Don't think I will knock you down from any malice on my part, Aron, but if the worst should happen, I must defend my right to destroy myself." "Do you have any food and water?" Aron shouted. "Enough for the time left me; I have more than I need," Father answered.

Three days passed. Every day Mother stood by the closed cellar opening: she shouted and begged him to come out, and when he wept and cursed her for not leaving him alone, she placed food and drink by the wall and said to him, "Father, here is food and drink," but he replied, "I don't deserve anything."

On the third day his voice sounded strange and weak, and the last resort was adopted: Aron Falkeid brought with him some men who tore down the brick wall and pulled him out by force. He looked more like a corpse than a living being; we could hardly recognize him. The eyes were no longer his eyes, he was sitting there with his lap full of hair which he had torn out of his head and beard. He held a knife in his hand, but he did not attempt to defend himself.

Aron took Father along with him, and from that day on he stayed in a windowless room in the attic of the Falkeid farm, the door being barred. He was ungovernable when he had his worst attacks, and no one knew when he would get them.

Mother went over to visit him every day for a half year; she washed him as if he were a child and she carried away his excrements so that he wouldn't eat them. When he no longer allowed her to help him but drove her away by force or crept into the farthest corner and turned his back on her, put his arms around his head and covered himself up, she visited him more infrequently, but not even then did she let an opportunity pass to alleviate his distress and share the horror that was in his mind. Because she loved him, she wanted to be part of his degradation.

While still a very young man Father had become very fond of Katharina, the only daughter of the pastor at Skjold, and she returned his love; her father, however, opposed with every means at his command her demeaning her class by marrying a man of such a humble degree. He forbade them from having any dealings with each other and gave his consent when a sea captain asked for her hand, but she refused.

Then he sent her to an army officer and his family in Bergen where entertainment and parties were the order of the day. She got to meet some of the finest young men in town, and many of them courted her, but she turned all of them down for the sake of Peder Jansen.

Finally, the pastor at Skjold went to Bergen to bring his daughter back. He was hoping that she was now of another mind, but he proved to be mistaken. She remained faithful to the promise she had given, and Peder Jansen did the same for his part.

A long time passed, no less than eleven years. Then it appeared that she was with child. Her father called her in and reproached her in harsh words for the great sin she was guilty of, but she looked him bravely in the eye and answered, "The sin is yours, Father, not mine!"

Then he began to question her as to when the seduction had taken place, and she answered him defiantly, "Some time when you were standing at the altar, and some time when you were drinking with your friends!"

The pastor of Skjold remained silent a long time, staring at his hands. Finally he again looked at his daughter and said, "Whether it is love or stubbornness that drives you, my child, I do not know. But I no longer am able to resist you in this matter."

Contrary to custom, they were married very quietly; she moved in at Hesthammer, and they lived together until the shadows began to descend on my father's mind.

I was the first child born to them. I was born with a caul; I was grasping it with both hands and held fast when I came into the world. They looked upon that as a good sign, and when Father was to decide on my name, he said: "The boy is to be called Cleng, for he clings to life and to victory."° That is just what the name means: a claw or eagle's claw, or he who clings to something.

As far back as I can remember I was never in any doubt that my parents loved me. But I had many whims and moods and often tried their patience more than I should have. I realized full well that I was misbehaving, and I felt both remorse and shame, but I covered it up with merriment and whimsy. My parents just couldn't make me out.

When I was two years old, my mother had twins, both boys, who were named Lars and Elias. It was about this time that one of Father's sisters lost her only child. Mother then said, "God has given me two; he wants me to share with the one who has none." Father's sister nearly went out of her mind from grief.

They drew lots, and Lars was the one whose name came up. Thus he was sent away from home right after he was born, and our paths separated. For that reason, he does not play a large role in my story. In time he took over the Hesthammer farm and was an able fellow, both at sea and on shore; in addition, he was a woodcarver and a rosepainter.

° In Norwegian a caul is called a "victory cap." Trans. note.

Elias died during the first year of his life, and our house seemed emptier than before. But four years later my mother had her last child; that was Kari, who later was married to Cornelius Nilsen Hersdal. I have a lot to tell about her; she and her husband were among those who crossed the ocean in the *Restauration*.

The Second Tale

For a thousand years or more the fjords of Western Norway have abounded in herring in late winter. Boats from Stavanger and from the surrounding districts came to Tysvær to take part in the fishing there.

The fishermen were wont to live aboard their own vessels or in boathouses, and they suffered much from the cold. The weather was unusually severe at Shrovetide in the year 1798. But no one can choose a palace where there is only a shack to be had, and the men ate and even slept in the boathouses and the open boats. But there were many who during the night would run up and down the hills to keep warm. The hoarfrost spun threads in hair and beard. The wooden-soled boots boomed against the rocks just as ice does when it is cracking. The moon looked green against a black sky.

So the fishermen welcomed invitations into the warm houses of the farmers. One Sunday evening several of them were gathered in the home of Aron Falkeid, our neighbor. Some of the people of the district were there too, I was the youngest in the group. I was not yet confirmed; the pastor had kept his word.

I have always been very fond of music and song, but the parish of Tysvær had very little of either. When I was standing on the bridge over the river, that day I saw people coming up from the shore in groups, and I heard the sound of clarinets and violins. The musicians were all fishermen from Stavanger. I guessed that there would be dancing in Aron's house, and the desire to join them became so strong that it overcame my sense of guilt at being merry in the very same house where my father was locked up in a cage. Finally I was standing in the doorway; from inside I could hear laughter and loud talk; suddenly, the fiddler plucked on his fiddle and tentative warbling notes came from the clarinet. Immediately the floor was filled with whirling polka dancers.

Aron Falkeid had just given his eldest daughter in marriage, and there was brandy to be had, more than usual. His son Aanen, who was a few years older than I, came out on the stoop and said, "Aren't you coming in?" I hemmed and hawed. "Are you afraid?" he asked. "Afraid!" I shouted, as if that word could not possibly describe me. "I have something that will give you courage," he said, "come with me over to the haystack." We walked over to it and he dug out a barrel of liquor. "We'll each have a drink," he said; "it's genuine French brandy."

I had had a drink before, but never anything as strong or anything that tasted as good; I drank until my head was swimming. The world looked marvelous, my soul felt joyful, and the twilight seemed red like a sunrise. We entered Aron Falkeid's large sitting room.

Among the fishermen who had come from Stavanger there was that evening one by the name of Lars Simonsen of Jeilane. He was the owner of his own boat and nets and was the headman of his crew; the cook for the crew was his fourteen-year-old foster daughter, Sara. She was a distant relative of his. Both her parents were dead, and he had taken her into his home as if she were his own daughter.

She was the first one I noticed when I stepped inside; she was sitting on a stool by the wall facing the door. Ever since her picture has been imprinted on my heart — yes, even unto this very day.

I would like you, too, Anne, to see her the way I remember her, and forgive me if I resort to words that we seldom use; but a time of sorrow and a time of rejoicing had come. If it is possible for a house to have a soul, and the soul looks through the window into the twilight, when the bright colors of day are fading and the blue of night is approaching, then her face was just like such a house. Her hands looked as if they were completely still even when busy with work. She cooked for the boat crew, she did the work of a serving maid, and from that work her hands ought to have been coarse and rough, but they possessed a shiny whiteness, like lilies; or has the loss I've felt made them look different to me now? I don't know; I've become an old man, and I no longer see Sara Larsdatter's hands before me in my dreams.

Those who were still steady on their feet continued to dance, and those who after a while became intoxicated staggered around or sat at the tables indulging in drunken talk. What I myself was doing I don't remember very clearly, besides the fact that I tried to dance and did not do well at all, not only because I didn't know much about dancing but also because I had consumed quite a bit. Someone shouted something nasty and indecent and made people laugh at me. I felt the blood rise in my temples, and a mist descended over the room.

Through the buzz of many voices I heard talk about the "possessed," and it seemed to me as if the walls echoed the words. I hardly realized that it was my own father who was being mentioned. Someone shouted in a husky, rattling voice, "Free the possessed, let him loose!" Suddenly everything became quiet in the room; the dancing stopped, the guests pulled back and stood along the walls. I suddenly realized that I was standing all by myself in the middle of the floor, and it seemed to me as if everybody was staring at me in an evil way. Once again I heard the shout, "Free the possessed, let him loose!"

It was I who had shouted. The people crowded around me, some of them shouted yes, others no. Then rose the echo from all the walls as if I were closed in among mountains: "The possessed, the possessed — !"

The girl I was dancing with put her hand on my arm; I noticed her veiled glance, her lips were moist, there were beads of perspiration on her forehead; and a sweetish and inciting fragrance wafted toward me from the low neckband of her dress. "I'll go with you," she said.

We went up the stairs; I felt as if the house was a storm-tossed ship; it sank down and heaved itself up again on giant waves, the stairs were creaking like a ship's ladder. The door to Father's room was closed with a bolt and a lock, but the evil stench penetrated through the wall. I unbolted the door myself, and I saw Father blink his eyes when the girl held up the flickering light. There was no opening or window in the walls; here time stood still, and day and night were the same.

His hair and beard were tangled; during the three years that he had been locked up its color had become like that of hemp. His eyes were like ponds covered with ice, his hands like the bark of trees.

The girl held the door open for him, and he crawled out; he walked on all fours, like an animal, and ambled down the stairs, hands first, and on all fours he entered the downstairs parlor.

The fiddler had been half asleep while his bow moved across the strings of his violin. He looked up: his bow stopped suddenly, and the dancing ceased; not one of the drunken people opened their mouths.

It began to dawn on me what I had done; I felt nauseated by shame and fright; I would have run away, but I remained standing there as if nailed to the floor; everyone remained standing stock still, as if spellbound by the sight. His twitching mouth could only be dimly seen behind the shredded beard. He had torn the hair off his face with his own hands; that is why his beard didn't have its former fullness. With his hands he made unintelligible signs in the air and upon his own body; he crawled over to me, he fumbled all over my feet and legs, he got up on his knees and then stood erect and felt my face, touching my mouth and nose and eyes just as blind people do when they try to recognize someone. And I saw in a flash that his glance was bright and showed the light of reason; he turned toward the large assemblage and said as if in great agony: "Where is the man who bears the compassion of God for His creature?"

No one answered, and he repeated the words: "Where is the man who bears the compassion of God for His creature?"

When he had said it a second time, he retreated into his own confusion, and with a sobbing laugh he crept across the floor to where Sara Larsdatter was standing; when he also had felt her arms and her face with his hands of bark and stared at her with dim eyes, she suddenly screamed, and after that one scream not another sound was uttered from her lips; from that time on Sara Larsdatter was mute.

She was the only one who knew what had happened to her that evening. She went out right after, and I followed her at a distance; when she had reached the boat on which she belonged, I turned around and went home.

The next morning, when I was going to pull up the lobster pots over at Kårstø, I heard people say that Sara Larsdatter had not uttered a word since coming back from the dance at Falkeid.

My sin against Father and against Sara was too big not to be atoned for. It didn't help much that not a word of reprimand was spoken by my mother when I confessed the evil deed to her. She said, "When sorrow overcomes us, sometimes we do things which we later regret. For I know it was the pain of it that drove you to it; I know you, Cleng."

I wept on her shoulder, but neither the weeping nor her kind words gave me release. I had entered into the realm of horror and darkness, and I didn't go to bed for three nights. I walked and walked along the paths in the forest and along the shore. Within me I heard frightening voices as distant thunder, and I wondered whether in our house there was a room in the attic or in the cellar which could be closed with lock and bolt.

An uncontrollable force drove me to the earth cellar, but I resisted when I felt compelled to enter.

On the fourth day, when I eventually lay down in the little attic with the slanting ceiling, the knots in the timbered walls seemed to me to become human eyes; their evil glance followed every move I made, and they saw my every thought. In spite of all this, however, I never completely lost my head, and fear never got the better of me.

Mother came up to me with a drink made from herbs, and as soon as I had emptied the bowl, I fell asleep and slept for two days. After that I didn't hear any of those evil voices any more; nor did I see things that do not exist. But I knew that I would never be able to forgive myself for the evil deed I had done to my sick father, and I constantly thought of whether I would ever be granted a chance to make amends for the terrible thing I had done to Sara Larsdatter.

Summer came; it was the month of June and I was taken on by a fishing boat as a crew member with a share in the catch. The fishing turned out well all around Tysvær, and many seine boats from other parts of the district gathered there.

One evening we were sitting, as was customary, on a rocky promontory, keeping an eye on the sea, looking for signs of schools of sardines. As usual the men passed the time by telling stories.

That night I heard for the first time the story of the miraculous crucifix in the church in Røldal. It would sweat every St. John's Eve, and whoever was allowed to rub a piece of cloth across it and then place the cloth upon his body, would be cured no matter what sickness he was suffering from, if that was the merciful will of God.

The thought of Father crossed my mind, even though I didn't see any possibility of being able to get him to the crucifix.

But I made up my mind to travel to Stavanger at once and go to see Sara Larsdatter, and secretly tell her of my remorse and ask her to come along to Røldal; I would set out the very next day, for the time was already approaching.

But the next morning the schools of sardines appeared in the fjord, and we had plenty to do. News about our catch spread throughout the entire district, and numerous fishermen gathered in the fjord. Among them was Lars Simonsen of Jeilane with his boat and his nets and tackle. This time too Sara was serving as ship's cook.

I was afraid that Lars Simonsen would recognize me and that he might complain to the authorities about the evil deed that had been done to his daughter. For that reason I stayed far away from him and his, but at the same time I did not let Sara out of my sight except when it was completely necessary.

In the evening she went ashore with a wooden bucket in her hand. I hurried on ahead to a spot where the brook was somewhat deeper so that one could just drop a bucket in and fill it.

When she approached and noticed me, she looked frightened but did not run away when I walked over toward her. I asked her whether she could hear and understand me, and she nodded affirmatively. Then I told her that I was sorry for what I had done, and I asked her to forgive me. She put the wooden bucket down and just stood there, holding her arms out in a deprecating and at the same time helpless gesture. I put my hands on her shoulders and felt that they were trembling and were thin and fragile, and I turned away for I was overwhelmed by feelings of tenderness and shame. Then she placed her hands against my face and she moved the tips of her fingers from my mouth along the traces made by my tears up to my eyes.

I asked her to stop for a brief moment; there was something else that I wanted to tell her. She sat down on a rock, and I told her about the crucifix in the Røldal church and asked whether she would come with me so that God could cure her. She backed away and shook her head as if to ward off a danger; she took hold of the bucket and prepared to go on her way. But I seized the handle and she loosened her grip, and I carried it over to the brook and filled it while I told her where Røldal was located and how much time we needed and what a pilgrim had to watch out for during the journey and during his entry into the church, and I asked once again and more insistently than before that she come with me for my sake. Through signs she made me understand that she was willing, and I asked her whether she could be ready the next evening.

The following day we met again in secret in the forest; and I explained to her everything that I had planned: where she should wait for me, and about the time of night we were to leave, and what she should take along.

The day had been bright and clear, but toward evening the clouds came drifting in from the sea, and a light drizzle began to fall. The air was as still as a sleeper's breath, and from the forest floor arose the aroma of herbs and flowers. I left her and walked home to prepare myself for the journey. Everything had to be done in secret; not until I was certain that everyone else in the house was fast asleep could I get started, and the nights around St. John's Eve are rather short. Darkness had already descended on the fields like a gossamery cobweb. I took off my shoes, and walked barefoot; the grass was heavy with dew.

I found the key to the storage house in the place where it usually was. The lock had been greased and did not make a sound. Father's traveling chest was hanging on the wall, half hidden under cobwebs. I opened it and put some flatbread, cured meat, and other dried food into it. From the storage house attic I brought down a coverlet and two knitted jackets, and in a wooden box I found a fish hook, a line, and a knife. On top of one of the beams I found that which was most essential for me to bring with me: two pine boards, for a pilgrim has to arrive at the church door on his knees and cross the church threshold in the same way. I also grabbed a small ax, and a silver rixdaler was put in a little bag I wore underneath my shirt.

When I was ready and was about to set out, Mother appeared in the storage house doorway: "What do you intend to do, Cleng?"

I told her everything, and she interrupted me before I could ask anything of her, and said, "You must leave. Not a soul will know that I am aware where you two are." And she gave me her hand: "Luck be with you, my son. He who carries a load for others, seldom carries too heavy a load."

I walked through moors and bogs toward the sea. The rain was falling more heavily, and the mist drifted like thick flakes across the fields. Midsummer nights are not so very dark so far north, but the rain and the fog made it impossible to see anything.

Without meeting a soul I reached the spot where I had hidden the boat the night before. I knew that people might be about in the area of the boathouses at all hours of the day and night. On board the boat I pulled a stocking leg over each oar as they lay there in the oarlocks, and the boat glided forward without any more sound than that made by the blades and the stem knifing through the water.

Sara Larsdatter was waiting for me at the spot we had agreed on. I didn't see her until the boat was gliding through the seaweed. Then she rose; she carried a bucket of water in one hand. Even though she was standing quite close to me she looked like a pillar of cloud, and in the mirage caused by the mist and the twilight she seemed much taller than she actually was.

Cautiously she approached the boat; the rocky surface was slippery. She had put a piece of sailcloth over her shoulders in order to keep the rainwater out.

The Third Tale

We soon lost sight of land because of the fog. It was important for us to get as far as possible away from the area near home before the sun rose. I counted on the weather clearing up; the signs which all people living by the sea learn to interpret from childhood indicated that it would be a bright and clear morning.

Almost unnoticeably the day broke; the rainwater looked just like a halo of pearls in Sara's hair. I had spread a new and dry piece of sailcloth over her shoulders, and had given her a goatskin to sit on.

She moved over to the center thwart and took hold of the shortest pair of oars; I myself was sitting on the front thwart with the heavy pair of oars. We were both rowing with even and tenacious strokes, and the boat put on speed; there wasn't a ripple on the water.

At sunup the drizzle lessened; toward the horizon the fog looked like a wall in retreat. The first puff of wind made streaks on the smooth surface of the water and breathed a blue tinge into it; above us we could just make out the sky behind a break in the gossamer clouds, and suddenly the early sun broke through and burned the haze into golden dust.

About this time Lars Simonsen would wake up to discover that his daughter was gone. Others would miss me. On finding that the boat had disappeared, questions would be asked and a search begun. But the ocean was wide and the fjords were numerous; who could possibly track us down?

A slight breeze came from the east; our course took us exactly in the opposite direction. To hoist a sail would not be very advantageous; stubbornly we toiled at the oars. Time passed.

By noon we had not yet had anything to eat or drink. We were close to a small island that was located right in the middle of the fjord. Since we saw neither people nor houses, we rowed toward shore, on the north side of the island. There was a powerful current along the shore; we pulled the boat up on a rocky incline until it lay safe, and moored it in a crack in the rock.

It was a sunny day, with a smell of salt from the sea. Above our heads the air was filled with screaming birds, and downy balls, just hatched, ran in front of our feet. All around were empty shells with traces of blood in them. I chased a baby gull, picked it up, and let my fingers run over its soft down; I did it as a sign of my tender feelings for Sara Larsdatter.

Our first meal on our pilgrim journey we ate behind a large rock. I cut pieces of dried meat from a shoulder of lamb, and we ate it together with unleavened bread; and we drank water from the wooden bucket, using a big shell that we found on the beach. The flocks of birds remained over our heads the whole time, like living clouds. Sara's hands were as graceful as birds' wings when she broke the bread.

After the meal we walked about on the island. It was quite large but flat. Barren hills alternated with lush miniature valleys with grassy fields; there were no trees, nor did we see any people or houses around us, but far to the east we caught a glimpse of a few small boats on the sound, even further away gray cabins by the shore and beyond them numerous farms, with fields and trees.

There were animals on the island: heifers and bulls, sheep with lambs, and goats with kids. The sheep were very shy, but the goats followed right behind us. I dug out some crumbs of flatbread from my pocket, and they ate from my hand. Their udders were distended, and I asked Sara whether she wanted to drink some milk. She nodded and lay down on the ground, and I milked a goat and let the milk squirt down into her mouth. The first squirt hit her in the corner of the eye and the next one hit her chin; the milk was running down her cheek and down into the hollow of her throat, but the third squirt came right into her open mouth, and I saw her tongue and her teeth, all red and white

We lay down to rest; the grassy slope was dry and sheltered by an outcrop of rocks. We lay side by side, not too close to each other; we fell asleep. When I awoke, I found that her hand had snuggled into mine. I had been dreaming that the fjord was crowded with boats; I ran up on the nearest hillock, but all I could see was a large sloop far out on the water. The wind had changed and blew from the west; now we could hoist the sail.

I went back and woke her, and we hurried back; on the way to the boat we passed a small inlet with a white sandy beach, on which there were a multitude of mother-of-pearl snail shells, the kind that children call "silver roosters" and believe to be more valuable than anything; she stopped to pick up some of the larger ones, and I too collected some of them.

It was ebb tide; when we had reached the place where we had left the boat, we took out the thwarts and used them as skids; together we pushed the boat into the water and hoisted the sail. There was a fairly strong wind blowing; she held the sheets, and I sat in the rear with the steering oar.

Then I told her the legend about the Røldal crucifix, the way I had heard it myself:

One day, several hundred years ago a blind man was fishing from his open boat out in the fjord. Because he was blind, he had a small boy to row for him. For more than half a day they rowed from one fishing ground to another without getting a bite; the boy became impatient and wanted to return home, and the old man at last was also about to give up. But just when he was pulling in his line and the bait was already a distance from the bottom, he felt that he had hooked something very heavy. He tugged and he tugged and wondered what it might be, and he asked the boy to look over the gunwale. The boy did so; at once he gave out a frightened cry and said that they had a corpse entangled in their line; but he soon realized that it was the body of Our Blessed Saviour, carved in wood.

When the old man was told that, he recited the Lord's Prayer, and they both exerted all their might and tried to lift the sacred object into the boat.

But time and again it slipped out of their grasp; when it was surfaced, the crucifix became heavy as lead. The sweat poured from the old blind man's forehead and filled his eyes. To reduce the burning sensation, he wiped his face with his hands; they were the same hands that had touched the crucifix, and no sooner had he done that than he regained his sight. At once he realized that it possessed miraculous powers, and without hesitation he decided to give it to a church so that others might share in its healing powers.

He spoke out loud the names of one church after the other, while he and the boy pulled and pulled, but in spite of all their exertions it remained in the water. Finally he mentioned Røldal church. Then the crucifix immediately became light and easy to handle as if an invisible and powerful arm had grasped it, and they lifted it on board the boat.

The wind died down somewhat, and the purple light of the evening was suffused over the mountains. On our left a deep fjord made its way in toward the dusk and the precipitous cliffs; there were several houses along the shore as well as a number of boats. But we rowed past and arrived at last at a wooded little island; we moored the boat in a well-hidden cove so that it couldn't be seen either from the sea or from the land.

We bailed out all the water in it and removed the thwarts, and up on the island we collected heather, spread it out on the floorboards, and made an improvised bed. We spread a goatskin and a piece of canvas over us, and we fell asleep immediately. We were both tired, and we felt secure; we believed that God's blessing goes with him who sets out on a pilgrimage.

When we woke up the sun was in the sky; its rays had the appearance of slanted columns connecting the mountain ridges with the surface of the sea; and along the shores drifted a bluish haze of night, slowly rising and vanishing. The island was completely overgrown with trees. Bird song rose up in bubbling joy, and the spicy fragrance from many kinds of plants and herbs mixed with the bitter, salty whiff from seaweed and kelp. It was a morning fit for the pure in heart.

Then, very close to us, we noticed another boat, one that evidently had arrived during the night; it was a boat with three pairs of oars; it lay heavy in the water. The people on board must have been sleeping, too; now they were getting up. They were two adults, a man and a woman, and a boy who might be about my age. The woman put out bread and butter on the floorboards, but both before and after the meal they thanked the Sustainer of Life, with heads bent in quiet prayer. Then the man rose and all together they sang an old hymn to the morning.

That they were poor was evident from their patched-up clothes and also their boat, on which the tar had been worn off in streaks and revealed the brownish wood underneath. But the sight of them did at the same time possess a touch of solemn remoteness, somewhat like the mirages I have later seen above the sands of the desert.

They had no sooner finished their hymn than the boy pointed at our boat, which they had not noticed until now, and they cast off and rowed over toward us and wished us a blessed good morning.

In the meanwhile I had glanced at the man's hands, and I don't know whether we answered him. His fingers had wasted away to such an extent that he could hardly grasp the oars, and I immediately understood that he was suffering from leprosy.

Let me tell you right now who the man was: His name was Ole Taraldsen Hetletvedt and he lived on the large island called Ombo not very far away. I have forgotten the name of his wife, but the boy, their son, was called Ole like his father. He was in time to become a schoolteacher and an adherent of Hans Nielsen Hauge's religious teachings, and he was one of those who sailed across the ocean on the *Restauration*. One of his sons, Porter C. Olson, has today a high position in the United States Army.

They had sardines in their boat — it was fully loaded. Because we were all curious about what the others were doing there, we started a conversation.

As for myself, I gave evasive answers. Ole Taraldsen told us that he had made the haul of sardines not far from Ombo. Now they were on their way to Hylen to sell their catch. "There are many people there this time of year," he said.

I played ignorant and asked him why that might be. He replied without hesitation that Hylen was the place where all the people gathered who were coming from the western parts and were on their way to the secret St. John's Mass at Røldal church. To Hylen they brought their sick and infirm, but they would also have in the back of their minds the possibility of a good buy of sardines or herring. Empty barrels and kegs they brought along with them, but other wares that they needed were to be had at the trading center, for ships loaded with grain and salt from the Baltic Sea ports and all the way from Odessa and Taganrog would call at Hylen. Even people from the East Norwegian districts of Telemark and Setesdal would come there, carrying their wares on their backs across all the mountains.

"But in addition to that," said Ole Taraldsen and held up his wasted hands, "I had in mind a trip to Røldal church, to see if any cure can be had there when the body of Our Lord begins to sweat on St. John's Eve. I've tried nearly all the remedies, but to no avail. There's not much left of my fingers and toes, but I had hoped to be able to hold my own until my sons can take over and do a man's work."

He fell silent for a little while, and then he continued, "Our pastor says that if the crucifix has any healing powers, it's a delusion caused by the Devil and a popish obscurement. That I don't worry much about, if only my fingers don't get any shorter than they are already; I certainly would like them to get back their full length, but for that I think a stronger faith is needed than mine."

I asked him how long it would take to travel to Hylen. "Are you going there too?" he said; he did not wait for an answer and added, "You have a light boat, I see, and if you have good weather you'll get there by midnight. As far as we are concerned, we'll be happy if we make it by tomorrow morning."

He got up and took hold of an oar, and pushed off; the three of them started to row. We had something to eat before we set sail; it was a fair wind. Sara dropped a fishing line over the gunwale and caught both mackerel and pollack. At a promontory we brought the boat alongside. No houses or people were to be seen; far above us were steep tree-covered hillsides and rocks and cliffs drenched by falling water. I stripped the bark off an old birch tree, Sara struck fire with a piece of flint, and we fried fish in the heap of the embers, ate our bread, and drank from the brook that ran past. Afterwards we cast off, and with a fairly strong tail wind we sailed into the fjord and reached Hylen before midnight.

Many boats were already tied up at the piers and landings, and more were coming. There were a lot of people walking along the shore, and from the surrounding mountainsides one could hear the echo of shouting, the stamping of boots, and singing.

At dusk we rowed the boat into an out-of-the-way place along the shore. We pulled it over the pebbles and stones on the beach and into a small cluster of trees; we spread heather over the thwarts and lay down just like the night before.

Next morning the six-oared boat belonging to Ole Hetletvedt had arrived, and it seemed as if he was selling his sardines at a brisk pace; there was no shortage of salt. He measured out the fish by the bushel with a bailer; sometimes he used a landing net and sometimes his hands. Blood trickled forth from the rotting sores on his eaten-away stumps of fingers.

That day still more boats arrived with sick people, and everyone spoke openly about the crucifix: the previous year it had been sweating more than usual, and many people had been cured. Strange tales were told about the lame who had begun to walk and the deaf who had regained their hearing, about the blind who had regained their eyesight, and others who had been possessed by evil spirits but had gotten rid of them.

In one of the boats two men lifted up a stretcher covered with a white sheet and a coverlet; nothing but a wax-colored and wasted face could be seen. In another boat a young mother held her deformed child in her arms; the child was crying, it had a harelip and cleft palate. All this I remember, and much more. At night a fire was lit on the earthen floor in one of the boathouses, and both the healthy and the infirm tried to get some sleep, but the wailing of the sufferers kept everyone awake.

Sara and I walked away from the others into the woods. It was dusk, the green hillsides looked dark in contrast to the surface of the fjord; the water reflected light from the sky and the red tinge still to be seen above the mountains to the north. I took Sara Larsdatter's hand in mine and pressed it against my mouth in order to stifle a cry but by her eyes I could see she thought it was meant as a caress. She pulled her hand free and walked away from me. When I got back to the boat, she had already stretched out and had covered herself snugly with the goatskin that we had shared the night before.

The next morning we set out across the mountains. We felt rested and refreshed and did not have much to carry, and along the road we passed many people, both the sick and the well. Many of them bore loads of grain on their backs; the strongest among them managed a full barrel of rye. Among the carriers we noticed a hefty woman carrying a barrel while she also kept busy knitting a stocking. The knitting needles glittered in the sun, the stocking swung and swayed and grazed the juniper bushes and the heather; uphill she almost had to bend double.

So far we hadn't used any money, but in order to cover the distance between Våge and Nes — where the boat goes on the Suldal Lake — we would need to pay something; that's what they had told us at Hylen. But I intended to use my silver daler for another purpose, and when we had reached Våge I immediately told this to one of the men who were to row us across; I asked him if they were willing to accept a goatskin for each of us. He straightway said that that was all right and even offered to row us back the same way without any further payment, if need be.

We were not alone in our boat; neither was the boat the only one. Four boats shoved off at the same time, all of them heavily laden. This was the busiest time of year; the snow had melted and one could now negotiate the Haukeli mountain pass; the plowing and the sowing were done and the haying had not yet begun.

Suldal Lake is long and narrow with steep mountains plunging down on all sides. Wherever green spots are found, small cottages seem to be balancing on them; I was told that there were more than one hundred cotters' families living along the lake shore. In summer they lived on berries and fish, in winter they would travel as beggars through the valleys, and were thus able to stave off complete starvation. But how many of them haven't starved to death down through the years, how many children haven't been like a flickering wick in an open door? The most recent letters that I have received from Norway say that now they are all leaving in a body and are crossing the ocean to America; they are following in our track, Anne. The parishes where they live pay for the voyage; they regard the price of a ticket to America as a lesser expense than having to clothe and feed them and all their relatives forever.

These poor people will make America rich; the next hundred years will amply show that.

Two different roads may be taken from Nes to Røldal. One of them runs through the Bratland valley. When people from that valley travel to Nes, they have to walk on ropes across the chasms, but one doesn't have to go up to such high altitudes if the route over the Suldal pass is chosen. The men who had rowed us, recommended that we take the route via the mountain pass, if we valued our lives.

We finally arrived at Nes; it was still three days before St. John's Eve. The richest man is he who has plenty of time; the following day brought a storm the likes of which one seldom sees in the summertime: an icy north wind swept down across the mountains, howling and shrieking and threw itself with full force down through the gorges and the mountain passes. The rivers ran black, topped by foamy white whirls, the rain slashed through the air like blue rivets, and up on the peaks and ridges the snow was falling.

We sought shelter in a boathouse together with many other people. The group was in a somber mood. All we heard were the complaints and the moaning of the sick, as well as the storm which was roaring outside, forcing the rain in through the open beams.

The wind slackened toward evening, and the boats transporting people arrived from Våge. The rowers' hands were all red; the travelers' faces were ashen. Their very lives had hung in the balance, and they were all relieved that the trip was over. I saw Ole Hetletvedt, his wife, and his son; they found lodgings in another boathouse.

It continued to rain most of the night, and there was a nip in the air. The boathouse was near the mouth of the river, and the gurgling noise of running water was the only sleep-inducing sound. But the deformed child was crying; the pale woman on the stretcher was moaning and whimpering; her emaciated hands were groping across the coverlet. No one asked her what she was suffering from, and no one tried to relieve her pain. And there were many others; muteness may also be like a cry. Sleep was a frightened bird flying up against the walls.

The sun rose in a clear sky, and there was a white cap on every mountain peak.

Each party ate by itself, and there was hardly any conversation between the groups. A blind woman sang a hymn in a broken voice; an old man and a child were both weeping. A bluish smoke rose from the dying fire on the earthen floor; the first ray of sunshine entered through a knothole in the wall and made a rose blossom on the face of the blind woman. Each one knew full well the pain that was his own; no one knew much about the others' sufferings, but they all knew that they belonged among the pilgrims.

"Two years ago the sweat of Christ made it possible for me to lift one arm," said a paralyzed woman who was being carried in a sling on her sister's back; "if the crucifix sweats this time too, I will be able, if God wills it, to move the other one too. Then I'll have no reason to complain, for then I can knit stockings and fold my hands."

Only once did someone mention the fact that we were within the parish of the pastor of the Suldal valley.

"Do you think he might have his men nosing around?" a man asked.

"Don't worry about it," another replied. "He just overlooks it. What else could he do? Can *he* help us? And even if he dared put all kinds of obstacles in our way — yes, even if he sent the Evil One himself — where the need and the suffering are great enough, every one will seek deliverance where deliverance is to be found, even if he had to crawl on hands and knees through the sulfurous smokes of hell in order to reach the cross of Christ."

When the meal was over, the people started off; they spread out, for they didn't think it wise to walk in groups, and also because some were ill while others were able to walk fast. Sara and I were amongst the first from the very beginning, and before long we were ahead of everybody else.

It was still rather cool, but it soon became warmer when the sun rose in the sky. We had to stop and catch our breath in the steep hills. The perspiration lay like a gray film on Sara Larsdatter's forehead, and she smiled.

Soon, very soon her voice would return and her tongue would be released from its fetters!

Summer farms were to be seen all about; sheep, goats, and cows were grazing on the grassy slopes. We were both thirsty for milk, but we did not want to ask for it; the silver daler that I was carrying hidden in a small bag on my chest was to be placed intact on the altar of Røldal church as a thank-you offering for Sara's cure.

The flowers made the cloudberry patches all white; the birds of the forest flew low above bushes and thickets. A cool wind came down from the mountains; it carried with it the aroma of the plants and flowers of the high plateau. At the top of the hill we took a rest; we were way ahead of the others. Far down we could make out the Røldal Lake with white-capped peaks forming a wreath around it; above the glaciers the sunlight dazzled the eye, the water was greenish-black with lighter colored ripples where sudden gusts of wind were chasing along, like fluttering silver veils.

The descent into the next valley was more fatiguing than the ascent had been; it is more strenuous to walk downhill than uphill.

At the Botnen farm on the southern shore of the lake one may hire a boat, but we wanted to get to the church unseen. So we chose to walk down the steep wooded slopes along the south side of the lake where there are only footpaths that are seldom used. But we even stayed away from the footpaths in order to feel completely safe. We didn't cover a lot of ground very fast, but at least we had plenty of time. There was still a whole day and a night until St. John's Eve, and no one would enter the church until the hour of midnight.

My little food bag had started to feel lighter. I cut a twig from a willow tree. We had a fish line and hook with us, and Sara dug out some worms by the wall of a mountain cowbarn. We tried our luck where a brook ran into the lake, and before we quit there were nearly a dozen small trout lying in the grass.

That night too we slept very little; we rested underneath the open sky. We shivered and moved closer to each other in order not to freeze, and because we were so close to each other we didn't stop shivering. We lay on the piece of sailcloth since we had given away the goatskins. The vault of heaven was tinged with green as a phosphorescent sea. Such are the nights in the North — luminous; the forest floor was fragrant of both sweet and bitter; a white mist hid the surface of the water.

Toward morning we made a fire and sat close to it, and thus felt much warmer. By sunrise we were asleep but were eventually awakened by people calling their cows. Women's voices were heard from the cowbarn, and the cows were running through the forest so that twigs and branches crackled. We hid ourselves underneath some tall ferns.

Later in the forenoon the cows returned to the place where we were, and I milked them for what little there was. But Sara did get something to drink, and the milk made her want to eat some food. She felt refreshed and joyful and happy again.

Evening came. Oh, if you could only see it, Anne, St. John's Eve in

Røldal: The gentle curve of the sky resting on the white mountains; plants and trees exuding a pleasant aroma, below us the lake keeping vigil with dim eyes. We made ourselves ready.

We were still hidden in the forest, close to the upper end of the lake. The church is located in the middle of the plain and is surrounded by many farms. In spite of the dusk we could see people walking to and fro. Glimmering light from candles flowed out of the church window.

Then I tied on the boards, first around her knees, then onto mine, and I began to say the Lord's Prayer and got as far as the fifth prayer, "Forgive us our trespasses." Then I noticed that her lips were moving, but without a sound, and I burst into tears and thought, "Soon, soon, it is going to happen."

We crawled out of the forest on our knees. Side by side we crept over tufts of grass and pebbles and rocks and then across meadows with wet grass; thick blades of grass cooled our hands and stroked our faces, for we were almost doubled over, and we drank from the balm of the earth and of the night. A bat in flight sketched secret signs in the air; lapwings were screaming above the marshes, a frightened corncrake called its young ones back.

We approached the church. There were people everywhere, but they hadn't all come there for the same purpose. Over by the wall of a house three jolly fellows were standing, passing a bottle from one to the other. There was much raucous laughter, and the sound of a fiddle was heard in the distance. Past us walked young couples, across the meadows and into the forest, for St. John's Eve is a time of longing, of passion, and of abandonment; that is the time that the maiden dreams about a bridegroom and a young man will win a bride in the dark of the forest.

The two of us acted like the serpent when facing the Almighty; we crawled on hands and knees past the joyful and the sorrowing and sensed that many people looked at us, but we did not heed them. Ours was a different kind of reality; we felt ourselves lifted up toward heaven on high, to where the apostle Paul had been snatched away, as well as many a sinner and saint ever since.

Of curious people there were many, but there were also great numbers of pilgrims. Some of them came from the same direction as we did, but more came from other districts. Everyone, however, was moving toward the church. Many people were crawling on the ground, some with boards on their knees, and others without. The sick were carried, and the cripples supported one another. In a large group of people, which had journeyed across the mountains from the east, the sick and the hale walked all together in a procession, the strong ones supporting the weak and the most wretched ones being carried or pulled along on stretchers. At the head of the procession walked a man with a wax taper a yard long; after him came an aged man and a young boy with an old regimental banner, and all who could raise their voices sang a hymn which I later on have heard sung at great and solemn occasions in Catholic churches south of the lands where Protestantism reigns. The air was so calm that the candle burned with a clear and quiet flame.

At the hour of midnight the bell in the church tower began to chime. Then the two of us with many others approached the church gate. In the church vestibule we helped each other to take off the boards from our knees, then, we got up on our feet and entered through the inner door.

The nave of the church was enveloped in darkness, but the choir shone as if the gates of Paradise had been opened wide; great and small candles had been lit on the altar. All the benches were filled with people, but many others gathered around the crucifix. The crowd was continually moving to and fro, but only a muffled sound was made by the many footsteps on the floor, and whispering voices sounded like a gentle soughing underneath the vault of the church. The censers were swung back and forth by a man standing right next to the altar railing and supporting himself on a pair of crutches. His white beard flowed down over his chest.

The room looked alive by the flickering lights which made it possible for us to barely discern the rose and vine-like ornamentation with which an unknown master had embellished the ceiling.

But above all, I remember Sara Larsdatter's face, transfigured as that of the Virgin Mary must have been when the angel announced to her that the Messiah was to be conceived in her womb and issue from her for the salvation of the world.

Someone with a deep voice started to sing a hymn, and many joined in. Then a small elderly man walked over to the choir door and in a low and whining voice read from a Lutheran collection of sermons. After a while many people became impatient; some people yawned, others talked in a low voice, and a woman whose mind must have been slightly impaired, was laughing, mumbling, and making faces. Here and there one could even hear people snoring. These sounds intermingled with the moans and the wailing of the sick who had gathered up front by the choir.

I felt drowsy for a short while; it was caused by the monotonous voice of the reader and by the warm air in which the aroma of incense mixed with the smell of rotting wounds and the sweat from many bodies.

The reading was finally concluded, another hymn was sung, and when the last stanza resounded through the room, the white-bearded man took the crucifix down from its place above the choir door and lifted it up in his arms, crying in a loud and trembling voice: "Our Lord Jesus Christ is sweating for us!"

First in line among those who sought to be cured was the leper Ole Taraldsen Hetletvedt; he stretched his wasted fingers up toward the cross, and the light from the tapers threw enlarged and flickering shadows on the walls of the church choir. His wife and his son Ole stood next to him; she held a dazzlingly white linen cloth, and she brushed it across the face of the Crucified One and then over her husband's hands and the sores in his face.

Then two men carried forward the sick woman who had been with us in the boat across the Suldal Lake, and after her the mother with the deformed child stepped forward, as well as many others. I observed their devotion and their pain, and hopes, and my heart wept and rejoiced. I lifted up Sara Larsdatter in my arms and our tears flowed together on my hands. Just when we got close to the crucifix, we saw that the woman with the pale face, the one who had been carried across the mountains and the seas, rose up from her stretcher, and she grasped the piece of cloth that had been laid across her face and pressed it to her mouth and kissed it again and again.

With the clean cloth that Sara Larsdatter had saved for this purpose, I too stroked the hard wood of the visage of Christ, and as I had instructed her to, she opened her mouth, and I stroked the cloth across her tongue and then across her throat, and I looked at her in hope and fear and expected that the first few words would cross her lips. She opened her mouth, and a choked and muffled sound issued forth, as if from the throat of a sick animal; and then no more was heard.

Hand in hand we left the church building. As in a dream I once again heard the chiming of the bells. The first gleam of the new day emerged above the mountains to the north. We walked through the meadows the same way that we had come, but no longer on our knees; I carried the boards under my arm. The grass looked gray because of the dew underfoot, and above the plains the night haze rose toward the sky like blessed souls clad in white.

When we got back into the forest, I made a fire and put the boards on it, and the sign of the cross which I had carved in them, glowed red and turned into ashes. We fried our last remaining fish in the embers, and we ate dry bread.

When the sun rose, we set out on the long journey home.

The Fourth Tale

A written summons from Pastor Ananias Dyrendahl had sternly requested me to appear in the church at Skjold on the eighth Sunday
after Trinity. I was to answer for my flight with Sara Larsdatter and for
everything evil and sinful that I must have done to her.

When I noticed that Mother made herself ready to accompany me on
the journey to the church, I said to her, "Stay home, Mother. There
will be many Sundays with sermons after this one." But she replied,
"This I want you to know, Cleng, that even if you had been on the way
to the gallows, your mother would have wanted to escort you."

It was a beautiful morning, with sunshine and blue waters. The fields
had begun to turn green again; the hay was already in the barn. But in
the outlying pastures and along the shores the grass was still uncut.

At a place called the Skjold Stream, the fjord becomes very narrow
and looks just like a river. Somewhat further on and on the left-hand
side and a short distance above the shoreline there was at that time a
small isolated haybarn; it was an old custom that churchgoers from
Hesthammer and Falkeid went inside the barn and changed into their
best clothes. Then they would have some food, provided they did not
intend to go to communion; one was not supposed to have eaten
anything when one was to partake of the Lord's Supper, for the hunger
of the body is a symbol of the urge and longing of the soul, and serves
as an admonition; thus they used to reason in the olden days.

There was an east wind when we hoisted the sail, a gentle breeze coming down from the mountains. In good time we reached the place where people used to change their clothes; we pulled the boat up on skids, and walked over to the barn. The door was locked with a bolt that easily could be shoved aside. Coming in from the daylight, we fumbled our way through the green dusk inside; a ray of sunlight made the dust seem luminous.

Mother placed our food on a fallen barn door; as was her custom, she read from Luther's book of sermons and together we sang a morning hymn.

Then we took our best clothes out from the chest and put them on, went into the boat and once again began to row. I thought of my father; I recalled our traveling to church years ago, when he was the one who did the rowing. His black coat with the silver buttons would be placed across one thwart, if the weather was fine; he would be sitting in his white shirt, and his black beard would flow down across his chest. Father was far from being a rich man, but he did own a best suit which many a man of means might envy him. That was also true in regard to Mother; she gave the appearance of being a lady of the upper classes when among others: poverty had not cowed her, and neither had people's gossip. If I close my eyes, I can still see her sitting right before me in the church boat, well-built, tall, and straight in spite of heavy physical labor and many childbirths. The dress she wore was of wadmal with red borders; she wore a white plastron with small silver brooches on it, and on her head a silken kerchief with red tassels. This kerchief she had received from Father as a morning gift, and it was only used on special occasions; she wore it on that particular day. I remember that it had slid down from her head while she was rowing — she handled her pair of oars easily and skillfully — and the part in her hair showed very clearly. Mother had curly hair, but before going to church she would comb it in sugar-water so that it would be nice and straight and look as if it were glued to her scalp; the women from our part of the country thought that that was beautiful. Beside her on the thwart lay a white kerchief in which were wrapped her hymn book and a little box with musk in it.

While still rowing, she looked me in the eye and said, "Do you dread this day, Cleng?" "I'm not happy about it," I answered. "It's not the wont of my people to crawl for anyone," she said; "we walk straight ahead without looking right or left; we tell the truth and speak up strongly rather than weakly." "That's what I thought," I replied.

"When we get to the church gate," Mother continued after a while, "people will be lined up on both sides. They think you are going to answer for some kind of indecent behavior. You have told me what happened from beginning to end, and there's nothing for you to be ashamed of. For that reason neither you nor I will lower our glance to the tips of our shoes when walking up to the church door, and we're not going to act as if we were sneaking into church. If we see people we know who usually greet us but won't look at us today, then we won't recognize them either. Should we see others who appear anxious to greet us, then we will reply with a nod or we will shake an outstretched hand and repay with the same cordiality that others show us. But we won't let our glance waver from side to side, in order to seek disapproval or approbation in word or expression. We would have been journeying to church today even if no summons had come for you, and in front of the cross and the altar one should not allow oneself to be weighed and measured by those who know only what is obvious; the measures and weights of the Lord are the only ones that count in that place."

These were exactly Mother's own words, and when we came to the boat landing and had pulled in the oars, she tied her kerchief around her head, held the white kerchief containing the hymn book and the musk box in her right hand, gathered her skirt with the left hand, and stepped ashore with great dignity, for there were already a number of churchgoers on the landing and several boats were on the way in. She let me make fast the boat, but waited for me, and on the way to the church and from the church gate and up to the entrance we did in every way just what she had suggested. In front of the entrance the crowd was so large that we had to wait until people drew to the side.

One man asked an acquaintance what wrong we had done, but he received no answer. Another man pointed to something on the right side of the church door, and said, "That's where the pillory used to stand; I can still remember when it was taken away."

"It was taken away much too soon," said another.

"That's where they had to stand, those women who had been found guilty of fornication," interjected a third person.

"It would have been more just if that punishment had befallen the male sex instead," a woman said.

"Your talk indicates the level of your intelligence," objected the man who had spoken before. "Women know what the consequences are; the greater reason for them to look out."

"But he's just a young boy — !" I heard someone say.

"The girl was younger," someone else remarked. What was further said merely faded into a low murmur. I felt my face flush.

There was much talk like that, but we were spared from hearing anymore. The crowd drew back in front of the church door, and we entered. A stool had been placed in the middle of the choir, in such a way that it was easily seen by the whole gathering; the sexton asked me to sit down. Mother walked inside and took a seat on the women's side of the Hesthammer pew; the men's side was empty.

Bells were ringing, hymns were sung; the pastor stood in front of the altar and then walked up into the pulpit. I didn't listen very attentively to what was being read and preached; I thought of the flatbread that I had thrown across the river, but it also occurred to me that he ought to remember me for other reasons than that. He had once lent me a book on arithmetic and algebra, and I had all by myself worked out some of the problems. I had shown my work to Pastor Dyrendahl one time I had been on an errand at the parsonage, and he had praised me for it.

No praise, however, had been given me by Father after I had carved numbers and signs in the floorboards and thwarts of our boat just for the fun of it; Pastor Dyrendahl was supposed to have heard of it, and it had made him chuckle. After that I left the boat alone, and instead found some pieces of chalk, climbed up on the roof of the boathouse, and decorated the flat stones in the same manner. Then Father laughed too, but Aron Falkeid said that I made a fool of myself in the eyes of the entire parish.

The pastor had asked whether I wanted to study Latin, but I had replied that I would much rather learn languages spoken by living people.

All this and more went through my head while the service proceeded along its appointed course; Pastor Ananias was very thorough in his exegesis of the biblical text. It occurred to me that he might even refuse to confirm me this year also; perhaps I would have to wait until I had a long beard, as was the case with those who were very slow to learn.

Suddenly I could see reasons why Pastor Dyrendahl might find it desirable to have me study for confirmation one more year: the last time I registered he had not been very satisfied with the gifts that I had brought. True enough, the clergy preach from the pulpit that we should lay up treasures in heaven only and not on earth, but it is easy enough to be a teacher as long as one has no intention of following one's own instructions. And Pastor Dyrendahl was no exception to the general rule. Do you think I judge him too harshly, Anne? But that's the way it appears to me even today.

At the time of registration most of the confirmands would be accompanied by their fathers, who would press forward to the vestry door, each one anxious to be the first to hand the pastor a gift, in that way making sure that their children obtained a place up front during the confirmation ceremony in the church.

The previous year everything had turned out in the customary manner: From one household they brought a lamb, from another, a tub of butter, or other welcome gifts. I had finished my studies for confirmation already the year before, but I couldn't be confirmed just because I had thrown the bread on the water. Nevertheless, I had with me a very generous present, and when I this year had shown up for the second time I came without anything. I felt rather ill at ease when the pastor, as was usual, in a loud voice had announced for all to hear what each one had given and then had said, "Cleng Peerson comes here with empty hands? Is he also coming with an empty head?" His intent was to humiliate me, but I countered, "Not if the pastor had something to push into it last year." "That I had," Pastor Dyrendahl replied, "but I didn't get anywhere with your hard heart."

Thereupon he spoke at length; what he said had a sting to it, but I was not at a loss for an answer. I said, "The pastor has gotten the very last head of grain and every penny of the harvest and the income on his assigned property, and we at Hesthammer are not lazy. But it didn't seem right for me to ask Mother for one more registration gift, for the pastor must know that there is no abundance to take from." Dyrendahl answered, "You shouldn't have been reluctant to ask your mother about a proper gift for me, for it is the duty of parents to be generous on behalf of their children." Then I felt the anger rise in me, and I said, "If Father finds begging to be in accord with his dignity, at least I don't do so."

"Father! Why do you call me father, young man?" Dyrendahl asked — his cheeks had flushed lobster red. I had just said it accidentally; the point of it was that people at that time — as is also customary in many Norwegian settlements over here today — often use this appellation for the shepherd of the congregation. But now he had gotten me angry with his miserliness and his hyprocrisy, and I was not able to contain myself: "Because I don't have any father!" I said; "I lost my own father when madness possessed him, and if the pastor didn't know it before now, he's going to find it out now: He succumbed because of the pastor's harsh demands for payment."

When the hymn had been sung following the usual service at the altar, the pastor at last called my name from the door of the choir and asked me to stand up and remain standing. I did so, and felt the skin on my face taut as when it is whipped by the salt spray of the sea and the water dries up and only the salt remains. My hands felt clammy and sweat ran from my armpits down along the side of my body.

The pastor made a short speech which he partly directed toward the congregation and partly toward me. First he dwelt on my good points, lifted me up high so that my fall could be the greater when he began to list my misdeeds. He didn't forget the bread I had thrown on the water and neither did he forget other thoughtless words that I had uttered.

When the minister had come to the end of his reprimand, he expressed the hope that my innate nature in spite of everything would be held in check by the inclination toward virtue and a moral life which the Almighty had instilled in our hearts.

Then the pastor asked me where Sara Larsdatter and I had been during the more than a week that we had been away, and what we had been doing all that time. To this I did not reply at all, and the pastor once again asked whether we had been guilty of acts that were irreconcilable with decency. I answered no. I was afraid that perhaps now he would mention my mother's fall from grace and social status, but he spared her. On the contrary, he asked for a more detailed account of certain circumstances surrounding Sara Larsdatter's and my apprehension: We had been discovered all by ourselves on a small island and there had been very distinct indications that we had been living there, since we had put up a small hut made of heather and twigs.

This was the island known as Finnborg, which was also the place I had ended up the time I wanted to journey toward the sunrise.

The pastor first inquired about our reason for staying there. I answered that I had wanted to bring Sara Larsdatter by sailboat to Stavanger in order to bring her home to her parents. But we had run short of water, and we had gone ashore on Finnborg since I knew of a spring there.

It was the pastor's farmhand who had found us; he and three other fellows had been sailing past the island in the pastor's boat. He had let Dyrendahl know that when they encountered us Sara Larsdatter had been resting her head in my lap, and that I had been holding her tenderly. The pastor asked me what I had to say to that. "It had nothing to do with tender feelings — I was forced to do it . . . ." I replied. "What were you forced to do?" the pastor asked. "To look for something in her hair," I said, and fell silent. But Dyrendahl was not one to be satisfied with hints and allusions. Why had I held her head in my lap, and why had I been busy with her hair? I replied, "I

could get at it better, I could see better, I got a better hold of them."
"Of what?" asked the minister. "Sara Larsdatter had become infected
with lice," I said. At that point I noticed that the congregation concentrated with greater enthusiasm on their prayers; the men bent their
heads forward and the women held the tips of their kerchiefs in front of
their faces, but nothing could hide the fact that they were laughing.
Mother sat erect, keeping a straight face.

"But — h'm — how had she become infected with these — these
creatures?" Dyrendahl said, clearing his throat and speaking
hesitantly.

"It was probably in the Røldal church," I answered, and just as soon
as the words had escaped my lips I realized that now I couldn't avoid
divulging what I always had wanted to keep secret.

"The Røldal church!" he exclaimed, and all the listeners looked up
in surprise.

I saw no other way out than telling him about our pilgrimage from
beginning to end. But that I couldn't do without confessing what was
even worse: that I while drunk had opened a bolted door and put my
father's wretchedness on public display. But before I was able to explain everything, I burst into tears from remorse and from shame.

As far as I could understand, the congregation had no knowledge of
all this. Perhaps no one knew that Sara Larsdatter had become mute
from that time on, since she had immediately returned to Stavanger.
However that may be: Either the pastor or the congregation did not
understand what I told them about the evil deed I had done to my
father, or they chose to make believe that they didn't understand; for
neither at that time nor later on did I hear a reproachful word from any
one. As for myself, I have always looked upon it as the greatest sin, and
many a time when I was crossing the oceans and traveling in foreign
lands and feeling like a homeless outlaw wherever I went, I would
think of the Fourth Commandment, and that I had not been able to
live in the land in peace and quiet just because of the evil I had done
unto my father.

The pastor asked me, "Do you then plead guilty of, or at least admit
being an accomplice in, causing Sara Larsdatter of Jeilane to lose her
voice?" And I answered yes.

"Strange, very strange," he muttered to himself, and asked me once
again, "And by your so-called pilgrimage you wanted to try to repair
the harm that you had caused?" Again I answered yes.

"But everything proved to be in vain?"

"Everything," I replied.

The white kerchiefs were once again fluttering on the women's side of the church, but the women were no longer trying to hide their smiles. Dyrendahl cleared his throat and said, "A pious thought inspired your action, my son," he said, "and God will look in mercy on anyone who repents his sin. But in regard to all other matters: Has it all been in vain what you learned as a child? And are you completely purged of spiritual fruits even though you are better versed in Holy Writ than many who have advanced in Christian understanding and living, since you give yourself over to a superstition that deserves no other name than a manifestation of the powers of darkness. Anyone who harbors the will to obtain the truth will realize that the worship of saints and the adoration of crucifixes and the expectation of supernatural cures are nothing but a delusion of Satan himself."

That's just about what he told me, and I replied, "But the mutes spoke at the command of Jesus, He cured the sick, and He even raised people from the dead."

"That is certainly so," the pastor agreed, "but those deeds must be considered as proofs that He was the promised Messiah. They are no longer to be found in His congregation, and this should indicate to us God's wisdom and will, and we must yield to His inscrutable ways."

But I said, "We can read in Holy Writ: 'You shall do greater deeds than those others.' "

"Watch out, Cleng," the pastor said, "so that you don't read yourself into perdition. For the *greater* deeds that the Bible speaks about are spiritual ones, not being done for the welfare of the body but for the salvation of the soul. And moreover, Holy Writ commands us to see to it that our entire behavior has to be seemly, and it teaches that God is a God of order. But what you have done, is to worship a wooden image as heathens do and believe the plain fact that the moisture, which covers the image because it is exposed to the breath by so many in an overcrowded church, is the sign of a miracle, that God lets the wood sweat in order to cure the ill and the infirm. Do you realize that you have gone astray?"

"No," I answered, and I mentioned the fact that a woman who had been brought to the church on a stretcher, had walked away all by herself, and that she had been so pale that she looked as if on the verge of death, but her cheeks had flushed the very moment someone had brushed the linen cloth across her face. But when the pastor asked me whether I knew what disease she had been suffering from and also whether I knew her name and where she lived, so that he could find out whether this had happened just as I had said, then I had to admit that I knew nothing about that.

With that the interrogation came to an end, and Pastor Dyrendahl concluded by saying that in spite of my great mistake and the ungodly aspects of my deeds, he still found that I was motivated by genuine repentance and the will to atone for the wrong I had perpetrated. For that reason he would not out of hand reject my request to be confirmed; neither would he — as he at first had planned — send a report to the bishop about what had happened.

When I walked out of Skjold church on that Sunday morning I felt more cheerful than when I had entered, and it seemed as if people looked at me in a different way. When we were on the way back across the lake, there were no boats trying to avoid us, and neither did we try to shy away from the others; boats with returning churchgoers seemed to be all around us.

Mother said, "You did very well, Cleng. Whoever is strong and confident in himself, can turn shame into honor." And a man whom we didn't know, stopped his boat and came close to ours and said, "Why should *you* wait to be confirmed! You know Holy Writ better than the pastor!" "The pastor knows the Bible, too," said another man, "but he twists every statement and every act written down to suit his own purposes."

Nevertheless, I was fond of Pastor Dyrendahl, and I had decided that a portion of what I would earn as mower after the haying had been done at Hesthammer, was to be given him as a present; I wanted to give it to him the very last time we were being examined prior to the confirmation. This, however, was to be done from an ulterior motive, for that was the day that we were to be assigned our places in church.

I brought my present, a tub of butter, yellow and firm and salted just right. But the tub was not as full as I had intended it to be, and the reason was this: I had been employed on an isolated farm that was very difficult to operate; many of the hayfields lay quite a distance from the main buildings. The farmer's wife always came out to us with the morning meal; it consisted of porridge made from barley, and boiled with water. One day she didn't find the wooden bowl that she was wont to use; I'm afraid it had been used to feed the pig. In any case, she knew what to do; what she lacked in cleanliness she made up for in inventiveness. She got out one of her husband's old leather pants, tied one of the legs at the bottom and filled it with porridge. She flung the pants over her shoulder, and walked out to us in the hayfield.

But I refused to eat; I lay down in the shadow of a tree, and when the farmer himself had eaten his fill and it was time to resume our work, I made no motion to grab the scythe. He asked me what was the matter, and I told him that I considered myself to be as badly off as the prodigal son who was allowed to eat the swills that the pigs did not want.

At this, they both got very indignant but I was angry myself; I quit their employ, and then they wouldn't pay me any wages. But I stood up for my rights, and in the end I was given a large piece of butter, which I divided into two equal halves and gave the pastor one of them.

The Fifth Tale

The city of Stavanger used to arrange an annual fair at the end of October. People would come to town from all over the county in order to buy and sell and amuse themselves, each according to his needs and his wishes. But our parish of Tysvær and the other places along the coast to the north did not have many superfluous commodities to bring to market.

That autumn I had decided to go to the fair, and in spite of all I was not going to arrive there empty-handed; I took along with me ten pecks of salted pollack, two barrels of apples, and a large churn of spiced sardines.

My main objective for going was to meet Sara Larsdatter again. I hadn't seen or heard anything of her since we had parted after our journey to Røldal, and for that reason I felt a bit uneasy.

I was in the company of a boy of my own age, Daniel Stensen Rossadal. We had come to know each other when we were studying for confirmation. Daniel was a quiet and thoughtful fellow, quite different from me; maybe that was why I liked him. More than a quarter of a century later he traveled with his wife and five children across the ocean in the *Restauration*. But this is one of the tales I shall tell you later.

We had a head wind, and dusk set in while we were still underway. Since we didn't think it wise to continue in the dark and along a route unknown to us, we sought harbor at a place called Kindingstadvågen in the parish of Finnøy. As soon as we had gone ashore, we met two men; they told us that directly above us there was a house that was operated as an inn whenever the occasion arose; people traveling by boat along this route would put up there. "But don't help yourselves to everything that the lady of the house will offer you!" one of the men said, and both smiled and winked, but we refrained from asking further questions.

On the outside, the house looked like any rural building; it was getting fairly dark and we could only make out its contours against the sky. But inside, everything testified to great affluence; the rooms were decorated with many things that must have come from afar; vases and bowls of porcelain and crystal, beautifully embroidered tablecloths and soft rugs, chests made of camphor wood, and conch shells. A whole lamb was being turned on a spit over an open fire, and a shelf across the fireplace was filled with bottles.

The housewife — as I supposed her to be — greeted us in a friendly manner. She was quite good-looking and was very talkative, full of fun and gaiety. I estimated her to be about fifty years old, and I thought her husband to be of about the same age; he was thin and short, and had a wispy beard. Later on I found out that they had both originally come from Sweden; the wife's maiden name was Anne Cathrine Sælinger, and her husband's name was Anders Nord. They had a daughter who looked more like her mother than her father; she might be about twenty years old, and every gesture and movement of hers seemed in a way very sensuous and provocative. It was she who whenever necessary, was turning the lamb on the spit, but at other times she was walking to and fro between the tables. Many were those who kept looking at her; but no fewer looked admiringly at her mother.

There were already a number of guests in the house, people who were going to the fair. Some people were sitting drinking by a long table, while they were waiting for the lamb to be served; it would soon be ready, the daughter said. Right after that she removed the spit from the fireplace and let it hang above a long and narrow dish so that the fat could drip down into it. Each man unsheathed a knife and cut himself a piece, and with it they ate flatbread and drank ale from Lübeck and French cognac.

As for myself, I hadn't tasted any strong drinks since that evil night at Falkeid, but now I once more drank whatever was put before me in order not to seem different; I was now quite grown-up in appearance.

When I was just about to become inebriated, one of the strangers said to me that I no doubt knew what kind of house this was. The daughter of the house was at the service of anyone who had the money and the desire. "But you have neither a beard nor coins on you, as far as I can see," he teased me, "and perhaps you haven't got much desire either."

I jumped up and ran after her all around the table; shouts and laughter reverberated like roars inside my head, and the fairgoers clapped their hands and urged me to continue what I had started. Just when I threw myself across a table, behind which she had fled, I overturned a large Chinese vase. It crashed to the floor, and bits and pieces flew through the air. I was lying there outstretched on the floor, and immediately Anders Nord pounced on me. I suddenly turned cold sober.

"This is going to cost you a pretty penny, you tramp!" he shouted. "What have you got in your boat, what are you bringing to the fair? That vase was worth at least a hundred dalers, and you're going to pay for it!"

I thought of how little the pollack and the apples were worth compared to the vase, but I was mostly chagrined over the fact that I had been led into a shameful way of behaving, one which had amused all the others.

Before I could say anything, Daniel answered him, "Cleng cannot take strong liquor, but he is a regular fellow, and he will make it up to you with work if the value of his wares is insufficient. But you may also help yourself to my goods; I have half a barrel of fine herring and two bags of wool."

Anders Nord made a grimace and laughed derisively: Did we really think that the vase was worth no more than a boatload of herring and pollack and apples? "Even if you gave me the boat on top of it, it wouldn't make up for it," he said. "I'm going to get the bailiff and the hangman after you; people have been hanged for less!"

Then Anne Cathrine pushed her husband aside and said, "We were the ones who made him drink and the girl is ours, and we took in the ones who put him up to it. The vase can be glued together, and none of you are to leave here one penny the poorer than you came."

She seized me by the shoulder, turned my face toward her, and looked me in the eye: "I like you, my boy," she said. "Today it's you who're running after the girls. It won't be long before it's the girls who'll be running after you. Then you can think back on this evening."

Such was my first meeting with Anne Cathrine Sælinger. A long time was to pass before I was to see her again, and many things were to happen in the meantime. Four years later she was divorced from

Anders Nord, and this is the way the divorce was effected: Both of them appeared in church, and following warnings and admonitions from the pastor, they each seized one end of a bedsheet and pulled it taut, and the bedsheet was cut right down the middle by an ax as a sign that they no longer had the right or the duty to share their bed.

I never saw the daughter again; she died young. Anders Nord died two years after the divorce, and he was always remembered as a bad character.

Daniel and I left the house and went down to the boat. We froze throughout the long and rainy night; the rain was mixed with snow. The wind let up toward morning, and the sky cleared. We set sail and reached Stavanger in the afternoon. A great number of boats of all sizes were already tied up along the piers. We found a place to tie up ours, and we carried our wares up to the marketplace, where lively trading was going on. I had sold most of the pollack and about half of my apples before dark, and Daniel had sold a quarter of a barrel of herring and a bagful of wool. We then decided to stop selling, since that was all we had brought up with us from the boat.

Then we walked around looking at the sights. There were swarms of people around the stalls, and there were many kinds of amusements that one usually encounters only in big cities, such as bear trainers and snake charmers and jugglers and quacks, one man who swallowed fire and a woman who was inside a barrel and let herself be sawed right through whereupon she immediately emerged completely uninjured.

We walked over to one of the counters where a big-boned woman with black down on her upper lip, shouted in a rough voice, "Hard-boiled eggs and sugar cakes! Big and small, come and buy!" I bought some from her and ate my fill.

A number of drunks were staggering in between the stalls, but I felt no desire to follow their example. Nor did I mix with the jolly group who were dancing in an open space near the marketplace. I still felt ashamed for what had happened the previous night, and I thought to myself, "If I allow myself to get drunk, there's no saying what may happen."

I had already begun to inquire among people standing next to the stalls and among the jugglers and clowns, but no one knew Lars Simonsen; nor did they know of any place called Jeilane.

At last the crowds were thinning out; the town's burghers all went to their respective homes and the traders to their lodgings, where they slept on the straw-covered floor for one skilling a night. There were fewer drunks staggering in the street; miserable syphilitic women were stealing around the corners, available for a skilling or a glass of brandy.

The night watchmen began their rounds; the first one came walking stiffly around a corner; he was carrying a stick and a lantern, singing the old watchman's song in a cracked voice. He then called out about the weather and the direction the wind was coming from and wandered on; his metal-shod stick pounded against the cobblestones. I also asked him whether he knew Lars Simonsen of Jeilane, and as if he had been awakened from his sleep he stood there a long time staring silently into thin air.

Then he said, "Is it the one who had his daughter put in jail?"

I felt a tightness at the throat. I said, "I don't know. What wrong had she done?"

"I've been told that she had abandoned herself to the Devil. The authorities were apprised of it, and she was called in and asked to explain. But no matter what they asked her she didn't say a word, and then she was incarcerated. A month later they once more interrogated her, but she displayed the very same kind of defiance and didn't open her mouth. She therefore was sentenced to stay in jail until she deigns to answer the questions put to her by the authorities."

"But she can't speak!" I said aghast.

"What do you know about that, you young scalawag? Her father said the same thing, but who'll ever believe that a person becomes mute without there being a good reason for it? Nothing like that has happened ever since the days of the priest Zacariah and then it happened at the command of the angel Gabriel. But angels do not walk about on earth any longer, neither here in this town nor in any other place."

Having said this, he continued on his rounds through the streets which became ever more deserted. As for myself I walked down to the boat. Daniel was already asleep; I lay down next to him and put the covers over me, but I remained awake a long time. I decided that the next day I would go to the town jail and ask to see Sara and tell her about everything that had happened since we had parted.

The jail was located just beyond the marketplace, next to the cathedral; it wasn't very far away. I asked the gatekeeper if I could see Sara Larsdatter, and he readily explained where she was. The main entrance was on the western side of the building; it also led to the two rooms where prisoners were kept, one room being above the other. He first led me down a dark and narrow stairway where it smelled of mildew and moisture. Sara was staying in the lower one, he said, and unbolted the door.

"Don't bump your head against the ceiling," he warned me. The room was no more than five feet from floor to ceiling; no prisoner could stand upright in it. It was hardly ten feet in width and about eight feet in length.

I had expected to find Sara all by herself, but a man was sleeping in the straw along one of the walls. His hair and beard were tangled and unkempt; spittle was running from the corners of his mouth, and his clothes and hands were partly covered with vomit.

That was what I noticed first; I didn't see Sara, and I thought to myself, "The guard must have shown me to the wrong room." But at that very moment she became visible in the light from the lantern, sitting hunched together in a corner and with her face turned toward the wall; her gray dress was almost indistinguishable against the stone wall. I called her name, and I noticed that she made a start; and then she turned toward me. She had become much thinnner, her cheeks were pale, and in the weak and flickering light the shadows underneath her eyes appeared darker than they really were. Her hair was unkempt and her clothes torn as if she had walked through a thicket of thorns, and I thought, "What's happened to her?" I said to her, "Sara, you're not going to stay here one day longer!"

I couldn't believe my own ears; she was able to speak and answered me, "Oh, will you try to get me out, Cleng?" I exclaimed, "Can you speak, Sara!" and she replied, "Yes," and burst into tears. But the guard said, "Then she has finally softened up. Now it may be possible to get a confession out of her."

The other prisoner started to roll over and to mumble in his sleep, and I asked the guard, "Do you put men and women in the same room?" He answered, "Only this one night. It's like this, with all the people coming to the fair the town is unsafe, and we have to take care of the most unruly of them. This fellow we know only too well. Every year he comes to town with brooms and dried fish, and he drinks up all the money he makes and then he goes berserk. But in prison he usually quiets down, and he hasn't hurt a soul since he was put in." I said to him, "May I ask Sara Larsdatter to come out with me to the room by the entrance so that I can talk to her alone? I'll make sure that she won't escape." The guard shrugged his shoulders and replied, "That's all right. Besides, where could she escape to?"

When we were alone, I asked her what had happened to her; at first she didn't want to say anything at all, but after a while she told me what had happened: The other prisoner had grabbed hold of her and pressed her up against the wall, and he had started to pull her hair and tear off her clothes. Terror-stricken, she had cried for help, and this had perhaps frightened him or maybe it was the fact that they had heard two men talk together right outside the building; one had said, "What's going on here?" And the other one had replied very excitedly, "I think they're killing each other! Let's get hold of the gatekeeper!"

They banged on the main gate, but the gatekeeper was a heavy sleeper; he too had had a nip or two since it was fair time. The prisoner, however, had thought better of it and had let her go: he crawled over to the straw mat, vomited, and went to sleep right after.

Not until then had she realized it: "I shouted!" And very cautiously she had tested her voice, with her mouth close to the moist stone wall; she had whispered, and when she had heard that she could whisper, she had talked a bit louder, and when she had heard the singing of the night watchman outside the building she had completely forgot herself and joined in singing the same verse until she had to stop because she had wept for joy. Then she had gone to sleep, her face turned toward the wall; she was still sleeping when the guard opened the door for me.

I said to her, "You just stay here another few hours, and don't worry about anything. I'm going to your father, and together we'll call on the highest official in town. I'll speak for you to the best of my ability, for you must get out of here at once."

I asked her about the way to Jeilane, and she told me, adding, "It's best that you wait until evening before you set out. Father is working in a shipyard all the way out at Kalhammeren. It's going to be difficult to find him there, and the owner of the yard doesn't like people to talk to his men during working hours."

"But you're not going to stay in the same room with that fellow one hour more than necessary," I answered, and we got hold of the guard and told him what had happened. "I'm sure she's used to things like that; one time more or less is nothing to make a fuss about," he pooh-poohed. But I asked him insistently and handed him a few pennies. Then he promised to move the drunk to the other cell right away. He accompanied us back down, kicked the drunk in the back, and shouted, "Get up, you filthy swine!"

That day I sold all the pollack I had left. I could also have disposed of my apples, but I put aside a quarter of a bushel which I wanted to give to Lars Simonsen; thus I wouldn't have to search for a topic in order to start a conversation with him.

The weather was cloudy and there was no moon in the sky, but it had begun to clear up. Windy blasts swept the autumn leaves along with it as well as dust and dirt; lonely twisted and distorted trees reached their bare branches toward the sky; I could see the stars in between the twigs and branches; they looked like grain being winnowed through a sieve.

After a while I reached the house; it was located in a hollow with steep slopes on both sides just like Sara had told me. I recognized the man who opened the door immediately; it was Lars Simonsen himself, but he didn't recognize me.

He hemmed and hawed when I asked whether he wanted to buy some apples, but when he heard the price he looked at one of them and bit into it. "You're not unreasonable," he said. "Step inside, and I'll get the money right away."

The room I entered was a joiner's workshop. A boy of ten or twelve was standing there; he was just about putting the finishing touches to a fine looking boat with mast and sails, a toy model, but in spite of that it was in every way a perfect ship, like the big ones that ply the waves of the oceans.

Little did I suspect that this boy was to become a famous seafarer, the leader of those who later were to cross the ocean in the *Restauration*. This was the first time I met Lars Larsen of Jeilane. Although not much more than a child, he was compactly built but not very tall, and like his body so was his face: It was already characterized by grown-up gravity which was softened somehow by a deep cleft in his chin — it is said that people with cleft chins can be relied on.

There was a pleasant smell in the room, from oak and pine wood and tar and glue. A train-oil lamp was burning in one corner; sawdust and shavings had been swept into a small heap as if the day's work was over, even though many kinds of tools were still lying about on benches and tables. Lars Simonsen gave his son an apple and took one himself; he bit it in two so that the core became visible. There were no worms in the apple, and the pulp was tender and sweet; he praised its taste and said once again, "You're a reasonable salesman."

Then I screwed up my courage and answered, "I'm not here for the sake of the apples, but because of your daughter Sara: I know her and I've got good news for you: she has regained her power of speech." Lars Simonsen said to his son, "Stay here and finish work on your boat!" And to me he said, "Come with me up to the parlor!"

There he kept silent while I told my story; I told him everything and did not cover up my own guilt. When I had finished he said, "From what you're saying, I can see that you believe I've known more about this than was actually the case. I'm ashamed to confess that on the evening in Aron Falkeid's house both I and my men were so drunk that we did not know what had happened. The next morning we did realize that Sara had lost her power of speech, and we were so terror-stricken that we immediately got ready and sailed southwards and home. But I regarded her fate as a punishment that the Almighty inflicted on me, and I ordered her to stay indoors all by herself so that the news about her condition would not spread further than was unavoidable.

"But when we made ourselves ready for the sardine fishing we sorely needed her as a cook, and she came along. The morning when she disappeared I was afraid that she had fallen overboard and had drowned while we were asleep. Later on we met others who were searching for you; they told us that a boat was missing.

"I was hoping that you two perhaps were together and were hiding somewhere. I didn't know of any reason you might have had for doing that, but when one is young one often does foolish things. As time passed, I got more and more worried about her.

"You're probably wondering why I didn't try to get in touch with you when they finally had found her. But I heard it said that you didn't open your mouth in reply to anyone who asked you questions, and I thought to myself: 'When Sara is alone with her father, she will, in some way or other, let me know what's happened. If I find a piece of white bark and a piece of coal or a slate pencil, then she will write it out for me unless something too terrible has happened.' But she put the bark and the piece of coal away and shook her head, and her silence made me imagine the very worst. In this I was confirmed the day I was called in by both the ecclesiastical and secular authorities, just a few weeks after we had gotten back home.

"An old adage has it that rumor can travel farther than a man, but a rumor can also grow while under way, and the rumor was that Sara was supposed to have participated in what the pastor called a witches' sabbath at Røldal church, where all kinds of deviltry had been going on. Observers who had been sent there by the minister in Suldal had noticed the young girl and her companion; they had even seen them crawl in the grass with boards on their knees.

"They ordered Sara to explain all this, but she didn't answer a word, and I said, 'She's mute.' 'I know her,' said the parson, 'she's been to my house selling fish. And then she certainly didn't lack for words.' And the magistrate said that that was the case: She had been to his house, too, and then they certainly hadn't noticed any sign of her being dumb. 'She must be very stubborn,' he said. 'But if it is so that she's become mute, she must certainly have given herself into the power of the Devil,' said the parson. 'I think if she's put in jail for a suitable length of time, the Evil One will probably leave her, or she will soften and be only too pleased to be able to use her tongue and confess the sins she's committed.'

"The city authorities agreed that such treatment was just and proper in her case after several witnesses had come forth and told shameful things about her of which I had never known. Her silence was looked upon as affirmation, and the parson said, 'If this had been a hundred years ago, she would have been sentenced to being burned at the stake. But since enlightenment is greatly advanced among us and superstition has ceased and a milder form of legal procedure has been introduced — it's for these reasons alone that she will get off so easy.'

"As for myself, there wasn't much I could say in her defense. I was stricken as dumb as she was. But if you, Cleng, will repeat to the authorities your story from beginning to end and you at the same time can refer to the pastor at Skjold and say that he believed you, then perhaps there's some hope that the pastor in this town and the secular authorities will do so too."

We went to see them the following day, and everything turned out the way we had hoped. Sara, too, gave under oath an account of what had happened, and what she said agreed with my testimony.

The following morning she was released from the jail. Her father and I were there to meet her, and we all went to her father's house. No sooner had we arrived than the wives of their neighbors came over with all kinds of delicacies, and they joined us in a festive meal. We all enjoyed it, except Sara. She had been undernourished for so long that she became ill and had to go to bed.

When the neighbors had left and the two children were asleep, Lars Simonsen and I were alone in the parlor. He asked me, "What kind of work are you doing? Would you consider learning the boat-building trade with me? Today I've made an arrangement to buy a small yard together with another fellow, and I would like to hire an apprentice that I can rely on."

I said, "I would very much like to work for you, Lars Simonsen, but first I have to return to my home and tell my mother, so that she won't worry about me, and I have to make sure that she can get along without me this coming winter, for my father is sick, as you already know, and he hasn't been able to do any kind of work for many years." He replied, "I don't look upon you as being less suited to working for me because of what you've just told me. Make the trip back to your home, and return here as soon as you can."

The following day Daniel and I set sail and made good time due to a southwesterly wind. We made certain that we stayed far away from the locality where Anne Cathrine Sælinger lived.

When I told my mother what I wanted to do, she said, "The last thing I would want is to let you go away, Cleng. But you're practically grown up now; you must decide for yourself what you want to do. There's only one thing I must ask you before you leave us. You're coming with me to visit your father. He is very fond of you."

During all the years Father had been confined to a room at Falkeid, Mother had visited him faithfully. On that particular day I learned that each time she was there she would wash him and clean his room, for he was as helpless as a newborn child and seldom did he utter an intelligent word.

But every time she was there Mother told him about odds and ends that had happened at home, anything she thought might please him: About the grass turning green and about how the grain was growing; about cows that were calving, and about good news from sea and from land, about people she had talked with and who sent greetings. "What does he answer you, when you tell him these things?" I asked. "He doesn't answer at all," she said, "and not until now has he indicated that he hears what I'm telling him and comprehends that I am with him. But one time last month it happened — as so often before when he became restless and shouted and waved his arms — that I pressed him close to me and sang a lullaby to him just as I did for you when you were a baby. Then he burst into tears, and I said, 'You're crying, Father.' 'Yes,' he said, 'I'm crying. Where are my children, where's Cleng? Does he keep away from me because of all the harm I have done to him; can't he forgive me?' 'You haven't done him any harm, Father,' I said, 'but he keeps away because he has feelings of guilt.' "

And that was true: Not since the evening that I let him out of his room had I been to see him. I felt ashamed, and I was frightened.

Together Mother and I walked to Falkeid to see Father, and for the first time since he had become sick did he indicate that he recognized me. Mother told him that I was to become an apprentice in a shipyard in town and also told him as much about my trip to the fair as she thought might please him to hear, but to all this he didn't reply at all. I myself was unable to utter a single word, for even though he didn't seem to be as miserable as the last time, I was appalled. I wished that I could control my feelings and show him kindness, like Mother did. She placed a cloth on a wooden tray, put the last flowers of fall, which we had picked along the roadside, in a vase, and lit a candle, and then she folded her hands and said grace before our meal. She began to eat and she tried to help him get some food in him, but he just sat there, silent and impassive, just staring at her. I was quite unable to swallow anything at all.

"Now you must start eating, Father," Mother said, and he replied with a sentence that I thought might have been taken from the Bible, "I am satisfied by the mere contemplation of thy face." Then she stroked his cheek very tenderly, and I comprehended what I had never before fathomed: All this she did not from a sense of duty nor from ordinary kindness; even in his debasement she retained the great love for him that she had had in her youth.

But when we had returned home, she said, "There are two things that I must ask of you now that you are going away: That you guard against excessive drinking and that you shun frivolous women."

When I didn't reply, she too remained silent for a short while; then she said, "Perhaps you think that your mother is not the one who should admonish you about this? You know that people used to talk about what I did, and even today they're passing judgment on me. There's not much I can say in my defense, but I know one thing: From the very first moment I met your father I was convinced that he was the one I wanted and he alone, and no sorrow seemed too heavy to bear and no pain would be too great if I could only suffer it all for his sake. Later on I must have done much that was regarded as sinful in the eyes of both God and man, and I did not escape my punishment. But the grief that befell me when your father's mind was beclouded I have never looked upon as chastisement from the hand of God, but rather as a gift of grace — so that I could share his agony. For I believe that even now he has the same warm feelings toward us all as he had before, but they are fettered and because of that he's tormented even more than we are. For love doesn't die even though it is not accepted and returned. Such love endures, but it has exchanged its joy for suffering."

Again she remained silent for a few moments and then said, "I have spoken to you about things that we seldom mention to anyone but the one we share everything with, and I don't know whether you understand all of this now, but whenever words are incapable of teaching us, days and years will later lead us to wisdom."

That's about what she told me, and she blessed me, and with her blessing I set sail and journeyed to Stavanger. I immediately started in as an apprentice for Lars Simonsen of Jeilane according to the agreement we had made.

Lars Simonsen was a good master and very skilled at his trade. I made good progress, even though the shipbuilding trade is not learned in a day, nor in an entire winter.

All the same, the following spring I left his employment, and signed on as a sailor on a ship; for I found it rather difficult to live with him and work for him.

The reason for this was as follows: I had fallen in love with Sara Larsdatter, but when I told her she said that she did not return my feelings. But she liked me very much, she said, because I had been fair with her in everything, and if I thought that that would suffice she was willing to become my wife only because of her gratitude toward me, but not for a while yet.

I replied that I too would like to wait, and that perhaps she in time would feel differently toward me.

When I told her what I had decided to do, it didn't make her happy. I asked whether she would like to get letters from me. Then she smiled at me and said yes.

"When will you come back?" she asked.

"When you are convinced in your own mind that it's as hard for you to do without me as it is for me to do without you," I answered.

Then she wept and said, "May that day soon come."

The evening before my departure I walked alone in the fields not far from the house at Jeilane and thought of many things. When I got close to a big oak tree which was standing in the middle of a field — the path ran right next to it — Sara Larsdatter suddenly emerged from behind it and stood there facing me. Without a word, just like she used to do when she was mute, she seized my hands and placed my fingers against her face, so that I could feel its form and shape: her eyes, mouth, and cheeks, and I recalled that she had done this once before. Quickly, I inclined my head, toward her neck and shoulder and smelled the fragrance of young womanhood, but I didn't give her a caress, and I ran on without saying good-bye.

When I got back to the house, she was not at home; neither did I see her the next morning when I left.

Many long years were to pass before we were to meet again.

The Sixth Tale

Everything that befalls a sailor in the way of danger and anxiety and the fleeting pleasures that he encounters — all of that you may read about in books, and ballads and songs have been written on that subject; why, then, should I dwell on these things here?

I was at sea for more than six years and sailed on many oceans. At first I wrote regularly to Sara and regularly she answered my letters, and I interpreted her words in such a way that they brought a message of a growing devotion. All the more I was surprised when all communications from her suddenly ceased; still, I continued to write for another two years and to send her small presents; then I gave up. I was quite certain that she had fallen in love with another, but distance and her being so unattainable made every memory of her the more precious and made the picture of her that I bore in my mind ever more distinct and clear.

Much can happen in seven years, but I kept to my promise: to keep away from strange women in foreign ports. This was not due to any great virtue on my part nor to the lack of desire; the temptations were neither few nor small, but there were people in this world who had put me under an obligation.

Nor did I concern myself with religion and piety, and I kept silent when the boatswain was singing during his evening devotionals — for he carried his piety more like a kneading trough pressed against his stomach than like a banner above his head, and the melody was sung in a minor key.

During these years I learned several foreign languages to such an extent that I understood what people said to me and could write and speak a bit myself. I knew English and French best of all, but I also had some knowledge of German. And also because I was diligent in learning all about seamanship I advanced to become boatswain after the old one died and departed from his evening songs and long sermons, and was lowered into the ocean.

Twice we suffered shipwreck. The last time it happened we were on the way home and ran aground on the coast of Norway a bit south of Egersund. You'll hear about this presently. The first shipwreck led to a singular experience, and I will now tell you all about it.

The shipwreck occurred at the Canary Islands off the west coast of Africa, during my sixth year at sea. The trade winds blow in that part of the world. They are steady winds coming from the northeast; only once in a great while does it happen that they turn into violent cyclones. Then even the greatest of ships are tossed about like pieces of cork on the waves.

Such a terrible hurricane descended on us; it was in the month of February. The ship was finally dashed to pieces on the jagged volcanic rocks that ring the west coast of Tenerife. The crew as well as the officers became the prey of the sea; only I and one other escaped with our lives. He was our only passenger. Clinging to a raft we reached the coast in the vicinity of a small town by the name of Puerto de la Cruz; it is located on a spit of land jutting out into the sea.

The passenger's name was Stephen Grellet. He had boarded the ship in Genoa in great secrecy, and I had had reason to believe that he was fleeing from someone.

A man may have various reasons for fleeing from his own country; but I didn't believe that Stephen Grellet had been guilty of any evil deeds; his face had a noble cast to it, and among us he conducted himself with great dignity and friendliness. He seldom conversed with us, but from the little I heard him say I assumed that he was a pious man. When he was alone and thought that no one was watching him, he seemed to be praying silently to himself.

We ran aground so violently that everything and everybody were thrown helter-skelter all over the deck. I didn't realize what had happened until I came to and was swimming among the huge waves, intermittently buried in them and with my head just enough above water for me to look around. It was evening; behind the tattered clouds I could see a full moon rise above the horizon.

Suddenly I felt I was standing on something that I thought was the sea bottom, but that something was moving. Just at the moment that it slid away from me, my hand touched a rope, and I grasped it with both hands. I thought it might be one of our rafts, and when the water for a moment was calm in between the crests of two waves, the raft rose to the surface.

The piece of rope was fastened to one of the logs in the raft, and lifted up on the crest of another roaring wave, the raft pressed itself in between two saw-toothed volcanic rocks and slid into smoother waters.

Until then I hadn't seen any sign of life, but now I discovered a man about half a cable-length away from me. I shouted to him, but no voice could carry through the roar of the storm, and he swam away in the other direction. Then he suddenly caught sight of a huge log and changed his course, and at the very same time he noticed the raft. The distance was not great, and he seemed to be a good swimmer. I myself was unable to steer the raft in any direction, but luck was with us, and before long I was able to reach out over the edge of the raft and help him up.

We both peered out across the water to see if we could discover any of our shipmates, but not a soul was to be seen, and neither did we see our ship. It must have gone to the bottom with all hands except us two.

In the meantime the raft had drifted nearer to land, and there were no longer any reefs to protect us from the sea; the waves were even bigger than further out, since we were now in quite shallow water. Not until a heavy rainsquall had come and gone and the moon was shining again did we see the shore. The raft drifted into a small cove. Just to the south we could make out a few lights, and the outlines of housetops were silhouetted against the horizon; it was the town of Puerto de la Cruz.

Presently the raft was tossed in among other rows of volcanic rocks onto dry land, and we found ourselves in the midst of a group of strangers.

If need be, I could make myself understood in the Spanish language, and I replied to their questions. But as far as Stephen Grellet was concerned, it seemed as if all that had happened had not affected him in the least; he fell on his knees, and facing the snow-clad summit of the mountain Pico de Teide, which rose above the layer of clouds and was crowned by the silvery-pale flood of the moonlight, he began to praise the Lord for having saved him. As for the French language I was mostly accustomed to the rude and vulgar shouting in the harbors and the swearing heard in bars and joints, and I was now deeply moved to hear the name of the Lord invoked in adoration and gratitude. The others, too, stood there solemnly while he was praying; some of them made the sign of the cross and recited "Hail Mary."

When we came into the town, we were taken to an inn where the inn-keeper put before us bread and fruit and something hot to drink, but we ate very little. Afterward he showed us a place where we could lie down. I finally fell asleep, completely exhausted from being awake for more than a night and a day. While I slept my dreams were filled with anxious thoughts about the fate that might have befallen our ship-mates.

The following day four of them drifted ashore, in addition to some wreckage from the ship; no one was alive.

Then Stephen Grellet asked me, "Do you think we fully understand why we two are the only ones who have escaped with our lives?" I answered, "I don't know." He said, "When the prophet Jonah was cast into the deep, God had even prepared his rescue in such a way by sending a sea monster to swallow him and later vomit him onto dry land, because God had in readiness for him a task which he was destined to do. It's the same way with us, boatswain. Are you fully aware of what your calling from God is going to be and what kind of deeds you've been assigned to undertake in His name?"

I answered, "I am an unlettered person, but I have known the most important articles of faith since childhood. Nevertheless, I have never tried very hard to live by them. May God help me so that I will show some improvement from now on."

Then he said, "The voice of the Holy Spirit in my heart commands that I shall set out for the summit of Pico de Teide and there ask the Almighty that He reveal to me what He wants me to do and that I from now on shall obey Him in all things. Will you accompany me?"

Deeply moved by the force emanating from him, I answered yes.

Our dead comrades who had drifted ashore, were laid to rest in the Catholic cemetery in the town. Both Stephen Grellet and I attended the funeral, and in accordance with the priest's request, I sang a hymn in my mother tongue before the graves were closed.

That evening Stephen Grellet said to me, "Tomorrow we will set out, if God wills it."

It was a quiet, soft dawn, as occurs so frequently on Tenerife; a bluish layer of fog covered the entire valley like an airy ceiling and reached far out over the ocean, and the rising sun made the waves look incandescent against the sharp and gleaming rim of the horizon.

We walked for several days. The ascent was steep, and we became footsore, but the fresh air was exhilarating. At times I felt downcast and at other times I felt more cheerful, and I asked myself whether it had been necessary to set out on such a strenuous expedition. We came into the layer of fog that enshrouded the mountains, and often we could see no more than a few feet ahead of us; it seemed as if it were a road without end. At last I began to feel impatient.

Stephen Grellet pulled out a map and showed me. "There's no doubt that we're soon approaching the rim of the crater," he said.

He folded the map, and we were just about to continue, when he shouted, "Look out!" We were standing just at the edge of the layer of mist, the sky above us appeared as a yielding bluish shadow, and at the next moment the summit of Teide became visible for the first time since the night of the shipwreck; bathed in sunshine, the summit towered over us, dazzlingly white.

Stephen Grellet stood silent for a while; then he turned toward me and said, "Friend, we're on our way to our consecration."

Although I understood little of what his words implied, I was deeply moved by their intensity and their sincerity. But he continued talking and his words were something like this, "My ancestors have lived underneath the peaks of the Alps for five hundred years and have looked up at mountaintops and have worshiped God, and a mountain peak bathed in sunlight and covered with snow is my earliest childhood memory. When we get to the chapel known as 'The Blessed Mary of the Snows,' I will tell you the story of my life."

One more day we continued walking, and the terrain was rougher than it had been during our earlier ascent. The path twisted and turned between black and jagged lava formations where there wasn't even a blade of grass and no bird song was heard. Nevertheless, the landscape seemed vivid because of all the colors of the rainbow being created by the refraction in the obsidian and the other rare rocks and by the sunlight being reflected in the towering stone columns and plinths. Snow covered the ground in the gorges and small valleys, but the air was not very cold. A warm breeze wafted across the wild and desolate landscape, seeming both frightening and fascinating at the same time.

Gradually we descended into the crater, and nature assumed a more gentle character, with green grass and small groves of pine trees. Finally, on a small ridge we saw a building with a cross on the roof; it was the chapel "The Blessed Mary of the Snows." Close to its wall, on the side facing the sun, we partook of a simple meal; then we went inside, but since there were no benches or chairs to be found, we sat down beside the altar, and Stephen Grellet began to relate his story.

"In a valley in the Alps, close to where the borders of three countries meet, there lived many hundreds of years ago a rich merchant whose name was Bernhard. He never needed to deny himself any of the good things in life that can be purchased with money. In addition, he had married a woman whom he loved with all his heart, and God had bestowed on them fine children; what more can a man desire?"

"I don't know," I answered. "But perhaps there's more one can desire for himself."

"Correct," he said. "A man can desire peace of mind here on earth and salvation in the life beyond. — And it so happened that the merchant began to worry whether he would attain to eternal life. It often happens that when a man stands at the acme of his life and his career, he is overwhelmed by a feeling of emptiness and loathing, and he says to himself, 'Now I am at the peak of my career, and I have achieved the main goals that I set myself in life. All around me I see things ripening, no matter in what direction I look; all things proclaim the achievements of their master. But it cannot continue like this. From now on a decline will set in, and I am quite helpless to prevent it from happening. Shall I then also from now on defy my heart, or shall I listen to the inner voice which begs me to break away?'

"The merchant Bernhard listened to the voice and obeyed it. He parted from his loved ones and turned his property over to others, and he made pilgrimages to many churches and asked the men of God what he should do in order to inherit eternal life. They gave him much good advice, grounded in the Gospel and in the lives and words of the saints as well as their own experience. They instructed him in pious exercises and they listed all the good deeds he could do with his riches. He followed their advice, but it gave him only a fleeting sense of satisfaction. Anxiety devoured his peace of mind, and emptiness devoured his anxiety, and he thought of seeking death.

"Then it happened that an old monk said to him: 'Tonight you are going to make your bed in the church, near the high altar. Bring along your eldest son and ask him to keep vigil, and when the hour has advanced until the third night watch, he is to call you, and you are to lift yourself up on your right elbow with your eyes closed; while you thus rise from your bed you are to open your eyes. What you then see will give you that which you most of all desire.'

"The merchant did as he had been told, and so did his son; when the merchant had been wakened and had got up on his right elbow and had opened his eyes, he saw the crucifix of the high altar bathed in the light of the moon, which just then was in such a position in the heavens that the rays came in through a very narrow slot high up in the southern wall of the choir and lit up the countenance of the Crucified One. The crucifix had been executed by a great artist who knew the terror and the purity of suffering. For that reason it also spoke urgently to the merchant about a love stronger than death itself, a love that he had never known before. Deeply moved, he rose and opened the little gate in the altar railing in order to worship at the feet of the Crucified One; just when he bent forward he could read an inscription in Latin that had been carved in the wood, a motto used by one of the old Crusaders: 'One for all; all for one.'

"Very rarely in life do we read words and at the very same time grasp their entire meaning; it happened to merchant Bernhard on that night.

"From then on he was not ashamed to be as the lowliest servant among prisoners, the sick and the poor, in such a way that even miracles and omens occurred wherever he and his disciples went. Many monks left their monasteries and joined him, and abbots and cardinals began to be worried about this new spiritual movement. For that reason they hurriedly put forth the proposal that a new monastic order be established. But the merchant Bernhard rejected all their plans and suggestions. He wanted to do his work in the freedom of the Spirit and would not be bound by any order, neither an old one nor a new one.

"Then it wasn't long before the merchant and his followers were persecuted, and they had to flee into the mountains. Many deserted him in this time of trouble, but even more remained steadfast — yes, even unto death.

"Their congregation survived for a hundred years, and related movements, such as the Waldensians and later on the Huguenots, served to strengthen and aid it. Some of the Huguenots went first to England and later on to the New World where they found a refuge where they could worship God in the light of their own conscience. Vague accounts of their fate and the conditions under which they lived would occasionally reach the land they had left behind and those who were still standing fast against the enemies of the faith.

"When the great revolution occurred, some people thought that the congregation would be able to live under more pleasant circumstances; others were afraid that it would lead to a time of greater trouble — and they were right.

"Then it happened that a young nobleman who was a lecturer in law at the University of Paris, accidentally heard the story of the merchant Bernhard, and because of curiosity rather than sympathy he decided to pay a visit to Bernhard's descendants and fellow believers. The congregation had gathered most of its members in a village high up in the mountains. He stayed with them a week.

"At first he had no thought of staying longer than that, but he was so deeply affected by their pious way of life that he said to himself, 'If God will only grant it, this faith shall also be mine.'

"He made up his mind to pray and to fast until the Lord revealed himself to him, and when he had patiently endured this regimen for almost a year, he received that reward which is called divine peace in mind and conscience. Soon after that he began to preach the Gospel, and many people said that he preached as spiritedly and forcefully as merchant Bernhard had in his time. Just as in those days, many converts were made, and the little congregation which for more than a hundred years had been greatly shrinking in size, once more began to grow. The enemies of the Gospel, however, heard about this, and they once again resorted to violence against the faithful, as they had in times gone by. Most of all they wanted to capture the leader.

"He, however, was of the opinion that he could achieve more by going into hiding, and he took his wife —she was well known for her piety as well as for her beauty — and their little daughter, and fled farther up into the mountains, to a ruined castle; it was inhabited only by a watchman who kept the worst decay in check. The watchman was also an adherent of the faith.

"But their pursuers tracked them down. They knocked the watchman down inside the gate, and when they had broken down the door to the innermost room in the tower and found the leader's wife there, they raped her and pierced her with a sword. They seized the child by its feet and threw it up against the stone ceiling. The child remained hanging there in a large crystal chandelier under the vaulting; and immediately below it, around a large table, they sat down to eat and drink.

"They finally went to sleep; then, he whom they had been seeking returned from the hunt. He found the watchman dead by the gate, and when he stepped into the upper room in the castle he encountered his wife's dead body; it was bloody and desecrated, lying on the floor. The murderers were sleeping heavily, their heads resting against the tabletop.

"Shaken by the horror of it all, he looked around to see if the child might still be alive, then saw at a glance his child hanging in the chandelier underneath the ceiling.

"Like fire from heavens it shot through him: 'An eye for an eye, a tooth for a tooth! I have the power, now I must use it!' But at the very same moment another Word of God came into his mind: 'To me belongeth vengeance, says the Lord,' and another one: 'Love your enemies, bless them that curse you, pray for them which persecute you.' And he bent down and kissed his wife's forehead for the last time and then lifted her gently up in his arms.

"He carried her far into the forest, and he tied a stone around her neck and lowered her body into a pond. While the water rippled shoreward and then became still, he prayed and thanked God for every hour he had had the privilege of sharing with her.

"Then he leaped into the saddle. The horse had carried the three of them all the way from the village into the forest; now it carried only him. He traveled at a fast pace without stopping across mountains and valleys and through foreign lands all the way to Genoa in Italy, where he secretly called on a French family who were sympathizers of his faith. They told him that his congregation encountered suffering and death everywhere, and he was confirmed in his intent to leave Europe and travel to America. All the stories he had heard about the country agreed that he would there find a safe refuge, and it was his hope that he, like William Penn in his time, would have the good fortune of being able to found a community of saintly people.

"He embarked on a ship, and while at sea he was in the greatest peril, but the mighty hand of God saved him in a miraculous way."

He fell silent for a moment, and my glance met his. He said, "You know who he is, my friend. Do you dare, then, to continue doubting that you, as well as I, have been selected to enter the service of the Lord?"

I was silent for a long time, and then replied, "Noble sir, you are mistaken in your assessment of the man whom you have shown such great kindness, for I am in every way unworthy and unsuited to such a high calling."

But he answered, "In His own good time the Lord will reveal Himself to you, my son. Will you now accompany me up to the summit of Pico de Teide?"

"Yes," I answered.

"Not very far from here there's supposed to live a man who rents out riding donkeys. We will look him up," said Stephen Grellet.

Together we walked out of the chapel, and while we were standing on the doorstep he spread out a map. We studied it thoroughly and soon found the place where we were. Thereupon we took our departure from "The Blessed Mary of the Snows."

We rented donkeys for a small sum, but in addition we had to pay for a local guide whom we were advised we ought to take along.

Although this mountain at a distance looks like a smooth, polished pyramid, the streams of lava have plowed deep furrows in it and have formed huge mounds, and the path winds through ravines, around tremendous rocks, and along the edge of dizzying precipices.

We rode for about twenty-four hours, and we arrived in the evening, as we had planned. A cabin had been built near the summit; we sought shelter there. We wrapped ourselves in camel-hair cloaks and goatskins, for the wind was blowing hard and the air was cold. Our companion made a fire and sat down beside it.

He woke us at dawn. Just like here in Texas, there too it's a short time between dawn and sunrise.

I don't have the ability to describe properly what we felt when the sun burst above the rim of the outer row of craters and let its flood of light virtually inundate us. But I remember that through a veil of drifting clouds we had a glimpse of the crater itself far below us; it was still immersed in bluish twilight.

Because of the ribbon of mist we couldn't see either the valley itself or Puerto de la Cruz way out on the promontory, but beyond the town we could glimpse the ocean. Gradually the mist became tinged with the red of dawn, but a shadow in the shape of a tower spread across it long after the sun had risen into the sky; it was the shadow of Teide's mighty crown.

Just when the sun rose I had the sensation of having witnessed this once before, way back in time, as in another life, and suddenly came to my mind's eye that morning on Finnborg, the island that I had looked for as a small boy in order to be there when the sun rose. Perhaps for the first time I clearly realized that at the different crossroads in life we often encounter the same signs, in order that we should reflect on what they imply and obtain wisdom from them.

When we had rejoiced at the beautiful sunrise, our guide said, "It's time for breakfast." In a spot from which the snow had been blown away, he dug into the sand with a flat piece of rock, and said, "Feel it!" We held our hands above the hole from which the heat rose from the interior of the earth. In the hole he placed an egg that he had brought with him, and covered it, and in this case it took exactly as long as it does to boil an egg over an open fire.

When we had finished our meal and our companion had gone over to the donkeys to feed them, Stephen Grellet and I sat where we were in silence. Due to the hot breeze emerging from the hole in the ground we did not notice the cold. At last Grellet said, "Columbus sailed from these islands on his voyages to the New World. As soon as I can obtain passage on a ship I will follow in his footsteps. The Spirit drives me thither. What do you choose to do, my friend? Do you hear the voice of the Spirit?"

I answered, "If I haven't completely forgotten what I learned when I was confirmed, it says in the Bible that the Spirit is like the wind; it blows wherever it so desires. I have not heard its soughing and sighing, but sitting here I can feel that I am being called back to my own land and people, and that call I want to follow."

Stephen Grellet said, "Surely, this is the voice of the Spirit in your heart. What task will the Lord set you to do?"

"I am not suited for any service for the Lord," I said. "But if my mother and father are still living I would like to see them. Before I left I also promised to be true to a young woman, even though she did not demand any such pledge of me. If she's still unattached, I shall once again propose to her."

He asked, "Is she a pious woman?"

I couldn't help smiling: "Far more pious than I am, but hardly as pious as you, my dear sir."

"May God bless you both," he said.

Shortly after this Stephen Grellet set off on board a Spanish schooner for America. Little did I know that we were to meet again many years later.

As for myself, I obtained passage on a ship from Tenerife back to Marseilles. Nothing could have suited me better, for in Marseilles I had put away all the gifts that I had purchased over many years — gifts that were intended for my mother and for Sara Larsdatter.

The Seventh Tale

In Marseilles I shipped on board a vessel bound for Norway. I took with me all the gifts and the other belongings that I had had in storage with the agent of the shipowner. Among them were a chest of camphor wood, and elephant tusks, Persian rugs and tanned hides of the longhaired baboon from Abyssinia, fabrics and tablecloths, cameo jewelry and pearls of amber, and many other things.

As so frequently happens, there was a strong wind from the northeast in the Gulf of the Lion and a storm coming in from the west in the Bay of Biscay, and in the English Channel we encountered calm and foggy weather.

When I was off duty I often took out the things I planned to give to Sara Larsdatter. The more I looked at them the more clearly I could see the picture of her in my mind's eye. I also looked at my own face in a small mirror on the wall and said to myself, "You've become manly looking and quite handsome, Cleng; many a maid would be pleased to get a fellow like you for husband. Then, why not Sara Larsdatter?"

At the latitude of the southernmost point of Norway, known as Lindesnes, while we were still far out in the Skagerak and not within sight of land, we ran into a storm approaching from the southeast; at times it had the force of a veritable hurricane.

I have very seldom had a worse experience at sea. We kept away from land because we were well aware that it would be a terrible gamble to try to find a safe harbor in such weather; it had started to snow heavily, and even in the middle of the day, we could hardly see ahead as far as the length of a ship, and much less after dark. The wind showed no signs of abating.

In this weather it became necessary to trim the sails, and I and a few others were assigned the task. I had signed on as a plain deckhand on this voyage just in order to get home the sooner; there was already a boatswain on the schooner.

In those days I was as agile as a cat, Anne, and steady on my feet; not many were better at climbing out on the yardarms.

Nevertheless, it was only with great effort that I got up on the topgallant yard. Above me I could see the top of the mainmast impale the drifting clouds; stars gave off sparks wherever small pieces of the night sky could be seen between the billowing sails. A shower had just swept past us, another one was just approaching like a black wall above the horizon. Both rigging and woodwork were covered with snow; everything had been showered with sea water which had turned into ice. Then, the capricious tossing of the waves suddenly made me lose my footing. During the brief seconds that I was falling — until I again almost miraculously managed to grasp a rope near the crosstrees of the topgallant yard — I once again saw Sara Larsdatter before me as in a vision, and like lightning it flashed through my mind, "If Divine Providence once again spares your life, then it must be because you are destined to share it with her."

Standing on the crosstrees I clung to the mast and waited for the trembling in my arms and legs to cease, and I did not climb down until I had completed my task.

But in spite of everything we did to try to save the ship and the cargo, we came to grief. The mainmast broke a few hours later, and right after that something went wrong with the rudder. Still, we kept the storm at bay for about twenty-four hours; in the end the ship was hurled against the barren and desolate coast south of the town of Egersund. But we didn't know where we were.

I have told you about one shipwreck, Anne, and I won't trouble you with the story of another. When one is in danger one doesn't have much time to think about it until it's all over. But even though the waves were bigger outside Tenerife, the sea was more choppy here, and much colder. We would soon have succumbed from cramps, if from nothing else, but this time, too, our misfortune brought some luck along with it, since the ship was tossed up on a low and rocky promontory, on the other side of which were the calm waters of a narrow bay. Thus our lives were saved and most of our belongings, but the ship's cargo was lost. The cargo consisted of grain and brandy, and the grain went to the bottom with the ship when it subsequently was thrown off the promontory and sank. But some of the casks of brandy drifted ashore.

The shipwreck had taken place at night, and for many hours we paced back and forth among the rocks and hills in order to keep warm. We saw no signs of people or dwellings. When dawn broke, we made fire from driftwood and other combustible material that we found, and we opened a cask and emptied it. The brandy made us feel completely exhausted, and I must have fallen asleep.

When I woke up, I was lying in the shelter of a large rock. It had begun to snow again; my clothes were already covered with snow.

Two men were standing over me; they had wakened me up from a sleep which might have ended in death. Both of them belonged to the district. They had been walking — as was usual after a storm — along the beaches to look for flotsam and pieces of wreckage. They didn't know anything about our shipwreck, nor had they seen any of the other members of the crew.

They helped me get up and brought me to their home. There they gave me something warm to drink and had me put on dry clothes.

I became sick and took to bed with a high fever; but I received the best of care. When I at last was well again, it had turned very cold and there was much snow on the ground. I let it be known that I would like to travel north as soon as possible, and the fisherman who had put me up and taken care of me, promised to get me a horse and a carriage. The owner of the nearest farm offered to drive me as far as the parsonage at Helleland; the pastor in that parish was both wealthy and hospitable, he said, and he would most certainly receive me warmly and see to it that I could continue my journey safe and sound.

Nothing noteworthy happened until we reached the parsonage; there, however, I was to meet a man who was later to play a role in my story. His name was Thomas Madland, and he was at that time a blacksmith in Stavanger. With his wife and six children he was one of the group that later was to leave Norway in the *Restauration*.

It was getting dark when we drove into the yard of the parsonage. The horses were foaming at the mouth; for the driver had made them run fast, and the terrain was rugged. The wind had formed large snow-drifts; it was very cold and there was no moon in the sky. Hoarfrost and ice covered the horses' manes and muzzles; their shoulders and backs were steaming.

The pastor emerged from the main entrance just as we turned into the yard. When he noticed how the horses were sweating, he swore like a trooper and asked us whether we weren't aware of the obligations attached to the fact that God had placed the dumb animals in our care. At that very moment I threw the fur cover to the side so that he could see the chest of camphor wood. He got very excited and wanted to know where we came from and what our business was.

Just a few words sufficed to answer his questions, and he immediately became very friendly and told me that in his youth he had been a ship's chaplain on the vessels of the East Asiatic Company, and later had served on a ship in the China trade.

"It was in the East," he said, as if apologizing for his rough manner in receiving us, "that the old coarseness in morals and behavior prevailed the longest. God look in His mercy upon a poor minister who learned the bad habit of swearing and has not been able to purge himself of such a great sin!"

Later on I was told that even though the Helleland congregation might have desired in their pastor — his name was Reynert — a man of somewhat more ecclesiastical dignity and manners fitting a servant of God, he was nevertheless loved by them and was considered a zealous spiritual shepherd.

He had the farmhand take care of the horses and ordered him to put them in the stable to be dried off with whiskbrooms, and the cribs were to be filled with the best oats. The driver and I were shown into the main parlor, where the fire was roaring in a large iron stove. On the table candles were burning in tall pewter candlesticks; white sand and chopped-up evergreens had been strewn on the floor. The fresh aroma of juniper mingled with the fragrance of tallow and incense. The minister's two daughters filled our cups from a large copper tea urn. Then we were served a sumptuous dinner, one that I shall not soon forget. I will mention the various courses to you, Anne, so that you won't think that the country your parents left had nothing but poverty to offer its people: We had smoked salmon and ptarmigan, cold cuts and ham, and many kinds of berries: lingon and cloudberries, cherries and black and red currants, and with it we had red wine imported from France, the kind that is most highly appreciated in Norway.

While having punch after the meal the minister offered us two of his own long-stemmed pipes and told us stories from his travels in many foreign countries, but he was also interested in hearing about my experiences. His two daughters entertained us as if we were members of the gentry; one of them sang, and the other played the spinet. They both wore dresses such as had become fashionable after the Great

Revolution; as far as that went, one could very well imagine that this was a wealthy home in France rather than a secluded parsonage in Norway.

I have already told you about Thomas Madland; he too was one of the company that evening and stayed to the very end. He had been living at the parsonage for some time, having done some decorative work in wrought iron; Reynert had a taste for art.

It was Thomas Madland who led the conversation on to a new subject; he mentioned a man by the name of Hans Nielsen Hauge. The name was completely unknown to me. His home was originally some place in the eastern part of Norway, over by the Swedish border, he said, but he had been traveling all over the country until he had been put in jail. Following a spiritual crisis and a strange revelation, during which he saw the heavens open themselves to him while he was plowing in his father's fields, he believed that he had been called to preach the Word of God. Although he did not preach against the established ecclesiastical order or the teachings of the Lutheran Church, he was nevertheless in disfavor with a great part of the clergy, and with the aid and cooperation of the secular authorities he was finally taken into custody.

The minister confirmed that that was exactly the way it had happened. He himself disagreed with Hauge, who in his opinion had given himself over to fanaticism, since no layman had the right to preach the Word of God in a public assembly and could not, of course, have the understanding and the knowledge to enable him to do it properly. But still, he did not think that Hauge's errors were so great that he deserved to be put in irons, he said.

Thomas Madland also told us that Hauge had visited the city of Stavanger and the surrounding districts, and he had gained adherents wherever he went.

This was what I learned about Hans Nielsen Hauge on that particular evening. After we had enjoyed the good food and the conversation — it was already very late — the two daughters showed us to our bedrooms. They were in charge of the household; the minister was a widower. They had prepared for us beds with pillows and sheets of the finest white Dutch linen and coverlets that were as light and warm as the down with which they were filled. It was indeed a change from what we had had on board ship, where the bunks had smelled of sweat and mold, and there were lice in the woodwork and cockroaches on the deck!

The blacksmith Thomas Madland had his own shop in Stavanger, but because he was very skilled in his trade he would at times take on special jobs for the gentry, for which he was well paid; he was nothing less than an artist in wrought-iron work. It so happened that he had just completed his assignment from the pastor of Helleland and was about to go back to Stavanger. Reynert was to drive him himself, and I was asked if I wanted to accompany them.

We set out a few days later. The snow still covered fields and forests; the cold weather had not abated. The sleigh was lined with bison and bear skins, and on the floorboard were hot stones to place our feet on.

The road led over hill and dale. The terrain was rough in many places, but none were actually very dangerous to life and limb, except one spot. Here the road sloped down toward an abyss at the bottom of which there was a river; the road was narrow and covered with ice. The driver advised us to get out of the sleigh, and we got past the spot while almost clinging to the rock wall on the other side of the road. There was nothing for us to hold on to but icicles hanging down from the escarpment above us, which resembled stalactites. We had pulled socks made from goat hair over our boots, in order to get a better footing in the snow and ice.

Then, suddenly, just what we had been afraid of happened — the sleigh began to slide sideways. The horse dug its shoes into the sheet of ice; frantic, it pulled back its mouth and showed its yellow teeth, while white steam poured out from its nostrils. It put up a tremendous fight so as not to fall into the abyss.

For a short while it looked bad for both horse and sleigh, but I didn't think of that. I thought only of the chest of camphor wood; it hadn't been tied very well to the sleigh and was just about to slide off. When we were on firmer ground, I asked the driver whether we could expect to encounter other spots like that, but he felt sure that the worst was now behind us. Nevertheless, I got hold of a piece of rope and tied it around the chest and also made a sling so that I could carry it on my back if need be. It was full to the brim with gifts, and I was constantly thinking about Sara Larsdatter and that I was going to place all those presents before her and ask her to reject neither them nor their giver.

We talked about many things while on the road. Thomas Madland was married and had three children, one son and two daughters. His wife's name was Sigrid; she was ten years older than he — she was almost forty. "But there's not a tooth missing in her mouth, and she has no wrinkles at all," he said, all the while praising mature women in preference to young women; although said in a jocular manner, it seemed to be the opinion of a mature and experienced man. I got the impression that he was very fond of his wife. I had no comment to make, but when he later on mentioned Lars Simonsen of Jeilane, I asked him if he knew Sara Larsdatter.

"She's one of those who don't make much noise," he said. "Many years ago she's supposed to have corresponded with a sailor, but it all came to an abrupt end."

"Perhaps he forgot all about her after being with girls in foreign ports," I ventured.

"Perhaps so," Thomas Madland answered. "It was discovered, however, that the shipowner's attorney for many years had misappropriated letters and packages, whenever he thought he could get away with it, and if that was what happened to Sara Larsdatter and her sailor, I don't suppose either one can be blamed for their being parted. The attorney is still serving his well-deserved sentence, and the Lord has at last once again looked with mercy on Sara Larsdatter."

When I asked him what he meant by saying that the Lord had looked with mercy, he replied, "Her marriage banns have been published. The wedding is to take place up north in the city of Bergen; I think she's left for Bergen already. — The one who marries her will get a lovely bride and a splendid wife."

I managed to remain calm and asked whether she was lucky in the choice of a mate.

"That I have every reason to believe," he said and told me how the engagement had come about.

One of the many adherents that Hans Nielsen Hauge had gained in the city of Stavanger was Lars Simonsen of Jeilane. It happened frequently that they got together in his house for prayer meetings, for reading of the Bible, and singing hymns. Sara too had attended, had become receptive to what was said, and had been converted.

"That's the way with Hauge's followers," Thomas Madland continued. "It's true that their glance is directed toward the heavenly regions, but earthly and temporal things are not neglected. Even in the matter of arranging marriages that are suitable and pleasing to God they want to contribute their share. Thus, Hauge is supposed to have said more than once to this or that follower of his: 'In this or that valley there is a beautiful farm for sale on reasonable terms. We could obtain a spiritual foothold there if you decided to live there, especially if you found yourself a pious girl to be your loving wife. If you wish, I will try to help you with both these things; an acquaintance of mine has some money that should be invested and another one has two marriageable daughters — both of them are industrious and virtuous.'"

Such had been the case this time too. A farm had been put up for sale near Bergen. And across the property ran a brook, large enough to run a mill. Hauge had looked at the farm and had confirmed that if a mill was built there it would provide a very nice income.

When he had found the right man to run the farm and the mill, he then had set out to obtain for him a sum of money and a girl to be his wife. The choice fell on Sara Larsdatter.

"But are they in love with each other?" I asked, and Thomas Madland answered, "Among Hauge's followers it is generally thought that if piety and obedience reign, they will in time be joined by that love which is so necessary for two people to be a good husband and a wife to each other."

In the meantime we had gotten as far as within seven or eight miles of Stavanger. I asked Thomas Madland if he could recommend a good inn where I could stay. He mentioned several, but finally advised me to go to the Admiral Cruys Bodega, a fairly new inn located in the part of town known as Skagen.

"In bodegas they usually only serve wines and liquor," I said.

"But not there," he answered. "It's only that the proprietress has a liking for anything that sounds strange and alluring."

"Is the owner a woman?" I asked.

"The bodega is owned by a certain lady whose name is Anne Cathrine Sælinger," he said. "She has become widely known for the good food and the wines she serves. Otherwise, her reputation is not the best, but I should think you're able to take care of yourself." He remained silent for a while; then he asked, "You are the sailor who corresponded with Sara Larsdatter? I don't suppose I'm mistaken in thinking that?"

"You're not mistaken," I said. "Thank you for your kindness to me, Thomas Madland. I'll put up at the Admiral Cruys Bodega."

The Eighth Tale

The sound of laughter and singing poured out of the open windows of the Admiral Cruys Bodega. Dusk had already descended on the narrow street; the houses looked like ships lowering their blue sails and finding an anchorage for the night.

I walked up the steep stairs to the front door, and through a sort of entrance hall I entered into a long low-ceilinged room with timbered walls. Hand-painted tapestries served to decorate the walls; shepherds were playing flutes, shepherdesses were sitting by purling brooks and tending their sheep. Shelves and mantelpieces were filled with models of sailing ships and other objects of the kind that world travelers bring home with them; it seemed to me that I recognized many of the things from the time that I had found shelter in Anne Cathrine's house on Finnøy. The Chinese vase was also standing there. Only faint lines on its glazed surface indicated that it had once been smashed; the lines gave it the stamp of venerability.

There were about twenty persons in the room, all of them men. From their appearance as well as their conversation I understood that some of them were sailors who had just returned home, others were skippers of cargo-carrying sailing vessels, and others again were citizens of Stavanger. Some of them were sitting with punch bowls in front of them, others were drinking rum or gin or the strong English porter which was a favorite beverage in Norwegian coastal towns in those days. Everyone was in high spirits, and became even more so when the waitresses came into the room.

I sat down at the only unoccupied table and ordered a drink which I knew would make me intoxicated in short order. When I was having a third glass, a no longer young but stately woman came into the room. I recognized her at once, and was surprised to note that she seemed younger than I remembered her. It was Anne Cathrine Sælinger. When she saw me, a smile lit up her face. She walked right over to me, shook my hand, and asked who it was that honored her with his presence. I told her my name and felt rather sure that she had recognized me.

"I see that the young gentleman has come from far away," she said. "Your dress and your polite manners give you away. I would feel honored if I may keep my new guest company." When she saw the label on the bottle standing on the table she added, "If you don't mind, sir, I would very much like to convince you that our wine cellar has other kinds of liquor to offer, of a finer taste, and with a slower and more elevating effect."

Thus our conversation got under way, but even though I could feel that I was slightly intoxicated I didn't say much. Not so with her; she started to tell funny stories that she claimed that her guests had told her; some of them were rather ribald although they did not completely overstep the boundaries of decency.

When the new bottle of wine was placed on the table and we toasted each other and her face became a bit flushed, it seemed to me as if she looked even younger than before. Her daughter appeared in my mind's eye, and I recalled what had happened that evening I had been with them.

Although slightly intoxicated, I did notice that her face was rouged, but not to excess. Her full lips had a greedy look to them, even though wrinkles had begun to knit a pattern of fine lines around her mouth. Her hair, which at one time must have been coal black, had turned gray, but still retained its sheen. Her body was buxom rather than gracefully slim; her dress was thin and displayed the soft contours that fashion demanded during the years following the French Revolution.

All this I noticed, and I was carried away by emotions that it is not proper for a man to feel toward a woman who might have been his grandmother. I got up in order to leave, but she said, "Don't you think you might be satisfied with a room in this inn, or have you already found accommodations elsewhere?" Then I recalled that this had been the real reason for my coming there, and I answered, "I would very much like to stay here." And she said, "You seem to be very tired; I'll ask the girls to get ready a room which I hope you will like."

She signaled to one of them to come over to the table and gave her orders, and when the girl a while later came back and said that everything had been made ready, we both rose from the table. Anne Cathrine walked me over to the door, opened it for me, and said good night in a very friendly way. I remained standing there and listened to her footsteps on the stairs.

The fire was roaring in the porcelain stove, and large birch logs were piled along the wall. I can still see the room before me: It was furnished with chairs and cabinets in Empire style — just then beginning to be very popular — the furniture being painted white with gilt ornamentation. The bed was of a different and older design; it was broad and was draped with a curtain whose heavy folds enclosed it on three sides.

I thought to myself, "In foreign countries a room furnished like this will cost more than an ordinary man's purse can tolerate." The very same moment I discovered a table with dishes containing bread, chicken, and wine, and I suddenly realized that I had not eaten for some time. I helped myself to the food, and while I was eating I wondered why Anne Cathrine Sælinger treated me like a guest of honor. But in spite of all that had happened to me, thoughts of Sara Larsdatter were constantly in my mind.

The next morning, when I was thoroughly rested and the sun was high in the sky, one of the waitresses came up to my room with coffee and cakes on an engraved silver tray. The mistress of the house had asked how I was. I felt flattered at hearing that, and told her that I was very well indeed. When the girl had left and had closed the door behind her, I jumped out of bed. From the chest I got out a suit that I had bought in Marseilles and which was to be used on festive occasions; when I had dressed, I spoke to the mirror and felt very satisfied with myself, "You have a clean-cut face and a smile that instills confidence, Cleng Peerson" — but at once I was overcome by a sense of shame: "Do you get all rigged up just for the sake of an old goose like her?" Even though this foolish vanity pricked my conscience, I felt gay and lighthearted when I stepped into the dining room.

Anne Cathrine was sitting at a table, conversing with an elderly man, whom I took to be a ship's captain. As soon as she saw me, she got up from her chair, excused herself, came toward me with a big smile, and said, "Oh, what a fine gentleman; he might have come direct from the general staff of one of Napoleon's armies!" And I answered, "That isn't too far from the truth, Madame Sælinger."

She asked me to sit down and seated herself opposite me, and after we talked about indifferent things, she suggested that we forget about formalities and address each other by first names. She asked if I had any relatives in Stavanger, to which I answered no. "No old sweetheart either?" she asked jokingly. "No, not that either," I replied. "But in spite of the way you are dressed and your cheerful expression I can tell that something depresses you," she said. "I suppose everybody has some kind of trouble," I answered.

She was toying with a large diamond ring which she wore on a finger on her right hand; she finally said, "I'm very glad that I can offer you a room as long as you might want it, and at a very reasonable price. I don't suppose you have any immediate pressing engagements?"

"I ought to visit my parents," I answered.

She looked at her hands; suddenly she raised her head and looked at me: "A man of your caliber will miss his mother. I can imagine that you are on very good terms." "It's always been that way," I answered.

"I know very well that I'm no substitute for a mother, but perhaps I could take her place as long as you're staying here?" she asked me. I felt a bit bashful and replied, "Yes, thank you, why not?"

Right after that I got up from the table, left the room, and went for a walk into town.

I didn't return until early evening. I had roamed through the streets of the town, filled to overflowing with a mixture of joy and sadness, with the bittersweet feeling of happiness one experiences when close to something beautiful and unattainable. Back in the inn, I ordered its best wine, for I knew that one's intoxication varies with the type of liquor. A feeling of quiet sadness will be maintained longer by the finest wines.

I had been sitting there about a half hour, and had consumed most of the bottle, when Anne Cathrine entered the room, just as she had done the previous evening. She said in a jocular manner, "Don't drink any more on an empty stomach! Come and have supper with me. The cook has a splendid lamb on a spit in the kitchen, and you've probably had nothing but salted meat and biscuits for a long time. Where's the ship that you sailed on? I don't know of any ship having recently arrived here from foreign ports?"

"My ship's lying at the bottom of the ocean," I answered; greatly surprised she asked, "Is that true?" "It's just as true as the fact that I've eaten other things than biscuits and salted meat the last few days," I said, and without mentioning the name of the minister or the place I told her about the meal that the pastor at Helleland had served.

"Please permit me," she said when I had told her about every item on the menu and had perhaps made it seem better than it was; "please permit me to show you what I can do in the kitchen and see if the Admiral Cruys Bodega is able to surpass what you've just told me? If you'll accept it?"

I said, "Why do you want to show me such great kindness?"

She replied, "I have become extremely fond of you. A woman will never become so old that she can't immediately see if a man has need of sympathy and understanding. And if I'm not mistaken, you're weighed down by a sorrow; there's a certain expression around your mouth and your eyes that's very revealing."

"Perhaps so," I answered. She opened her purse and took out a coin, saying, "Here's a two-skilling piece. I'll keep my hands behind my back and pass the coin from one hand to the other. Then you'll guess in which hand I hold it, and if you guess correctly, you'll tell me all that's happened to you; but if you guess wrong, then I'll tell you my story. Afterwards you tell me about yourself, if you so wish. Are you game?"

I didn't feel very much like it, but I was afraid that she would think it was discourteous of me if I refused, and when I tried to guess which hand held the coin, I guessed wrong. She began to tell me her story, and included all kinds of things, but it was mostly about her marriage to Anders Nord. It was quite apparent that he had not been a faithful husband; she tried to excuse him, but in such a way that the excuses seemed more like accusations. She concluded, "In spite of everything I hope that he died in the Lord. He received the sacrament while still conscious, and the last thing he did was to emit a sigh just like the sighs made by the followers of Hans Nielsen Hauge."

She lifted her glass and looked straight at me; I couldn't tell whether there was sadness or merriment to be read in her eyes. She said, "Let's drink a toast to his salvation, Cleng Peerson." I raised my glass and felt as if it was an act of blasphemy, but felt strangely moved all the same. "You lost your husband too early, Madame Sælinger," I said. "Alas," she replied, "he gave me little joy." And as if she didn't wish to dwell any longer on this subject but was content to have titillated my curiosity, she changed the subject: "The food is served! Let's go into the dining room."

It was in truth a table that in every way surpassed that of the pastor of Helleland! When the meal finally was at an end and we had conversed about many things and frequently toasted each other, she said, "You asked — or did you not — why I seemed so elated and happy tonight?"

"Yes, I did," I replied, even though I didn't know of having said anything of the sort.

"Now I will tell you the reason," she said. "For one thing, it makes me happy to think of the fact that today it is five years ago that I received my divorce from my husband, and secondly, because it is two years ago that he was released from the troubles of this world. Today I have at last been told that certain obscure points in his will have been interpreted to my advantage. I have become the owner of everything that he left: shares in ships and in trading companies both here and in Bergen, in addition to all his money, which amounts to several thousand dalers. We have been drinking to his salvation, but we can also drink a toast to my prosperity, and to the possibility that I get someone to share it with!"

She smiled again, but I was at just as great a loss as ever at interpreting her smile as I had her words, and I decided to thank her, wish her good night, and leave.

Her eyes filled with tears; she bent across the table and whispered, "Cleng, my young friend, I must confide this to you: within five years death will have caught up with me too."

I half believed, half doubted what she said, and the change in her demeanor made me feel even more uncertain. She raised her champagne glass so that the liquid gleamed against the light; sounding bitter and jolly at the same time, she said, "Drink with me, Cleng Peerson! I don't intend to sit idly by and just wait for the tolling of the bells and the three shovels of earth!"

We both emptied our glasses, and she filled them once again.

It is difficult for me to relate what happened after that, because I remember very little. When I woke up it was daylight. My head felt sore as a red-hot cannonball, and my throat was drier than a dusty highway. I was lying in a board bed, where the drapes were of heavy silk with a woven pattern of dancing cupids. At my side lay Anne Cathrine, still in a deep sleep.

Appalled, I sat up and wanted to steal quietly out of the room before she woke up. But just as I was getting out of bed, she opened her eyes.

I had expected to hear the most angry reproaches, but quite to the contrary: she smiled at me in a friendly manner and extended her hand. I didn't know what to think, but I apologized for having inadvertently entered her bedroom.

She replied, "It's easy for me to forgive you that, Cleng. But you well know that if you hadn't promised to marry me, I would never have let you."

I became greatly dismayed at hearing this and said, "I haven't been guilty of having done anything that is shameful, have I?"

"Have no regrets, Cleng," she answered; "and don't grieve over it. I can be a good wife to you the few years that I have left to live."

Filled with despair and with shame, I once again asked her to forgive me. Then she was moved to tears, and she said, "Anders Nord treated me as if I were a dog in the yard or a louse on the wall. I'm not going to blacken his memory, but he was not a man who could give a woman solace, and I'm not the kind that becomes cooler with age."

Time and again it occurred to me that she must have been lying to me, but I was in a degrading and defenseless situation, a situation which became the more so when she rang a bell and one of the maids opened the door to our room. Anne Cathrine asked her to serve us breakfast in bed; a few minutes later she entered with newly made coffee and hot rolls.

While we were eating Anne Cathrine said, "You have provided me with the greatest joy, for you have flattered my vanity as well as having brought back my youth, and in the midst of all this you have displayed a noble disposition. I know only too well that I'm no longer as desirable as some of the young women that a sailor can have, but perhaps I nevertheless dare hope that you were seeking something else besides the wealth that you will inherit from me?"

And what else could I have done, except to assure her that what she believed was indeed the truth?

When we had eaten I got dressed and went out. I walked through the narrow alleys in the direction of the harbor. A ship was just then being made ready to set sail. Then I saw two men, one of them quite old, the other very young, walking along the quay together with a young woman, and they all stepped on board the vessel. I recognized them instantly: they were Lars Simonsen and Lars Larsen and Sara Larsdatter; it was quite evident that they were on their way to Bergen to the wedding.

They put their baggage down on the deck; it consisted of chests and boxes; she stood up straight and stroked her hand over her forehead so that her kerchief slid back. The sun made her hair gleam like gold; around her lips there was a touch of sadness. She had grown into a beautiful woman. With loathing I thought of what had just happened, and I recalled what Stephen Grellet had asked me on the summit of Pico de Teide, "What service will the Lord ask you to perform?"

Because I felt such great agony, I could think of no better relief than drowning my shame in a greater shame.

I returned to the Admiral Cruys Bodega, and for days and weeks I gave myself over to passion and licentiousness. Just as the prince in the fairy tale was changed into a white bear, so also was I changed through the magic of Anne Cathrine Sælinger. Even though I detested her, she tied me to her through physical intimacy, and there was no princess who could release me.

It was almost spring. The wild geese were flying north high above the roofs of the houses; the starlings woke me up long before daybreak. Leaves of grass appeared between the cobblestones; the lindens surrounding the cathedral were covered with shoots, and the young maidens had started to carry parasols when they were out promenading.

I had been as if bewitched; but suddenly one day I could once again look at the world around me: the sky with light clouds drifting in from the west and the sea with its rippled blue surface. I was reminded that there was a fjord upon which I must sail and a home that I must find again.

Anne Cathrine did not object when I told her that I wanted to visit my parents. She couldn't have helped realizing that I would never again cross her path, not to mention take refuge under her roof.

She prepared the best provisions for me to take along, and in an unobtrusive manner she wished me a happy journey.

A sailing vessel destined for the north country brought me across the fjord; I continued my journey on foot.

It was early evening when I approached Falkeid and Hesthammer. There had been a slight drizzle; it had covered both land and sea with a thin veil, but the sun was shining again. The rays from the setting sun looked like a fan of mother-of-pearl and gold reaching into red cloudy cupolas towering up one behind the other, as if one huge room behind the other were rising in magnificent splendor behind the heavenly gates.

Solitary houses were to be seen in the little valleys and around bays and inlets; uniformly small and gray, each was seemingly hiding behind the mountain in whose shelter it had been built. Thin smoke rose from chimneys and smoke vents and mingled with the air; a light breeze wafted across the hills and mountains. In the birch forest, gleaming after the rainfall, the buds were bursting; the sun which sank toward a clear horizon, with clouds above, seemed to lift everything up — houses and trees and the distant blue hills — making everything look larger than it was.

The loveliness of that evening was enhanced by the fact that I saw again the many places I had known in my boyhood and youth.

That is one reason I recall that evening, but it is not the only one. Man himself every day creates the world anew in his own image. I saw a man and a woman walk hand in hand along a green path.

No, Anne, it wasn't two young lovers that I saw. They were my parents; my father was bent and old, my mother was still as erect as ever.

Let me first tell you what I already knew from my mother's letters: that Father had been living at home for more than two years. But I didn't know that this past winter he had suddenly and without warning lost his eyesight.

This was the first real spring day of the year. Mother had for that reason taken him by the hand and brought him out into the fields, so that he could feel the sun and the wind against his face and enjoy the aroma that flowers in bloom spread across the land.

They were walking in the fields belonging to the Falkeid farm, along the edge of a meadow beyond which there were some rock outcroppings, and I caught sight of them just as I reached the top of the rocks and was walking down into the brushwood. I recognized them immediately, even though they were walking with their backs toward me.

Father was holding a stick in his right hand, and with his left he was holding on to Mother's arm. I was wondering why she time and again was bending down, as if she were picking up something from the ground and holding it up to his face.

I knew about a deep fissure in the rocks nearby, and from the top I hurried down through this opening. A big rock blocked the exit at the lower end — we had often played there as children.

Just as I had reached the hiding place behind the rock, I heard their voices, and then I could see them. I understood from Father's groping and unsteady walk and from the way he held his head that he must be blind. Mother bent down once again: "Here we found the first buttercup that time too," she said, and she picked one and stroked its petals against his hand, saying, "Can you feel it?" And he said, "Yes, I can feel it." And she held it up to his face, and she said, "Can you smell the fragrance?" He replied, "I think it reminds me of the smell of wet earth."

He was carrying a small bouquet of flowers in the hand in which he also held the stick, and now Mother bent down once again and exclaimed, "How wonderful, the first white anemone! We'll pick it with root and all." And she let him touch it and said, "Can you feel the root? You remember the shape of the root of a white anemone?"

I thought of the many years he had been locked up in nothing but a cage.

He touched the root, and it sounded as if a subdued and gentle laughter was revived within him: "Here I used to walk in the springtime holding Cleng by the hand when he was a little boy. He would pick white anemones and bring them to me. His fingers were just like these roots, firm and cool and moist from the earth."

Mother seized a birch twig and made it almost touch his face. Of all the trees on the Falkeid property this was the first one whose leaves turned green; its shoots had already opened up. She said, "You can smell the fragrance of the tree?" And he replied, "Yes, the same fragrance was about you the spring we were married." "It was here that you picked flowers to make me a bridal wreath," Mother said. "I kept the wreath in a drawer in my chest. Now it has moldered away."

They walked along a path back across the fields, and I could no longer hear what they were saying, but the sound of their voices seemed to hover in the still air. Not until I caught sight of them again, all the way over by the river, was I able once more to hear the birds singing all around me.

I followed the same path across the fields. The sun had set, there were dewdrops on the grass; the red clouds were dimly reflected in the river when I crossed the bridge.

The Ninth Tale

Much had changed since I had left home. The fact that Father was much better and could live at home constituted the greatest change. True, he could at times be seized with melancholy, as in the past, but he didn't become completely unmanageable. It was rather as if he would quietly walk into a room completely unknown to us and would close the door behind him and remain there. He was not yet an old man, but he had the subdued demeanor of the aged — or of a sick but patient child.

Lars and Kari, my brother and sister, had grown up since I had seen them last. Lars visited our home for about a week right after I arrived, and we did some of the work on the farm together. It was the first time in many a year that I saw the grain sprout in the fields.

But when the haying was to be done, I couldn't stay put any longer. I heard about a shipyard on a nearby island which needed a skilled worker and went over there on a small sailing vessel.

There was plenty of work to be had in the shipyard. By midsummer a large half-decked cargo vessel was ready on the slipway. It was to be delivered to a man living on Sør-Talgje, an island lying in the direction of Stavanger, and I was given the task of taking the boat to its owner and being responsible for the entire delivery.

There was a stiff breeze when we sailed out of the fjord, and we reached Talgje by nightfall; it was Midsummer Eve. When we dropped anchor, people were flocking down to the shore, as if they were going to church; they had finished their day's work and had put on their Sunday best. The vessel's owner was already out in the harbor in a rowboat; he had seen his new ship from afar.

The ship was inspected from all angles, and it was loudly praised by everyone. Then someone suggested that the new owner should let as many as desired come on board; they wanted to test the ship under sail.

Finnøy is the name of the island lying on the other side of a narrow arm of the fjord. "Let's go over there and celebrate Midsummer!" someone in the crowd said. "Why not," agreed the owner, and when everyone was ready he took the rudder himself.

Just across from the southern tip of Talgje there's a good harbor right below the Reilstad farm. We set our course for it. The harbor was almost deserted; only a few old men were puttering about. They praised the vessel and the weather and told us that almost everyone had gone up to the Berge farm. They were going to have a bonfire there.

"And the mistress has arrived," they added.

Who the "mistress" might be I didn't offer much thought. I was looking forward to dancing with the Finnøy girls; it was said that they were the prettiest in that entire district.

We all walked up together, and we had no sooner arrived at the cairn where the wood for the bonfire had been built up, than I saw Anne Cathrine. Now it was evident who the "mistress" was. She also caught sight of me; she came over and greeted me in a friendly way. It didn't seem at all as if she were surprised at seeing me there.

She had arrived the day before, she told me, and also said that she used to live there in the summertime. The business at the inn was slow; the two maids were able to manage things.

She had on a calico dress; around her shoulders she wore a flower patterned shawl with big tassels. Just as the first time I had seen her the thought struck me: How beautiful she must have been once! But I knew only too well that she was no longer concealing any youthful charms underneath her dress.

Toward me she acted in a motherly manner, but also with a touch of coquetry. I felt a bit awkward and wondered whether some one might know of what had been between us. The other young fellows had already chosen their partners, and the dancing had begun. She said, "*You* ask *me* to dance, Cleng," and I couldn't get out of it. We joined the circle of dancing couples; she danced with so much grace and dignity that I had no reason to feel downhearted, but still that's the way I felt. It seemed to me as if people round about were putting their heads together, nodding knowingly, and laughing at us.

Food was to be served, and many splendid dishes were put on the table; neither was there any shortage of beer. I was told that most of this had been paid for by Anne Cathrine; she was the hostess and had arranged the festivities. But the women from the nearby farms had brought with them some of their finest delicacies.

At last the bonfire was burning and lit up the surroundings. The dancing ceased; we all stood there watching the flames reaching for the sky. It was a calm and warm evening; the sparks floated in the air, resembling small stars, an ever rising shower of fire etched against a thin veil of clouds which still displayed a tinge of red. Specks of dust and ashes landed on our hands and faces; then I noticed that Anne Cathrine was standing beside me. Whispering, she asked me whether I had a place to stay for the night: "My summerhouse is down below, not far from here, you know, by the Kindingstad inlet; there's a vacant room that you may use," she said. "You're welcome to use it."

"I have to deliver the new ship to its owner," I said. "But tomorrow I'll stop by and see you, if you would like me to."

I did not return to the boat, for I knew that the owner would sail back to Talgje during the night, provided there was a suitable breeze. Instead I crawled into a boathouse where I lay down in the hollow between two rows of lobster pots, and covered myself with a piece of an old fish net. It was far from being a soft and comfortable bed, and it grew colder during the night. From near and far I could hear singing and loud talk. For that reason it took some time before I fell asleep; I lay there thinking about a Midsummer Night spent in the Røldal church several years ago, and I was wondering how Anne Cathrine could possibly be suffering from a mortal disease, her being so lithe on her feet.

The next day was a Sunday, and I set out for her house at about the time people would be going to church. She greeted me in the most cordial manner. The table in the dining room had been set; it was covered with the finest linen cloth, cups and plates were of English porcelain, and as before there was no lack of delectable dishes.

She didn't mention our past relationship with a single word, and neither did I, but toward the end of the meal, after we had been conversing about unimportant things — she was talking most of the time, while I was rather silent — she suddenly turned to something entirely different: "Over at Talgje I own a piece of property along the shore," she said. "I've thought about building a shipyard there. There's going to be great demand for ships in the years ahead, both large and small. Napoleon has just started on the task that he intends to finish, and many a fine ship will go to the bottom before he is done. When we get married I thought you could supervise the work in the yard."

I must confess that I was somewhat taken aback. In spite of everything that had transpired between us, it seemed unthinkable that I should enter into marriage with her. At that time she had reached the age of 63; I myself was 23. This all happened in the year 1806.

I carefully tried to direct our conversation onto other things, but in vain, and when I finally asked when she planned to build the shipyard, she replied, "Just as soon as the haying is over. I was hoping that you would have wanted to supervise the construction of it."

"But I have promised to stay until Christmas in the yard I'm with now," I lied.

"Very well," she replied and there was a sharp edge to what she said, "I'll have it built with the aid of others, but I count on your taking over at New Year's. Then we can celebrate our wedding in the spring. I would very much like the wedding to be one that will be talked about far and wide."

I felt embarrassed and ill at ease, and left just as soon as I could do so in good grace.

It so happened that when I was walking along the road I met a number of people returning from church. Among them I met a young fellow whom I knew slightly. His name was Johannes Jacobsen Stene; he was about three years younger than I. Johannes's home had originally been in the Suldal valley where his father had been a schoolmaster, but right after confirmation he had signed on with a small cargo vessel sailing to ports in the Baltic, as far as Riga and St. Petersburg. Now he was the skipper of a sloop belonging to Sven, the farmer at Kindingstad — and it was on Kindingstad's property that Anne Cathrine's house was located.

Already at that time it was being said that he and Sven Kindingstad's oldest daughter, Martha, were interested in each other, and that proved to be true: about two years later they got married. What we first and foremost should remember him for, Anne, is the fact that he was the one who contributed most of the money when the *Restauration* was purchased, and he himself was along on the ocean crossing, he and his wife as well as their children — everyone with the exception of one boy who fled into the woods and hid, making it necessary to postpone the ship's departure for about a week. A lot of people combed the terrain searching for him, but to no avail.

But these are events that belong further along in my story.

We happened to be walking together for some distance, and he said to me, "Have you been visiting Anne Cathrine?" Evasively, I replied that I had called at her house on some business. "It's being said that you and she maintained a house of ill repute in Stavanger," he said. I felt my face muscles tighten, and when I attempted to answer him by pointing out that one should not put one's trust in evil rumors, I hardly managed to utter a single word.

"I'm not asking you whether you've given her any promise of marriage, and I'm not asking whether there's been anything between you," he said; "but you should know this, that when she was married to Anders Nord and also later she set her cap at young fellows, and you'll not be the first one to be laughed at if you get caught in her trap. But if you take my advice, you'll get away from her while there's still time."

With these words we parted. Months went by. I spent Christmas with my parents and brother and sister, but I didn't mention with a single word that I was in danger of becoming the bridegroom of a woman who was old enough to be my grandmother.

I was giving some thought to whether I should go back to sea, but I felt that I was bound by what she had said and that our life together had placed an obligation on me. After New Year's I traveled to Stavanger. Anne Cathrine showed me ledgers and securities and gave me an idea of her financial situation. I would never have thought that she was so rich. "And these are times when someone who wants to increase his capital can do so," she said. "The shipyard will earn a one hundred percent profit, and the war is going to last a long time."

While we were busily engaged with these things, she suddenly began to moan. She held her left side and leaned back in her chair. I held her up, but when she fainted I had to call the maid in a hurry. Together we carried her into another room and put her on the bed.

"She's had another attack," the maid said. "And the intervals are getting shorter all the time. That's the way it was with her mother, too, the last few years before she died, she's told me."

I had become more and more certain that Anne Cathrine had been telling me stories when she talked about her infirmity, but now I didn't know what to believe. When she regained consciousness a little while later, she looked wan and pale and had bluish rings under her eyes. It struck me that she looked much older than she had an hour before. She bit her lip, as if trying to conquer the pain; she smiled bravely, and when she had been given a glass of water and a powder, she asked that she get some pillows to support her back so that we could finish our discussion about the business.

I don't think that the wealth of this world had a greater hold on me than on most people, and later in life I scorned the power of Mammon; but we all have our weak moments, don't we, Anne? For the first time in my life I heard a devil whisper in my ear, "All you have to do is to endure it a few years; and then you'll have all this wealth to yourself."

I can tell you the rest of the story in a few words: Right after Candlemas I went back to Talgje and took charge of the shipyard. We laid down the keel of our first ship, and the work went on apace. In the meantime, Anne Cathrine began the preparations for the wedding. Three times the banns were announced from the pulpit in Hesby church. As if in a trance, I allowed it to happen and hardly comprehended that I was the one who was involved. Once again I thought of fleeing, and I had frightening notions, such as obtaining poison at the apothecary's and killing Anne Cathrine. I had made the slight acquaintance of the apothecary's assistant — his name was Enoch Jacobsen — and I knew that he mixed medicines and sold them behind apothecary Zetlitz's back. But I couldn't make myself go through with these or other plans. Silently, I swallowed the crude jokes made by the men in the shipyard, alluding to the age difference between Anne Cathrine and myself.

But away with the memories of all these troubles! Instead I want to tell you how the wedding turned out, but not because I take any pleasure in recalling it; but I thought that you might like me to tell a little about it. Then you can compare it with your own — and later on with my second wedding, when we get that far in my story. That wedding took place at Bishop Hill eighteen years ago; that time, I was forty years older than the bride, while the first time the bride was forty years older than I. Happy is the one who finds a partner who is right for his age and appeals to his heart.

Anne Cathrine had originally intended that the wedding should take place in Stavanger, but when she found out that we were both being laughed at on the island of Finnøy, where everything was more in the open, she, stubborn as she was, decided that we were going to ride to Hesby church, and that we were to invite as many of the best people in the area as the rooms at Kindingstad could accommodate.

The wedding took place on April 7, 1807. From my family, my mother and my sister Kari attended. Mother was about fifteen years younger than the bride; that fact made my embarrassment even greater. But Anne Cathrine was in a joyous mood and behaved in every way as a young girl in love. She pinched my cheek and playfully pulled at my beard, which was still soft and thin.

When she came down from her room dressed as a bride she looked splendid in spite of her age. She had on a black dress, over which she wore a white and sheer apron of striped drapery. A white starched scarf was pinned below the bodice, and around her waist she wore a red belt with dangling silver brooches. The bridal yoke was studded with many kinds of decorations: many-colored ribbons, flowers and brooches and pearls, gold and silver threads.

The five-pointed bridal crown was made of silver, and had many brooches fastened to it. As was customary, her hair had been braided high up and tied tightly around her head; it was surrounded by the bridal crown, the inner ring of which was lined with a piece of red cloth which had been stitched to her hair. There was also a wreath of artificial flowers around the crown, and from the flowers a wave of wide ribbons welled forth down her neck, reaching as far as her hips.

My mother had helped her put on all the finery. When they both came down and Anne Cathrine had gone into the parlor, leaving my mother and me alone for a moment, she looked at me and said, "You could have gotten a worse-looking bride, my boy."

It seemed to me as if her glance simultaneously contained pity and contempt and great tenderness. But I don't think she knew anything about what had been between Anne Cathrine and me; perhaps she believed what was being said: That I married her for her wealth and figured on her passing away before long.

The owner of the Kindingstad farm served as host and master of ceremonies. He jokingly said that it was about time for him to practice the duties of a good host. It was now generally known that Johannes Stene was to marry his daughter Martha. According to custom, he offered everyone drinks and almost forced people to sit down at the table by shouting at them, shaking hands, and making all the gestures that were needed. It was considered proper to hold oneself back, but the differences in rank were quite evident when the guests sat down to the table.

When everyone finally was seated, he tapped the handle of his knife against one of the beams in the ceiling; that was the sign for the guests to fold their hands and silently say grace before the meal. He himself said grace in a loud voice. Thereupon, everyone rushed to serve himself, each one using his own spoon. The first dish consisted of very hot milk mixed with beer, in which were floating buns, sugar cakes, and aniseed pastries. With this was served bread with butter and cheese and cold cuts until everyone had eaten his fill. Voicing thanks to Providence and to the hosts, everyone got up from the table. A few belched loudly; this was one way the people ever since olden times had shown their appreciation of the food, but now this custom was going out of fashion.

Then we immediately got ourselves ready for the trip to the church. When a young bride was to enter into holy matrimony, she would take leave of her mother and her father in the doorway, tearfully embracing them and thanking them for all that they had given her, and the parents would bless her and wish her happiness in her new home. My bride had no one to say good-bye to. I helped her to mount the horse; the previous day she had slid and fallen on a wet floor and had sprained her hip, and she was walking with a pronounced limp. But she managed to sit properly in the saddle, and all went well even when the shots were fired and the horses reared.

First in the procession rode two musicians; one of them played the violin, the other one blew on a clarinet. It was a mild spring day; the wind played with the multicolored ribbons that billowed out from the bride's crown, and the sun shone brightly, there being a few white, drifting clouds in the sky. I heard people talking and laughing behind me, and almost numb I thought to myself, "It's you they're laughing at." But I didn't turn around; I looked straight ahead, even when we were passing farms along the road and people shouted and greeted us. Anne Cathrine did the same. More joyful bridal couples must surely have been riding to Hesby church.

What the minister said and what he read, what hymns were sung and what happened otherwise — I can't remember a thing. But we did get married, and we rode back to Kindingstad, where the wedding feast continued with an abundance of food and drink.

After the meal I walked in and out of the rooms. I felt ill at ease, but perked up when an unexpected guest arrived in the early evening. It was a fellow from my home district, Daniel Stensen Rossadal; you'll remember that he and I traveled together to the fair the time I stayed in Anne Cathrine's house at Kindingstad.

Daniel's arrival made me very happy. Even though we had not had much to do with each other, I knew that he was a fellow one could trust.

It so happened that we walked together across the fields and down toward the shore. He said, "I have greetings to you from Sara Larsdatter. She has just become a widow."

If only I had known this a day earlier —

No one could understand how it had happened, he said; Sara's husband was working on a mill that he was putting up; the brook was overflowing, because the snows were melting in the mountains. In one way or another he must have had a beam fall on him, and it seemed as if it had held him down under the water so that he had drowned.

"She asked me to give you her best regards," Daniel Rossadal said once more.

"If you're traveling up north, you must give her my warmest greetings," I said.

"I'm going north next week," he replied. "She's thinking of coming back to Stavanger, she told me."

We parted; he went on board his ship and set sail for another island or village. As for myself I didn't return to the house where my wedding was being celebrated. I set off across hill and dale and hardly knew myself where I was going; but the moon showed me the way — it was in its third quarter.

Toward morning I realized that I was on the farthermost point of land, not far from Hesby church. I thought to myself, "Here I'm standing on a gray rock, and inside a gray rock I'm going to live for the rest of my life."

I didn't notice someone walking behind me, but suddenly I felt a hand grasping my shoulder. It was Johannes Stene; he had a dog on a leash.

"Are you sitting here, Cleng?" he said.

"Yes, I'm sitting here," I answered.

"This road won't take you any farther," he said. "You may as well come back with me."

The moon cast a pale light over the sea; in the east the sky showed signs of a new day.

I got up without making any reply. We stopped outside Anne Cathrine's house. The sun was just then rising above the horizon. Sheep and lambs were grazing in the green fields, and from the treetops we could hear the singing of numerous birds.

The guests had departed, and the house was empty. When I walked up the front step I ran into my mother. She was ready to set out on the return journey.

"I didn't think I ought to leave until I was certain that you were alive," she said. "What have you done, Cleng?"

"Yes, what have I done?" I said.

She put on her coat, bade me farewell, and walked down to where the boats were tied up.

Upstairs, in the room that had been prepared for our bedroom, I heard Anne Cathrine pacing to and fro. I walked up the stairs. She was sitting there, fully dressed, still in her bridal outfit, but the crown was lying on the bed, which was freshly made up.

Her eyes were just like two running sores: "What a disgrace has befallen me!" she moaned. "What shame you've brought on us both. I'll hate you, Cleng, as long as there's breath in my body."

The Tenth Tale

A few days later we brought on board all Anne Cathrine's wedding gifts and other belongings of various kinds and sailed to Stavanger. We made our home in her house; we shared the premises, but we rarely were together at meals, and never did we sleep together.

One day I met Thomas Madland; I hadn't seen him since we had been together on the journey from Helleland. Brimming over with happiness and enthusiasm, he told me that his wife had born their fourth child, a girl, three days earlier: "It's five years since the last time," he said, "and we were afraid that there wouldn't be any more. Come and have a drink with me."

He took me into his office; he filled my glass several times. He asked me if I would like to see the baby, and without waiting for an answer he got up and walked ahead of me through several rooms — the house consisted of two older buildings that had been joined into one. Without knocking he opened the door leading to the bedroom where his wife was lying. She was just then nursing the baby, and as we entered she moved so that the baby let go the nipple, and the milk squirted into the child's face. Quickly, she covered up, but I was filled with a deep sense of tenderness, both because I saw a woman at her most womanly and because I've always loved children and even newborn babes have seemed lovely to me. I bent over the little one and praised its hands and nails, and both parents were struck dumb with happiness.

From there we walked to the smithy, and Thomas Madland, who was a very good blacksmith and proud of his profession, showed me various pieces of work on which he and his men were engaged at the time. Among them were a few powerful iron calipers. They had been ordered by one of the shipyards in the district; and he mentioned the name Lars Simonsen of Jeilane. I asked about Lars Larsen, and Thomas told me that he was working at the shipyard part of the time and the rest of the time he worked on a ship sailing to France and back.

"He's home just now," he said, "and Sara also arrived here two days ago. She's become a widow since the last time she was here; did you know that? And she has her child with her; it was born around Christmas time, according to her father."

Hurriedly I said good-bye to him and rushed back to the Admiral Cruys Bodega. In Anne Cathrine's sewing box I found a pair of scissors; I first trimmed my beard in front of the mirror in my own room. Then I had the barber shave me and apply oils and ointment to my face, which was very sore from such unaccustomed treatment. Then I put on my Sunday best and set off for Lars Simonsen's house at Jeilane.

It was getting dark, but I knew the way although it was many years ago since I had walked along that road.

I knocked on the door to the workshop; I noticed that a light was burning inside. Lars Simonsen opened the door. Lars Larsen was standing by the carpenter's bench; when he turned around I recognized him immediately; but he had become a grown man since last I saw him. Lars Senior had changed very little.

It was very dark outside. They probably couldn't make out my features; neither was my voice familiar to them when I facetiously and in an altered voice asked them whether they weren't going to ask an old friend to come in. I resorted to this kind of prank just to hide my apprehensiveness.

"I don't think I know you!" Lars Simonsen uttered. "What's your name?"

Then I told them my name, and they immediately asked me to come in.

We talked for a while about where I had been on land and sea and about their shipyard; but the fact that I owned a shipyard myself and was a married man I never mentioned. Finally Lars Simonsen turned the conversation to Sara and told me all that I already knew. He said, "You want to say hello to her, don't you? And I hope you can stay long enough so that she can get up a good meal for us."

We walked up to the parlor, and for the first time since I had gone to sea I stood face to face with Sara Larsdatter. Her face flushed and a dizzy feeling came over me, but our glances met and steadied us. Her face was like an open book; there are no secrets that can be hidden from the eyes of a loved one.

She immediately began to serve the evening meal. When the table had been set, we men sat down and so did she, and we all ate together. We conversed about ordinary everyday events, and I could see clearly that Lars Simonsen had about him an air of gravity that I hadn't noticed before. When the meal was over, he got hold of his spectacles and a book and read from Holy Writ. And then he recited a fervent prayer, in his own words. After the prayer he put the Bible aside and poured a single glass of brandy for each one of us, and when we had emptied our glasses and talked for about a half hour, Lars Simonsen got up first, and right afterwards so did Lars Larsen; both said good night, as if there had been an unspoken agreement that I had come to see Sara only.

When I too after a while rose in order to take my leave, she said, "Take your time, Cleng; it's still early. And running across each other this once we do have something to tell each other, don't we?"

The shyness that had characterized her when we met, was now completely gone. I sat down. Without further ado she asked, "Why did you stop writing to me?" I said, "As far as I know, it was you who stopped." Then I told her what I had heard about the steamship agent who had been discharged for stealing and for disloyalty. And she said, "If your letters had reached me, I wouldn't be a widow today."

The years had changed her, but not so much that her face didn't have that clear quality and her body that soft and dignified maturity that one sees in women who have recently given birth to a child. I said to her, "An unfaithful functionary can do more harm than he is aware of himself. For I don't think I err when I say that what I read in your last letters, I can still read in your eyes."

She replied, "A maiden is very much like a sleeping child. The child wakes up when someone touches it or it hears a beloved voice — but only slowly."

"Yes," I said, "that's the way it must have been. But you got married?"

"You too got married," she answered impetuously; "and it's even being said that you married because of greed for money and property."

"You must think about me whatever you wish, Sara," I said.

"We will think about each other as well as we can," she replied. She was silent for a moment, then she turned toward me and said in an agitated voice, "I had a pious and god-fearing husband; I certainly could have gotten one that was less worthy. But I would have derived more joy from *your* beating me with whips and sticks than I did from his goodness! May God forgive me, but I didn't cry the day I was told of his death. I had just heard that you had come back."

I was about to exclaim, "Anne Cathrine will be dead in two or three years," but instead I said, "We could go away together. I have my friends abroad. We could travel to Newcastle or St. Martin or to Amsterdam or Marseilles — " and not until I noticed her sad and indulgent smile did I stop reeling off the names of cities and places. She said, "No, we can't run away. For the sake of our salvation we cannot do it, Cleng. And remember that I have a child. This will have to be the only time we meet; now our ways must part."

She was breathing heavily and began to wring her hands: "Dearest, do me the kindness not to come to my father's house anymore; otherwise, I must move back to the place I used to live! And when we meet in the street, then pretend that you don't know me!"

I burst into tears at her words and asked why we couldn't be friends, since neither could be blamed for what had happened. She turned her face the other way, and I saw that it was distorted with pain. When she again looked at me, she had regained her self-control and her calm. She answered, "So that we both will be able to bear our burden."

I rose, and she did likewise, and as we were standing there facing each other, I said, "We ought to have kissed each other at least once, Sara." Willingly she stepped closer, but she abruptly freed herself from my greedy hands, and when I again tried to hold her close, she held me at a distance by placing her palms against my shoulders; she looked me in the eye and said, "There are two steps along this road, and we have taken the first one. Leave now, Cleng, otherwise I don't know how we can control ourselves any longer."

Then I noticed wet spots on the bodice of her dress, made by the milk that had begun to flow. Happy and bashful, she said, "The child is waiting."

I remained standing there, and she lifted the child out of its crib. For the second time that day I was with a woman nursing a baby, but Sara did not cover herself. I saw the head of the child up close to her breast, as if it was still a part of her body.

A wonderful quiet descended on us, and I thought to myself, "This is the way it is to come home. Thus it is when a young husband sits down with his wife and rejoices with her over what life has given."

She put the child to bed and got up to say good-bye. She said, "I'll come with you," and she accompanied me as far as the big oak tree well beyond the house. Letting her hand go, I had already turned to walk on, when I suddenly felt her cool lips against my temple, as if the wing of a butterfly had brushed against it.

Never again could I make myself stay in Anne Cathrine's house. With the advent of summer she moved out to Finnøy, and I stayed at the Talgje shipyard. We met only when it was strictly necessary.

In the early autumn rumor spread like wildfire. Norwegian sailors had seen a great number of ships southwest of Lindesnes; they were large ships of war, heavily armored and accompanied by supply ships. People were not mistaken in assuming that this was the British fleet. Many conjectures were made as to its destination, but no one knew for certain.

In the war going on at that time the united kingdoms of Denmark and Norway were on the side of Napoleon; Norway had had no choice in the matter; we had less control of our own affairs than the most pitiful slave does today on an American plantation. England was the opposing nation. England and Denmark had clashed already in Viking times but they had since then had close and friendly contacts; now they had become enemies. There were dire consequences for both sides, but Norway took the brunt of the hardships; we were small and weak in comparison with the power of Great Britain, and we had no one to help us.

It soon became evident that the British fleet was on the way to Denmark. The ships anchored in the Sound and threatened Copenhagen, but before that they had discharged several thousand soldiers on the north coast of the island of Zealand; from there they moved on toward the city.

An envoy from the British government demanded that Denmark for its own good should enter into an alliance with England, or, alternatively, in some way give what he called a "pledge of security." It had so happened that Napoleon at midsummer had concluded peace with Prussia and Russia, and England remained the only powerful enemy of France. With his generals Napoleon had discussed plans for crushing English resistance. It was decided that they should take over the entire Danish-Norwegian navy and use it for an invasion of Great Britain.

The plan was kept secret, but the British government had nevertheless gotten wind of it, and, using the expression "necessary pledge," its envoy requested that all fully armed ships be put at the disposal of the British.

When the Danish government rejected these demands, orders were immediately given to go into action. The end was a miserable defeat for Denmark; it was said that the British dragoons were chasing the Danish militiamen with their riding crops, and that their warships bombarded the capital until the city begged for mercy. The British took with them the ships of the entire navy in addition to treasures of many kinds; even the churches were plundered and the sacred vessels taken away.

Right after that we heard of a good deal of privateering, between Denmark-Norway on the one side and England on the other, and the two powers tried to outdo each other in robbery and violence. The operations could be called nothing else but piracy, and it was done under the protection of the law.

In our two countries one could apply for a royal letter of marque and thus obtain the absolute ruler's blessings to go out and engage in piracy. This happened on both sides — those are the ways of war. May God look in His great mercy on our United States so that the North and the South will not oppose each other in a civil war!

But if the truth is to be known, it was England that began this despicable business, for already during that summer the British captured all the Norwegian ships they possibly could, on the seas and in port. But in autumn our boys made up for lost time; they didn't lag far behind, either, as far as bravery or brutality was concerned.

Any seaman was free to take out a letter of marque for a modest sum, and he could then freely help himself to all British property afloat. This situation continued throughout the war, and it brought in its wake greatly improved circumstances for the people along the southern coast of Norway, to such an extent that they lived in great affluence. But people were starving and suffering in the interior of Norway; one year of famine followed another.

As for Lars Larsen of Jeilane, it so happened that a short time after I had been to their house and had met Sara again, he signed on with a ship going to St. Martin, where they unloaded lumber and dried fish and brought grain back to Norway. On its return voyage the ship was captured, and Lars Larsen ended up in an English prison ship. This happened in the fall, about the time that Copenhagen was bombarded. When the news reached Stavanger and Lars Simonsen was told about it, he took it very hard, and a few days later, while standing by his carpenter's bench, he collapsed and died.

Some time after the funeral, when Sara was living alone, I visited her again and asked her to run away with me and flee the country. She answered, "I can't do that, but I'll wait for you until you are free again."

It so happened that I received a call from the pastor of Finnøy to come to see him. Anne Cathrine had lodged a complaint against me because I didn't fulfill my marital obligations toward her. It was only too true: Weekdays as well as holidays I lived in a small room that I had had furnished in the loft in the main shed at the shipyard.

The minister let me off rather leniently. He asked whether I weren't fond of Anne Cathrine, and to that I answered no, but when he wanted to know why I had married her, I said nothing. He sat silent for a while, as if reflecting on what I had said; then he nodded and said that I might leave.

I knew that he had recently become a widower. His wife had been married to his two predecessors as pastor in that parish; she had passed away at the age of 98.

Anne Cathrine had shares in several ships, I have already told you. Now she and her partners had first one vessel and then another rebuilt and fitted out for privateering. These ships had to rely on great speed for a fast attack and a quick getaway; for that reason they were lightly built and they had short masts, so that they couldn't be seen at a great distance.

Nothing untoward happened until the autumn of the next year, 1808. One day toward the end of September a boat from Stavanger tied up at the shipyard at Talgje. There were four men at the oars: Knud Halvorsen — he was the son of the owner of the Reveim farm at Madla, near Stavanger — and next to him on the forward thwart sat the fisherman Elias Eliassen Tastad. On the center thwart sat the apothecary's apprentice Enoch Jacobsen, and next to Enoch, Anders Reianes, who was a farmer and fisherman on the island of Rennesøy not far from Talgje. Anders was the oldest one, close to 30 years old; Enoch was the youngest, about 18 years of age; all four were unmarried. I knew Enoch and Anders slightly; the other two I did not know at all.

They had a seine with them in the boat. And the reason that they had tied up at the shipyard and wanted to talk with me, was this:

Anders Reianes had been to town with a shipload of crabs. When he had made delivery of the crabs and was sitting in his boat eating the food he had brought with him, an acquaintance of his from Nedstrand came over to him. As is usual, their conversation dealt largely with fishing. The other man mentioned that big fat mackerel were swarming all along the shore of Nedstrand.

Elias Tastad was sitting on a jetty nearby, mending fish nets. He could hear what the men were talking about.

"Yes, now we should have been up in the northern part of the fjord, hauling in all that mackerel," he shouted over to them. "Here's the seine all ready, but my boat is still wet from the new pitch I've put on it."

"If you supply the seine, I'll supply the boat," Anders Reianes shouted back to him. "We can leave within a few hours' time, if you wish. But I have to leave a message for my family so they won't worry about me. My brother works in the shipyard at Talgje. We'll stop by there. He always goes home on Saturday night. But three men aren't too many for a seine gang; we ought to have at least four, or even five."

"I know two fellows I bet will want to come along," Elias Tastad answered, mentioning the names of Knud Halvorsen and Enoch Jacobsen. Enoch was a cousin of Elias's; he had worked for the apothecary since he was twelve years old, but pharmacist Zetlitz was not very satisfied with him, since he had been guilty of some dishonest dealings. For that reason he had just been dismissed from his job. Now he was loafing around doing nothing. Enoch was a sensitive but also a hotheaded fellow. His tendency toward melancholy he covered up with a certain insolence in his dealings with the world.

As for the rest of the crew: Knud Halvorsen had just moved in to the city and had started as an apprentice for an umbrella-maker. Anders Reianes belonged to Hans Nielsen Hauge's congregation, of whom there were a few on the island of Rennesøy.

The four of them told me what they were trying to do, and Anders Reianes asked me whether I would like to come along with them. I immediately answered yes. I was very anxious to get as far away as possible from Anne Cathrine and everything that reminded me of her.

The last time I had been over to see her, she had mocked me in public and had asked whether I had actually been so simpleminded as to believe her when she had pretended that she was suffering from a deadly disease: "All women know the art of fainting at the right moment! Have you ever noticed any other symptoms of any other kinds of infirmity in me? The time when there was still some spirit in you, you certainly found out that I could keep up with you! But if you ever come and demand your right as a husband, it might so happen that you will have to grovel and beg and still be turned back by a closed door."

All this she said while Johannes Stene was in the same room. He turned his back to her and walked out of the house; he was a decent and fine fellow.

I got ready in a hurry, and we started off the very same day. We arrived at the village of Stranda, which is located on an eastern arm of the fjord. From way back it has been considered the finest village in its parish. If we made a big catch, we would be able to sell the mackerel more easily there than in any other place; and if we needed salt, we knew we could get it there, if there was any salt to be had at all. Due to the war there were already shortages of several necessities. People came to Stranda from all around the fjord country in order to trade and exchange wares, and ships called from distant lands to pick up cargoes of lumber.

It so happened that we made a big catch the very first day. The mackerel was hauled on board the next day; it was fortunate that a ship from Danzig had just arrived with a cargo of salt.

Stranda had quite a big population. Among other things the village boasted an inn, with rooms to let and beer for sale, and a country store; the inn was a long, low building a little back from the shore.

We walked up to the inn. The shiny dalers in our pockets made us feel ready for a real night out, and we wanted to enjoy the best in food and drink. First we had pastries and beer, but it wasn't long before the brandy bottle was on the table. Anders Reianes kept up with us up to that point, but then he got up and asked us to show moderation, god-fearing man that he was. The Haugeans never brought shame on a giver by misusing his gift.

As for me, I kept on drinking at a steady pace. I sought solace in forgetfulness from all the pain and ignominy caused by my unhappy marriage.

That may have been the reason that I was especially touchy, and when Enoch started to tease, as he always did when he was drunk, I got angry. He called me money-mad and also made the kind of remarks a man is apt to make when drinking has loosened his tongue. I was already quite befogged, but I seem to remember that I threatened him and said that he'd better watch what he was saying, otherwise I would see to it that he was silenced. To that he answered that he readily believed I was able to silence people; there must have been some grounds for the rumor that I had scared Sara Larsdatter dumb.

I replied in the same vein. Round town it was being whispered that a mother had come to the pharmacy and wanted some medicine for her child whose throat was contracting from cramps and whose breathing only came with great difficulty. Enoch had been inebriated — he was also stealing and drinking from the pharmacist's alcohol — and he had mixed a medicine which caused the death of the child. Zetlitz had made every effort to hush up the whole thing so as to protect the damaged reputation of the pharmacy, but it was all in vain.

For that very reason I told him that if it was a question of being silent, there were some people lying six feet under, their mouths filled with dirt, who might bear witness against him. He immediately pulled out his knife, but I was just as quick and grasped his wrist, the result being a fist fight at close quarters. I forced his arm away from his body while he resisted with all his might, and when he suddenly weakened and gave up we were both holding the knife as it was sunk all the way to the shaft into his left thigh.

This I can remember very clearly: the knife imbedded in his thigh and the blood that was spreading like dark rose petals, soaking his clothing and making my palm warm and sticky.

I looked around as if I had just awakened from a bad dream, and appalled I heard my own voice, husky and unrecognizable: "Can I possibly have done this?"

"God help us: Yes — I'm afraid you did it," Elias replied.

Just then Knud Halvorsen came into the room. He bent down over Enoch and carefully worked the knife loose, and the blood came out in spurts from the main artery that had been severed.

None of us had any clear idea of what we should do, but I recall that we took Enoch's trousers off, and we could clearly see the wound. It was almost the length of a finger and so wide open that the flesh turned inside out along the cut and looked just like bloody entrails. Knud pressed his hand against the wound while Elias tore off his shirt and tied it tightly around the thigh above the wound. But the blood did not stop welling forth.

Enoch was deathly pale; his lips looked like streaks of gray in among the blond down on his lips and chin. He had been conscious until then, but now his eyes closed. Just a little bit of the white of his eyes was visible, and a tremor went through his body, as happens just before life fades away.

I had become sober and clearheaded; I asked if there were no one about who knew how to stop the flow of blood; but the innkeeper just shook his head in confusion and mumbled something about the sheriff and about murder. At that very moment we heard an ugly rattling sound from Enoch's throat, and someone or other shouted, "He's dying!"

Then I seized him in a powerful grip, and lifted him up, and carried him out through the open door. In the lamp light I noticed that my hands were splattered with blood.

The Eleventh Tale

What happened after that occurred so quickly that I don't have a clear recollection of it. But I must have carried Enoch down to the boat, and the four others must have followed us, and we shoved off and started to row. What I remember clearly is that we were a distance out on the fjord; there was an oily sheen and a phosphorescent glimmer on the surface of the water, and on shore someone was shouting something or other. I didn't comprehend what was being said, but I know what I was thinking; perhaps we all thought the same thing. We were scared and bewildered. "What shall we do now?" said Knud Halvorsen.

Elias replied, "We'll row over to Ombo, to Ole Franck."

None of us had heard that name before, but a drowning man will clutch at a straw, and we comforted ourselves with the thought that this unknown man would be our deliverer.

Right across the fjord, in an easterly direction, lay the big island of Ombo; its dark and indistinct contours rose up against the sky; the moon had not yet risen above the mountains, but there was nevertheless a pale silvery light coming from above.

Ole Franck and Elias Tastad were related; how close I do not know. In his early youth Ole had been to sea and had served in the navy; he had lived in Denmark for a while, and that is where he got married. During the British bombardment of Copenhagen the year before, he had assisted one of the surgeons and had thus learned how to treat wounds. His wife was one of the civilians who were killed during the bombardment. He had been very fond of her, and had even assumed her Danish family name, Franck; before that time his name had been Ole Kro, Kro being the name of the farm on which he was born.

When the bombardment was over and the Danish fleet had been seized and his wife put to rest in Danish soil, he left and moved back to his home district. He lived with Elias Tastad's parents for a short time, but soon went back to Ombo, which was his birthplace. He built himself a new house on an old deserted cotter's farm. Elias had helped Ole build the house; so he knew how to get there.

When we were about in the middle of the fjord, the moon rose above the mountains. The Nedstrand mountains seemed to be receding in the moonlight, but the shadow of the steep sides of the Ombo mountains appeared threateningly close.

Was Enoch still conscious, or was he perhaps dead? A stream of anxious thoughts passed through my mind. Then we heard him moan and complain of thirst. "We'll have water for you very soon. We'll get there in a minute," Elias said. "I know of a brook not far away."

We rowed in towards a narrow inlet. We saw no signs of houses or fields or meadows. There was a brook coming down from the hills, just as Elias had said. I filled my own cup with water and supported Enoch's back with my left hand and put the cup to his lips with my right; and he drank from it, but only very little. With a low whimper he sank back and his head slumped weakly to one side. He had lost consciousness again.

Hurriedly we pulled the seine over the gunwale and carried it into the woods and hid it. Then we put driftwood down on the ground as skids and pulled the boat up in the shelter of dense junipers; they were tall as a man and were growing almost all the way down to the waterline. Then we took the skids and tied them together with the aid of the sail and thus made a stretcher for Enoch.

This done, we set off. A stranger would not have been able to see even a trace of a footpath, but Elias walked at the head of the stretcher and knew where he was going; at the start I held up the rear end of the stretcher. Right before me was Enoch's face; I could look straight into it. His head tossed from one side to the other, in rhythm with the lurching of the stretcher. He didn't let out a sound anymore. Yellow leaves flitted through the air when a gust of wind came down the mountainside; one of the leaves settled on one of his eyes, and the moonlight which filtered down between the branches and the sparse foliage, made his face appear almost unreal. It was as if we were seeing him on the other side of a grating, inside an isolated but illuminated room.

The path meandered through dense forest and across marshes from which a milky white haze was slowly rising; the air was cooler here, and the withering leaves of grass glistened from the hoarfrost.

Finally we were standing on top of a mountain ridge; below us were gently sloping hills. Elias pointed at something, but I couldn't see anything but wilderness and more hills; the little house was well hidden in the forest. Not until we got a bit closer did the walls of recently felled timber become visible against the dark tops of the fir trees. There was not a cloud in the sky, and Elias didn't follow the footpath any longer but selected a course which allowed us to be hidden by the trees as much as possible. It was almost three o'clock in the morning.

We stopped outside the house for a moment; we were in the rear of the house, near the main doorway; a small window high up on the wall gave the impression of being the eye of an unfriendly stranger. I felt the blood hammer in my temples.

Elias knocked on the door, gently at first, then more forcefully. We heard a sound inside and then we could make out a face behind the windowpane. The man must have recognized Elias, for he immediately pushed the bolt aside and opened the door.

Getting straight to the point, Elias told him that we had with us a fellow with a knife wound in his thigh. "We are not free from blame for what's happened. You must help us as well as you can."

Ole quickly raked the ashes from the live embers, threw twigs and juniper into the fireplace, and the fire began to crackle. He lit an oil lamp hanging on the wall above a long table, and he motioned us to place Enoch on it. Carefully we loosened his clothing; Ole got out ointments and pieces of cloth.

While he cleaned the wound and dressed it, he could only utter a brief command and indicate with a nod what he wanted or when he needed a hand. When he eventually was finished, he gave me a piercing look — his eyes were light blue, and his glance was sharp as a knife.

"Well, well, you murderers," he said; "we may have saved his life — unless septic fever gets him. But it's time that I hear a bit more about this, isn't it? One doesn't sink a knife into a man for nothing."

It was Elias who told him how it had happened; he neither exaggerated nor concealed anything. When he had finished, Ole Franck said, "You're afraid that the sheriff and the bailiff will get you, I suppose?" I nodded, I was standing closest to him. "Does anyone know that you're hiding here?" he asked. Elias assured him that there was no fear of that.

Ole cleared his throat. "It so happens," he said, "that I am going to make a trip to Stranda today. I thought I should put in provisions for the winter. When you live in isolation and don't own any farmland, you must husband the little money you have, that is, if you *have* any money. Over at Stranda I'll probably hear what people are saying about all this and what the authorities intend to do about it. If I find out that everyone takes a fairly reasonable view of the matter, then I'm willing to go pretty far out of my way to help you. In that case you can stay here until this fellow is strong enough to go home. But if it should so happen that he dies, then the culprit will have to come out of hiding and take the punishment that he deserves. And whenever I'm *out* of the house, you're going to stay *inside:* bolt the door and keep the windows closed! And I don't want anyone to look out the window even if the Queen of Sheba is riding by."

Enoch had been transferred from the table to the extra bed in the house. Ole Franck had put more juniper on the fire, and hung a pot filled with water on the chimney hook to make some barley porridge. He also put boiled herring, flatbread, and salted meat on the table, together with a large dish of sour milk. He walked silently to and fro and got everything ready; he had a knack for housework, and I followed him with my eyes. He was rather short, his face was clean-shaven and lean, his skin was sallow. His eyes were light blue, as I've already mentioned, his eyebrows were thick and dark, and he had a high forehead — he was turning completely bald — except that he had lots of hair, thick and without a touch of gray, by his ears and in the neck.

While we were eating, the light of morning crept over the timbered walls bringing new shades and tints and making the room appear different from what it had seemed like in the light from the fireplace. A panther skin was hanging on the wall above Enoch's bed; two conch shells, shining like mother of pearl, stood on a table. A cuckoo clock with pendulums and weights counted out the hours — very slowly, it seemed.

When we had finished eating, we put the horn spoons back in their place underneath the crossbeam. And Ole Franck made ready for his trip to Stranda. As soon as he was out of the door, we slid the doorbolt into place according to his instructions; through the window we saw him disappear into the forest where the hillside begins to slope down toward the sea. The sun had already risen; the sky was blue and clear above the horizon in the west, and the delicate colors of morning resembled an outstretched wing arched above the ocean.

Ole didn't return until evening. He was carrying a heavy load; he had with him ship's biscuits and salted meat, peas and pearled barley and other kinds of food that can be stored away for a while.

First he walked over to Enoch and nodded when he saw that everything seemed to be fairly well with him.

He finally spoke: "I'm sure you would like to know what the people of Nedstrand think of you, fellows."

No one could deny that.

First he mentioned the rumors that were circulating. The reason that the boat had left Stranda in such a hurry, it was being said, was that Enoch's end had been drawing near and we didn't want any witnesses around when he drew his last breath. The sheriff had been notified and had been told what the innkeeper knew: that we were from a place somewhere to the south, near Stavanger, but he didn't recall having heard any of our names.

The sheriff had called together a whole group of men to help him, and the authorities in Stavanger had been alerted. "But when he doesn't find you there, that doesn't mean that he'll give up," Ole said.

"This is the way I see it," he continued. "It seems that Enoch is out of danger, but he won't be able to kick the ceiling for a week or two. And even though he may not want to report you to the authorities, they may feel obliged to go into the affair more closely."

"I'm not going to report anybody," we heard Enoch utter; he was awake and had heard what was being said.

"And no sheriff can find his way here so easily," Elias added.

"Oh, he can find us here faster than anyone thinks," Ole said, "when it becomes known that you have relatives on Ombo. Besides, I can't keep you hidden too many days. I'm not going to be here this coming winter."

"But all those provisions?" Elias asked.

"They are to be used for another purpose," Ole replied.

And this remark serves to introduce a new chapter in my life story.

The previous spring Ole Franck had purchased a sloop in the town of Kristiansand; the hull had subsequently been rebuilt in a shipyard in Egersund, and the ship had been suitably fitted out as a privateer with the right sails, guns, and everything else.

Ole had also obtained a letter of marque, he now told us, and he was well on his way to being in the privateering business in the near future.

For various reasons he had kept all this secret from the people in the district. He had been promised a crew in Egersund, but a short while ago he had been told that several of those who had signed on had now backed out. When the sloop arrived from Egersund — and it could happen any day now — it wouldn't have more men on board than was just sufficient to sail it up north and make delivery.

"Now the question is," said Ole Franck, "whether you fellows might consider signing up in their stead? It's my opinion that it might be a good thing if we could make it seem as if there were a great distance between the authorities and Enoch. And when we come back with Englishmen in chains in the hold and a ship full of confiscated cargo, there's no reason why we can't hope that everyone will want to forgive and forget. In times like these it must be considered to be a great service to the fatherland to bring valuables into the country. If you dare to join me, I'll risk signing you on."

I didn't care too much for privateering, but in view of the entire situation it seemed to me that I ought to be only too happy if the others were willing to stand by me through thick and thin.

Enoch was sleeping just then, but as soon as he woke up and heard mention of privateering, he sat up in bed and assured us that it wouldn't be long before he was up and about again. This was just the thing that he had been planning for some time, he said, and he was of the opinion that the wound would heal faster on sea than on land, and it would be a very long time indeed before he would go back home!

"If the septic fever doesn't get you, you'll get to sea, all right," said Ole.

That's the way things turned out. One more week passed by before the sloop arrived, but one morning at daybreak the *Avenger* dropped anchor in the inlet below the house. We could see her mastheads jutting up beyond the hill.

That day too we stayed inside for the most part. Everything had to be made ready, and we had our hands full. Right after midnight we weighed anchor. There was a pretty strong northwest breeze, and the weather was clear. We set sail, and we held to a westward course.

The next day was clear, with typical autumn weather; it was now the beginning of October. The waves reflected the color of the sky, they were blue like tempered iron. The crests of the waves had a golden tinge as the sun rose, and later they turned pure white when the wind blew more briskly. Soon the salt spray soaked the entire deck.

Those of us who had previously sailed on the ocean, looked upon this as rather pleasant weather, but Knud got seasick and vomited, and things weren't any better with Elias. A big wave suddenly washed over the rail and tore across the deck; it swept him along so forcefully that he collided with the mast and hurt himself. Ole Franck called him a landlubber and said that he had a lot to learn about the sea. Elias sank down on a coil of rope and looked as if even prison would be a place greatly to be preferred.

As the day wore on, the wind freshened and became a veritable storm. The ocean opened wide its jaws and showed us its teeth; it bit into the hull, and for a moment we were dancing and swirling above the abyss. Then it spewed us out again; it grasped us once more in its gleaming, crooked teeth; the ship's planks and ribs were creaking loudly.

At last it was evening. The colors of the air and the sea took on a chill tint, the stars appeared like a heavenly phosphorescence above the mastheads. The short day hurried westward under more canvas than even the Flying Dutchman dared make use of.

We had plenty to keep us busy up on deck. Ropes had to be made taut, sails had to be furled, and hatches had to be battened down; the strong wind was now at hurricane force; to be at sea was no longer child's play. Giant waves surged in on us, like multitudes of horsemen on white-maned steeds. The ship's keel cut its way right through, as with a drawn sword, and the sails stretched dark banners over the field of battle.

When the new day dawned, both the ship and the crew had fought, and fought hard. Knud came up on deck — his face looked as if it were made of glass. The wind slackened as the day wore on, but the swell was still considerable. The *Avenger* had not been damaged, and once the sea was smooth, we all recovered our spirits.

We stayed within the limits of the Skagerak; we were cruising up and down that body of water. Thus a week passed, and we had not had any contact with any Englishmen. In this respect our venture must up till then be considered very unsuccessful. But Enoch continued to improve. When the weather was good he would at times come up on deck, but he still had a tight bandage wrapped around the place where he had been wounded.

Early in the second week we at first set our course in a southeasterly direction, and then directly east. We were cruising off Lindesnes, at times within sight of the Norwegian mainland; once we were so far south that we could make out the Skagen peninsula in Denmark. Each and every ship that came from the Baltic or from the ports on the west coast of Sweden had to pass this part of the ocean, and we were confident that in the long run the English ships could not slip past us.

That proved to be true.

It was early one morning, in the middle watch, at seven bells. A haze covered the ocean, and the air was chilly, as it may be even in good weather that late in the autumn; but when the sun rose, the flakes of mist disappeared little by little, the way smoke gradually gets less in a bonfire. Only in a few places did the misty flakes remain hovering above the water during the early forenoon hours.

That fact was to prove our undoing.

It was about eight o'clock when the lookout shouted that there was a ship to leeward, but we noticed immediately that it couldn't be a convoy. Ole Franck grabbed the binoculars and said that it was a squadron of so-called "chopping blocks." And we all knew that that type of ship didn't leave port for any old reason.

The chopping blocks were a smaller type of ship that were in use along the coasts of Norway. They had been named thus because of their construction, making them especially well suited to attack enemy vessels lying becalmed off the coast. When the observation posts on shore discovered a convoy, all the chopping blocks would be manned with ten to fifteen experienced sailors who would row or sail their ships out toward the merchantmen. The one ship that seemed to be the most valuable prize or the one easiest to attack was selected for boarding.

Long before the chopping blocks were within firing range they would fire off their cannons and the crew would shoot their pistols into the air; the attackers would also swing their sabers and carry on in the best pirate tradition. When the privateers finally boarded the enemy vessel, there would often be hand-to-hand fighting and many broken skulls if the crew dared to offer resistance.

The prize would be towed in to the nearest port, the crew was put in jail, and the cargo, according to the rules of war, would be sold, usually at a very low price. It was said at that time that the women of a certain district in southernmost Norway were using powder sugar instead of sand for scouring and were wearing silk dresses on weekdays.

Soon the chopping block armada came so close that we could observe it with the naked eye. It was composed of about a score of ships, each with a substantial crew. The *Avenger* turned about and sailed directly toward them, but we didn't proceed at a very great speed; the sea was almost completely calm. When we got close, we laid by, and they sent a rowboat over to us.

The men told us that a convoy consisting of four enemy merchantmen and one navy brig were on the way from Gothenburg. According to the information they had obtained, it would not be long before the convoy would come into view. They wanted to wait for it here, and they had nothing against our joining them in capturing the convoy, for it was quite possible that the forenoon would bring with it a strong wind, and the chopping blocks would not be able to accomplish anything against fast-moving ships.

An hour or more passed; then Ole Franck announced that he could see the convoy through his binoculars. It appeared over the rim of the horizon toward the southeast, far out to sea. Soon we could just make out their sails, smaller than the palm of your hand. Later the hulls emerged from out of the haze; there were four vessels in all, just as the chopping block sailors had told us. As far as I could see, they were sailing pretty far apart; the one nearest us was still several nautical miles away.

A sudden gust of wind made ripples on the surface of the water. The chopping blocks at once hoisted their sails, but they didn't gain much speed. Although there was a moderate breeze, the cargo vessels didn't manage to change their course until the privateers had gotten so close that fleeing seemed next to impossible.

At that very moment we noticed something that was more of a surprise to us than perhaps to the others, namely, another chopping block armada approaching the convoy; it must have come from the area east of Lindesnes. Even though there would be more of us to share in the spoils, the chances were now much better that we could make a real big haul — especially because it seemed that we wouldn't encounter much resistance: the navy brig that supposedly was to accompany the convoy was nowhere to be seen.

When the *Avenger* had come within range of the enemy, Ole Franck gave the order to fire a broadside. The first salvo did less damage than expected, and additionally we got an unpleasant surprise: the navy brig appeared out of a flake of mist not very far away. But it was located just right to receive the next broadside from the *Avenger,* and we didn't let the opportunity pass us by. This time it seemed that luck was with us. When the gunsmoke drifted away, the brig had turned her stern toward us and was evidently in full flight. It set a course due south, toward the wide open ocean.

In the meantime the wind had freshened; there was a moderate breeze coming from the east. Ole Franck thought that this maneuver on the part of the brig was a rather strange one, since it was improbable that our first salvo had damaged her; all our cannons were small and light.

The freighters were heavily loaded and were not able to change course as fast as the brig. They seemed to be completely defenseless. We selected the one that was not only the biggest but also was sailing farthest from land; the chopping blocks evidently were set to capture the other one. Ole Franck ordered another round of fire, but it was only intended to frighten them and remind them of the fact that the time had come to lay by and surrender without making any trouble.

To our great surprise, however, it looked as if the ship had no mind to give up without a fight. It fired at us twice with all its cannons on the starboard side, but we didn't suffer any damage as far as the crew or the vessel was concerned. At the very same time the merchantman suddenly changed course. The wind had increased and its sails were bulging. Slowly the ship turned its stem in a southward direction and set a course for the open ocean, just the way the navy brig had done.

Ole Franck told us later that he had just been about to order the launch to be lowered when it became clear to him that we had foolishly anticipated a victory that was not to occur. The merchantman made its bold maneuver at just the right moment; the wind freshened, and the ship proved to be a first-rate sailer. We too hoisted all sails and pursued it, but we kept falling behind. Nevertheless, we kept up our pursuit for about an hour; then, unexpectedly, we seemed to be gaining on them. Ole Franck ordered us to take our places at the guns, so that we would be ready to fire at a moment's notice.

When we came within range once again, the *Avenger* fired once, then once more. But when we heard cannons roar a third time, the sound came from another direction.

For the last quarter of an hour we had had nothing on our mind but the merchantman. In the meantime, however, three other ships had approached from windward; they proved to be two smaller naval vessels and a big merchant ship.

The first cannonball whipped into the sea about a half cable length from the bow of the *Avenger*; the second one sent up a spray that descended on our deck; the third one smashed the fore yardarm.

But Ole Franck didn't intend to lower the flag. We fired once more but missed. The wind was now much stronger, and the *Avenger*, which was but a piece of cork on the ocean compared with her adversaries, didn't lie as deep in the water so that she rolled heavily in the rough seas; this made our taking aim so much more difficult. But both the enemy merchantman and the navy vessels had everything under

126

full control, and the next shot scored a direct hit in our hull, right above the waterline. Still, we made ready for another round and were just about to fire when we realized that one of the Englishmen was in a position to give us a broadside at any time and at very close range.

The cannons roared, and the very first salvo smashed the *Avenger's* mast as far up as the topsail. The piece that had been shot off tumbled down over the ship's side; sails and rigging were completely tangled.

That was the end of the battle.

Then something unexpected happened on board our ship. Enoch had come up on deck in spite of the fact that he had been told to stay below, and then he suddenly fell forward across the starboard railing, with the upper part of his body dangling in the air.

I didn't know what went through my mind: that he might have been hit by a splinter, that the wound had opened up, that he had fainted — but I was fully aware that the next time the boat heeled over he would be flung over the rail and into the sea.

Before I managed to grab him, however, wooden beams and pieces of metal were flying through the air; flames leaped up, and the smell of smoke burned in my nose. Nevertheless, I had plunged forward, right through the rain of splinters, and just as another wave made our sloop list over, I got hold of him by the ankles — it was almost too late — he was about to slide over the bulwark.

He was unconscious as he lay there on the deck; I lifted him up and carried him down to his cabin. He opened his eyes. "You saved me," he said, and once again he passed out.

The navy brig had lowered its launch when I got up on deck again. It had a full crew and headed straight for the sloop; military buttons and sabers gleamed in the sunlight. Ole Franck was at the wheel; he saluted when the first officer came up on deck. The officer had a pistol in his hand, aiming it at Ole. When the rest of the uniformed men had gotten up and over the bulwark, the commander in chief ran quickly across the deck while the others covered him with their guns.

When he reached the place where Ole was standing, he pushed his pistol against his chest and started to shout something or other very rapidly in English. Ole probably understood some of the words but he didn't get the drift of it, and after having made the officer understand that he needed an interpreter, he waved me over to him. The commander first asked whether all our men were on deck, and I replied that we were, with the exception of one man who was sick.

"He's also to stand in line!" said the commander. "I'm sure he's not in such a bad shape that he can't stab a dagger in our back if he has the opportunity. Fetch him!"

It was an order. When I once again walked below I could feel the point of the pistol between my shoulder blades. Enoch had regained consciousness.

"The commander wants us all to stand in line," I said. "Are you able to, Enoch?"

"Yes, if you hold me up," he replied, but we hadn't walked many paces before he collapsed. The officer who had followed me below, stuck his pistol in his belt and helped me; when we got up on deck I carried Enoch amidships so that he could lean against the mast.

The British commander ordered us to line up, and he was insistent that Enoch should stand up without help; but after the boy had fallen down twice I got permission to support him. Since I once again had to serve as interpreter, it fell to Knud Halvorsen to hold him up, with the aid of Elias Tastad.

In a fierce manner the commander requested information about who we were, what we had been doing, and what cargo we were carrying. To tell him this required but a few words, but we weren't done with the questions and answers before the *Avenger* began to list. Without our knowing it the last bullet had hit the ship at the waterline; now we realized at once that the sloop was sinking.

We received orders to bring everything of value up on deck; but except for personal belongings and the usual seaman's outfits, so little of value was brought up that the commander became suspicious and ordered three of his men to search the ship. When that had been done and nothing more had come to light, we were ordered to bring everything down into the launch; we had to row while the British sailors aimed their pistols at our faces as well as our backs. But Enoch didn't have to row. Very pale, he leaned against the gunwale; a large splotch of blood was spreading over his trouser leg.

On board the brig we once again had to line up, but after a brief interrogation we were ordered below. The last thing I saw was the *Avenger*; it was lying there with its stern sinking below the water's surface and its bowsprit pointing up at an angle; the distance between the ships was no greater than that I could distinctly read the name.

The room below was evil-smelling, and it was so dark that we stumbled across one another. We were going to experience more wretched conditions than these in the coming years, but habit is a merciful companion. After a while we were given some bread, which we shared between us, and a can of lukewarm and bitter-tasting water; the one can was to suffice for all of us the first twenty-four hours.

As soon as we had gathered our wits, we began talking together in a low voice. We all realized that we were on the way to a prison ship, and we had heard so much about conditions on board such ships that we were far from overjoyed. But we tried to keep our spirits up. The war wouldn't last very long, we told ourselves. Who would ever have thought that most of the survivors of our imprisonment were not to return home until six years later, in the year 1814?

The ship's bobbing up and down told us that the wind was freshening; the brackish water on top of the keelson splashed this way and then that way. We noticed that the smell was getting worse — we had almost gotten used to it. It was more difficult to get used to the rats; they ran across our hands and faces. We knew that they would get aggressive as soon as we fell asleep. I had once served on a ship with a seaman who had had the tip of his nose eaten off by rats.

We lost track of whether it was night or day, and no sounds from the deck reached down to us. At last our weariness got the better of us. Enoch was the last one I talked to; he didn't have much to say, but what he did say was enough: he expected death to come and that was all. I told him about the two times I had been shipwrecked and had gotten away with my life; then I told him the story of Stephen Grellet, but before I had finished, he fell asleep and was snoring loudly.

I stayed awake. A strange feeling, akin to joy, began to rise within me: the world which Anne Cathrine inhabited was so exceedingly far away; no longer was I to be troubled by the knowledge of being near her or being worried about managing her property. I was a prisoner, but for the first time in many years I had a feeling of being free. "When I return, she'll be gone forever," I thought to myself. "And if not, I'll sign on a ship and stay at sea until doomsday."

My arms and legs didn't feel stiff anymore, they had got used to the hard boards. I thought of Sara, that we would perhaps meet again some time in the future, and a shaky hope gave peace to my mind.

Overwhelmed by a happiness that I couldn't fathom, I finally fell asleep. I fell asleep to the sound of rushing water, as I had done so often before on the wide ocean.

The Twelfth Tale

Thus began the year we spent in an English prison ship. For the first few months we dreamed about returning home the next spring; for we took great stock in the rumors that were circulating about battles and alternating defeats and victories between the two warring sides. But most of these events had never actually occurred, or they were distorted in the retelling, their contents offering much more hope than was warranted by the facts.

The privateering captain took us to Leith in Scotland, where we were imprisoned from the fall of 1808 to the fall of 1810. In the spring of the latter year I attempted to escape with two other men, but we didn't make it, and since the chances for a successful escape following this attempt were as small as the punishment would be severe, I wasn't tempted to try again, at least not until we had been moved to the river Medway, near the mouth of the Thames, not far from the city of Chatham.

I'll soon get to the account of my second attempted escape and how it ended, Anne, but first I ought to give you an idea of how they treated us and how we lived on board the prison ship. Conditions on board were on the whole very similar at Leith and at Chatham, but winters were colder in Scotland, and we suffered more from the cold in the wintertime than we did from the heat in the summertime.

Let me tell you about the voyage from Leith southward, since it once again made me fully conscious of our situation. One of the most dangerous aspects of degradation and misery is that after a while one will adjust to it.

But since the humiliation we now suffered was even worse than before, I became even more conscious than ever of the pitiful conditions that were our lot.

The first autumn storms hit us while we were on our way south in November. The wind increased to a hurricane, and it looked as if the ship would sink. Hardly any of the prisoners had any hope of staying alive, and some of them cursed the Almighty while others were praying; we were lying on slimy and stinking coils of rope, dirtier than vermin and clothed in rags that didn't even cover our emaciated bodies. We were weak from scruvy, and in addition we were suffering from seasickness — we could never stop vomiting. On top of all this, we suffered from a stomach ailment caused by impure drinking water. When the ship heeled and flung us from one side of the hold to the other, we would pile on top of one another, some of us half-drowned in the brackish water above the keelson, others without any defense against the greedy rats with their red and hairless legs and long claws; unseeing, we crawled about in the dirt and the vomit.

Among my fellow sufferers were Elias Tastad, Enoch Jacobsen, Ole Franck, and Anders Reianes. In addition to them, Anne, it had so happened that Lars Larsen of Jeilane had also been put in with us.

Half asleep, half awake, I had a feeling that what was happening around me was not real. I could see before me my home and my old neighborhood and recalled how Mother had been leading my blind father by the hand that spring I had returned home from sea, and I was full of longing for my home — even my life as Anne Cathrine's husband seemed attractive compared to the miserable conditions that had befallen me.

We could neither hear ourselves speak nor cry out due to the crashing roar of the sea when the waves struck the ship and almost inundated it. But the third night the storm abated. It was just as if we all woke up from a trance. Enoch Jacobsen uttered words that I had never heard him use before; weeping, he shouted out, "My body and soul are in the power of the Devil! What can I do to be saved?"

At first I thought he was delirious, for more than anyone else he had during our entire time in prison continually mouthed swearwords and curses and filthy talk. But when he called Anders Reianes by name right after, I realized that his mind was clear.

Anders answered him, "We all deserve our suffering, and it's right and proper that we kiss the rod and praise the Almighty. For He reaps where He hath not sown and gathers where He hath not strewn. But to those who desire salvation, He hath said, 'Believe in the Lord Jesus Christ and ye shall be saved.' "

I've told you before that Anders was a member of Hauge's congregation, and during the past two years he had led an ever more pious life among many unbelievers.

This is what I heard, and I don't know whether they continued their conversation. But there was a great change to be noticed in Enoch. When we reached port and he was no longer terror-stricken, his mouth was once again running over with all kinds of evil talk. Nevertheless, his inner self had been more greatly affected than anyone ever knew; that we were to find out later.

When our ship had anchored near Medway, outside Chatham, we were beaten and cursed and ordered up on deck. Trembling and shivering from exhaustion and from the cold, we had to line up to be counted. Then the sailors pushed us down into launches that had been brought alongside. Each launch had a boarding net on each side, and a platoon of marines was stationed fore and aft. We had to row ourselves. Under strict surveillance we rowed in a westward direction, and we entered the mouth of the river Medway. The banks of this river are rather flat, and here and there along the course of the river were mudbanks from which rose clouds of stinking steam, spreading like smoke across the water.

At about the time that darkness set in on this gray November day, the launch passed a spit in the river and we entered into a wide open basin, which looked almost like a lake. Ships were anchored in row upon row, about twenty in all, and with their tall and dark hulls silhouetted against the evening sky they reminded one of nothing so much as giant coffins. When we got close, we could see that all kinds of projections had been put up on them, such as funnels and other fittings which jutted up in the air. They had been equipped to provide space for the greatest possible number of prisoners.

We who had been captured on the *Avenger* were first put on board the prison ship *Bahama,* but later on we were transferred to a ship named *Fyen.* This ship had belonged to the Danish navy and had been seized by the English in the port of Copenhagen in 1807. As for me, however, I escaped before the transfer to the *Fyen* took place, and what I am writing here concerns the conditions under which we lived on the *Bahama.*

The *Bahama* had previously been a proud ship of the line; that was evident from the beautiful lines of the hull and the long rows of gunports, and also from the bright colors that had been used and from the towering masts. But now the entire ship was marked by decay and rot.

When we got closer, we could see blue smoke rising from the funnels; it wafted up in spirals and then spread out like a fog above the water; it filled our noses with a sour smell.

As the launch came alongside the ship, we were ordered to stand up, and we could look through the boarding nets as a grid; everyone stared silently at the dark hull. Then I suddenly became aware of a new sound; the buzzing of a thousand voices that reached down to us. The ship was already packed with prisoners; they had noticed the launch.

Some kind of platform had been built around the entire hull, quite close to the water's surface. The platform was used by the guards on patrol duty; they were armed with muskets. We pulled the launch toward a floating jetty, from which a long gangway, canvas-covered on both sides, led up to the tall bulwark. The boarding nets were lowered, and the quartermaster in the launch made a sign: We should get ready to go on board.

It so happened that I was the first one to go on board. When I had gotten up high enough, I could look over the bulwark and down on a part of the ship that had an oblong shape and reminded me of a big barn. Behind a bulkhead with numerous embrasures I could make out the outline of the forecastle. All the pipes sticking up from it reminded me of a gigantic pin cushion. Standing behind the bulkhead by the embrasures were armed guards, and marines were pacing the forecastle. Behind another wall, fortified in the same manner, jutted up a projection which probably used to be the quarterdeck; that was the part of the ship set aside for the officers.

In the space between the quarterdeck and the forecastle, a crowd of people were milling around; never before had I seen so many persons gathered into a limited area, and I had an inkling that we were going to live under even more miserable conditions than those we had suffered at Leith. A stinking smell, which I recognized only too well, hit me in the face.

Like us, these prisoners too were marked by suffering and humiliation. But I had gradually become accustomed to the thought that this is how it had to be, and I probably didn't feel as bad about it then as I do now when I bring it to mind. Look at them, Anne, look at the way we were, dressed in the most miserable rags and tatters! — between the rags we could see nothing but gray skin, ribs jutting out, bony arms and legs, and skinny thighs. Bearded and mangy and pale were we all, nothing but skeletons covered with skin, seemingly resurrected from the grave by the Devil, in order once again to suffer through a purgatory without hope.

When the prisoners on board the ship realized that this new load was to be added to their number, they began to jump and dance like savages, they swung their arms in the air, twisted their shoulders, they shouted and shrieked.

We all had our names placed on the ship's roll of prisoners: Each new prisoner stepped up to the desk and gave his name and nationality, and this was put down on paper. Then we were told that any attempt to smuggle out letters would be punished with solitary confinement in a dark dungeon. Attempts to escape rated the same kind of punishment but one of longer duration; that is, provided one was still alive after being caught.

The prisoners on board the ship had come from a number of countries. The majority were Frenchmen, and they were staying on the upper gundeck. About the same number of Americans were kept on the lower gundeck, and farthest down, on the orlop, there was another group of Frenchmen; they were called Rafalés and Manteaux Impériaux, people who had lost all sense of personal dignity and had given themselves up to shameful vices. They sold their food rations in order to obtain money to gamble with and parted with the rags that covered their bony frames for the same purpose; some of them were practically naked; few of them had on more than one piece of clothing. Those were the most miserable creatures I have ever seen, and the impression they made on us Norwegians made us make up our minds that we should stay clear of them. I turned immediately to the clerk and asked him to bring a request to the attention of the commander: that we might stay on the lower gundeck with the Americans. This he agreed to.

From earlier experience I knew that it was important to be able to hang our hammocks in a place where we could hope to get sufficient air. I recalled only too well the nights with their choking fits in the prison ship at Leith.

We found out that the only vacant area on the *Bahama* was very close to the latrine, but the ventilation was nevertheless bearable, and I supposed that we would be able to stand it. We fastened the rope ends of the hammocks to hooks that had been put up for that purpose, and as soon as we had the opportunity we crawled into our hammocks and spread over us the clothing that had been handed to us. The hammocks formed a continuous layer of canvas between the deck below us and the deck above, and we were lying so close together that one man could hardly turn without the others having to do the same.

Here and there in the huge oblong room there was a dull light from the lamps. Some of the prisoners had their own tallow candles, but this was prohibited, and whoever was caught received automatically three days in solitary at half rations.

About the time the prisoners were ordered to go to bed for the night, the guards would close with chains all openings and passages along the lower gundeck. We had long ago got used to the rattling sound in the dark; but during one of the first weeks we had spent on the prison ship at Leith, one of the prisoners would shout loudly every evening when he heard the chains, and one night he broke away and jumped into the sea; we never saw him again.

Filthy air, fleas and lice, a multitude of cockroaches and bedbugs made the nights seem long. But the cold was worse. We froze and we scratched ourselves; it was only due to our lethargy and the fact that we were used to it that we were able to endure it. It was always a relief when the gates were opened and the chains removed at seven sharp in the morning. Then we would stretch our aching limbs and get up to be in line to be counted.

In some ways the days seemed to be just as long as the nights, even though we Norwegians and Danes as well as the Americans made an effort to keep both our hands and minds occupied; in that way we could also earn a shilling now and then. Those on board a prison ship who had a little money in reserve were rich, and the rich man would always get a chance to hold his head up and improve both his own conditions and those of his fellows who were close to him. He could thus obtain better and more food than that which the guards had to offer. The usual prison food consisted of carrots, which were often half rotten, and sea biscuits infested with weevils, at times also of watery soup with a bit of onion or barley in it. Only very seldom was there any change in this menu.

Those who had money could also subscribe to *The Statesman* or some other newspaper; most of the prisoners became quite proficient in English in the course of the five or six years of their confinement. Those who knew the most would at times give instruction to their mates, or one might get help from a friendly soldier on guard; the relations between the prisoners and the crew improved steadily.

Nevertheless, we were in the power of a capricious Providence, and our living conditions were far from as amenable as the authorities had intended. Corruption flourished. In spite of the fact that the English Parliament had appropriated large sums of money for clothing and food for the prisoners of war, we were dressed in rags and were starving on top of it, while the guards — and many others, too — became fat and rich. Almost one hundred thousand prisoners of war were on board the English prison ships; the ships became a source of considerable income for a large group of Englishmen, for the reason that each middleman had a chance to steal money, food or clothing, and most of them succumbed to the temptation, the result being that the prisoners received very little of what originally had been intended for them.

But the number of prisoners did not stay at one hundred thousand; many of them died due to the miserable living conditions. Smelly, brackish water seeped through the rotting planks in the ship's sides, the walls were moldy, and water was dripping from every beam. No one escaped the "prison cough"; many were affected by one kind of disease or another, usually in the chest or in the stomach. Being already in a greatly weakened condition, many of them were driven into an early grave. Tuberculosis took the biggest toll, but cholera too returned again and again and kept on until the stomach discharged nothing but blood. Some tried to settle their stomachs by crushing bricks and mixing the dust in the food, and some were of the opinion that this helped.

The meals got a bit better after a while, however. Those who had some money to use as payment and to bribe the guards were able to induce them to buy some food ashore. But the slightly improved conditions did not make anyone turn to the Almighty in order to thank Him. Instead, the desire to act wantonly was aroused, and carnal desires soon got the upper hand. When they had money, the prisoners could purchase the favors of the streetwalkers, and many of them did. But what usually takes place in secret between a man and a woman here occurred right out in the open and without any shame or embarrassment.

All this debauchery was the reason for the spread of syphilis, and since even the most minimal requirements for cleanliness could not be met, many of those who kept away from immoral behavior were also infected.

This is the way things were on board, but as conditions after a while got less vile, and the prisoners at times got shore leave, they indulged in similar riotous living on land, and others would even seek physical pleasure with other men.

But while all kinds of shameless greed got the upper hand, there were also many things done which were inspired by the nobility and grandeur of the human spirit. Nevertheless, it should be noted that some of the men were alarmed by the misery and human decay that they saw around them, and they sought inner purification through piety and self-denial. These pious men received both spiritual and temporal help from the outside. But this did not occur until after I had escaped, and it is about this escape that I will now tell you.

The Thirteenth Tale

Surreptitiously I had revealed my intention to try to escape to a few of my countrymen, but they advised me against it and didn't want to join me at all. They were of the opinion that the war would soon be over; besides, they thought the risk was too great, and they had in fact good reason to think so. We had witnessed more than once an attempted escape which had ended in sudden death.

It was also being said that even if the war were to last for some time yet, the prisoners would be gradually set free. We had already seen proof that such a thing could happen.

Still, I was not able to sit there and do nothing. One day I gave a hint of my plans to an American prisoner who had become a very good friend of mine. His name was Joseph Fellows. He had earlier told me about his own country's war of independence against the English and about the republic that had been founded in the New World on the other side of the ocean; in that country, high and low were equals before the law.

It was Joseph Fellows who for the first time awakened in me the hope that I could perhaps become a citizen of the United States of America. When that hope was in time fulfilled, Joseph became one of my faithful assistants. It was he who sold the first lots in Kendall Township on Lake Ontario to the immigrants. But this is quite another story — one which I shall tell you later.

It was on New Year's Day 1812 that we for the first time had a more thorough conversation about a possible escape. We were up on deck; the rays of the sun breaking through the fleecy clouds made the sky red, and flakes of mist were drifting over the water; the evening was drawing near.

We heard church bells ringing on shore, the only sign of it being a holiday. Around the harbor and out in the river the hustle and bustle did not differ from a working day. Just then a number of barges and small boats loaded with provisions were approaching the prison ships; they were selling food and brandy. All kinds of ships of various sizes were making their way up and down the river, some going out to sea or up the Thames to London, others destined for the docks at Chatham.

Joseph Fellows immediately agreed with me that we should try to escape. I found that he was much better informed than I; he had thought of solutions to problems and difficulties that I didn't even know about.

"I suppose you can swim, can't you?" he asked.

"Like a fish," I answered.

"You can't afford to do worse," he said. "Do you see the two windmills on the hill over there?"

It was not difficult to see them; their arms stood out dark against the sky.

"Between them and us, about fifty yards from the shore, there is a mud bank. Can you see it?"

"Yes," I replied; "and I know only too well that it is soft as syrup and that we have to push right across it."

"Then you must also know that most of those who try to get away are so exhausted from their swim that they can't go on. Maybe you've noticed at times when the shutters are opened in the morning — have you seen the dead men lying there?"

"Yes," I answered; "and I know that the British like to have them lie there a day or more while sea gulls and ravens peck their eyes out, making us lose any desire to try to leave."

We didn't speak any more about it that day, but during the following week the plans for our escape filled my mind as soon as I opened my eyes in the morning, and I began to discuss them piecemeal with Joseph.

On each prison ship there was a so-called prisoners' committee, and it had always been a convention that if anyone wanted to try to escape he would first have to get permission from the committee. In addition, he should have enough food and money with him, and finally he should take precautions against informers.

Our rules prescribed that all this and even more had to be done, but nevertheless it had now become the custom that those attempting to escape didn't let the committee even hear a whisper about it beforehand.

We, too, failed to inform the committee. But we made thorough preparations. Above all, it was important to obtain a sufficient amount of money; for that matter we had already taken care of that. We had woven baskets of straw and had made various decorative and useful objects of bone: dolls and chessmen or ship models, which had been sold to fellow prisoners or to guards and officers, or even to people on shore.

It was also possible to obtain money in other ways: by offering for sale a highly desirable spot to hang one's hammock or by selling a holder for a lamp or lamp oil — even as little as a thimbleful; but any one with a little self-respect would rather *give* such things away than sell them. I, on the other hand, had put away money that I had earned by mending shoes and clothing. Necessity is the mother of invention, and after a while I had become a fair tailor as well as shoemaker; the demands on one's skill weren't very great!

But I was knitting most of the time. Whenever I could get hold of some yarn and had some free time, I would walk about with some knitting in my hands. If a man wants to save himself from complete decay and degradation and retain his dignity while being ill treated by fate, then he should resort to some kind of manual work. Knitting has provided me with pleasure and diversion in all the years that have passed since that time; I don't go along with those who say that it's only something that old women should spend their time on.

Two weeks went by. We had everything ready, but the right moment for escape had not yet come. But one Saturday evening, toward the end of February, everything seemed just right. There was to be a big celebration on board the *Bahama*; it was the fiftieth birthday of the commander-in-chief. His name was Higgins, but no one ever used his name; he was always called the Chief.

That particular Saturday he had spent on shore; not until early evening did he return to the ship. The captain's gig appeared in all the colors of the rainbow when it came alongside the pontoon jetty at the ship's side: the oarsmen were dressed in blue flannel uniforms with the insignia of the commander-in-chief in front and in back, in silver, gold, and red. He was sitting in the cockpit himself — the colors of his hussar's uniform were gold and scarlet — and all around him sat a cluster of cocottes, of the kind that only engaged in what was called "dignified" relations. They were dressed in ruffled silk dresses trimmed with fur and feathers. They were all talking loudly, screaming and laughing; they had already been drinking.

Besides these, there was a giant of a man sitting in the boat; I never heard him called anything but Goliath. Goliath was the Chief's personal servant. He, too, was dressed in his Sunday best, which also was multicolored and gay-looking.

The Chief had announced that a prize of ten pounds sterling would be given to any prisoner who dared fight Goliath during the upcoming festivities, that is, provided the prisoner won. The prisoner would run the risk of getting a thorough beating; in addition, Goliath had been given the privilege of throwing the prisoner over the bulwark and into the Medway, if he should be in that mood. The prisoner, however, was given the same privilege.

The commander led the way up the gangplank of the *Bahama*; then came the cocottes, and Goliath came last. The Chief looked straight ahead as he walked to the fore part of the ship, but the cocottes shrieked, making all kinds of noisy and indecent gestures, as they passed by the rows of emaciated men who had become excited from viewing this spectacle and had gathered from all parts of the ship, yelling and shouting after them. Goliath uncovered his chest and his arms and showed his powerful muscles, and he shouted derisively at us just the way the giant of the Philistines once had shouted at the children of Israel. In reply, several hundred fists were raised in a threatening gesture, and a collective shout went up from the crowd.

After them came servants with baskets filled with the finest fruits, with cheese and wine. The host and his guests sat down behind a fortified bulkhead on the quarterdeck. The table was set, gleaming crystal goblets were filled with wine, and they all emptied their glasses.

"This is the night we've been waiting for, Cleng," Joseph Fellows said.

Everyone seemed to have a marvelous time on the quarterdeck, and when the Chief offered any prisoner who would accept Goliath's challenge a large goblet of the finest wine prior to the fight, many of them eagerly pressed forward. The guards had to unsheath their bayonets and keep them back with force.

It was growing dark. We were ready to make our escape when night had fallen and the party had become even more riotous.

We hoped that the commotion around Goliath would attract the attention of everyone, and in that respect we were far from disappointed. While the Chief together with the cocottes and the other guests were eating and drinking in full view of the others, Goliath walked to and fro and mocked the prisoners even more than before.

The quarterdeck was illuminated by burning torches, which also threw light on the horde of prisoners; otherwise, darkness had descended all around us. Like ghosts from the underworld, their heads and shoulders were silhouetted against the light; here and there we could see a raised fist. Their shouts increased in volume, and the dense darkness from which it rose, as if from a black abyss, imparted a stamp of horror and unreality to the entire scene.

The first one to challenge Goliath was now allowed to enter the area where the fight was to take place. The ship's physician was assigned the task of acting as umpire, and if the fight developed in such a way that one contestant seemed to be about to kill the other, he had the right to intervene and part them.

Joseph and I looked at the fight in a different light than did the others. For that reason we paid less attention to the fight itself than to the commotion that it caused; neither did we stay to watch the finish. But a long time after, when all the Norwegians were free again and I met Elias Tastad in Stavanger, he told me all about it: Many prisoners had tested their strength against Goliath, but they had all suffered the same fate. Having starved for so long, they had no strength to match his, and the imagined strength that one thinks one has after having imbibed a glass of wine on an empty stomach had endowed them with a foolish arrogance, which only made them look ridiculous and made them go down in defeat so much more quickly.

Then a man appeared who had seen through the trickery; it was none other than Knud Halvorsen Reveim.

Knud was a giant of a fellow, tall and powerful — even though he couldn't measure up to Goliath in size — and he had been able to endure the hardships of imprisonment much better than most. When he volunteered and was offered the goblet filled with wine, he refused to drink it. That made Goliath angry, and he didn't become much better disposed when he felt the strength in Knud's grip. Even Goliath began to feel the strain and was tired.

The end of it was that Goliath nevertheless won, and having gotten all excited, he lifted Knud above his head and tossed him out across the bulwark. This too was permitted, and if the defeated party could swim he would still have a chance to stay alive.

It so happened, however, that at the very moment that Knud was flung across the bulwark, he tried to grasp the top of it from the outside. He didn't completely make it, but it caused Goliath to lose his balance and fall across the bulwark and down on the platform that had been built all around the ship. The prisoners believed that something serious had happened to him, but he immediately reappeared. He

climbed up on deck and raised his tremendous fists up in the air, and
the prisoners noticed that they were covered with blood. They thought
this meant that he had killed Knud, and in a second they began to act
like wild animals. They pushed forward and broke down the barricade
in front of the stand on which Goliath was standing. The officers immediately fled down below deck together with the cocottes and the
other guests; in the melee a few warning shots were fired, but no one
was harmed.

But Goliath met his end when the prisoners broke his neck with their
own hands. Then they broke down the doors to the cabins in which the
officers and the cocottes had sought shelter and violated the wanton
women. But because the prisoners restrained themselves and did not
attack the officers, only their leaders were punished by being hanged.
The rest had to suffer beatings by the cat-o'-nine-tails — many of them
until they collapsed — , and the entire prisoner contingent was put on
half rations for a week and in addition had to carry out fatigue drill for
three hours every day.

About Knud Halvorsen I can relate that with a few strokes he
reached the pontoon jetty which was lying by the side of the ship. A
ladder was put over the ship's side, and only a few minutes after he had
been tossed overboard, he was once again standing on deck, safe and
sound.

While the prisoners were venting their rage on Goliath, Joseph
Fellows and I climbed over the bulwark and then crawled over the railing of the platform. Well hidden from the sight of any one on board
ship, we threw off our pants and jackets — the only garments we had
on — and tied them to our packs. Beforehand we had rubbed our
bodies with grease.

We carried our packs in shoulder harnesses; they contained our most
essential belongings wrapped in canvas — among these was another set
of clothes that we had just acquired — and thus equipped we slipped
into the water. It felt ice cold at first, but we quickly got used to it and
the grease also protected us against the cold. Just the same, I felt
spasms as if I had a cramp when we began to struggle against the
strong current.

We swam close to each other, neither losing sight of the other. There
was a chill wind, and the choppy sea struck us in the face and filled our
mouths with nauseous brackish water. We didn't say a word until we
were safely beyond range, but when we thought we were safe Joseph
asked, "Are you all right?" I answered, "Yes. And how about you?"
"Don't worry about me," he assured me.

The dark surface of the water seemed to have no end, even though we saw lights on shore and were quite certain we were swimming in the right direction. "I think we're close to the mud bank now," Joseph said at last. "You can keep it up for a little while yet?"

At that very moment our feet touched the bottom. A heavy, sweetish smell enveloped us, and half swimming, half crawling we moved along the edge of the bank. Speed was the essence. If we allowed ourselves as much as a moment's rest to catch our breath, our feet would be stuck in the mud.

Our arms and legs seemed as if they were paralyzed from fatigue. I asked Joseph whether the mud bank stretched all the way to the shore. He replied he didn't know; the river was always changing, not only its course but also its width.

We continued on, however. We could feel the bottom under our feet for most of the time, and in a few places it felt firmer than did the outer edge of the bank; if it hadn't, we would probably not have made dry land. But in some places it was just as difficult to proceed, whether we were trying to wade or to swim. We had almost no strength left, but when at last the shore loomed fairly close we continued with renewed courage.

Still in all, Joseph went under when he had merely a ship's length to go; he sank down to the bottom so quietly that the only thing I noticed was a movement in the mud similar to boiling porridge and a few bubbles that burst on the surface. But I acted quickly, plunged my arm in as far as I could and got hold of his pack. I grabbed it and pulled him along, and when I had struggled ahead a few yards that never seemed to end, I was suddenly standing on firm ground.

He looked as if he were dead. I dried the mud away from his nose and mouth and started immediately to rub him with a wisp of dry grass. He quickly came to. I rubbed his whole body dry and helped him get dressed, and when I had put on my own clothes, we discussed what we were to do then.

Right above us there was a village, and we immediately agreed that we had to stay far away from human habitation. Consequently, we set off toward the right across the open fields. Only a few minutes later we walked right into a big haystack. We burrowed ourselves in it and made sure that we had left no traces. It was snug and warm, and we considered ourselves quite safe, but we nevertheless took every precaution. We never went to sleep at the same time but kept alternate watches, just like at sea. We spent about thirty-six hours in that manner. We didn't notice anyone pursuing us, and there were no other signs to indicate that we were wanted men.

We discussed back and forth where to go from there and make good our escape. From the very beginning the assumption had been that we would have to try to get over to France; but without using a disguise of some kind or other we considered it impossible to safely get as far as one of the towns on the Channel coast. I knew the area well from my years at sea, and I said to Joseph that Ramsgate might be the most suitable town for our purposes. He fully agreed to my plans.

During a previous leave from the *Bahama* I had gotten to know about an inn on the road between Gillingham and Chatham. It was in a locality where the houses were few and far between. After dark and unseen by anyone, I could steal up close to it and investigate the possibilities of obtaining some food. The small supply of provisions that we had managed to take along from the *Bahama* was almost gone.

We decided to try just as soon as darkness had set in, and luck was with us. I was the one to make the attempt; Joseph stayed behind in the haystack.

Just when I reached the yard at the back of the inn, a troop of cavalry soldiers arrived unexpectedly. They took the packs off their horses, and from what I could catch at my position behind a hedge, I understood that they had an ample supply of provisions in their packs. It was all piled up in a shed behind the main building, and one of the soldiers was told to stand guard.

But even before the arrangement with rotating guards had begun to function, while a powerful storm showered rain and hail on the roofs, I rushed forward and nabbed a pack from the supply stacks.

At that very moment the servants at the inn and some of the soldiers were busy with finding space in the stables for the horses; anyone not busy with assigned tasks had sought shelter in the inn.

I might perhaps have had the chance to grab a fully saddled horse, but I was afraid that they would see immediately that one was missing, and I did nothing about it. Besides, Joseph had promised that he would get hold of a horse. Ever since we had come ashore, a beautiful brown horse had been grazing in the field below the haystack; but we didn't see any sign of an owner. We didn't have any harness; for that reason I picked up one of the harnesses lying in the yard. It was a good thing that it kept on raining and hailing while I ran back across the open fields.

But the shower didn't last long; between the drifting clouds I could see a dark blue sky and flickering stars. The night wind made the air feel as hard as glass. Having sought protection from the storm, the horse was standing close to the haystack. Joseph was holding it by its mane and rubbing its back with whisks of hay when I came back. It was neighing happily; they had already become good friends.

We put the saddle on it and hitched it to an empty and rickety wagon which had been standing near the haystack. Then we began to load the wagon with a lot of hay from the stack, but we did it very carefully, hoping that no one would notice it. Everything was ready, and we set out. It wasn't so dark that we couldn't find our way across the fields. We made a long detour around all habitation and at last got on to one of the main roads that connect London with the towns along the Channel coast.

We had agreed that if anyone were to question us, we would pretend that we were farmers going to market to sell hay, this being a commonplace business. And if others were to think that we had an outlandish accent, we were to say that we originally had come from Scotland. When on leave in Chatham, people had always thought that I was a Scot.

During the journey we talked about what we would like to do in the years to come, if everything went well. Joseph said that as far as he was concerned, he would take the first boat home to America. He would then immediately apply for an audience with the President and bring with him documents proving that the American agent for war prisoners in England did nothing at all to prevent the prisoners from being treated like animals. It wasn't only that food, clothing, and money were misappropriated, but the agent only read and then burned the letters which escaped prisoners had sent him with the request that they be forwarded to the American government. Neither did he offer any help if such a letter was found on an escaped prisoner who had later been caught by the British, even though he knew that as punishment the entire prisoners' committee would be placed in solitary on reduced rations, while the other prisoners had to give up all their tools and would even be deprived of the right to swapping and bartering.

"This war may last at least another year," said Joseph; "and I feel it to be a matter of conscience to do what I can to prevent my countrymen from living and dying in such disgraceful conditions."

He continued to speak about truth and freedom and about the enlightenment of the heart through the Holy Spirit and about his reliance on the Almighty; and he spoke in such a way that I learned to respect his views. But I said little on that score and consequently received brief answers; nevertheless, it was quite clear to me that he had been influenced by some people who called themselves "Friends," who were called "Quakers" by others. This was the very first time I heard the word "Quaker." Joseph told me that he had come into contact with them while on leave on shore, and they had asked him whether he thought it might be possible for them to come aboard the prison ships and hold what they called "silent meetings" and otherwise help the prisoners in a material way. They spoke about the Gospel and the inner light and about the good deeds that are pleasing to the Lord, such as helping widows and orphans, clothing those who are cold, feeding the hungry, and visiting prisoners and the afflicted.

He also said that even if the war ended, there would still be many kingdoms in Europe where the citizens would be obliged to obey the ruler first and God second. Thus it had always been, but the Almighty had time and again worked on stubborn minds who then would hold the freedom of the heart in higher regard than all material welfare. Among them was one of his own ancestors, who had made the voyage from England to America in the *Mayflower* about two hundred years before.

And while we were sitting on top of the hay wagon and were approaching Ramsgate, he told me the story of the Puritans who had settled in America in the year 1620. About ten years later when I was in the harbor of the City of New York together with Joseph, welcoming the friends and relatives who had arrived in the *Restauration,* my thoughts went back to the conversation we had had during the trip from Chatham to Ramsgate.

Joseph once again talked about what he would do when he came back to New York, where his father was a land agent. He would take a job with him, since it would provide him with a fair income; but also, he said, because he would have the satisfaction of being able to help the immigrants from many lands who were seeking a place of refuge and a new home in America.

"But New York is a city full of sharks and heathens, who don't even stop at tearing the clothes off a poor man's back, taking the food out of his mouth, and stealing every penny in his purse, if they see the chance," Joseph said half in jest; and half seriously he added, "But tell me in good time when you're coming."

Hardly any of those war prisoners contemplating escape didn't know the name of one or more skippers in the Channel ports whose help could be invoked if one wanted to flee the country — provided one had enough money to pay cash for their services. Such was the case with us, too. We preferred to get in touch with a skipper who also owned an inn. Such a place will always be visited by people on horseback or in carriages, and the innkeeper will for that reason always have need of hay.

The skipper was at home, and we made believe that we wanted to sell him our hay. He saw through us immediately, and just as soon as he had assured himself of the fact that no one was listening, he got right to the point and asked where we wanted to go and how much we would be able to pay for the crossing. I mentioned a certain sum, but he demanded a good deal more — just how many guineas I'm not able to recall. Then I said that we would rather buy a rowboat for half that money and get across by ourselves.

But he laughed and said, "You don't know much about the Channel! The current is as strong as a river, and the waves rise up so fast they can sink something much bigger than a rowboat."

Then I told him that I had sailed up and down the Channel in all kinds of weather and knew all about the difficulties it presented to the sailor. Thereupon he accepted the payment we had offered. "If I get the horse and load of hay in the bargain," he said.

It had been our firm intention to have the horse sent back to its rightful owner, but when we saw no other way out, we agreed to the skipper's demand. We knew that he too was taking a big risk, for anyone being caught transporting escaping prisoners, would be condemned to imprisonment on the same harsh terms as those accorded war prisoners.

The skipper hid us in the attic of his inn for the rest of the day, and his wife served us plenty of food; she was the one who was in charge of the inn. When night fell, a little boy guided us through narrow alleys down to an out-of-the-way section of the harbor; that's where the skipper's vessel was moored. On the boat deck there were piles of nets and other kinds of fishing gear.

Without saying a word he brought us up forward and locked us in a tiny cabin. Shortly after we heard much clatter and creaking; we knew that they heaved anchor and threw hawsers from shore to ship, and from the sound made by blocks and tackle we knew that the lugger sail was being hoisted.

We finally sailed out of the harbor and could hear the waves of the Channel beat against the side of the ship. Half asleep, I imagined I could see the yellowish water which I had seen so often during my watches. And even though we were still in great peril, I was overwhelmed by a joyful kind of weariness and soon fell asleep.

There is little to tell about the rest of the voyage. Without running into any kind of trouble we reached Calais, where we left the boat. That was also where I said good-bye to Joseph Fellows. He subsequently secured passage on a ship from Le Havre to Philadelphia. But I continued on to the port of St. Martin. From there I sailed to Norway in a schooner whose home port was Bergen.

About my homecoming and what happened then, I will relate in great detail later on. But first I want to revert to the prison ship, Anne, and let you know what occurred there following my escape.

The Fourteenth Tale

Most of my friends remained in prison for more than two years.

About Enoch Jacobsen I can relate that his formerly worldly ways little by little changed, and he adopted a serious and reflective view of life. He would at times sink into a deep gloom and take a somber view of everything. Even before my escape, while we were still together on the *Bahama*, he would sometimes be so overwhelmed by despair that I feared for his sanity. It must indeed have been the Almighty himself who moved him, although no one would know that from Enoch's own words. The only time I heard him invoke the name of God was during our trip from Leith to Chatham, a journey which I have already told you about.

After our safe arrival at the river Medway, I never again heard Enoch mention the name of God. But in spite of all his cursing and obscene talk he was constantly meditating about the way to salvation. This he has told me himself.

In his great need, he finally opened his heart to another human being: Anders Andersen Reianes. Not long after Enoch had a long talk with Anders, it so happened that they as well as many other prisoners were transferred from the *Bahama* to the prison ship *Fyen*. There were six hundred prisoners on the *Fyen*, even though the ship was smaller than the *Bahama*, and the conditions under which they lived were more miserable than ever before.

But prior to the actual transfer Enoch came across a copy of a Danish translation of Robert Barclay's *Apology for the True Christian Divinity.* It belonged in the very modest library on board the *Bahama*. The fact that Enoch had not taken notice of it before, was due to his by and large having been indifferent to reading and that the commanding officer had refused the prisoners admission to the library; but Enoch got hold of the *Apology* through one of the guards, who was a religious man and felt great kindness toward the Norwegians.

The force and clarity with which Anders spoke about God's Word gave Enoch assurance about his future salvation. But when he read the *Apology* and found out that it dealt with the same kind of experiences that he knew from his own life, he concluded that there must be people in England who lived in accord with these teachings, and he felt an intense longing to meet them and to speak with them. In spite of all the gratitude he felt toward Anders Reianes, it was clear to him that they in many ways had not had identical experiences. Anders was a thoughtful man, and his faith was firmly grounded in the teachings of Martin Luther; Enoch, on the other hand, was filled with emotion, powerful feelings that at times would fling him into the darkest abyss and at other times would lift him up and give him an inkling of the bliss conferred by salvation.

When he was transferred to the *Fyen*, he had to leave the *Apology* on board the *Bahama,* in spite of the fact that he would very much have liked to become even more absorbed in it and possibly learn by heart those chapters that he considered most priceless. But on the *Fyen*, through the goodwill of one of the guards, he borrowed an English dictionary from the commanding officer, and with its aid he wrote letters to a certain person who belonged to the Society of Friends in the city of Rochester and asked him to visit them on board the ship if their spirit were moved by the Lord to do so. The letter was very clumsily written, but the addressee nevertheless understood its meaning. He took with him a fellow believer, and they had themselves rowed out to the ship and asked for permission to come on board. Later on they came again in the company of several others.

They were not able to converse with Enoch, for it was only very recently that he had made an effort to learn the English language. But each made himself understood with the aid of signs, and they soon realized that they were united in a sincere longing to learn the nature of God.

From that time on he was very eager to improve his command of English. He made money by selling ship's models he had carved from bones obtained in the galley, but he didn't buy food or clothes; neither did he spend a penny on entertainment, as he had done previously. Instead, he bought an English grammar and a dictionary.

But his progress was very slow, and he soon discovered the reason for it; it was due to the fact that he didn't know the grammatical rules of the Danish° language either. He then put English aside for a while and concentrated on Danish, until he had laid a foundation which would make his study of English so much easier. Before very long he surpassed most of his fellow prisoners, not only in regard to the written language but also the spoken.

Elias Eliassen Tastad was one of the very next to join the Society of Friends. Among all us Norwegians he was looked upon as an undemanding fellow, always considerate of others. That became very evident when he later on, as the leader of the Quaker congregation in Stavanger, declined to go with the *Restauration* across the ocean because he — as he said himself — feared that the flock would scatter if the shepherd left them. And he assumed this attitude in spite of the fact that he had to suffer persecution and many kinds of hardship intended for him by both the Church and the King's men. But what I want to tell you about this belongs to a later part of my story.

Like Enoch, Elias Tastad was an emotional man, but he had a firmer character, so much so that great thoughtfulness was linked with his very deep feelings.

He, too, wrote a letter to the Quakers on shore, informing them as to the state of his soul; he wrote something like this: "I am very sick in my spirit because there is no way to heal it. I have sought, but I haven't found; I am like a man who has no strength in his legs. Oh, how often I wish I would meet an experienced and faithful friend who can say a few words of comfort to me, so that I can become more patient while I am awaiting the hour of purification and the time that my wounds be healed!" I was given this letter to read at one time, and I repeat what I can remember from it.

Thus, the foundation had been laid for a small congregation of Friends on board the *Fyen*. At first they got together for silent meetings in a closet having space for only three people. Later, when they had grown in number, they met in Enoch Jacobsen's cabin, and when the flock had increased even more and they were about a dozen

---

°Danish was the written, although not the spoken, language in Norway at the time. Tr. note.

in all, they received permission from the ship's officers to come together in one of the saloons. There they worshiped quietly or they praised the Lord in loud voices, and often they would tremble and quake so that they couldn't sit still. Some people say that it was for that reason that the Friends from the very beginning were called Quakers, while others are of the opinion that the origin of the name may be sought in the fact that during a court case against the Friends the founder of the movement, George Fox, admonished the judge to tremble before the Living God.

The flock gradually grew larger, so that when peace finally came the number of those who adhered to the Quaker persuasion had reached about thirty. A third of them were Danes, the others were Norwegians.

The little flock of believers met with great opposition when they officially established their own congregation, a veritable Bethany in the surrounding Sodom. They were mocked for the sake of their faith, by the ungodly and by the self-righteous. Nor was there any lack of blows.

But in the midst of all this they obeyed the words of the Master: "Love your enemies, bless them that curse you, do good to them that hate you, and pray for them that despitefully use you and persecute you."

The followers of Hans Nielsen Hauge, too, derived joy and comfort from the silent meetings of the Quakers, even though they didn't agree with every aspect of their teachings. Nevertheless, there was greater harmony between them than has been believed in later years.

Rumors about an early peace between England and Denmark-Norway began to circulate in the spring of 1813, and the conditions under which the prisoners were living steadily improved. It was now quite common for anyone who behaved well to be given permission to go ashore. On the first day of the week the Quakers among the prisoners could visit the congregations of the Friends in neighboring towns.

At this time, too, those mentioned above and many others sent a plea and a request to the captain of the *Fyen* for representatives of the Society of Friends to come on board and preach the word of God to them. Such petitions were favorably answered several times, and many prominent men of the Quaker faith spoke to thousands of prisoners about the True Light.

Among the speakers was Stephen Grellet. You will remember, Anne, that he and I were the only ones who were saved and were thrown up on shore on the west coast of Tenerife, and that he later on took me along to the chapel "The Blessed Mary of the Snows" and to the summit of Teide.

I have told you the story of his life down to the time I met him. It remains for me to tell you that he got safely across the ocean to America, where he was greatly attracted to the teachings of the Quakers. In view of his former persuasion, it is easy to understand that he would feel himself attracted to the Society of Friends. Impelled by the Holy Spirit, he later traveled to England, where he distributed bread and the Gospel to the prisoners. Once he spoke to seven hundred war prisoners at Chatham. Elias Tastad was among the listeners that time, and it was Stephen Grellet's powerful testimony that set his mind and heart afire and infused him with light and warmth forever afterward.

Many years later — in 1818 — Stephen Grellet came to Norway, where he also visited Stavanger. That was the first time I met him since we had parted in Puerto de la Cruz.

Enoch Jacobsen was not among those who heard Stephen Grellet at Chatham. Because of his pious ways and behavior, his good knowledge of English, and the intercession made by the Friends with the commander, he was released from prison in the summer of 1813. But he was not allowed to go back to Norway, in spite of the fact that he was longing more intensely than most others to see his family again in order to ask their forgiveness.

Enoch went to London, where he got a job at Samuel Southall's umbrella-making establishment. Mr. Southall was one of the leaders of the Society of Friends in London, and it was through him that Enoch was put in touch with prominent men who were later to become defenders of the Quakers in Norway and to plead their case before the ecclesiastical as well as the secular authorities. The most distinguished man among them was Sir William Allen, a highly respected scientist and philanthropist, member of Parliament and throughout his long life a friend of many of Europe's crowned heads, among them both King Carl Johan of Sweden-Norway and Tsar Alexander of Russia.

Sir William Allen visited both of these men on a later occasion; when he spoke with influential men he would always intercede on behalf of the weak and the poor among his brothers. On his first trip he also stopped in Christiania and Stavanger, where he preached the word of God to high and low and helped his fellow believers in their need. He was in truth as welcome in royal palaces as in the poorest huts. But about this, too, I shall tell you in greater detail later on.

The majority of the prisoners were set free and returned home in the fall of 1814, but Enoch Jacobsen and Lars Larsen of Jeilane stayed behind in England for almost a year. Enoch continued to work in Mr. Southall's umbrella-making establishment. He decided to stay on because immediately after the conclusion of peace he got word that both his parents had died; therefore, he no longer had any reason for hurrying home, and he was also convinced that it was important for him to take the opportunity to learn more about the basic teachings of the Quakers. In fact, he, together with Lars Larsen of Jeilane, was selected to receive special instruction in their doctrines.

All the Norwegians who adhered to the faith of the Quakers, were in agreement that upon their return to Norway they would found congregations, each in his own town or district. They were quite convinced that the suffering they had experienced in prison for the sake of the Gospel could be equally great when their new-found faith came to be transferred to the soil of their old homeland. They well knew how both Hans Nielsen Hauge and his followers had suffered for their faith, having even been beaten with sticks and put in chains, even though they had never left the Lutheran State Church. The Quakers had reason to expect even worse treatment.

Lars Larsen got a job in the house of Sir William Allen's mother, the noble and distinguished Lady Margaret Allen. She was just like a mother to him, and he was very fond of her. He had lost his own mother when he was very young.

Everything that Lady Margaret and Sir William told him about the origins of Quakerism through the work of the pious George Fox, about its doctrines and its creed, and what he saw himself of their god-fearing ways in their homes as well as at their meetings — all this bolstered him mightily in his decision to follow in their footsteps and establish a Society of Friends as soon as he returned to Stavanger.

About the other prisoners — those who left England in the fall of 1814 — I can tell that they were brought home on board two Swedish frigates and they disembarked in Christiania.

Many of those who hailed from Stavanger settled down in the capital; among these were Knud Halvorsen Reveim and eventually, Enoch Jacobsen. Knud set up shop as a watchmaker and umbrella-maker. Enoch Jacobsen, too, became an umbrella-maker; he and another Quaker rented lodgings in the house of a merchant by the name of Hans Erichsen, who was married to Hans Nielsen Hauge's sister. Thus you see, Anne, that there were many different contacts between Quakers and Haugeans, and it is hardly to be wondered at that most of those who crossed the ocean in the *Restauration* were nominally Haugeans but really Quakers. They didn't want to stand too far apart in these matters, since they feared that their troubles would multiply if they also outwardly disassociated themselves from the Church, especially its sacraments and rituals.

Lars Larsen of Jeilane returned to Stavanger after a while. There, Elias Tastad and others had prepared the ground for the new faith.

Most of the returning Quakers went back to their old hometown in Norway, and in truth, they all held on to their beliefs, although quietly and in private. Permanent congregations were founded in Christiania and Stavanger only, and from Stavanger Quakerism spread far and wide throughout the county.

But I shall continue my own story from where I interrupted myself. You will now hear the account of my own return to Norway during the winter of 1812.

The Fifteenth Tale

It was about the middle of February, 1812, that we sailed from St. Martin through the Channel and up into the North Sea. When we approached the coast of Norway the wind became quite strong and it began to snow heavily, and when we had passed the outermost island on the coast between Stavanger and Bergen — its name is Utsira — we had to tack outside the mouth of the fjord for about twenty-four hours, since at the entrance to the shipping lane the water is filled with subsurface rocks and skerries. Many ships have run aground here, and many a life has been lost.

But twenty-four hours later it stopped snowing, the sky was clear, and the wind slackened. No harm had come to the boat or to the crew; only the rudder had been damaged a bit. The captain did not think it advisable to continue on to Bergen, but it was decided that we were to continue straight ahead in the direction of the Hardanger Fjord, toward a place by the name of Ølen. The little seaside settlement of Ølen saw a lot of activity in those days, primarily shipbuilding. It was to be expected that there would be an inn there and a place to rent a horse and carriage.

I didn't get a glimpse of my native land until the storm died down. The heavy snowfall had covered every slope and every headland, and everything was gleaming white from the shore to the tops of the highest mountains. I had only been away three and a half years, but in retrospect the years in prison seemed interminable, like time itself.

We arrived in Ølen without any mishap, and skilled shipwrights repaired the damage to our vessel in short order.

But before the ship was ready to sail subzero weather set in. The fjord was covered with ice in a single night.

I put up at the inn. I didn't mind that the food portions were rather small; I wasn't used to any luxuries on the prison ship. But I didn't know that the entire population was destitute because of crop failure and famine. Still, this first winter of great need and distress was tolerable in spite of all; the winters that followed were worse. The valleys in the interior suffered most, since there the frost would come in early autumn.

In the valleys the news spread rapidly that a war prisoner had returned. Many a family had a son or a husband who was missing; so people would gather around me, and they never got tired of asking questions.

Without being initially completely aware of it I began to embroider on one, then another event; being sort of fired by the listeners' desire to believe the most outlandish things, I would at times forget all about the truth and tell about things that just entered my mind, or I would make myself the hero of events that I had just fleetingly heard about.

But I was soon to get other things to think about than bragging and telling stories. One day it was reported that large flocks of wolves had been seen approaching the neighboring district. The following day we heard that the wolves were not far from Ølen. It is not at all unusual for wolves to come down to inhabited areas in Norway, most often in the wintertime, either a loner or a few together. But in this case — it was said — the flock numbered several hundred, and they were so aggressive and wild that God help any creature meeting up with them, whether man or animal.

The heavy snowfall might have been the reason why the wolves came down to the lowlands, but old people who had seen many curious things in their lives claimed that the wolves smelled the herring. During the past year an abundance of herring had once again come in to the coast, and this happened to be the time of one of their periodic arrivals.

When the rumor about the wolves began to spread, everyone became very frightened, not least because so many men were away from the district, most of them taking part in the herring fisheries; others had not yet returned from the war against the Swedes, and a great number had landed in prison in England. Under many a roof a lone wife would sit with none but children and oldsters and would have no other means of protection than a scythe or an ax.

Like so many others, the innkeeper had listened open-mouthed to my stories, especially the one relating how I had been released from prison for two weeks in order to be appointed by the king as Master of the Royal Wolf Hunt, and had later, in token of their gratitude, received double food rations during the balance of my imprisonment. An old man among the listeners had asked me, "But are there wolves in England?" According to what he had heard, the only dangerous animals supposed to be there were wild boars and unicorns. I assured him that no country in the entire world was more pestered by wolves than the British kingdom, more especially by water-wolves; they would just as soon stay in the water as on dry land and they would swim along the shore like large schools of porpoises, for they had become accustomed to eat fish, just like the otter. And it might not be ruled out that such a thing might happen here, too, I added, namely, that the wolf would conquer the ocean just like the seal and the whale in the distant past had left dry land when food became too scarce.

And when I noticed that my tale brought fear to the eyes of some while others were still doubting, I continued and made my tall story even more incredible: I bragged about the marvelous idea that I claimed had come to me on board the prison ship, and which I had mentioned to the guard, and which he in turn had told to the officers, and they had informed the captain, and the captain had spoken to even higher officials so that it got all the way up to the king, and that the king then had had me come to the court and had asked me to carry out my idea. Wherever a flock of swimming wolves, approached, I said, we would man a number of rafts and rowboats, every vessel available, and we would attack the wolves with long poles that were forked at one end; we would hit them over the neck with the forked end of the pole so that it held onto them like a clamp, and then we would have to keep the wolf submerged until it met its end. In that manner we had killed so many wolves, I told them, that the entire wide avenue that leads from the river Thames up to the royal palace had been covered with wolf skins in honor of the Prince of Wales when he returned from a naval expedition against the Spaniards.

On account of such hair-raising stories I had become a welcome guest, for I attracted many customers, and the innkeeper sold quite a lot of brandy and beer.

One day he came to me and said, "You're a man who has got yourself and others out of many a tight spot; now you've got to take care of the wolves for us; if you don't, we daren't even think how it will all end." I felt quite uncomfortable at this suggestion, for I had no idea of how to handle a thing like that. "I must think this over during the night," I replied, even though I well knew that a thousand and one nights wouldn't give me anything more than time to invent new lies and stories.

Nevertheless, it so happened before morning that I had decided on a plan. The plan seemed to me to be as crazy as killing water-wolves with forked poles, and I had precious little faith in it, but I thought to myself, "I'll just make my escape in the heat of battle, and no one will ever see me again; and even though I may not be able to save a single human being, no one will suffer any injuries from a plan such as this."

The innkeeper himself came into my room the next morning, carrying a breakfast tray. A messenger had reported that the wolves had now come so far that they could be expected at any moment. He asked whether I had thought of some method to rescue them.

"You may be sure of that!" I answered.

Since there was a shipyard at Ølen there was no shortage of ropes and cordage. Down by the boat landing there were also large piles of dry junipers ready to be shipped to Bergen. There was a shortage of both coal and wood in all the cities, and juniper makes an ideal firewood; the needles blaze up immediately, and the wood is resinous and hard, burns long, and throws off a lot of heat.

I also knew it is a short distance from Ølen to Sandeid, where the Ryfylke Fjord cuts far into the land — it was less than seven miles.

I then told the innkeeper of my plan, and he said that he thought it was no less fantastic than what I had related about the hunting of the water-wolves.

While I was eating my breakfast another message arrived to the effect that there was no doubt that the wolves had smelled the herring, for all the beasts were running with their heads straining toward the west and were howling incessantly. The flock had had the dark appearance of a newly harrowed field as seen against the snow and the moonlight, and not a soul dared to defy it.

"If that's the way it is," I said, "they want to reach the ocean, and they have to run along the isthmus between Ølen and Sandeid. It's well known since way back that a wolf daren't jump over a rope stretched across his path. If we take all the cordage at the shipyard and in all the homes and the boathouses, it will probably be sufficient to reach right across the entire isthmus, and if we're short I'm certain that people in other districts will put in some of theirs. A special messenger has to be sent around to everyone, so that the work of blocking their path can be started as fast as possible from both sides of the isthmus."

I asked for volunteers to report to me, and even more men than were needed immediatly placed themselves at my command. When I noticed that, I shouted, "Whoever has a gun and knows how to use it, mustn't leave it home! And everybody else, every living soul of you, is to report with a hay fork or a scythe or some other farm implement! It'll be of good use as long as it has a point or an edge. And it won't do any harm," I added, "if a farmer who has a carcass lying in his yard takes it along, whether it's a dead dog or a sheep's stomach. Then he should place it at a good distance outside the ropes and so that it attracts the wolves. But you've all got to be very careful so you don't frighten them before they have come close enough to be done away with. It's only if we can kill or wound a part of the flock that we can hope they'll be so scared that they'll run away for good."

I myself didn't think for a minute that this could be carried out, but no one raised his voice in opposition. On the contrary, everyone got ready as well as he could, and at noon another big crowd from the district was gathered outside the inn; some were dressed in nothing but rags, poor miserable things shivering from the cold and from hunger; others wore one jacket on top of the other so that they could hardly move, — and their footwear was either high boots of the very finest type, or completely worn-out shoes held together by withies and straps, and many wore wooden shoes. Among the types of weapons they carried were also all imaginable kinds, such as scythes and old spears for killing bears, and even an old rusty bronze sword that had been found in a gravemound.

The bonfire was still crackling in the yard, and everyone crawled toward it as close as they could. The cold had become more severe in spite of the fact that the sun was shining all day from a clear sky. The hoarfrost was melting in the men's beards, and the hems of the women's skirts softened in the heat; they had been as stiff as flatbread and trees' bark.

The most vigorous and courageous among the men were ordered to attack the wolves from behind when they approached the barrier, and then to pursue them on skis toward the barrier, driving them with burning torches in their hands if necessary.

"And all you others will carry a juniper bush in addition to what you are now carrying," I said and pointed at the piles that were ready for shipment. "But before we set out, each one of you must get some strength from the provisions you have brought along. But we won't leave here until those who have been selected for the task have finished putting up the rope barrier from shore to shore, between Ølen and Sandeid." And that's how things were done.

Then, they all sat down to eat. All those who had brought more than sufficient food shared with those who were greatly in need, and the inn-keeper treated all those who wished, to a drink or two.

Another messenger had come from the east and said that the packs of wolves were getting very near. If the wolves did not take it into their heads to change course, it was possible that they would reach the barrier before midnight.

With that, we set out, and the men all assumed their positions along the entire roped-off area.

We completed all our preparations around midnight, and about the time that one figures that the dog watch begins at sea, we could hear the first howls. Even though I had always doubted that wolves could smell herring dozens of miles away, I certainly found out that they were able to locate the carcasses.

The moon had risen above the mountains to the east. Then we could just make out the shadow of a drifting cloud making a fleeting pattern on the snow at the top of the hill toward the north, and what looked like a moving black flake sailing across the white hills which sloped down toward the isthmus. The frost and the east wind carried their howls to us.

The men shouted to one another down the line to be ready with the ropes and to those who had weapons to be prepared to use them, and to those who were carrying juniper bushes, to make sure that they would kindle. Small bonfires were scattered over the snowy ground.

It was the biggest pack of wolves that I had ever seen. As the beasts were darting back and forth in the moonlight it seemed to me that they numbered several hundreds, even though it may be that the distance and the light conditions made us overestimate their number. One pack ran toward one of the carcasses, while others rushed toward another one. Just as they threw themselves on the carcasses and started to tear at them and fight among themselves, the order to fire was given, and shots rang out. Some wolves were killed, others merely wounded, and those who up till then were unharmed, threw themselves on their fellows as soon as they smelled blood; they tore them to pieces even before the last howl had left their throats. Others turned about and set off in the direction from which they had come. But then the skiers with torches held high pursued them immediately, and the wolves found themselves trapped between the rifle fire and the bonfires.

Then the order was given: "Cease fire!" and the rest of the waiting crowd stormed ahead. Each used the weapon or the side-arms he had received. And no old woman was too sick or any child too weak to run toward the wolves with a flaming bush. The result was complete chaos, and among all the wonders that occurred that night, the biggest wonder was that nobody was killed.

That the attack succeeded beyond all expectations must be due to the fact the wolves were insane from hunger; their savagery and their bloodthirstiness exceeded even the frenzy of the people running toward them with weapons and torches.

Several hours went by, and the ice-blue night yielded to a red morning. But redder than the light of the sky was the snow, stained with blood. Carcasses of wolves, completely torn to pieces, were spread all over; they were counted, but I have forgotten the number. I only know that the tracks of the few that survived could be traced eastward toward the mountains; one had fallen dead here, another there during their flight. But there was seldom much more left of them than the skin, the paws, and the head.

From that time on there was never any mention of wolves in that entire region, at least not as long as I lived in Norway.

I was praised for my daring and wisdom, but felt a great sense of shame, since the work had been done by others. And when the people in both districts wanted to do me honor, giving me what little food and drink that they had, I answered that I had relatives and friends waiting for me; I couldn't postpone any longer letting them know that I had returned home and was among the living.

A ketch from Stranda at Nedstrand lay at anchor at Sandeid. As soon as there was a sign of wind, they would set sail, the skipper said.

We didn't have to wait. The very next morning there was a strong breeze blowing from the north and out toward the mouth of the fjord.

The Sixteenth Tale

There were many places in Norway where I would much rather have gone ashore than Stranda. The name of the place reminded me of things that I preferred to forget: a knife in Enoch Jacobsen's thigh and a cowardly flight. I certainly could expect that more than one person would recognize Cleng Peerson; and didn't the authorities still want to see me about a certain matter?

But I had no qualms about drinking some of the skipper's gin: "This is the last treat you get on board this ship," he said, "and when you go ashore here at Stranda, you will only be offered the cheapest kind of Norwegian brandy or at best some Lübeck beer, and I don't think I have much to tell a sailor about what kind of a drink that is."

Still steady on my feet, but with my head raised high above the petty troubles of this world, I went ashore. It just crossed my mind that Cleng Peerson had let his beard grow since the last time he was here; besides, he chose for the occasion to adopt a dialect and intonation which had a touch of the speech in Bergen. Anyone that might recognize in this fellow a knife-wielder scared out of his wits, would have to have very sharp eyes.

I walked straight up to the inn, where I ate and drank, but not to excess; actually, there were not many dishes to choose from. Here too, the scarcity of food was apparent. The skipper kept me company.

If I had been a humble and sincere fellow, the events of the past might have made me sober-minded, but intoxicated by victory in the battle with the wolves and by a freedom which still felt as if it were newly won, I didn't look upon the good things that befell me as gifts from the hand of the Almighty. My arrogance increased even further when the skipper of the ketch told everyone about my recent deeds.

Boats from many places round the fjord had been sailing into the harbor, and hungry people were making the rounds of every house. Some of them were begging; others offered to exchange silver or precious objects for dry bread, and others tried to sell their very virtue.

The skipper of the ketch began to jaw about this when we had been sitting at the inn for some time and the brandy had taken effect. There were rumors, he said, that one of the city of Stavanger's wanton ladies had made herself at home on board one of the boats which was used for overnight lodging in the harbor; but she was supposed to be choosy and not available unless one paid well.

I had resisted such temptations in the docks of Antwerp and in the harbor of Marseilles, and during our imprisonment only a few Norwegians had abandoned themselves to loose living. But it wasn't only the skipper's strong gin and the innkeeper's plain brandy that made me lose my bearings. In the course of the conversation I found out that Anne Cathrine was still in the best of health and was running her business with a firm hand. The shipyard at Talgje had been further enlarged; she had shares in more privateers than ever before and was making big profits from this dubious business on the seven seas.

With that I had another drink in order to soothe the pain and to drown my sense of shame, and from my mouth came all kinds of empty and shameful talk. "If it's true that that woman's staying where you're telling me, then she won't be alone tonight!" I promised the skipper. Drunk and excited, I got up from the table, and we left the inn together. The moon was up, and there was a strong southeastern breeze; nevertheless, the cold didn't seem to be as biting as it had been. The snow had piled up in big drifts in between the houses, but all the jetties were ice-covered.

The skipper pointed the boat out to me, and laughing loudly he patted me on the shoulder and wished me luck. Then he walked back to the inn, rather unsteady on his feet. I remained standing there for a while, following him with my eyes.

At the end of the jetty I passed two teen aged boys; they were quite drunk and bragged to each other about their great deeds on board the vessel that served as overnight lodging. Hearing them robbed me of any desire I might have had of getting closer acquainted with what was hidden behind the cabin door of the tarred and ice-covered vessel; but my own boasting prevented me from going back to the inn. I stepped on board the boat.

Almost the entire ship had been roofed over, as is customary in that kind of vessel. The door to the cabin was closed. I opened it slightly; my heart beat faster, not because I felt any strong desire but due to my anxiety, which my intoxication was not able to suppress.

Right inside the door, in the left-hand corner, there was a small stove. The fire had not been put out; it made the room seem pleasant and cozy and infused everything with a faint reddish tinge. On both sides of a narrow center passage there were two rows of berths, each row having two levels; I could just about make out the berth at the end of the passage, since the light from the embers did not reach that far.

There was another door on the far wall; it no doubt led into a separate cabin. From my position I couldn't see any sign of life, and for just one moment I thought of seizing this last opportunity to make my retreat. Then in the moonlight that flowed in through the skylight I saw a woman lying in one of the innermost berths. The thick greenish glass of the skylight gave her face a phosphorous tinge, and for a moment I thought she must be dead, a victim of hunger or disease.

But when I came closer, I noticed that she was breathing regularly and quietly in a deep sleep.

She seemed so very different from what I had imagined: her mouth and chin gave the impression of helpless innocence. But what I mostly wondered at, in spite of all, was that this unknown woman had a blindfold firmly tied over her face and eyes. Her full, dark hair was loosely spread across the headboard and covered her forehead and her cheeks.

But although this encounter was both unexpected and odd, it seemed to me that there was something familiar about the woman's facial features, what little I saw of them.

As I touched the bedclothes in order to cover her over, she was disturbed in her sleep and whimpered, but I couldn't make out any words. I walked softly over to the exit, but she woke up, and I heard her voice, frightened and anxious: "Is anybody here?"

"I just wanted to cover you better so you wouldn't freeze," I said.

It was as if an electric shock had passed through her entire body; she suddenly grasped the blindfold as if to tear it off, but she immediately put her hand down again.

"Shall I get you something to eat?" I asked, feeling a bit uncertain, since everything had turned out so differently from what I had expected.

"Oh, no," she replied, and she turned her face toward the wall.

"Perhaps I should put more firewood in the stove?" I asked.

"No," she answered again, her voice barely audible.

Once again I had the strange feeling that there was something familiar about her and that I was in the presence of something invisible, as if every word I uttered was carefully listened to and weighed. My voice was husky from sobs that had filled my throat without warning, and I asked, "Isn't there anything I can do for you?"

"Please be so kind as to go away," she said, not as a command but as if that would be the fulfillment of her most fervent hopes.

"Yes, I'm leaving," I answered. But when she at that very moment started to sob, I remained standing there, feeling as helpless as one who would like to bring comfort and doesn't know whether one can or dare do so.

Then she called me by name: "Cleng," she said, and I could have mentioned her name even before that if I had been able to believe my own ears, for I had recognized her voice. It was Sara Larsdatter.

I couldn't think of any sensible reason why she had been driven to a place like this, but as I was standing there by her bed I felt as if I were a guilty person next to an innocent one.

She took the blindfold away, and her eyes were blinded by tears. I knelt down by her bed and kissed the tears away from her face; the salty tears quenched a thirst I never before had stilled.

She said, "Since the time you and I sailed past here on the way to Røldal church, I have over the years dreamed about a day when I could make myself beautiful just for you, Cleng. — And then you had to find me like this!"

"Sara," I answered her; "you will always be beautiful in my eyes."

"If so, I know that you have more kindness in your heart for me than I am worthy of," she replied.

I rose and touched her cheek and felt her tears moisten my fingers, and I said, "I'm leaving, but I will return soon. I'll go and get you some food."

When I came back I didn't find her in the cabin, but the door leading to the other room was open, and I heard sounds inside; they were strange and frightening, like suppressed moans.

As I bent down in order to enter through the low door-opening, I noticed that in that room too there were berths, four in all, and Sara was standing in front of one in which a small child was lying.

Hardly a quarter of an hour had passed since I had seen her face for the first time in many years. Hunger and pain had put their stamp on it; nevertheless, I had recognized her immediately. But it seemed to me that this brief moment had changed her face more than had the many years that had gone before, as if its very shape had been changed in the way that a swirl in the water changes its glittering surface and everything reflected in it, into a new and strange picture. Her lips trembled as if she were to scream but could not; but when she spoke, her voice was surprisingly calm.

"He is dead," she said quietly, as if she were afraid to wake the child she was bending over. "Can I possibly *now* believe that God will forgive me for what I did in order to keep him alive?"

The dead child was Sara's son.

There were two other children lying in there: a boy of ten or eleven and a girl a bit older. I was told that they were brother and sister; their names were Talleiv and Guri.

They were orphans, and had no relatives at all. They had originally been living in Telemark.

And with this I shall spin out another thread in my narrative, Anne. I will tell you the story of Talleiv and Guri.

When the war with Sweden broke out, their father had been called up and went with his company east to the Swedish border, and a little while later their mother died from consumption. But a brother of their father — he was living in the same house and was rather eccentric — said to them, "I'm hardly able to clothe you, and even less food can I give you, but if we take along the food we still have and equip ourselves in the best way possible, I think we should be able to get across the Haukeli mountain pass before winter comes. On the other side lies the ocean; winters are milder over there, and there's more food to be had."

This was late autumn. The very first night with frost had spoiled their harvest, but the uncle put a half-eaten leg of mutton and some pieces of flatbread that had been baked from the grain of the previous year — the last they had — in their traveling bag, and then they set out. The snow had not yet settled in the mountains — they were very lucky in that respect — , and they got across the mountain plateau while the ground was still bare. They caught fish in pools in the brooks that were not yet covered with ice, and the uncle would also once in a while shoot a ptarmigan. They quenched their thirst by eating frozen lingonberries; there were plenty of them that year.

Having crossed the mountain, they first arrived in the valley of Røldal and then in Suldal, but hunger and poverty were just as bad in these districts in the interior as east of the mountains, and the man —

his name was Sjugurd and people had given him the nickname Aust-mann — did not have much of a talent for supporting either himself or the children. When he was asked about what he could do, he replied, "Castrate a pig and shoe a horse," but these were things that every farmer knew how to do himself and were unwilling to pay for; much less would they give food to have them done.

Sjugurd Austmann was not one of the most quick-witted, but he nevertheless soon realized that they had to do one of two things: either they would have to go back to Telemark or continue on toward the ocean. But in the meantime winter had arrived in the mountains and the snow was yard-high; there was only one direction in which they could go. And that's how it had happened that he finally had ended up at Hylen together with the children. The man who had driven them in his wagon that far saw to it that they could travel further on the first ship available.

The boat was to call at Tandrevoll in the Sjernarøy islands, but the skipper was reluctant to get stuck with three hungry people in addition to the ones he already had to feed. Therefore, he put them ashore at Tjul; that is the name of an island that lies right across the sound from the Tandrevoll farms. The farmer at Tjul was called Martin, a name which had been used for the eldest son as far back as anyone can remember.

Martin's wife was alone in the house when Sjugurd Austmann and the two children walked up from the boat landing. It was said that when she saw him she got a shock which she never got over; she was a frail and delicate woman and besides she was with child. But Sjugurd's appearance was such that it was far from a pleasure to look at him. It wasn't so much that his clothes looked like rags hanging on a pole; ac-tually, his equipment was more frightening: he carried a huge sharp-edged ax across his shoulders, the blade reflecting the sunlight. But the worst thing was the man himself. The color of his hair had a yellow and greenish glint to it and resembled most of all dry grass; it stuck out to all sides, just like the hay from a haystack, and it hung down over his forehead and his eyes and down over his neck. On the right side of his face a red and very wide scar extended from his temple down past his ear. One eye was very large and seemed constantly to be staring at peo-ple, the other eye was almost closed; one eye was brown and the other blue, and his glance seemed threatening and frightened at the same time. Each nostril was only slightly smaller than his mouth, and his nose sort of pulled his lips upwards so that the yellow and pointed teeth were protruding. His chin was not visible, for his lower lip was hanging down so far that it covered it, and he was practically beardless. People said that only two things were missing for Sjugurd to be the ugliest of creatures: he didn't have a harelip nor did he have horns.

Sjugurd, however, was not aware that his appearance frightened people, for he had never held a mirror in his hand. If he came to a pool in a brook, he would get down on his knees, close his eyes, and drink if he were thirsty, then he would get up and continue on his way.

The boy Talleiv didn't seem to be much handsomer than his uncle. His hair was dry and unkempt, just like Sjugurd's, but its color was different. It was black as coal: its color, however, was not endowed by nature alone, but so many heavy layers of pitch had been mixed into it that they formed something like a cap, and to this cap had been fastened an iron ring. Sjugurd had fitted out Talleiv this way, because the boy was suffering from scabs and since all other kinds of remedies had been tried, Sjugurd had finally decided to use one of last resort: when the boy's hair had grown to sufficient length and the cap of pitch was firm and large enough, a hook was fastened to the ring, and the boy had to get up on a table or a stool and he was hung up securely by the ring and the hook in a beam in the ceiling. This done, they would suddenly pull away what he was standing on, so that he fell to the floor by his own weight, or they would even go so far as to pull his feet. Thus, the cap, the scabs, and his hair, and, even at times, strips of his skin would be left hanging on the hook. The Indian method of scalping is almost to be considered a caress compared to this.

But when the suspended boy had come to, his bloody head was rubbed in with a salve and rags and bandages, if such were at hand. It is said that this kind of treatment has cured a great number of people; but it does sometimes happen that the cure is harder to bear than the illness.

But Talleiv had beautiful eyes: big, brown, with a velvety and frightened look; this set him apart from his uncle.

Both the grown man, who must have been close to fifty, and the boy, who was only ten, went in for drinking bouts and fighting when there was an opportunity. It was Talleiv who had slashed Sigurd's face and made the big scar. They both boasted of it once when Martin Tjul out of the goodness of his heart had given them too much to drink.

But Guri was as unlike the two of them as the sun differs from the earth; her nature was as bright as her hair and skin; and when her eyes looked into yours, it was as if a flower opened up. She seemed trustful of everyone, as if no one had ever done her any harm, even though she was so well acquainted with many types of evil. It was for her sake alone that Martin Tjul's wife promised all three of them a roof over their heads.

I, too, have seen the look in her eyes, Anne. I met her glance for the first time when she opened her eyes in the cabin that winter night. Since then I have met only one other human being whose eyes have looked at me with the same trustful expression. That was you, Anne, when we met in the street outside your dead parents' house in Milwaukee, and I answered you in Norwegian when you poured out your troubles to me.

It was arranged for the three of them to stay at Tjul through the winter; they were to work for their food and lodging. Then it became apparent that Sjugurd possessed a few more skills than he had professed in Røldal and Suldal. Martin Tjul had got a good lumberjack in him; Sjugurd swung the tremendous lumber ax as no one had done before. There were plenty of birch and oak trees at Tjul; the birches were split into firewood, and the shipyards found good use for the oak. And Sjugurd could do more than that: no bull was so wild and no pig so ornery that they didn't fall dead as a result from a blow with his ax, and when his knife had punctured the heart of the animal and had been pulled out, Sjugurd would lie down and place his mouth to the wound and drink the warm blood.

Thus he was a very useful man on the farm, and he was easy to deal with as long as he didn't touch the strong stuff. But one day Martin treated him to a drink and then had teased him, and he had gone down to the boathouse and there he had cut two mackerel nets and a square sail into so fine shreds that it could be put into a pipe bowl; on top of that, he had trampled on and smashed about fifty lobster pots. And when he couldn't be restrained even after all that, Martin drove him off his farm the very next day, and Guri went with him even though everyone had become very fond of her and would have liked to see her stay. She couldn't stay, she said, because she had to take care of her brother, and Talleiv had demanded that he go along with Sjugurd; for even though they outdid each other in doing wrong and crazy things and would often torment each other so that either one or the other would fly into a rage, Talleiv couldn't get along without Sjugurd, and Sjugurd was even less able to be away from Talleiv.

Martin Tjul gave them an old soggy rowboat that he had intended should be burned on the midsummer bonfire; that was all it was good for. Even though the weather was fine, the boat seemed as if it were about to sink. Sjugurd was rowing while Talleiv and Guri were bailing with all their might. Thus they proceeded from islet to islet, from island to island, and after four days at sea the boat was no longer so leaky that their lives were in danger. But by that time they had come as far as the city of Stavanger. All the other places where they had tried to go ashore they had been chased away with sticks and threats.

All this happened in the autumn, at the time of the fair, one year after Sjugurd and the two children had crossed the Haukeli mountain. A juggler who traveled about with a monkey and a trained bear, caught sight of them in the crowd. Things had gone badly for him; his monkey had died a few days before, and the bear did not thrive and didn't want to dance because he had lost his sidekick. But now he perceived better days ahead. "If I could only get hold of those two and exhibit them for money," the juggler thought to himself; he felt completely certain that uglier people than these two did not exist in this world or any other.

He waved them over to him, but Sjugurd pretended that he hadn't noticed, not until the juggler raised a bottle in his hand. Then he pushed confidently ahead through the crowd and also pulled Talleiv and Guri with him into the juggler's tent. When they were well inside, the juggler gave them something to drink and asked whether they knew how to perform any tricks. Sjugurd hemmed and hawed and answered yes, perhaps so. Then the juggler offered him twelve skillings a day and Talleiv half of that if they would let themselves be put on display. "But you should be able to say or do something interesting when I introduce you to the spectators," he said. Sjugurd replied that he could make grimaces if that was good enough, and when he had made no more than one attempt, the juggler immediately increased his pay to fifteen skillings. "In addition, I know a lewd song," he said, "but I don't have a singing voice." "Go ahead and try," said the juggler, and when Sjugurd had finished he had approved the song; it was coarse enough, all right, but his voice was not good at all.

"But, how about you, my child?" the juggler turned toward Guri. She looked down and blushed, for the song was in truth very explicit. He asked her again, and when she asked to be excused, he at first threatened and then tempted her, but then he left her alone and asked Talleiv to sing, and he was willing. She asked her brother not to do it, but he wouldn't listen to her.

Then Guri said to the juggler, "Then I'll sing the song myself."

When she many years later told her husband — she was married to Elias Tastad — why she had offered to do it, she put it this way, "Talleiv was the youngest; he was a child who had no knowledge of what he sang, and it seemed to me that if I refused to sing I would be like one of those who corrupted the children of the Lord, one of those who deserve to have a millstone around their necks. But also because I was his sister and knew that he had been given an ugly face and a difficult disposition to live with in this world, it seemed to me that singing the song would be more degrading for him than it would degrade me, and that it would sound dirtier in his mouth than in mine."

Just the same, she was spared — though I do think that the Lord would have looked in mercy upon her and held her innocent, for the three of them were near death from hunger; they hadn't eaten at all during the forty-eight-hour trip from Tjul to Stavanger. The juggler forgot about the song; actually, he preferred something else that seemed far better as soon as Sjugurd had mentioned it to him.

It was close to the time that Talleiv was to lose his "pitch helmet," as it was called, and Sjugurd explained to the juggler what this was all about. Hurriedly, a pole was put into the ground, a crosspiece was fastened to it, and an iron hook was nailed to the crosspiece. A table was placed underneath, and Talleiv was ordered to get up on the table. Then the juggler announced in his loudest voice what was going to happen, but every spectator had to pay two skillings before the event. A great number of spectators gathered, a few hundred or perhaps more, but some left as soon as they heard what was going to happen.

Both the juggler and Sjugurd collected money from the spectators. Talleiv in the meanwhile was standing on the table; he was pale as ivory. "Give him a glass of brandy," Sjugurd told the juggler. The juggler did so; he brought the bottle with him from out of the tent after having been inside and filled his money box with all the coins that had been collected.

The hook was fastened to the ring and the table was quickly pulled away from under Talleiv's feet, but the pitch helmet wouldn't give, and the boy was screaming like a stuck pig. Many of those who were watching, became incensed, some because they didn't think they had gotten their money's worth, others because they thought this was going a bit too far.

The juggler ordered the boy to get up on the table once more, and told Sjugurd to tug at his feet, so that the people would actually witness what they had paid for. But this was going too far even for Sjugurd. He had a sudden attack, of the kind that he would have once in a while, especially when he had been drinking; but this time he had only had one glass of brandy. Martin Tjul, who had read the old sagas, called such attacks the berserkers' madness. In Sjugurd's case, it first started with his body becoming rigid like a wooden log, then he would turn up the whites of his eyes, and he would be foaming at the mouth.

In that state he would always be seized with some kind of fury. On this evening at the fair he pulled out his knife and waved it about him as if it were a scythe and he were mowing a field. He mowed the place empty of people. When a couple of strong-arm fellows came up and wanted to restrain him, he let out a roar and ran through the crowd outside and down to the harbor and dived right into the water. His corpse was found the following morning.

This put a scare in many people, and most frightened was the juggler himself. He crept into his tent and hid, never giving another thought to the two children. For hours they were standing on the edge of the jetty from which their uncle had jumped. Some men who took pity on them, got hold of a boat and used water binoculars to search for him, but it was already dark and they couldn't find anything.

The children had no one to turn to, and no one gave them shelter. The town was overcrowded with transient people, just like Bethlehem on that first Christmas Eve. The night was chilly; the northwest wind swept across the harbor and pressed through the narrow alleys where the children walked up and down in order to keep warm; now and then a snowflake fell from the sky, but mostly the sky was clear, with glimmering stars.

The night came to an end, and they survived. Guri was even in a happy mood when the day broke, and she comforted her brother. He especially suffered from hunger and thirst, and he froze even worse than before; hailstones whipped down on the cobbled street and on the roofs of the houses and into the children's faces.

Guri said, "We'll have to ask for something to eat," and they started to walk from door to door, but it was all in vain. Those people who had seen them at the juggler's tent the previous evening, closed their door on them for that very reason, and those people who had not seen them before, probably shut them out because Talleiv's looks scared them. No one had ever seen a head like that, and no one had ever before seen such a helpless look in the eyes of any of God's creatures.

When they came down to the harbor about noon, they saw their uncle's lifeless body being pulled out of the water. His face was pale and less ugly than it had been while he was alive. Two men placed a piece of sailcloth over him and carried him through the streets to the morgue. One grabbed his arms, the other, his feet. They didn't need a stretcher, since he was stiff like a log.

One of the city's two policemen walked ahead, representing the authorities, and the children followed a distance behind, but they didn't dare walk into the morgue. And the door was shut.

Since all other doors in that town seemed to be closed to them, they walked up a steep hill on the south side of the little lake by the cathedral. Still another hailstorm pounded the streets. They saw a large oak tree and ran over to it and sought shelter on the lee side of its trunk.

While they were standing thus, Sara Larsdatter happened to pass by. They had stopped not far from her house. She was on the way home; she had spent some hours in a warehouse in town salting mackerel.

This is what had happened to her since her husband's death: The farm near Bergen had, according to the contract, gone to the Haugean congregation; she didn't inherit a skilling from his estate. Her father's shipyard was not run very efficiently by the men who had taken over after her brother Lars had become a prisoner of war in England. She was then given the advice that she ought to sell, which she did. But money didn't go very far in those evil times, and it wasn't very long before she was almost destitute. By doing odd jobs she managed to earn enough for herself and the child; but need and want were never far away.

And when she saw the two children and recognized them as the two she had seen the night before when she had crossed the marketplace, she took great pity on them and asked them to come along with her. And they slept their first night under Sara Larsdatter's roof.

The Seventeenth Tale

That night in the houseboat, Sara told me about everything that had happened to her during the years we had been apart. And I told her a few things about life on board the prison ship. About the fondness we felt for each other no words were necessary; but between us there was a drawn sword.

When the new day dawned, we saw through the half-open cabin door a large rowboat entering the harbor. Two elderly people were at the oars: a woman on the front thwart, and a man on the center thwart. I recognized them as the boat passed us. They were my mother and my blind father. Mother still wore the stamp of dignity and strength as she had always had, but Father looked almost as miserable as when he had been locked up in the Falkeids' attic. Whiskered, skinny, and clad in rags, he just sat there and tried to follow my mother's strokes of the oar; his own strokes were very feeble.

The distance from Tysvær to Stranda at Nedstrand is several dozen miles, and I was wondering what purpose they might have in coming so far in such a small boat in the middle of the winter.

They found an unused boat landing, and when Mother had moored the boat, she took Father by the hand and led him up among the houses. If it was their intention to continue their journey, I would have to make my presence known to them; but when I noticed that they spoke to a man they met and then walked into the inn, I turned back to

Sara. She was busy washing her dead child; from my sailor's bag I got out a sheet to put around the boy. In our hands he looked like a bird or a skinned rabbit.

When he had been made ready for burial, we placed him in an empty berth.

But Father's and Mother's boat was not the only one coming into the harbor at Stranda on that day. Toward evening a larger boat with four pairs of oars arrived; it was brim full with men and women, even infants, and some very old people.

We were told that they were cotters' families from the area around Suldal Lake. Even in good years want was always at the door there. Now it had crossed the threshold and made itself master in every house. Storehouses and bins had been swept clean eventually, and when every piece of food had been eaten, they knew no way out other than slaughtering the few domestic animals that they owned; first the sheep, then the goats, and finally the cow. But most cotters' families have many more children than they have livestock; it didn't take very long to scrape the bottom of the meat trough.

When February came, they bolted doors and windows and traveled to Sand, begging and threatening their way from door to door for over a week. Some people set out cocked guns, and many of them were wounded; a girl of thirteen bled to death, but the sheriff and the pastor made believe nothing had happened.

Then they heard that the fishing for spring herring had begun in the open sea, and one night they stole a large rowboat and rowed with all their might toward the mouth of the fjord. They thought, "If we get that far, we will once again be able to eat our fill, and we can salt the herring if we obtain salt, and we might be lucky enough to make it last until spring."

They dropped a troll line and caught a large cod, and they ate it raw.

After sailing for forty-eight hours they reached Stranda at Nedstrand. Some of them looked like no more than shadows; they didn't open their mouths, neither in supplication nor complaint. Others had become quite wild from hunger. Ravenously, they threw themselves at anything that could be eaten.

A young widow had lost both her children during the voyage; they were twins, four years old. She had been a vigorous and beautiful woman; now only skin and bones were left. Her mother's milk had ceased to flow; the children were suckling nothing but blood. They both died with her nipples in their mouths, and when she noticed that they were no longer suckling, she put them both down on the floorboard. Then she lifted the large, empty breasts, placed them over her shoulders and buttoned her dress. They had accomplished all that might be accomplished, first for the sake of charm and beauty, then for the sake of passion, and finally for the sake of life, and from then on she would carry them the way one takes away a useless burden. She didn't open her mouth when the two men who had assumed command of the boat, decided to draw lots as to whether the children were to be dropped into the sea right away or remain in the boat until they reached shore. It turned out that they were to be lowered into the sea. When one of the men recited the Lord's Prayer, she folded her hands but when they were carefully lifted over the gunwale she looked at the dead children as if they were no concern of hers. Not until one of them uttered a feeble sound just as he sank below the surface did she rise to her feet and stretch out her arms toward the child. Standing there she noticed that he stirred just a bit as he sank down next to his brother. There was not even a ripple on the surface of the sea. Finally, they both appeared as two light-colored flakes deep down, like the belly of a large fish.

The cotters' boat didn't arrive at Stranda unarmed. Some had knives in their belts, a few had an ax slung across the shoulder; there was also a muzzle-loading gun to be seen. But most of them left their arms in the boat when they disembarked. They were hoping that their hunger would be stilled without their having to resort to force and violence.

No one who saw them could help being appalled, and if they had shown up one by one, it is probable that any one with compassion in his heart would have done all he could to help. But this was such a large group that no one could possibly help to the extent that it would have any effect.

First they walked from house to house, but the people locked and bolted their doors. Then they returned to their boat and got hold of their weapons, and through intimidation they got into first one house, then another, and finally, the inn. When the innkeeper spoke about calling the sheriff, they said that they intended to continue on the next day, out toward where the herring was, and they wouldn't stay long nor would they harm him if they only were allowed to eat their fill that evening and the following morning.

Nevertheless, the innkeeper called the sheriff, but when he showed up he thought it the better part of valor to go easy with such a superior force. He contented himself with announcing that each and every one would be held accountable if he were to be guilty of any misdeed, but privately he advised the innkeeper to serve them all the food he had.

"It's as empty and bare here as every other place," replied the inn-keeper.

"The sheriff's storehouse isn't empty," answered the other, "and if you can only keep secret where the food is coming from, then you can send a few of your servants out to my place and get meat, flatbread, and flour, so that these poor people can eat their fill tonight and once again tomorrow morning, as they have requested."

While all this was taking place, I had stolen into the inn and taken a seat down by the door. The cotters from Suldal and their companions filled up the entire room. One little boy was chewing on a piece of leather that had been part of an oarlock, another boy was scratching with his nail the inside of a strap from a horse's harness and was eating the fat that is exuded by the horse's hair. A few babies were sucking on pieces of charcoal.

Next to the far wall sat my father and mother. I thought to myself, "Mother won't notice me in all this uproar, and even if she did she wouldn't recognize me with this full beard. If she nevertheless were to hit on the idea that it really is me, she wouldn't believe her own eyes."

I felt quite safe; it had already begun to grow dark, and the light was very poor in the large, low-ceilinged room.

But I had only been sitting there a short while, when she got up, walked straight over to me, took my hand, and said in a low voice, "Imagine seeing you here, Cleng!"

"But how did you recognize me, Mother?" I asked.

"That I don't know," she answered; "but I sort of had a feeling that you were here even before I saw you."

"Does Father know it too?" I asked.

"No," she replied.

"I'll go over with you and tell him who I am," I said.

"Wait just a little while," she begged. "I must prepare him for it, otherwise the joy might be too sudden for him. It's drawing near to the end for your father, Cleng."

I was just going to ask why they had come to this place, when she got up and walked back to Father. The hungry flock from Suldal had not yet been informed of the sheriff's offer; none of them knew that they were to eat their fill before the evening was over. Most of them just sat there, saying nothing and abandoning themselves to complete powerlessness and silent despair. But some of the smaller children were whimpering, and some of the men who had been drinking brandy, spoke in loud voices; they cursed and threatened, and one of them prayed to Almighty God that He help his mother. She was lying prostrate on the floor, her head resting against his boots. Her black kerchief had slid down over her face; only the toothless mouth and the pointed chin were visible.

Then Father rose and said, "If only those who complain could be silent, and if those of you who pray and curse will stop it, then I'll have something to say to you."

He looked like a dead man, just risen from the grave. A deathly silence descended on the room; even the small children stopped crying.

In spite of age and misery, his bearing was still erect. His hair, hanging down on his shoulders, the flowing beard, which now had become snow white, and the unseeing, wide-open eyes gave him a stamp of holy madness. That is the way that the saintly hermits must have looked when they emerged from their caves and went into the cities in order to foretell the end of the world.

His voice was broken but it had retained some of that ring and fullness which I remembered from his prime; the milky white and extinguished glance seemed to radiate a strange power; each and every one got the feeling that his glance was directed at him and no one else.

"You see before you an old man dressed in rags," he began, "and a woman, younger in age, attired in a dress she has no reason to be ashamed of. I myself am blind; I can't actually see that it is so, but I know it."

Mother's face darkened from the pain inflicted on her; she looked directly at him; there was no trace of dismay in her glance; it was filled with tenderness and calm.

"I have been carrying a heavy cross on my shoulders," Father began once more. "For many years pain was my companion night and day, and more than once I implored my wife to erase me from the land of the living, because all the suffering of this world had been laid on me. It was as if Jesus, the blessed one, had been born anew into the world in my body in order to bear all its agony and suffer for all its sins."

He stopped speaking; the light made the blind eyes seem to flicker; there were beads of perspiration on his forehead.

"Since then I have learned that suffering is not the heaviest cross that a man can carry. Emptiness is heavier. With me, pain drove me into insanity, and at the bottom of insanity lurks emptiness. But when the insane man realizes that, he will redirect his soul toward reason, if it only can find the way. But if he doesn't find the way, then he is imprisoned by emptiness; and everyone leaves him, all that he has loved: wife and children, property that he can touch and experience, the earth beneath him, the hope that is in his soul. No matter whether he is blind or sighted, this world with all it contains becomes to him like shadows without a name."

He started to wring his hands; the muscles in his face were twitching. When he had regained control of the agitation that filled him, he began to speak again:

"Thus for almost three years I haven't been able to sleep, by day or night, because my soul was a sieve of emptiness, and I have said to this woman: 'Oh, if I could only experience a joy or a sorrow which would make me feel certain that I am still alive! As I am standing here, I am like a wind that whistles through a keyhole, nothing more.' Therefore I said to this woman: 'Do you want to take me along with you so that we together can seek a place where human beings are happy or are suffering; if I could only be restored to life just once before I die, in order to know joy or pain or tears, otherwise I fear that in the great beyond even hell will be closed to me.' Then this woman answered me, 'Let us row into the inner reaches of the fjord; perhaps we will meet people who have gone through great distress and trouble and nevertheless have kept a pure heart and an undivided love.' "

Then I rose and said, "Do you recognize me, Father?"

"No, I do not know you," he replied.

"I am your son Cleng."

"My son Cleng does not exist for me. His name is like ashes on my tongue; his memory is like the needs that we have no knowledge of. But if you yourself believe that you are among the living, then let me hear your story."

And I told about Sara Larsdatter and her dead child and about Guri and Talleiv. And here I will repeat for you, Anne, what has not before been written down, just about the way I told it to the group in the inn, but without giving any names:

"We who are gathered here know that it may be a very difficult task to obtain for oneself and one's family the daily bread during these years of need and suffering. Still more difficult is it when a household is suddenly doubled in size and even more. The woman that I'm telling you about, experienced that her workdays became long and the nights short. Her hands were rough from salt as long as there was fish to be salted. Thereafter she walked from door to door, but found that nobody needed her to work for them. Stavanger has recently had a generous share of beggars, and she didn't want to increase their number. The idea never occurred to her that she might sell her honor for bread, even though she knew that many a woman had taken this way out, as does happen in evil times.

"One day very reluctantly she had to face up to the fact that she and her charges were starving. Then she went to see the skipper of a small cargo boat whom she knew slightly and asked whether he needed a cook on board the vessel. If she could be given meals for herself and her three children, she would do all the work without any wages. It was a lot to ask, and he hemmed and hawed, but at last he said yes.

"The boat carried herring barrels from Sand to Stavanger. Everything went well on the first trip, but after two weeks he made other demands on her, and she refused to submit to him. He asked whether she thought that he needed four mouths to chew his food. And when she didn't answer, he next asked where she would prefer to be put ashore. She didn't reply this time either, but the nearest harbor was Stranda, and there he put his boat alongside and commanded them to go ashore.

"Then they went from door to door in the wintry weather and asked for work and shelter. But who will take in a strange woman with three children in a time of misery and starvation? At last she took refuge in a boathouse, and she had the girl watch over the other two children while she walked on to other houses and knocked on other doors. She knocked in vain, but when one of the farmers heard that she had three children left behind in a boathouse, he came along with her. It was late in the day; it was growing dark, and they groped their way across fish traps and nets. Next to the innermost wall he discovered that someone had put up something from pieces of wood and sailcloth, and the earthen floor was covered with heather and grass. The two boys were sleeping inside; one of them was as beautiful as an angel and the other one was uglier than any child the man had ever seen before. The girl was also sleeping, leaning against the wall. A small tallow candle flickered in a pewter candlestick, and on a wooden tray which had been placed on the cover of a small chest there were a half-eaten salt herring and a mug of water. The water was turning into ice, and chill blasts of wind entered below the ceiling so that nets and ropes were swaying.

" 'You can't stay here,' said the man. 'But I know of a boat where you can come and live.'

"He helped her get on board; by then her own child was delirious.

"Trembling in every limb and ashen of face from keeping awake nights, Sara was sitting by the bed of the sick child. That's where the skipper of the cargo vessel found her the next time he was traveling west, and what he previously had demanded but not received, he now took without asking. He left behind him bread, herring, and beer when he went ashore, and later on he got drunk at the inn and spent some time with his companions and bragged loudly about the evil deed that he had committed.

"What he had told them incited them all, and five men went on board the vessel, and they all forced themselves on Sara Larsdatter.

"Violated and ravished, but unbowed and pure in heart, she demanded pay for the sake of the children, and the five men walked back to the inn before they had sobered up and bought meat and bread from the innkeeper, and brought it down to her. She divided it among the children and also ate some herself.

"By putting herself forth as a living sacrifice she was enabled to keep the three children alive, even though her own child seemed to get ever weaker. One night she was standing by its dead body. She was silent a long time; then her misery burst up through her throat, but she couldn't weep.

"The other two children had awakened and had fallen asleep again. She closed the door to their cabin, and she lit a tallow candle and placed it in the candlestick, and while the night wore on an old friend kept her company. They had been fond of each other from childhood on, but they were not able to marry, and when they had spoken about this and many other things she began to cry while looking him in the eye, and she said: 'For years I have dreamed of the time when I could be beautiful just for you, and you were to find me like this!' He replied, 'Wherever there is a great love, the greatest beauty is also to be found. But why did you have the blindfold on?' She replied, 'Perhaps it was because I felt that no one could wholly own me as long as they couldn't look me in the eye.'"

Then Father rose to his feet and shouted, "I know you! You are Cleng, you are my son!" And he fumbled across the table until he touched Mother's hands and face and once again he shouted, "I know you, too! You are both alive and born again in me, and again it has been granted me to taste suffering and joy. Yes, I know you, Katharina! When I sat in a cage in Aron Falkeid's attic and was more pitiful than any animal, then you came to me and placed my head in your lap and sang to me until I fell asleep, as if I were a child. But I invoked the names of all the devils and cursed your name. How could I scorn such a great love?"

When he had calmed down again, he exclaimed in a broken voice, "I can weep again! Oh, I'm able to weep again! Praise be to God for my tears!"

And he bent over and kneeled down in front of her chair, and he hid his face in her lap, and again he shouted, "God be praised for that love which is stronger than death!"

A tremor passed through his body, it seemed like a big tree trembling under the blow of the ax before it falls. He fell down again and breathed his last, embraced by her who had carried him forth to a new birth.

The Eighteenth Tale

As the sheriff had promised, the hungry flock from Suldal were twice allowed to eat their fill: that evening and the next morning. Many of them ate until they got sick, but the sheriff reminded them that if they didn't continue on their way as agreed, there would be trouble. Thereupon they hoisted sail and set their course in a westward direction.

We, too, departed; our destination was Tysvær.

The two who had died we took along with us. We placed them in the forehold, the child lying next to my old father. I took hold of the one pair of oars myself, and Mother took the other pair. Guri and Talleiv sat on the rear thwart and Sara was in the stern. Later we all took turns rowing, so that no one would get tired and all would be able to keep warm.

The weather had changed; rowing along the shore we saw the water running down the cliffs and precipices from the glaciers. A thin veil of clouds made the sky appear white, except toward the west where we could see a narrow, bright blue stripe above the horizon.

Five of us were among the living; we had two dead persons along. A great number of people came to the funeral, but we invited only the close family to come with us from the churchyard to our home.

I met my sister Kari again; she was now engaged to Cornelius Nilsen Hersdal. They got married later that year and had four children when they left for America on the *Restauration*. Cornelius's brother Nils also came along; he is the one who later was called Big Nels.

The herring fisheries turned out very well that spring; the herring kept coming in to shore throughout the month of March, also around Tysvær, and I joined a seine gang. Most of the time I was able to sleep under my own roof, but many had to find shelter in the house-boat or in a drafty boathouse. On a moonlit night, one could see men running across the rocks and knolls trying to keep warm. It was a very cold spring that year.

The total herring catch was estimated at about a hundred thousand barrels, and it was only the herring that saved the coastal population from starvation during the following years. The grain harvest failed far and wide. The grain that was not destroyed by the rain was ruined by the frost.

The frost showed no signs of loosening its grip even when spring arrived, and I was not able to sow by the time I had planned to do so. Then I decided to pay a visit to Anne Cathrine; I had something to talk to her about, and it could no longer be postponed. While under way, I suddenly realized that it was our wedding anniversary; five years ago we had entered into holy matrimony.

I treated myself to a drink in the boathouse before I tackled the hills leading up from the harbor at Kindingstad. The liquor made my feet more nimble and made me light of heart, and I may even have hummed a tune and not given much thought to how my aging spouse would receive me.

When I entered the open door, she rose, supporting herself on two sticks, and with a smile that was not very pretty, she said, "So it finally pleases you to step under my humble roof. You are getting to be famous: you're supposed to have been hunting more than one kind of game since you returned to this country. But if you think that your Anne Cathrine is one of the tame animals in the Ark, it might just be that you're very mistaken."

I didn't answer, and she continued in the same manner, "You left the country in a great hurry," she said.

"I didn't have much reason to stay," I replied.

"That's true," she said. "There are some people here who consider you guilty of manslaughter. The authorities will find it difficult to avoid indicting you; no one has heard of or about the pharmacist's ap-prentice Enoch Jacobsen in three and a half years."

"I can provide proof that he's still alive," I said.

"And even in the best of health?" she asked.

186

"He's neither better nor worse off than any of the others locked up on the prison ship."

"I think it's going to be pretty difficult for you to get proof that he's alive, until the war is over," she said; "and *that* may take many years yet."

"Let's hope not," I answered.

"Oh yes, let's sincerely hope that it will," she replied. "To me this has been a good and beneficial war. Just look here!"

She sat down by the table filled with documents. I remained standing at the end of the table, but she said, "Pull up a chair and sit down next to me! As far as I can recall, you weren't afraid to get close to me before we were married."

The documents were ships' papers of various kinds, partly shares in ships, partly bills of lading, and so on. She placed them before me, one after the other, and jotted down numbers in a ledger lying on the table next to her. At the same time she explained that during the last few years the various ships in which she owned shares, had earned so and so many thousands of rixdalers in peaceful trade, while others were privateers and had captured prizes valued at so and so much money. "*Our* ships," she said, but whether that meant that she looked upon me as part owner or whether she meant the other share owners, I couldn't make out, and I was very careful not to ask her about it.

Nevertheless, one thing was quite clear: she was speaking the truth. The war had brought her large profits and no losses. And even though I felt disgust when I looked at her greedy hands leafing through the documents and her unrestrained joy from owning far more than any person would need, I felt as if I was a beggar and a parasite. I said to her, "I'm applying for a divorce from you, Anne Cathrine. It is probable that no greater disgrace will come to you if I choose to abstain from your company than when your first husband did so." To this she replied, "Have *I* broken the vows of matrimony? *One* of us two has the right to apply for a divorce, and that person hardly bears *your* name! Not only have you shirked your husbandly duties, but it is being said, and it's supposed to be reliable information, that you willingly have shared with others that which your legal spouse ought to have had wholly to herself, if what the law and the prophets say is still valid. But I haven't thought of applying for a divorce from you, and if you're smart, you'll realize that *that* too is to your advantage, Cleng. Soon I'll depart this life, and then it becomes yours, all that wealth that I gathered while you were in prison doing nothing but laze around and waste your time. As you know, I'm now close to seventy. It would be strange indeed if I have much more than twenty years left to live."

"That's enough, Anne Cathrine!" I shouted at her. "That's more than enough!"

She made believe she hadn't heard me.

"You may be so fortunate," she continued, "that you will bury me before you yourself have reached fifty. Then you'll still be a man in your prime, and if your pious Sara is so constant in her love as she has shown herself to be up to now, you will have much joy and pleasure to look forward to."

I rose and left her without saying another word; I went on board the boat and went to sleep. It was already evening. The next morning I hoisted sail and set course for Tysvær. My sister Kari was soon to be a bride.

The wedding was held on the Saturday following Ascension Day.

Who would ever have thought that spring would not be in full bloom on that day, after such a long and hard winter? But that was not nature's intention: on Ascension Day there was a heavy snowfall, and the next two nights the cold was so great that the river that runs between Hesthammer and Falkeid froze over. In the woods the foliage had everywhere turned rust-brown.

The bridegroom and his father had arrived at Hesthammer the night before, but the guests didn't begin to show up until Saturday morning, about the time the bride was expected to come down from the second floor, where both mothers, as was the custom, had helped her put on all her finery.

I looked at sister Kari, and I recalled another wedding and another bride. The silver brooches on her breast gleamed, and calm and erect she wore the bridal crown; it mustn't fall off her head. If it should do so by accident, that was interpreted as being a sign that the bride was not a virgin. And when I saw how she sparkled from sheer joy, I thought to myself, "If only this had been my day of happiness too, and that Sara Larsdatter had been given a crown to wear!"

As was customary, the ale bowls were passed around before we set out for church. The men brushed their moustaches away from their lips and the women looked out for the fringes of their shawls while the bowl went from mouth to mouth. The ale was not of the weak kind, and there was much laughter and bantering while each one skoaled the next in line; some of them took the trouble to read the inscriptions on the wooden bowls and found that they were excellent.

Then all took their places in the boats. There was a following wind and the men were all good rowers; seldom has a bridal procession taken such a straight course and reached the church in such a short time.

When we rowed past people on the shore, they shot off their guns in order to greet us and some of the rowers fired off their pistols in reply. Some took a nip because of the cold, but no one was unsteady on his feet when entering the church.

The parish had gotten a new pastor; his name was Thomas Morten Henrik Swensen Magnus; he was a man who didn't lack for names. He was probably about thirty years old at that time, still unmarried, but he did have an eye for the fair sex. Later on he married someone of his own class, the youngest daughter of the judge in the district of Ryfylke. Swensen Magnus was extremely conscious of his clerical dignity; nevertheless, he was neither condescending nor pretentious as long as the common people danced to his tune; but pity the one who would try to interfere or create confusion in the affairs of the church! For that reason he was known as a staunch opponent of the Haugeans, and he was later to become the most severe persecutor of the Quakers in Stavanger county. Many people were to suffer greatly in both body and soul because of him, and in no other place in the kingdom of Norway did emigration to America for reasons of faith and conscience become as extensive as that from Tysvær and Skjold.

People said about Swensen Magnus that he made out better in a verbal argument and with his pen than he did as a preacher in the pulpit. For certain recurring occasions, such as weddings and funerals, he had three set speeches, and people could choose among the three according to how much they were able to pay. Kari and Cornelius had selected the middle one; it was generally known that that speech gave the best value for the money. He would at times insert insults in the least expensive speech, and it was also said that the most expensive one was not to any appreciable extent better than the middle one, for Swensen Magnus was in any case quite unable to reach the heights of oratory.

On the way back from the church he joined our company. He was not the man to scorn good food and drink. When he had taken his place in the boat and had been treated to a few drinks, he became quite elated and wanted to take the oars. One man had to yield his place to him on the thwart. Some people hid a smile; they didn't think that this sailor of the Lord could stand his ground as an oarsman, but in that they were wrong. He kept time with the others, even when he had consumed so much brandy that he began to sing a lively ditty about the girls in Copenhagen.

He continued in the same vein in the bride's home, dancing with the bride after the bridegroom. The bridal dance is stiff and solemn, but the pastor increased the tempo so much that Kari almost lost her crown.

Snuff was passed around after the meal, and some of the men puffed on their pipes, but there was a shortage of tobacco during those years. It was much easier to obtain brandy, but in my parents' house it had always been the custom to drink with moderation.

Otherwise, everything passed off as is customary at a rural wedding. The guests celebrated the entire day and part of the night. Distances were long between the farms, and beds were made on the floor both in the parlor and in the attic. Toward morning, when most of the guests were asleep, I made a solitary round of the farmyard. As I passed behind the cowbarn, I could hear that the cows were lowing and seemed very restless. When I got closer I noticed that the door had been left ajar and I also thought I could hear someone sobbing. Very carefully I moved closer. Then in the light of the early dawn, I saw the bride and the bridegroom standing inside. He was holding the bridal crown, but she had gone into one of the stalls to caress one of the cows. She wept and moaned over the fact that she had to leave them, and she stroked its bony back and said, "Poor starving animals. And we have been gorging ourselves on food and drink. It would have been better if we had gotten married without having such a feast, Cornelius; then we wouldn't have had to have the pastor in the house, either." But Cornelius said, "The air is mild tonight, Kari; there are bare spots in the field already. Let's untie the animals, so that they can graze wherever the fields are green."

While they were busy with that, I opened the door and made believe that I had just come, and I helped them so that soon all the cows and the calves were out. They were so starved that they could just about walk, but we supported them. When we had reached the bare spots they began to graze, and they grazed until the black earth showed through all over.

I remained standing there, but the bride and groom returned to the house, to enter into their chamber. I took a long walk in the woods; I followed a creek bed far into the forest. At last I came to the spring where I had filled Sara Larsdatter's cask a long time ago.

I was not surprised to see that she also had come to the same spot. I sat down on a rock next to her, and we sat like that for a long time, without saying a word, until the sun rose and its light spread like a red banner across the fields and trees. The dripping icicles above the spring glowed like the candles in the Røldal church on that St. John's Eve of long ago. A southerly wind whispered in the tree crowns.

"Are you going to stay home this summer, Cleng," she asked at last.

"As soon as the plowing and the sowing are done I'll be going to

Talgje and take charge of the shipyard. You'll recall that's where I worked before the time I was in the English prison ship. And how about you, Sara?"

"I don't know. We have a house outside the town. It's standing empty."

"Nothing would give greater joy to Mother and me than your staying here," I said; "especially now that Kari's leaving."

"But Guri and Talleiv?"

"We'll be glad to have them too. The bins have never been completely empty at Hesthammer. And they won't be empty in the future either, I suppose. But Guri will no doubt be able to get a job on one of the farms; she's soon a grown woman. Isn't she going to study for her confirmation next summer?"

"I overheard the young farmer at Rossadal ask your mother whether she thought Guri would like to work for him," Sara said. She was silent a little while; it seemed to me as she was struggling to hold back her tears. Then she added, "I think it will be best that I also leave here. It so happens that I'm with child."

Tenderly I touched her cheek; it felt like silk to my touch.

"My friends among the Haugeans would never have imagined that Sara Larsdatter would ever get into a situation like this," she said. "In Holy Writ they have read about which kind of women are to be stoned according to the law."

I replied, "In Holy Writ there is also a passage about a woman who was held in low esteem by both the just and the self-righteous. She wept when she faced the Lord Jesus and washed his feet with precious ointments and dried them with her hair."

At this point in our conversation we heard the sound of voices from among the trees. In a little while the pastor and Guri Olsdatter appeared in the open field not far from us. The pastor was feeling very gay; he gesticulated wildly and loudly praised the morning, the sun, and the bird song, and he spoke animatedly about nymphs of the forest, about dryads and untouched and primeval nature. Guri could hardly walk straight and was babbling something. When she stumbled and almost fell to the ground, he steadied her and they walked arm in arm.

"Easy, easy, my little friend," he said, "easy, easy, little friend. True that the wedding at Cana was blessed by our Lord and Master, and personally he saw to it that the good wine was served at the end, when the guests already were quite drunk; but you see, little girl, this, like so many other passages in the Bible, has to be interpreted in the light of its symbolic meaning, and I shall explain this mystery more fully to you when you commence the preparation for your confirmation."

They moved away and disappeared in among the trees, and we could no longer hear their voices.

"It looks as if our minister has had enough," I said.

"And Guri has had *more* than enough," Sara said; her voice shook. "The worst of it is that it was the pastor who kept on filling her glass. That I saw with my own eyes. She ought to be grateful that she's walking in the woods with a decent man; otherwise this night might have proved to be her undoing. She has suddenly grown up this spring."

"Yes, she has," I replied. "We will advise her to accept Daniel Rossadal's offer to have her stay there this summer."

And when I think back on that morning, Anne, I must mention to you a piece of news that reached us the year the Sloopers had arrived here in America: Guri Olsdatter had been expelled from the Society of Friends because of her drinking, and almost a score of years were to pass before she was restored to favor, even though she was the wife of Elias Tastad.

She went to Rossadal right after Whitsuntide, and I sailed about the same time to Talgje, as had been decided, and did not stay in Anne Cathrine's house.

Sara and Talleiv remained at Hesthammer.

Talleiv was a difficult boy, as he had always been. He thought up as many tricks and strange ideas as there are days in a year, and many more were to occur to him before the beginning of summer.

One day, just before St. John's Eve, he and Sara had rowed out on the fjord to fish. They had sailed farther out than usual and had come upon a fishing ground where the line never even reached the bottom before the fish swallowed the hook. Sara had never before heard or seen the like of a catch like this even though she had spent much time in boats since early childhood. She insisted that they continue as long as the fish were biting; but they hadn't taken along anything to eat or drink, and as time passed Talleiv became more and more impatient. He cajoled and he threatened, and he wouldn't listen when Sara tried to talk sense into him. Since there was such a great shortage of grain, she said, one just couldn't refuse when the sea proved to be so generous. The fish continued to bite eagerly; the line had cut and bloodied her hands and fingers; but she took no notice of it.

Then Talleiv removed the bung from the bottom of the boat and tossed it out in the water, and he said to her, "Are we now going to row back?"

The water poured in and she seized the oars. "Put your thumb in the hole," she begged him.

"I can swim a dozen miles if need be," he said. "It doesn't matter to me if the boat goes down. But how about you, now?"

He knew that Sara didn't know how to swim, and he was quite likely going to take advantage of that fact. She started to row as fast as she could until her back ached; she asked him to change with her so that she could sit with her finger in the hole for a while.

"You're rowing well enough; I can't compare with you," he laughed.

The water reached almost as high as the gunwale, and the floor-boards were floating about. The fish that were still alive were swimming around in the boat. Then Talleiv took a piece of cork out of his pocket and plugged the hole. He said, "*Now* I'll change with you if you want to bail."

And while she was bailing for dear life he sat on the thwart, laughing scornfully at her, stroking the oars once in a while.

But Sara was already feeling sick, and she didn't get inside a house in time. When they reached the shore, Talleiv just ran away from her. She crept on all fours into the boathouse, and there she gave birth to a premature baby that showed no sign of life.

It so happened that the pastor's farmhand had been to Kårstø that day, and on his way back he found her lying bleeding on the floor. First he went to fetch help to get her indoors; then he sailed to the parsonage at Skjold where he told the minister about what had happened.

Pastor Swensen Magnus was fully conscious of the fact that he had been installed in his office in order to uphold the true fear of God and the correct moral conduct among the members of his flock, and he sent a message to Sara Larsdatter enjoining her to show up in church during the regular service on the seventh Sunday after Trinity and be called to account for lewd behavior, for the sin of fornication, and additionally for such treatment of her own body that it had resulted in the loss of the life of the unborn child, and, furthermore, to be prepared to state the name of the father so that he too could be called to account and pay the fine of 24 skillings ordained by the church. She herself had to bring with her 12 skillings, since woman, according to the Word of God, was a frail vessel and more susceptible to the raptures of the senses and therefore ought to be shown greater leniency in regard to the fine.

As for myself, I never heard anything about this. Not that anyone had neglected to send me word; Mother had prevailed upon two young fellows to sail from Skjold to Talgje in order to tell me about all this in spite of the fact that it was right in the middle of the haying season and little time could be spared. But just at that time I was in Stavanger to deliver a vessel to Johannes Stene. His name has already been mentioned; later he was to become the main shareholder in the *Restauration*. Johannes had recently moved from Finnøy to Stavanger and had started in business for himself.

When the young fellows didn't find me home, they delivered the message, contained in a letter, to Anne Cathrine. She opened the letter, read it, and burned it.

On the Saturday before the seventh Sunday after Trinity I felt such great alarm and disquiet when I woke up that I couldn't concentrate on any kind of work. Fearful that evil things had happened at home, I made ready and sailed in the evening. Around midnight I was standing in front of closed doors at Hesthammer.

I shouted, but received no reply. I walked around the buildings, into the barn, shouted once again — and then at last I saw Talleiv come crawling out of the hay. He was sullen and cranky, and his bad conscience made him even more taciturn, but I found out that Mother and Sara had rowed to church that very evening.

This was no real cause for alarm, but I hardly took time to bolt down some food before I was back in the boat. The wind had abated; the moon, a white sickle pointing downwards, etched red stripes in the surface of the sea; the water dripping from the oars was red like blood. I had a salty taste in my mouth, and it was as if my life blood flowed out of my hands and down the oars and colored the sea itself. I knew that wherever I would end up in this world, the sorrow I bore because of Sara Larsdatter would transform the heavens above me and the earth under me.

"Could it be that something evil is about to happen?" I thought, and I recalled a Sunday of a summer many years ago when I had rowed this way and had myself been called to account in the church because of Sara.

The moon followed a low arc and set, and the land and the sea looked like cold iron under the stars that brief hour before dawn. The small barley fields on the shore took on a tinge of ripeness even though they were quite green; the summer had been a wet and cold one. The haying had begun; hay bricks were rotting and the racks were leaning over.

When I saw the large number of boats lying in the landings by the church I realized that the turnout was greater than at any confirmation or Christmas morning service. Around the stables horses were tied up, row upon row, and a huge crowd was milling around the church building. I was late; the service had already started. The windows were open, and I could hear the sound of the pastor's voice, but it was not possible to make out the words.

"What's he saying?" I heard someone ask another in the crowd. "Is she saying anything in reply?" "No, she hasn't answered one word the whole time." "Listen, he's raising his voice; he must be angry." "Can anyone wonder at that?" I heard someone else say.

But I didn't intend to wait outside any longer. I pushed forward and wormed my way through the crowd; when someone bawled me out I answered, "Make room, make room! I have an important errand, I'm bringing a message to the pastor!"

Not until I had pushed my way through the church vestibule and into the church proper — the center aisle as well as all the benches were filled to overflowing but there was an open space in the choir — did I catch sight of Sara Larsdatter up front, all alone. The minister was standing directly in front of her; he held an open book in his hand, as if he were conducting an examination.

Following a brief pause he resumed talking: "Thus we do not possess any decisive proof that Sara Larsdatter willfully brought about the conditions that led to the very premature birth of the child," he said and let his glance sweep over the large congregation. "For that reason we shall as far as this point is concerned — inasmuch as we heed the fact that the first and the last Commandment of Christianity is mercy, and also the new and more humane laws of our modern times — waive any charges."

He raised his voice when he continued, "It is a sign of the leniency introduced by the new laws and customs that we today have summoned Sara Larsdatter to appear in this church so that she — in addition to the fine fixed by law at twelve skillings — should be given an opportunity to confess her sin and if at all possible state the name of the one she rightfully thinks should be listed as the male parent of the dead child. Answer, Sara Larsdatter, so that we can remain true to our stated purpose not to let you suffer any injustice!"

Sara opened her mouth as if to say something, but no sound passed her lips. She looked around, obviously frightened and confused.

In the meantime I had pushed my way up the center aisle and was now the third person standing in the choir. In the full view of everyone I took out a purse from my pocket, opened it, got out a silver daler, and placed it on the pages of the open book that the minister was holding, and from the book's pages the coin slid down into his hands.

"A silver daler?" he exclaimed. For a brief second our eyes met, and I could detect a trace of uncertainty in his glance. "You are Cleng Peerson?" he said, making it sound more like a plain statement than a question; "are you the man who made Sara Larsdatter pregnant?"

"No," I replied, "but I would like to pay the fine for the guilty one."

A loud murmur was heard among the large assemblage.

"Once before I stood up here in the choir for the sake of Sara Larsdatter," I said. "Then I was fifteen years old. Today I am thirty. During all these years my heart has been filled with affection for her, but external circumstances have made it so that we could not be joined in marriage."

I had never thought that I could ever speak out loud about these things, but an irresistible force drove me on. First I reminded my listeners about all that had happened, from that evil night in Aron Falkeid's parlor until Sara in late autumn that same year had been liberated from the jail in Stavanger; and I included as much about the journey to Rødal as I thought necessary. I recounted her story up to the time I found her in the houseboat.

I forgot all about the church, the congregation, and the minister; I only saw Sara Larsdatter. At first she stood there looking down at the floor. But when I mentioned my love for her our eyes met, and once again it seemed as if she wanted to say something, but not a word crossed her lips.

Sunlight poured in through the windows, and the rays just then lit up the altar painting with the two Marys: on one side the mother of Christ at the time of the annunciation by the angel Gabriel, and on the other, Mary Magdalen, the sinner, weeping, anointing the feet of the Saviour, and wiping them with her hair.

And I said something like this: "I have not studied to become a minister, and I cannot interpret the words of the Scriptures. But I spent two years preparing for my confirmation and what I was taught in my childhood I have never forgotten. Look at this picture! I do not have in mind to compare Sara Larsdatter with the Mother of Christ, but they have this one thing in common that in order to consummate a task of love and sacrifice it was necessary for them to appear as debased women in the eyes of the self-righteous. Nor is it my intention to compare Sara Larsdatter with Mary Magdalen; still, they do have that one thing in common: that our Lord and Master is aware of their love and honors them above the Pharisees and the learned. Jesus Christ also met another woman who didn't deserve greater respect than that which our pastor and our authorities show Sara Larsdatter. To her He said,

'Neither do I condemn thee; go and sin no more.' And to those who had stones in their hands and were about to kill her he said, 'That one of you who is without sin, let him cast the first stone.' These words shall be heard again here today.''

I gave Sara Larsdatter my hand, and as we walked down the aisle, people drew to the side. Once again I heard the murmur of many voices; a wave of approbation had begun to swell.

We walked hand in hand out through the gate in the churchyard and down toward the shore. Tears were pouring down her cheeks and she smiled at me.

"Are you happy now, Sara?" I asked.

She did not reply.

"Are you happy, Sara?" I asked once more, not because I needed any confirmation but because she had been silent the entire time and I longed to hear her voice.

Then there was a movement of her lips that I recognized, and she put her fingers to her lips. I had seen this once before: in Aron Falkeid's parlor more than fifteen years earlier.

Once again Sara Larsdatter had turned mute. And from that day on she remained silent until the day of her death.

The Nineteenth Tale

Once upon a time I had had the kind of faith that moves mountains. But it was no longer so. When I again traveled to Røldal in the autumn of that same year, I did not harbor any secret hope that it might benefit Sara. I probably didn't even know any reason why I should go on the morning that I woke up with my decision made; it was merely a resolution arrived at between sleep and dreams: "Get up and leave."

The valley of Røldal hibernates during the winter, being surrounded as it is by mountains on all sides. But the people make up for it in the summer, at three big festivals: first at St. John's Eve, with the secret night service for pilgrims; then the fair when people from near and far gather there. This is a celebration of dancing and drinking and long knives, when men do not heed life nor limb and when women are not careful of their virtue.

The last festival is the "pastor's holiday," and that is reckoned to be the valley's most important celebration. I arrived there at that time quite by accident. It is true that I had heard about it before, but I didn't know that it was held at this time of the year.

The "pastor's holiday" has been so named after the service of thanksgiving that is held after the crops have been brought inside and every farmer can look to the future with confidence. Røldal was at that time a church annex under Suldal, where the minister lived; on this occasion he was visiting his congregation in Røldal for the last time before the onset of winter. The snows came early in that district, and the Suldal Lake was covered with ice even before that.

Since way back the "pastor's holiday" was a time of joy; the merry would dance and play, the pious would give thanks to God, and everyone would consume what the earth had produced as well as the bread of life at the church altar.

But I think you will understand, Anne, why this particular "pastor's holiday" turned out to be quite different in many ways, when I tell you what had happened during that summer. And it will at the same time illustrate how a large part of the people of Norway lived during those days of privation before the wars came to an end and our country won its freedom and the Lord once again opened His bountiful hand.

I have told you that winter had returned with all its ferocity around Ascension Day, when we celebrated the wedding at Hesthammer. But in addition, Witsuntide also brought with it snow, and not only in the mountain valleys; even the outermost points toward the ocean were covered with snow. Cows dropped dead in their stalls, and the people chewed on the bark of trees, like rabbits, for the sap was rising and it was sweet.

The weather improved in June; the sky was cleared by the southerly wind, and the sun was shining throughout twenty of the twenty-four hours, for the day is that long even in that part of the country; people are able to lie in bed and read their book of sermons at midnight if they wish. But even before St. John's Eve continuous rains began to drift in from the ocean with the westerly wind, slowly wringing its wet bag empty. The air was frigid, and on the mountain plateaus the snows held their own.

The rain and the moisture caused the grass to grow tremendously both in the outlying fields and the meadows, and this of course was a good thing for the cattle; their grazing reflected both on their condition and yield. But when the rains didn't even let up at the time when haying was to begin, people became worried about what might happen. Still, they got out their scythes, for the grass in the meadows was bent to the ground from the rain and the moisture.

But perhaps the grass had been better if it hadn't been cut; now the haystacks were mouldering and the fields turned yellow, and when the hay finally was brought wet into the barns, it lay there like huge cakes and decayed into a cheese-like mass.

The grain did not fare much better. The straws grew very long but they did not receive any strength from the sun and the wind, and the ears were light and the pith was of poor quality. The farmers along the coast, however, had fairly good crops, but in the valleys no living person could remember that there ever had been a crop failure like this one; still it was said by some that once, very long ago, there had been a harvest that had been worse. At that time people and cows and sheep had been walking side by side and had been gnawing at anything that was growing, and no animal that was dead from accident or disease was thrown away as carrion.

You have seen how a tornado can lay waste both a farm and the entire prairie, Anne, and you have seen how the hail can lash the wheat and how grasshoppers can eat up an entire crop. But in the part of the world where we are now living, the grain fields are almost endless. If great damage is done in one state, it may be that in another there will be a hundred-fold yield. In the country which your parents left it is only the mountain plateaus that are endless, and the arable land is merely like the wrinkles in the face of a giant. That is why man is helpless when powerful forces stir.

On my way to Røldal I took the same route as that followed by Sara Larsdatter and myself once very long ago.

The rain continued to pour down incessantly; the rivers were foaming, brown as well as white, the brooks were all overflowing their banks. But the evening I reached Røldal it cleared up, and the people mustered new courage. If they could now be blessed with a week's sunshine, it would be possible to cut the grain, they said, and if it was still dry when brought into the barn and made to last longer by the addition of the bark of the elm tree, it might still be possible to use it as food for humans.

A mild southerly breeze was blowing throughout the afternoon; toward evening it subsided, and when night fell, there was an icy wind coming from the mountain to the east. Then everyone knew what might be expected, and those who owned the grain fields on the flat land down by the Røldal Lake were in greatest danger, for in the fall the night frost takes its greatest toll in the lowlands.

When it looks as if such things may happen, there has traditionally been only one remedy to fall back on: people cover the fields with smoke. They set about to do just that, and everyone helped the one who needed it most.

It so happened that I was helping a young widow to save her crops. Her husband had been killed in the war against the Swedes; she had been left with two children on a very small farm; it was located on the shore of the lake, facing south, near the spot where Sara and I had been hiding when we put on the kneeboards. Yes, I verily believe that we must have crawled on our knees every inch of the length of that grain-field.

The young widow and I carried juniper branches to each of the four corners of the field — some dry branches, others were green — and we also placed some in the middle of the field; and when the air sharpened at midnight, we lit the dry branches and placed the green ones on top of them, and we ran back and forth with bushes in our hands and swung them over the fires so that the smoke would stay down, close to the field, and cover it with warmth and make the cold less severe. A new moon hovered above the mountain and threw light on the merciful haze that lowered itself over the fires and the crops.

The moon set behind the mountain, it turned darker after midnight; only the stars were flickering, and at dawn the sky looked phosphorous. A white mist was still covering the field, but it was not a mist of mercy; the heads of grain were gleaming with hoarfrost when the sun rose. I picked one up and rubbed it; it was slimy and had no pith.

We had been keeping watch together all night, and the two children also stayed awake; now the sun rose in the heavens, and we were all standing with dead ears of grain in our hands. Who was going to take mercy on them? Unless a miracle occurred, they would not survive the next winter. I opened my food chest, and we divided the meat and the bread. She thanked me and blessed me, but she didn't plead for help nor did I make any promises. I left her and the children and walked over into the woods to the spot where Sara and I had been sitting an entire day and had shared our fish and bread. There I took leave of what had been completely inalienable to me. Then I knew why I had come to the valley.

This happened on a Thursday in the week of the "pastor's holiday." The young people used to come together to dance and make merry on Saturday night, but on this night there were no laughter and singing, nor dance steps to be heard. But some of those who still had liquor in the house drank themselves into a brief forgetfulness.

Sunday morning was clear like a fine day in autumn, purified like a human face that has known trouble and affliction. The hungry as well as those whose hunger had been stilled went to church, and it was completely filled. As I looked at these people, with my glance turning toward the Man of Suffering and Sorrow on the cross, and I knew that all around them and this house of the Lord lay the graves, and surrounding all this were the frozen fields, I thought to myself, "Who shall lead them to freedom? Is there still to be found in this world a place that is flowing with milk and honey?"

Yes, I had to call this to mind, Anne, for on one of the last days of this year of our Lord 1858 I heard that a group of people from Røldal have in mind to pull up stakes and set out across the ocean, partly because of the troubles they have had on account of their faith and partly because of the troubles of this world. That "pastor's holiday" happened almost half a century ago, and I ask myself whether perhaps one or another who at that time was a little boy or girl and sat in the church — perhaps the widow's children — are among those who now in their advanced age are seeking freedom and a better livelihood in the New World? I do know that the following year those two children buried their mother. She was placed in a large mass grave for those who had starved to death; when the warm weather returned and the frost in the ground was gone, each of the dead received his own resting place.

Among the other things I recall from that day were the comforting words spoken by the minister, dealing with the story of Christ who fed five thousand in the desert with bread and fishes, and thereupon he himself made evident to our eyes this miracle of love: while the congregation was listening to the reading from Scripture, the people on the nearest farm were preparing great quantities of food. Without the congregation's knowledge he had brought with him flour and dried reindeer meat, and when the last hymn had been sung and the bells had tolled nine times, the people walked out of the church, and the first thing they saw were the steaming pots and kettles. As the Saviour did in the past, the minister spread out his hands to bless the gift, and meat and porridge were ladled out. The members of the congregation sat down, some on the churchyard stone wall, others on the graves, and they ate and their hunger was stilled.

But because he did not wish that anyone should give him the thanks and praise that were due God alone — even though the pastor's fields too were frozen and there were few hams left in his storehouse — he very quietly stole away, and rode back to his home in Suldal.

But if you ask me, Anne, what happened to the people of the Røldal valley that winter, I can tell you that the old people and the very young ones who just had been weaned, were the first to die; but the toll was also high among the mothers who were still nursing their babies; first their babies were given their milk, then their blood, and it is said that they were finally chewing their nipples. There was also a man who was well versed in Holy Scripture and had read this passage: "Happy is the man who seizes and crushes your babes against the stone wall"; it was told that he acted according to the letter of the law with his own child, and he did believe that he had earned the happiness that the Bible promised, for what he did was done with great love. It was his first and only child, just born into this world; his wife bore it and then expired, and both were placed in the same grave.

But don't let me paint a dark picture only; there are also some brighter moments to be noted: late that winter herds of wild reindeer came down into the valleys from the mountain plateau, and the white grouse cackled in every thicket, and they shot more game than in many a year.

Suldal was worse off, for that valley was further away from the great mountain plateaus, and many an experienced mountaineer didn't have the strength to walk all the way up into the hills to hunt. That conditions could get beyond human endurance I had already learned during the previous autumn when I was on the way home from the "pastor's holiday" in Røldal. Many of the cotters' cabins along the Suldal Lake were empty; some of the people had died; others had gone to valleys were life might be more pleasant or toward the coastal districts, like the group of hungry people we had met at Nedstrand the year before.

Nevertheless, most of the farmers stayed as long as they could. At that time there were more than one hundred cotters' cabins along the shores of Suldal Lake, and for the poor people shortages of food were a well-known phenomenon even during good years, but this winter they had to put up with all the agonies of starvation. God forbid that I shall ever forget the emaciated children sitting on the promontories, as we rowed along the shores of the lake! — children with enlarged heads and a vacant look in their eyes, stretching out their hands to us and begging for food. But we had nothing to give them, and we steered away from shore and rowed in the middle of the lake so that we would be spared listening to their pitiful cries.

For many years they would visit me in my dreams. Their white bones have been resting in the Suldal churchyard a long time. Only a few found their way over here from their bare cliffs and mountains, only a few have plowed the rich earth of America and gained life and strength from it.

I had heard that if one went from Våge down to Hylen — the usual route for the traveler — one could not help stumbling over dead people or be surrounded by those who were still alive; for that reason I chose the road via one end of Suldal Lake over to Sand. The ferryman at Lågen was given the very last salted herring that I had with me.

I have wanted to tell you all this, Anne, about the hardships our people suffered during the last night watch before the hour of freedom struck and a new day dawned in the history of our fatherland.

But in spite of all that I have seen of suffering caused by physical need, I also knew that one can experience an even greater agony: the one that befalls a man when his spirit is forcibly enslaved and his conscience is violated. Even though it is true that most people seem to be satisfied when their food pail is full and their bed is warm, as is the wont of dogs and pigs.

But some people are steadfast, and about those who don't allow themselves to yield and be cowed but endure everything, have faith in everything, and hope for everything, about those my next tale will deal.

The Twentieth Tale

Peace was concluded in 1814, and the men in the British prison ships returned home. The Norwegian prisoners returned to a country that had just recently severed its ties of dependency on Denmark and had gained national independence, even though it had become united with Sweden under a union king. This arrangement has — as you know — lasted without change for almost half a century.

Among the first to return to Stavanger were Elias Tastad, Ole Franck, and Even Samuelsen; they were among those who were later to establish a Society of Friends in that city. The last-mentioned does not figure in our story, but his name should be mentioned here in the same way that the Apostles Peter, James, and John are always mentioned together, even though James occupies a very modest position in the Gospels.

Lars Larsen of Jeilane had, as mentioned before, served in the household of Lady Margaret Allen and had been with her son Sir William and had seen with his own eyes the acts of mercy that he had performed in the slums and prisons of London. On every Sabbath and also at other times of the week Lars would take part in the silent meetings of the Friends; he got to know their customs and their religious views and was strengthened in his faith in God's Word, as expounded in the Quaker teachings.

For you to understand what I am going to tell, I will have to give you here a brief introduction to the history of the Friends and their doctrines.

The founder of the movement, George Fox, believed that God primarily reveals His will in the human soul, and he preached a religion in which experience meant more than dogma. When he was active, about the middle of the seventeenth century, there was, if possible, even less religious toleration in England than in our own country, and, by the next generation, 20,000 of a total of 100,000 Quakers had been imprisoned and about five hundred had succumbed in jail. Many of them left their country and went to America. They bought large tracts in New Jersey, and there they intended to build the City of God on this earth. You know that the founder of the state of Pennsylvania was the Quaker William Penn.

Around the turn of the last century the Quakers were a small and timid society; they isolated themselves from the world and looked upon themselves as a chosen Zion, destined to suffer and be outcasts.

But when despondency was about to completely paralyze their will and joy in life, a few of them mustered up courage, and through their prayers and persevering struggles a new flame was lit among them, and this revival also ignited the men on board the prison ships.

Here are some of their principles, so that you will be familiar with their convictions and know how they endured until many of them saw no other way out than to leave their home and country — this was not in order to be spared from carrying their cross, but to plant their cross of worship in a new earth, even though only a few among them were fearless, and fewer still possessed a great measure of courage and confidence.

The walls in their houses of worship were to be without pictures or any kind of decoration; because God is an invisible spirit He is to be worshiped without the intermediary of visible things. Neither did they have an altar with candelabras and candles, and no carved altar-piece, for Christ had given them His light in their souls and carved His picture in their hearts.

They didn't use an organ, nor church bells, and no singing; in their view, all this hid rather than revealed the countenance of the Lord; but He was clearly visible to their spirit. And the new kind of hymn, which is called the hymn of God and the Lamb, can only be sung by a heart that has been born again.

None of the Friends were to act as pastor, to be raised above anyone else and wear clothes that set him apart; for every child of the faith is a member of the sacred clergy and belongs to a chosen people, clothed in the attire of Christian justice.

They acknowledge Him as their Master in all things; for that reason they did not bend knee to any lord on this earth, be it bishop or king, and neither did they take their hats off when they greeted someone. "Not even our mothers do we greet any other way," they would say.

But in spite of all this they were subservient to both the secular and spiritual authorities as long as their own conscience was not infringed on.

They gathered together at silent meetings, as I have already told you, two or three times a week, sitting down and waiting for the Spirit to come to them. When it came, they lifted their voices invoking or praising the name of God, giving testimony or admonishing one another. At times the coming of the Spirit would be like a forceful wave of energy passing through the body and the spirit, at which time they began to shake and tremble.

Just as they had no visible altar, there was no chalice or wafers for communion, nor any baptismal font; for they looked upon bread and wine, like baptism in water, as being merely preparatory symbols, useful only until the congregation of the Lord would comprehend the world of the Spirit which so clearly lay behind the symbols.

They furthermore taught that no true Christian must ever go to war, for Jesus Himself has said that he who takes the sword shall perish by the sword. The Friends should also abstain from making use of oaths, for Christ in the Sermon on the Mount has very clearly revealed the will of God in this matter. Before a judge they were to say: yes, yes, or no, no.

With great zeal they wanted to work for the kingdom of God and carry the Gospel with them wherever they went, no less in deed than in word.

Like our Lord Jesus Christ, the Friends were also to perform good deeds, rejoice with the joyful and weep with those who were sorrowful, always feeling assured that not even a cup of cold water given in the name of Jesus would go unrewarded on the day that the Lord will judge everyone according to his deeds.

Such were their teachings, Anne, and such are their doctrines and their life even today. Feeling both remorse and hope, I myself felt attracted to them, but like Peter, when he at a distance followed his Lord from Gethsemane and denied him outside the palace of the high priest, thus I too have denied their faith, attempting to get out of it by using excuses such as this: "You are at heart different from these pious people; for that reason you cannot follow them; you must set your own course."

Much more could be said about this, but let it pass. I would rather tell you about Elias Tastad's homecoming, as he has told it to me himself. His mother received him with embraces and tears of joy, and because she herself was a pious woman and soon understood from him that he was in accord with her in this matter, she begged him to go to communion with her. But when Elias told her that he did not at all accept the bread and the wine as the flesh and blood of Our Lord, she became afraid that he must have become involved in some kind of English heresy.

She had already announced that both she and her son would come to confession, and when she showed up all by herself, the dean of the congregation — his name was Støren — asked her searching questions about her son. She answered him by repeating what Elias had said. Then Dean Støren's countenance became impassive and forbidding, and he said, "What kind of ungodly teachings might it be that have darkened his soul?"

The very next day Dean Støren paid a visit to their home. Elias was not in, and the dean asked his mother whether Elias perhaps had brought back with him various kinds of books. She then showed the clergyman an English Bible which he thumbed through rapidly; then he inquired once more, "Doesn't he have any other books?" She answered, "That he does, but they have been borrowed by others."

"So soon?" the dean asked, raising his eyebrows. And in very severe terms he gave instructions to the effect that Elias had to come to his office on a certain day at a certain hour and bring with him all the printed material that he possessed.

When Elias came ashore — he had been out on the fjord putting out his nets — his mother repeated to him what Dean Støren had said. Elias immediately went to fetch the books that he had lent out, and he showed up at the dean's at the appointed time. The books were Barclay's *Apology*, William Penn's *Key*, and a book about baptism which I haven't read, but which I often saw in the homes of the Friends.

Elias placed the books on the table in front of the dean. Pastor Heyland, the coadjutor of the town, had also shown up. The coadjutor asked him whether he knew the Bible and more especially the New Testament. "Yes," Elias answered, "but I hope in future to gain greater insight and understanding of Holy Writ than I have attained up to now."

Then Heyland said suddenly, "Why don't you take your hat off? Don't you know that one has to show respect for the clergy?" When

Elias told them the reason why he kept his hat on, both pastors began to reproach him for many things. Aghast at their severe words, Elias nevertheless mustered up courage and referred to Christ's Sermon on the Mount, but Dean Støren objected that he had misunderstood its contents and added that no one who didn't know Greek would ever be capable of understanding the true spirit of the Sermon on the Mount.

About Barclay's *Apology* the dean said, "This book contains many errors."

But Elias answered, "It was written by a man who lived in full understanding of truth, and it has been translated into Danish by a minister who was converted and embraced the living faith."

"Do you mean to say that our dean and myself are not of the living faith?" asked Heyland.

"It is not up to me to judge *you* or answer for you any more than *you* can assume the same kind of authority on behalf of *my* conscience," Elias replied.

Following a thorough interrogation, during which Elias never was at a loss for an answer, the dean said, "Elias Tastad, I must advise you to leave Norway and go back to England. Here you will find no sympathy for your views, which do partly agree with the Word of God, even though the delusion is more evident. But you will undergo much suffering. However, England is already full of sects, and there you will no doubt be able to live in peace."

Elias replied, "I don't seek peace, but truth."

Thereupon they continued to interrogate him in regard to the Scriptures and found that they could stump him on a number of questions. Pastor Heyland especially spoke to him angrily and with great fervor and said that Satan himself had taken up abode both in *his* heart and in each and every one who adhered to the teachings of the Quakers.

Dean Støren was more moderate in his judgment, and in order to show his friendly disposition he asked Elias to go on an errand for him and deliver a letter to Bailiff Løwold. Elias was very happy to do this, but when he came into the anteroom of the bailiff's office, he came upon a lieutenant, who served as the bailiff's secretary.

When Elias spoke to him without doffing his hat, the lieutenant rose and hit him with the back of his hand so that his hat flew off his head and knocked down a marble statuette next to the wall; it fell to the floor and was smashed to pieces.

The lieutenant immediately demanded that Elias should pay compensation for the damage done, but Elias refused to do so. Then the lieutenant threatened to report him to the bailiff, but nothing came of that. Elias delivered the letter, picked his hat off the floor, put it on, and left the room.

Somewhat later it happened that Elias was at Reveim at Madla, right outside the town, in the house of a man by the name of Iver Halvorsen. Iver was the brother of Knud Halvorsen and worked a farm at Reveim. Elias had looked him up earlier and brought greetings from Knud. He spoke at the same time to Iver about the new faith, and Iver had been greatly stirred and was convinced of its truth. He was the first one to be converted by the returning Quakers.

While Elias visited Iver this second time, Pastor Heyland arrived and spoke to both of them with great wrath and told Elias that if he didn't leave the kingdom of Norway within twenty-four hours, he would find himself in great trouble, for no teachings but those of Luther were to be tolerated. Then Elias entered into a discussion with him, and he tried to prove that the Friends in many ways were closer to Luther than was the established church. Feeling indignant at such audacity, the minister rose to his feet and slapped Elias's cheek, but when Elias turned the other cheek, in accord with the Sermon on the Mount, the minister stayed his hand, since he too recalled the words of the Bible. But he told Elias that if he wanted to adhere to his faith he should go to England, for there were no Quakers in Norway.

"There are some, and there are going to be more," Elias replied.

Then the minister was seized with an attack, for his heart was not very strong, and Elias and Iver carried him into the adjoining room and placed him on the bed. They put moist pieces of cloth on his forehead and they loosened his waistband so that his stomach assumed its natural dimensions. Then he rapidly regained consciousness and declared that he respected Elias for the firmness of his convictions.

"But," he added, "if you stay in this country you will be the cause of a bigger clash than that caused by Hans Hauge, and he has so far been an inmate in eleven prisons. But you are a young man and you should not face such a bitter fate."

But Elias answered, "I have spent six years in an English prison ship."

Heyland voiced great pity and compassion for what he had suffered, but Elias answered, "I thank the Lord for letting it happen that I was made a prisoner, for through my imprisonment I was led to freedom. And I'm not going to England or any other country; here where I was born I'm going to stay, even though it means jail or death."

To that the minister said nothing, whereupon Elias returned to town. He and a few others came together for silent meetings after the fashion of the Quakers; however, this did not become generally known and was therefore not contrary to the law. The old ordinance governing religious assembly in Norway was still in force and was to remain so for many years.

Elias wrote several letters to Lars Larsen during the year the latter stayed on in England. He told him about the opposition he met with and about the struggles that they must be prepared for when the time came for them to resign from the Lutheran Church and establish their own church organization. For this had not yet been done.

The first real Quaker meeting was held in Lars Larsen's house some time after he had returned to Norway, during the winter of 1816. But before I write about this and the new state of affairs brought about by these developments, you must hear more about what happened to Sara Larsdatter and about several others.

While I was living in the city part of the time, and partly at Talgje, Sara Larsdatter stayed with my mother. Talleiv was the only man at Hesthammer, and in spite of many strange notions and tricks he gradually began to conduct himself better, so that he was of greater use and became less troublesome. Even his looks improved a whole lot when the scabs on his head disappeared, but the scabs on his soul never quite left him. People still remember him, I'm sure, because of all his curious notions and also because he became a skillful auk hunter, but this doesn't belong in our story. Here we take leave of Talleiv; he lived in a cabin by the shore, remained unmarried, and died before he had turned forty.

I have already told about his sister Guri that she was hired by Daniel Rossadal and worked on his farm. She stayed there several years. She grew ever more beautiful and had a friendly although slightly fickle disposition, and ever since early youth she harbored a weakness for strong liquor. She was able to keep her urge under control for long periods of time, but again and again it happened that it overpowered her even though she prayed to God to give her strength.

Elias Tastad fell deeply in love with her in spite of this, and she became his wife. Many trials and tribulations befell them in their marriage; about this I shall tell you more later.

I was at Talgje when I first was told about Lars Larsen's having returned home — we had just laid down the keel for a new vessel — but I immediately sailed in to town to bid him welcome. And then I traveled to Tysvær to tell Sara that he had come home. From her expression it was hard to tell how she felt about it. At that time she had been mute for about four years, and it was just as if the muteness not only had silenced her tongue but also had little by little exerted an influence on her body and soul. As I remember her from that time on, she seemed to be dreaming, as if she was resting in a gentle half sleep where no feelings — be they pain or joy — affected her as deeply as before.

Mother would miss her, that I knew; but I would just the same state my errand: would she be willing to come back to Stavanger and run the house for her brother?

She nodded her assent, and made us understand that in such a case it would be necessary for Guri to take her place at Hesthammer. And so things were arranged.

Since the time Sara had left the house at Jeilane in the winter of 1812, it had been standing empty for almost a year. Then vagrants and tramps began to find shelter there; they caused damage to the house and it fell into decay. Elias Tastad and I walked out to the house one day; the door was shut and the windows were boarded up, and when the door at last was opened we could see for ourselves that the place was worse than a pigsty. The occupants were still lying in bed even though it was past noon; it was their wont to sleep during the day and carry on their work at night. They all refused to leave the house, and we got nowhere with them until the authorities evicted them and the police chased them out of town. When they left the house at Jeilane — this was about a week later — they cursed the city of Stavanger with all its people and all its regulations, and they loudly blamed themselves for not having burned down the house while there was still time.

Our first impression was that there wouldn't have been much damage if they had done so. But after we had inspected the house from cellar to attic we realized that it would still be worth the trouble to fix it up; the timbers were in splendid condition, yellow as honey, and without worms. Elias's mother washed down all the ceilings and walls with lye, hot water, and soap until every knot and every nail were gleaming. Being expert carpenters, Elias and I started on the repairs. We made a new roof, and the outside walls were freshly tarred; and, without asking, I took all that I thought Sara and Lars would need of kitchen utensils from that which had been put away since Anne Cathrine had shut down her business in the Admiral Cruys Bodega. Sara was to have a kitchen that even the finest ladies in town might envy.

Lars came along to Tysvær when we sailed to fetch Sara. Guri Olsdatter was already there to take her place on Mother's farm. On the return trip we had a fair wind and reached Stavanger in a few hours.

Lars had to make some purchases in town, and Sara and I walked ahead to light the fire and cook a meal.

It was winter, but the sky was cloudless and the air was mild. When we had gotten as far as the big oak tree not far from her house, I took her in my arms and stopped short. Perhaps she remembered that we had been standing here before; I, to be sure, remembered it only too well.

I gently stroked her cheek, and when she didn't seem to mind, I asked her whether she was still fond of me. She nodded.

"If Anne Cathrine dies soon, do you want to marry me, Sara?" I asked her.

She shook her head. "Why not?" I asked.

At that very moment the air reverberated with a song that I knew well; it was the shrieks of the singing swan. I looked up and saw the big white bird in flight against a red sky, and when I pointed to it and Sara too saw it, she made a motion with her hands that I shall never forget. First, each of her hands seized the wrist of the opposite arm and held them as in a vise. Then she once again pointed at the swan, which was flying in a westward direction and was about to be hidden behind the foliage of the oak tree — the rays of the evening sun were reflected in its feathers.

I knew what she meant. And when I took both her hands in mine, she blushed and let me hold her in a tight embrace.

After that moment we never again felt so close to each other.

A short time after he had moved into the house at Jeilane, Lars called the first meeting of the Friends. I myself attended that first time and also later on, but I never asked to become a member of their society; neither did any of them utter a wish that I do so; but both Elias and Lars often spoke to me about the way of truth and the inner light of the soul.

The congregation in Stavanger was to remain a small flock for a long time. It is only during the last several years that large numbers have joined, after the laws of Norway regarding separatist sects and dissenters had become more lenient and the ordinance governing religious assembly was rescinded. At that time neither the men of the State Church nor the Friends themselves made it easy for others to become a Quaker. When someone requested that he become a member, he had to undergo a test and an examination, and in addition, he had to have letters of recommendation from trustworthy people regarding his Christian way of life.

Moreover, when new members called on the pastor to offer their resignation from the State Church they would have to be prepared for a severe reprimand. The pastor would also ask them whether they didn't know that they were committing an illegal act and were in fact rebels against the state and its legal system.

But during the early days nothing worse happened to them than threats and they were frightened, but none of them were fined or put in jail. The secular authorities seemed indeed to hardly notice them.

But they did so in earnest when Knud Halvorsen got married according to the Quakers' ritual; that happened in Christiania late in the year 1816. The woman whom he had fallen in love with was called Anne Olsdatter, the same as you, and when their friends had gathered at the appointed time and place, the wedding ceremony transpired in such a way that the two engaged people took each other by the hand, and following a ritual which included the reading of the Bible, prayers and promises which had been accepted and approved by the Friends in England, they pledged each other fidelity until the end of their lives. Then a marriage contract was drawn up, signed first by the bride and the bridegroom and then by all the guests, one after the other.

Five days later Knud handed the contract to the magistrate's office and asked for an endorsement. He was told that this could not be done since it was contrary to the laws of the realm. The magistrate, moreover, let it be known that he had found it proper to report the situation to the ecclesiastical authorities.

Thus the Friends were exposed to the scrutiny of the authorities, and their time of troubles began. I shall be brief when I tell you about them, but you should know something of all this.

Many wise men put their heads together. There was no doubt in their minds that it was a scandalous and offensive thing for Knud Halvorsen and Anne Olsdatter to live together after having been wed according to such a ritual. But that was not all: the very presence of these two people represented a danger to the morals of the nation. Thus, the decision was made to the effect that both ought to be driven from the country for the same reason that in the old days ladies of easy virtue were shipped from the coastal towns of Norway to the West Indies.

Others were more sober-minded, and they maintained that the newly won national independence ought to have as one of its consequences greater freedom for the individual also. They stressed the fact that this was not a matter of anyone desiring to lead an ungodly life, one that might give offense; the question, its very essence, was whether religious freedom too is a basic human right.

A royal commission was appointed; it was charged with investigating, with the aid of the clergy, where in Norway any Quakers might be living and in what number. The total they arrived at was very small, and it seemed as if the Society of Friends in Christiania was about to be dissolved.

As soon as Knud Halvorsen read in the paper about the setting up of the royal commission, he wrote a letter to its members and said that as long as the Quakers could not count on toleration on the part of the authorities, they would have to consider leaving for a country in which religious freedom existed.

True, he didn't have America in mind then, but England. As a matter of fact, his wife and many other Friends had already gone there, and now he left for England himself; this was in the spring of 1817. But it was not their intention to leave Norway forever. Knud Halvorsen hoped that the religious laws would soon be changed; then he would return home with his wife and his fellow believers.

In England he was in close touch with the original Society of Friends and gave its members insight into conditions in Norway; already that summer an appeal was sent by leading English Quakers to the royal commission, asking for freedom of conscience for the Friends in Norway.

The commission, however, reached the decision that Quakers, in principle, were not to enjoy any kind of civil rights. But since the king had charged it with the formulation of a proposal for a final arrangement, this was done. The Quakers were to be allowed to live in only some of the cities of Norway, ten in number, so that they could be under constant surveillance. As long as they stayed in one of the prescribed towns they were to be exempted from taking oaths and from military service, direct taxes to the clergy, the Church, and the military establishment; in the same manner, they were not to be bound by church regulations regarding communion, baptism, funerals, and weddings. But no one could be accepted as a Quaker until his twenty-fifth birthday; thus the exemption from military service would not be an attraction for anyone to join them. The agreement also strictly prohibited attempts to convert anyone to the Quaker faith through worldly promises, threats, ridicule, or underhanded means. If such things happened, they would lead to banishment from the country and no appeal would be allowed.

The commission had completed its work before the end of the year 1817, but in the process of arriving at a final legal formulation and sanction, the number of cities which were to be the places of refuge for the Quakers, was reduced in number; thus, Stavanger was taken off the list. Perhaps this was a result of ignorance about real conditions; but, in any case, the County of Stavanger proved to be the only place in the country in which the movement grew, as it has continued to do up to our own day. According to the last letter I received from Elias Tastad — who is still living, even though old and feeble, just like me — today they number about a hundred and fifty. There might have been more, but he himself has seen to it that the gate was made narrow; his wife, though, has been restored to favor since she — as he says — through the merciful help of the Lord seems to have conquered all desire for strong drink.

I shall soon tell you why for a time she was so steeped in this kind of wretchedness. She was seeking relief and trying to erase a great sorrow from her mind.

The Twenty-first Tale

In the month of March, 1818, we had completed work on a vessel in the shipyard at Talgje; it had been contracted for by a man in Egersund, and with the buyer himself on board I myself skippered it on the delivery voyage.

At that time the city of Stavanger awaited a new pastor, and he had arrived at Egersund on his journey west. Besides his charming wife Christine he had along a skinny, long-legged sister whose name I have forgotten. The minister's name was Alexander Lunge; he was a distinguished-looking gentleman, and I soon found out that the young couple were extremely fond of each other, at least as far as tender caresses are a sign of love.

Pastor Alexander bore the stamp of his office and his station in life wherever he went; he had a dignified appearance and was at the same time condescending in a friendly manner; his personality was such that while he always elicited one's sympathy, one nevertheless found it difficult not to be irritated by him. I myself didn't feel any greater urge to keep silent in his company than in that of others, and we had many lively discussions on the way to Stavanger, mostly of the good-natured kind, but some also had a sting to them. For it fell to my lot to escort the pastor and his wife from one city to the other.

In Egersund I took lodgings in Madame Nissen's hospice; Pastor Lunge and the two ladies also put up there. They had sailed with a fair wind and calm weather from the eastern part of the country; but now the weather suddenly changed to a strong wind from the north with snow squalls, and this kept up day after day.

We therefore had to settle down and wait for the wind to abate.

The first evening we spent under Madame Nissen's roof, we sat in her cozy parlor playing whist. Lunge had his sister as his partner, and I had Christine. A steaming punch bowl had been brought in, and the hot drink made us all feel cheerful.

Pastor Lunge asked me about the part of the coast along which we were to travel, and I told him that it was among the worst in the land. When he inquired whether I would consider sailing along the coast of Jæren in the kind of weather that we were having, and in that case take them along, I answered that I would leave as long as I thought it justifiable, but in this storm with snow and poor visibility I would think twice. He had probably heard that I was not unskilled when it came to ships and sailing, for he said that he would not hesitate to entrust himself and his dear ones to a boat skippered by me.

I thanked him for his confidence in me and said that I felt I was fairly good at handling a boat. "Then the question is whether the pastor can hold the ship of the church on an equally steady course for heaven when *he* will serve his new congregation," I said. Lunge comprehended the serious rather than the humorous side of what I said; he wrinkled his brow and asked whether I perhaps was one of those who displayed exaggerated piety. "Hardly," I answered; "otherwise I wouldn't be sitting at the card table tonight, and least of all with a minister. But still it is very possible that I may be the cause of your Reverence's hair turning a bit gray." He responded with an uncertain smile but was immediately placated when Christine stroked his shock of hair and said, "You've already got the first ones, Alexander."

She and I won one round after the other. Lunge played an exceedingly poor game. He excused himself that his mind was on his inaugural sermon which had been scheduled for Palm Sunday and confided to us that he had been meditating over the text during the weeks they had been under way and thought he might embellish it with impressions and examples from his own entry into the city of Stavanger as well as from the journey. But the way things looked now he wouldn't get there in time, "and thus I can't make use of a significant oratorical point," he said, but the very next moment he consoled himself with the thought that these illustrations would hopefully not be too old to use the following Easter.

"Most certainly not, your Reverence," I replied, and reminded him that the account of Jesus' entry into Jerusalem had not faded after almost eighteen hundred years. Then the minister threw the ace of hearts on the table and for once won a trick, while he at the same time turned toward me and said modestly, "But there is a difference."

It was four days before the storm subsided a bit. No sailing vessels were available, but we hired a large rowboat with crew, our intention being to get to Sirevåg or Ogna. From there on the terrain is not so rough, and we hoped to be able to continue the journey overland.

The sea was calm as long as we had the island of Eigerøy to port, for the sound that separates it from the mainland is very narrow. Lunge, who thought that we would continue to sail through placid sounds like that, began to grumble at the fact that we had not set out earlier. But when we got further out, when the waves of the open ocean came straight at us and the boat shipped a lot of water, with the breakers thundering against a bare and ragged coastline, he immediately changed his tone. At the very same time a snowstorm swept its white brush across the white crests of the waves, and the sound of the booming breakers ahead drowned out the roar of the storm. The two women began to cry, while Lunge upbraided me for not having prepared them for this.

"This is just what I warned you against," I answered.

Then, very meekly, Lunge said that if I considered it to be hazardous to forge ahead, he would be of a mind to turn back for the sake of the women, but I asked him whether he knew the hymn "I Walk in Peril Wherever I Go."

"Yes, I do," he replied; "but I also know that passage in the Bible which says, 'Thou shalt not tempt thy Lord, thy God.' Please ask the rowers to turn back."

"That you have to do yourself," I said. He so did, but they pretended that they didn't understand him.

Then he shouted with great force, "I command you!" But I said, "The boys have difficulty in understanding the speech of the educated classes." One of them, however, uttered something like, "We give the commands here," and gripping harder he spat into the air; the spittle stuck in the minister's sideburns, looking like fine down.

The men rowed for quite some time before they made a sharp turn around a promontory and entered a narrow inlet, and all at once the waves were gone, as if cut off with a knife. Then one of the rowers said, "That was a narrow escape, God help us." He probably said it to frighten the minister, although the trip had not been without its dangers.

Pastor Lunge opened a small chest and got out a bottle of brandy. First he treated the rowers and me to a drink, and then he and the two ladies had a nip.

The place where we had sought shelter was called Sirevåg; a solitary cabin was standing on the shore. The cabin was locked, and no one could have been living there. But a boy came walking down the rocky slope toward us; he must have seen the boat and been curious about it. We asked him whether he could provide us with horses, and he replied that that he could. He left again, and for about two hours we just stood there under the lee of the cabin wall. It was bitterly cold; the wind howled and the snow kept on falling.

At last the boy returned leading three lean horses with plain wooden saddles. The boy went ahead on the narrow path, and we set off on horseback through a wild and rough terrain. The minister rode with the dignity that befitted a government official, and his young wife rode very gracefully, for she had a soft and supple body. But when Alexander Lunge got a good look at his skinny and long-legged sister astride her horse, he began to roar with laughter and shouted, "Dear sister, your face looks as if you hoped for a literal fulfillment of the passage in Holy Scripture about the bruised reed that shall not break!" As for me, I set out on foot and walked until we reached a place that is called Ogna. We spent the night there and also the following day while some of the local people went back to Sirevåg to fetch the chests and trunks belonging to the minister.

In the meantime we arranged with the owner of the farm that he would provide us with a horse and wagon, for from that point on the terrain is much more level. He finally showed us something that resembled a two-wheeled cart. The axles were made of wood, and Lunge made the remark that the wheels seemed to be octagonal. "Square," I said. The seats were merely two planks nailed to the sides of the cart.

When we had driven almost a quarter of a Norwegian mile, the pastor's sister had to get out and vomit; the cart was pitching worse than a ship in a heavy sea. She was green as cheese, and she said that she preferred to go by horseback. She sat astride the horse; it had no saddle at all. But just because the horse had short legs and she was long-legged, the tips of her boots just about cleared the tufts of the heather.

At long last we reached Nærbø, where travelers usually change horses. We hired new horses with more suitable saddles and began a more pleasant stage of our journey. The weather, too, improved; the rain let up, the wind had changed, and the clouds were drifting in from the south; and now and then a glimmer of sunlight lit up the brown and desolate landscape. To the minister and his ladies it seemed drab and dreary.

As we were approaching Sandnes, Pastor Lunge, riding ahead, saw a few houses and a glimpse of the sea and shouted gleefully, "We've reached our goal!" But I had to disappoint him, for if Stavanger doesn't have much to boast about, there is no doubt that Sandnes has less.

Nevertheless, the minister felt more elated from that time on, and he made joking remarks about our being just like the children of Israel wandering through the desert — he pointed at the jagged mountains on the other side of the fjord and at the moors to the left where here and there a wind-blown tree reached its bare branches toward the sky. An acrid smell of burned turf filled the air.

When we at last had got as far as a place known as Støttebakken, the town of Stavanger loomed before us. We could see the city's splendid cathedral with its twin towers sharply silhouetted against the bright evening sky. In front of it we could see the little lake surrounded by lindens, and behind the Kongsgård Inn rose a forest of masts; a great number of ships were lying in the harbor. This was just the time that the ships were returning home from the voyages made in winter.

The horizon was ringed in by blue and distant mountains, and the minister shouted joyfully about everything he saw.

The Reverend Alexander Lunge and his family slept in Dean Støren's house the first night he spent in the city of Stavanger. I myself put up at Mrs. Faust's inn, and across her groaning table I told her about the trip from Egersund, more or less following the account I have just given you, Anne.

I took it easy at the inn for a few days. There was a somber mood to be detected throughout the city, for Agent Kielland's second wife had just died, and no one deemed it proper to approach him on any practical matter until she had been buried. It was generally understood that the agent would find the Lunge family a place to live.

It was during the funeral that Pastor Lunge appeared in his cassock for the first time in the city of Stavanger, and on that occasion the agent gave him an honorarium of twenty dalers. The two men greeted each other by the open grave.

Later Mrs. Faust told me what had happened when Dean Støren had accompanied Lunge to see Kielland about a house for the new pastor and his family. When they arrived, the agent had put on his uniform, even though he was looking into the running of his general store (not exactly important official business), where all kinds of products were sold, from sugar and rum to tar and salted herring.

When they had been introduced and the agent had taken off his spectacles and wiped them and put them back on again, he stared hard at Pastor Lunge and especially at his wife, whom he asserted he had not noticed during the funeral, a matter which he personally deplored very much.

When Dean Støren had told him why they had come, the agent stood up straight in his tight trousers; then he lit his long meerschaum pipe, let his glance rest on the young couple, and said condescendingly and with great dignity, "When a government official comes to Stavanger, he will not lack for a place to live." Then he offered the minister's wife his arm and led the way up to the second floor — for Kielland was staying during the week in the same building he had his store — and over to one of the windows. He pointed at a two-story house right across the street and said, "That house is at your disposal. If you wish, you may move in immediately."

Agent Kielland owned both that particular house and several others; he reigned just like a king in the town.

The pastor and his family moved in the following week, and Lunge gave his inaugural sermon the first Sunday after Easter. The old cathedral was completely filled; the entire congregation with the district governor and Agent Kielland in the lead walked around the altar and placed their offering on it. It consisted of paper money in small denominations; the bills made large heaps, but at the welcoming party which Agent Kielland gave some time later for Pastor and Mrs. Lunge — and at which this was mentioned — the minister made a charitable remark to the effect that if the quality of the money was not very great the offering had made up for it in quantity.

The Haugeans had much the same thing to say about Alexander Lunge's inaugural sermon. They had all attended the service together with all the other members of the congregation. The Quakers, however, had then, as always, attended their own meeting in the house of Lars Larsen of Jeilane.

The Twenty-second Tale

It was the privilege of Cleng Peerson too to be a guest of Agent Kielland at his manor, called Ledaal, at the welcoming party for Pastor Alexander Lunge and his wife Christine. And because I wish not merely to give you an insight into the living conditions of the plain and poor people in our old country, Anne, I therefore ask you to come along with me.

When Kielland invited me, it happened in this way. We met somewhere in the city; he was coming from one of the streets near the harbor on his daily morning walk, while I was coming from Skagen and was on my way to visit my old friend, the blacksmith Thomas Madland. It was a day in June, a fairly warm day with an easterly wind and sunshine. Kielland threw out his hands, praised the weather, and claimed that even down there he could smell the aroma of the chestnut trees up by the Kongsgård Inn. Actually, the chestnut flowers had withered a long time ago, but Agent Kielland was a bit nearsighted and wore gold-rimmed glasses even on weekdays. In addition, he liked to down a glass of gin or two in the morning. That made him feel elated; he was usually inclined to feel very melancholy, a fact that was known only to his immediate family.

The first time I had the honor of meeting Agent Kielland was immediately after my return from the English prison ship. It happened one day while I was walking down the street. My mind was filled with thoughts of many kinds, and for that reason I noticed little or nothing of what was going on around me, when I was suddenly brought back to reality by a stranger who stuck his silver-mounted walking stick right in my stomach. Even though I had never seen the gentleman before, I realized immediately that it must be Gabriel Schanche Kielland, royal agent, merchant, and knight of the Order of Dannebrog.

To my great consternation, he also knew who I was. What I had just been pondering was whether I ought to report to the magistrate's office in connection with my having knifed Enoch Jacobsen prior to our enlisting on the privateer and landing in an English prison. It therefore seemed doubly alarming to be accosted right in the middle of the street; I felt as if I were an unmasked criminal, even though he addressed me in a very friendly manner:

"You've just returned from England, Mr. Peerson?" Agent Kielland said. He proved to be exceedingly interested in hearing about conditions on the opposite shores of the North Sea and asked me to come with him to his office, which was not far away. He poured some Madeira wine, and we discussed a number of things. On that occasion he also mentioned that it would please him very much if I would pay a visit to his home, for which I thanked him. But because of matters that you will soon hear more about, Anne, the visit never came about, and our paths were not to cross for some years after that.

Now, at last, we were again standing face to face in the middle of the street.

"You owe me a response to the invitation you received six years ago, Mr. Peerson," he said.

"Perhaps you should renew the invitation," I answered.

"That's done herewith," he said. "Tonight I'm giving a party for the town's new minister and his charming wife — and for you, Mr. Peerson! The clergyman and his family, I understand, had the pleasure of having you as their escort from Egersund. That alone should be good reason why we can look forward to having you also in our midst tonight."

I thanked him but told him truthfully that I didn't own a presentable suit.

"Mrs. Faust will take care of that for you," he said. "Come along, we'll go to her inn right away."

Mrs. Faust served as the city's midwife, but her main business was running a large and well-reputed inn.

The lady received us in a friendly manner, and Agent Kielland informed her about the evening's social affair and suggested that I obtain suitable attire.

Mrs. Faust might be around fifty. She was taller than most men; she held herself erect and was a bit plump but was unostentatious in manner and at the same time very dignified. There were a number of things that she was criticized for; people whispered that she would needlessly make use of tongs, and also that she would often send a less capable substitute to poor people but wanted to be in charge herself in the homes of the affluent.

But even if there were any basis for such accusations, her good points outnumbered the weak ones. She would easily win people's trust. High and low would confide in her, but she would always keep the information to herself. In that way she became privy to everything that happened; she was the town's confessional.

At Agent Kielland's request, Mrs. Faust got out from a chest in the attic a suit of clothing that was indeed fit for a man of high birth: short, yellow trousers with white stockings and low, black shoes; a green coat with a high collar and coattails that reached below the knees; a dark purple velvet vest and a snow-white silk cravat, and in addition a top hat. When I had put the clothes on and again stood before her, she said, "Shame on anyone who will not call Cleng Peerson a gentleman! He deserves indeed another lady by his side than Anne Cathrine!"

Then she combed my hair and shaped it with the aid of ointments, oils, and powder. Believe me, Anne, neither before nor since have I worn such a splendid outfit. You only know the Cleng who has been wandering across the prairie and in the big forests; but you should have seen him then! Well, I was in my prime, then, about thirty years old.

"Tonight you will meet both married and unmarried ladies," Mrs. Faust said, "and I'm sure it's going to be an occasion you won't soon forget. And don't refuse if Agent Kielland asks you to tell about your stay in the British prison ship or about your fighting the wolves at Ølen, for ladies of quality just love to shudder."

"I might tell them other stories that will make them shudder much more," I answered; "but when I go to a party this time I'm going to listen and not speak. We must leave that to Pastor Lunge; the party's in his and his wife's honor."

"And for you too, Cleng Peerson," she said. "It's going to be you more than anyone else who will lend glamor to the evening. And now I can confide in you and tell you that I know quite a bit about your doings ever since the time you set out on a pilgrimage to the Røldal church — not forgetting your feats during the battle with the wolves at

Ølen. I spoke about this to Agent Kielland even before you met him the first time, and I reminded him again of it today."

I understood that I had had a secret friend in her and asked whether she would join in the festivities.

"Yes," she said. "And you should know, Cleng, that Agent Kielland has shown us a special favor since he is going to send his own carriage to fetch us. A messenger who arrived while you were dressing, asked whether that might be convenient, and I thanked him on behalf of you and myself. I hope this will fit into your plans."

The carriage arrived on time. Two splendid horses, white with black spots, were harnessed to the carriage, which was also white with gilt ornamentation. First I helped Mrs. Faust take her seat; she filled two-thirds of the width of the seat, but what was left was more than sufficient for me.

The time for the party had been set at six o'clock, and it was to be held at Agent Kielland's estate; its name was Ledaal, and it is located a short distance outside town. Just before the war he had built a large house in the manorial style, unquestionably the most stately building in the district, with the exception of the cathedral. Ledaal was the only private residence in the district that had been built of stone, and much of the building materials had been brought to Stavanger from afar, from the island of Bornholm in the Baltic. In addition, the house was well supplied with all kinds of utensils of iron and brass, through advantageous purchases in Scotland. The builder had been the most competent carpenter available, a man who had learned his profession in Bergen and Copenhagen.

I had often heard about the merry parties held at Ledaal during the carefree days before the war, when Agent Kielland used to propose a toast to Voltaire and the French Revolution. His guests used to call him "The Jacobin," a nickname which made him feel very flattered.

Such were the topics of our conversation while Mrs. Faust and I were being driven to the party. She went on to tell me about Agent Kielland's charitable works in the city during the war years. In spite of a good grain harvest on Jæren there had been shortages of flour, since the farmers had been forced to give up large quantities of oats and barley to the military forces at Kristiansand; similarly, large quantities of herring had been ordered for the famine-stricken districts in the eastern parts of the country. But Kielland had bought up grain for his own account, one year even at a total cost of several thousand dalers, and had stored it in his warehouse at Sandnes and then placed it at cost at the disposal of the Poor Relief Commission. This was a great boon to many persons in need, especially the great number of wives who had been left alone with a flock of children while their husbands were imprisoned in England.

Agent Kielland became a greatly beloved and venerated man among rich and poor alike.

The invitation had mentioned that the party would be held in the garden, weather permitting. But while the guests were arriving, there was a light drizzle; consequently, the party for the most part took place indoors.

It is indeed long ago, Anne, and if I were to describe the large and small rooms the way I remember them, the picture I draw for you would be pale and inaccurate. Let me just say that Ledaal equaled the best manorial houses you can find in the New World, and surrounding the house Agent Kielland had laid out a park in the French manner. Just at this time of year everything was blooming; it was hard to believe that such lushness was possible in the harsh climate of the North. As for the interior of the house, I chiefly remember that above each door Agent Kielland had had these four letters inscribed: HEHI, which in Norwegian stand for SHE IS NOT HERE — in blessed memory of his first wife.

The evening was a success in every way. The little daughter of the customs inspector played the piano, and in addition, a quartet received much applause, in spite of the fact that they were all amateurs. The violinist was a tailor by profession, and a shoemaker — who of course had gained much practice in hammering pegs into shoe soles — beat the drum, while a quartermaster played the clarinet. The makeup of the quartet was not a result of any lack of musical virtuosi in the city; rather it was due to a predilection of Agent Kielland to make it possible for the common people to gain entry into the social life of the town; for even though he, in line with his entire intellectual bent, was an aristocrat and showed it in his dress, his manners, and way of speaking, he appreciated being considered a man of the people, professing a republican outlook, and enjoying a reputation for doing good deeds without petty considerations — a reputation which was indeed deserved.

There was dancing to the music of the orchestra. First I asked Mrs. Faust for a dance, and then Mrs. Christine Lunge; later on I danced with others, and feeling very animated from the wine and the sight of the beautiful gowns of the ladies I was lavish with my compliments. As a consequence I had an attentive group of listeners — especially among the fair sex — when Agent Kielland asked me to tell something about life on board an English prison ship and about the battle with the wolves at Ølen.

I am afraid that I have forgotten what kind of dishes were served, but I recall at any rate suckling pigs roasted on a spit, tropical fruits, coffee, and a very fine Madeira. Following the years of war and hunger, a period of relative prosperity had come to the coastal towns of Norway. And any change from hard times to more prosperous is always seen first in such things as food and drink and women's dress.

This in turn served to heighten the spirits of everyone, through toasts and through speeches: the first one for the new clergyman and his family, then one for my contributions toward the welfare of the nation as a killer of wolves and as a privateer — the latter I regarded with no little embarrassment; I have never been able to see anything meritorious in the fact that I landed in prison because of my own foolishness. Later, toasts were also made to the university, for all those who still suffered privation, and for Agent Kielland's library, which recently had received a valuable shipment of books from the Gyldendal publishing house in Copenhagen. All this was laced with patriotic anthems and drinking songs.

But best of all do I remember the conversation about the religious life in the district. Alexander Lunge, being a newly arrived clergyman, was very much concerned with this topic, and besides hearing what Dean Støren and Agent Kielland had to say in the matter, he also got to know the views of Pastor Swensen Magnus. That the last named was one of the guests was occasioned by the fact that he was a house guest of Dean Støren while attending to important official business in town. Agent Kielland had heard of this and had said that it would give him great pleasure to have the pastor of Skjold and Tysvær as one of his guests that evening.

There were many other men that I would have much preferred to have met in circumstances like this, and I think that he felt the same way. For that reason we kept our distance most of the time. Nevertheless, I must admit that I tried to catch what the four gentlemen at the card table were saying, especially when Swensen Magnus spoke; even though I didn't feel uncomfortable at the party, my heart was with my poor friends among the Quakers. The table had been placed at an angle between two large rooms, and I took a chair, feeling comfortable since I was well hidden by the drapes.

In the beginning the conversation was mostly concerned with business and trade. In spite of his goodwill toward plain people,

Kielland complained about the multitudes of plebeians who had invaded the city and had gone into business and were amassing fortunes.

The name John Haugvaldstad was mentioned in this connection — he was the leader of the Haugeans in Stavanger. Mr. Kielland told briefly about a meeting he had had with this man on board a British frigate at Tananger during the war, and he had only good things to say about him as far as that occasion was concerned. For it was not Haugvaldstad's desire for the heavenly treasures but his pronounced appreciation of the earthly ones that bothered Kielland.

Be that as it may, the event that Mr. Kielland alluded to took place the first time that I myself had the honor of meeting him, and it all transpired in the following manner.

You remember, Anne, that he stuck his silver-mounted walking stick in my stomach and in that way made me stop short? Well, when we had conversed a while in his office, we looked around inside the general store, which despite the shortages of foodstuffs during the war years was still rather well stocked. Then we suddenly heard the booming of cannon.

"They are shooting from the fort at the Kalhammer promontory!" he said.

Kielland was the commander of the militia and would be in charge if the city were attacked by enemy ships. He immediately ordered his two finest riding horses to be saddled.

"You're coming along," he said, turning to me. It was an order.

The horses were ready and in front of the steps in less than five minutes. We swung ourselves into the saddle and rode as fast as possible through the narrow streets and up the hills toward Ledaal. Agent Kielland inquired whether there were any reports from any of the forts and then ordered two of his own horses to be saddled. And he rapidly changed from his civilian dress into uniform. A uniform was provided for me too. Before we were ready we could hear the booming of guns from the two other forts of the city.

"We'll ride to the Kalhammer promontory," he said. "I don't feel secure about that fort; I myself was against its being fortified. It is located so far away that if it is taken by the enemy, he can turn its guns around, toward the city and destroy it completely."

At that time Agent Kielland was a man about sixty, but he handled his horse like a spirited cavalry officer, and we galloped along at top speed. There was no road leading to the fort, only a narrow path winding along naked rocks and swamps toward a small hill, where there was an observation post with a guard house and signaling equipment.

The flanks of the horses were covered with foam when we finally got there. One of the guards immediately took charge of the horses, and Agent Kielland asked the commanding officer what was going on. He was obviously very excited, but he tried to hide it. The commandant immediately made his report. Fortunately it did not concern any enemy ship — a fact which they finally had ascertained — but a peaceful Danish merchant vessel on its way from Bergen to Gothenburg; it had tried to put in at Stavanger because it had been shot at by a British frigate somewhere to the west of Tungenes. Fortunately the Kalhammer guns had not damaged the ship nor wounded any of the crew by the time the mistake was discovered, he said.

"I don't call that luck, to miss a ship which one believes is an enemy vessel!" Agent Kielland snorted with rage. "But no matter, the enemy can be expected any time. What has been done to give *him* a broadside?"

"Our entire fleet of gunboats is already on the way out toward the open sea," said the officer of the watch. "They passed the promontory a little more than fifteen minutes ago; the sailors were rowing all out."

"Very good," Kielland said; "I hope to God that others will also work all out before the new day dawns. Stavanger has a fleet of gunboats, and if they don't let themselves be heard tonight, they don't know what honor's about! But — already!"

The faint sound of cannon reached us from a westerly direction. Right after that we saw a cavalry officer riding at top speed across the hills in the fading daylight. He came to a halt in front of Agent Kielland and the commanding officer, saluted while still in the saddle, and announced that he brought a report from the guards at Tananger. A British frigate was patrolling the coast, and there was every reason to believe that it would attack as soon as the opportunity presented itself.

The harbor at Tananger is the busiest on this part of the coast, and it was absolutely certain that lives would be lost and there would be heavy property damage if it was bombarded. There are a number of houses in the area; in addition, central supplies of foodstuffs and military equipment were stored there during the war.

"Under conditions such as these it is my duty," Agent Kielland said, addressing me, "to be present at the battle and if necessary take an active part in it in order to bring it to a favorable conclusion. We'll ride out there right away!"

Just as soon as the cavalry officer had exchanged his horse for a new one, all three of us set out in a southwesterly direction. The clouds were reddish — it was already twilight. When we at last reached the spot where the Hafrsfjord cuts far into the land through a narrow sound, the moon rose above the horizon. The tide was running out and there was a swift current, and the eddies were waving from shore to shore like dragons with flaming crests.

When we had spurred our horses into the water and had crossed as far as the middle of the narrow sound we caught sight of the gunboats going south. They looked like dark slithering shadows, silhouetted against the gleaming surface of the sea.

We reached the shore on the other side and rode on as fast as the horses could carry us; they began to get tired. We rode across cultivated fields, across heather-clad and rocky hills; in some places we followed the wagon roads, which were soft and muddy during the spring thaw.

When we finally got as far as Tananger Bay, we could see the first flashes from the gunports of the frigate. The gunboats immediately answered in kind; they were now within range. Five in all, the entire navy of the town, they formed a ring around the frigate. Agent Kielland had had two of them built for his own account, other citizens of Stavanger had contributed money to pay for one, and two of them had been sent there by the government.

They all fired at the same time, but before the frigate could get ready for another salvo, they had disappeared in the shelter of the islets and skerries while loading their guns; and then they fired anew from their sheltered positions. There were also indications that they had made several hits, but the frigate was quite capable of retaliating. Still, the gunboats seemed to be undamaged. I knew that an attacker had to have a lot of luck on his side if he were to hit them; it was very difficult to aim accurately, since the gunboats were lying so low in the water.

Following several rounds it became clear that it was the frigate which had gotten the worst of it, and as sometimes happens, the small vanquished the great. When the frigate's hull had been hit several times, above and below the waterline, it finally seemed as if it were ready to surrender.

In his capacity as head of the citizens' militia, Agent Kielland had a boat lowered. With two strong men at the oars, we were rowed across the bay, and together with officers and crew of the gunboats we boarded the frigate.

Kielland addressed the captain in English, and when the latter immediately stepped forward, Kielland told him who he was and in a loud voice declared the frigate to be a prize. Everyone on board had to consider himself a prisoner.

The captain asked whether they would be put in a prison ship or in an ordinary jail.

Kielland did not answer right away, and I knew the reason: there were no ships available of the kind that the captain had alluded to. And even though the town jail had recently been enlarged, there would not be room enough for the British crew. Besides, there were always other people in town who had to be sentenced to jail.

Agent Kielland spoke again, "It has always been the custom of Norwegians to be fair to their antagonists in an honest fight," he said. "For that reason, and being faithful to the traditions that are honored among us, we have made the following decision: all the guns on the frigate are to be dismantled and are to be turned over to the Norwegian militia, through the commanding officer for the citizens' militia in Stavanger. Everything else that you can do without, keeping in mind that the ship still has to be seaworthy and have enough provisions for a voyage across the North Sea, is considered to be our prize and is confiscated. Finally, the captain is to sign a document in which he gives his word of honor that he will abstain from privateering in the future or from acts of war of any other kind vis-à-vis Norway, unless he is ordered to do so by the military authorities in his homeland."

This was a very good solution, the way Agent Kielland looked at it. But the captain of the privateer looked upon it as a manifestation of a highmindedness that he couldn't fathom. He saluted Kielland smartly, and then he saluted me — he obviously looked upon me as the second in command.

When all the necessary formalities had been taken care of, he requested us to provide him with a doctor as soon as possible. One of the frigate's crewmembers was lying below deck, severely wounded. Agent Kielland replied that a physician from Stavanger might be able to arrive within a few hours, but then the captain made us understand that in that case it would look rather hopeless for the wounded man. Agent Kielland inquired as to whether the crews of the gunboats might include someone who had training as a military orderly or had medical experience of any kind at all.

At once a man in his forties stepped forward. He was slender, with a kind face, almost like a woman's, and his voice was in accord with his appearance. He declared in a humble voice that he was ready to offer that bodily and spiritual care that God in His mercy might grant.

As he uttered them, the words took on a sad and at the same time comforting sound. But I thought to myself that an unusually well-disposed fate had come to our aid as long as it had let men of that type join us and help us defeat the English frigate.

Later on I got to know him better and learned that his great meekness was combined with courage and a fine intellect. But many people would misjudge him because of his appearance. The man's name was John Haugvaldstad. He was immediately conducted below deck and to the bed of the wounded man; Kielland and I followed. The captain walked ahead and showed us the way.

The reason why John Haugvaldstad happened to be on the gunboat was as follows: right after his return from the spring herring fishing — he was one of the most enterprising fishermen in the area and owned several valuable fishing gears — he had signed on as a volunteer on board the navy ship *Najaden*. The reason was this: about a score of sailors had recently been drafted from the coastal district that he belonged to. One of the boys was very sick, but when the places on board ship were to be filled, he was all the same, upon the strict orders of the commander, brought forcibly on board. John Haugvaldstad was a witness to this occurrence. He felt extremely sorry for the sick young man and signed on as a volunteer in his place.

Evil tongues would have it that in spite of his Haugean makeup, he would cheerfully have signed on as a watchman in hell if this would only take him away from home, for his wife was just as great a vexation to him as a boil in the throat. Still, I don't believe, Anne, that that gives us any cause to deny that this man had both nobility of mind as well as courage — even though many besides him have found that warfare is less of a strain than the battles that are waged between four walls.

When Agent Kielland a short time after learned the details as far as this entire matter was concerned, he immediately let John Haugvaldstad out of the service and had someone else called in in his place.

In this late evening hour John Haugvaldstad was standing by the wounded man's bed, with a lit candle in his hand. Death had already put its stamp on the soldier's face. He was a young man, hardly twenty years old. Whether he was delirious or whether his mind was clear, I do not know, but time and again he called for his mother: "Dear mother, where are you?" Haugvaldstad, who didn't understand English, asked what he was saying, and I explained it to him. Haugvaldstad asked me to interpret for him, and he told the young man something like this: "We cannot send for your mother, but our Saviour and Redeemer, the Lord Jesus Christ, who shed His blood in order to save us sinners, He is now present and will heal the injury to your soul. Those who put their confidence in Him, will not be put to shame." With these and similar words from Holy Writ did he speak to the boy, who still seemed to be conscious even though he didn't respond; neither did he say anything when the captain bent over his berth and called him by name.

He died within minutes; when he showed signs of being ready for the great journey, John Haugvaldstad fell down on his knees by his bed and recited the Lord's Prayer and thereupon with great solemnity pronounced the Apostolic Benediction.

Gabriel Kielland was standing erect but with his head bent during the prayer and the benediction; his stern face seemed chiseled in stone, but when Haugvaldstad rose to his feet and prayed for friends and enemies in this evil war, Mr. Kielland too was visibly moved.

The British marine was laid to rest in Norwegian soil.

The guns on the frigate were dismounted in accordance with the orders, and some of the commodities on board were confiscated, but Agent Kielland showed moderation. Five days after the battle the frigate sailed out of Tananger harbor. Kielland and I were standing on a rocky knoll by the entrance to the harbor and watched it through our binoculars until its sails disappeared below the horizon.

A crowd had gathered around Gabriel Kielland to listen as he continued to complain about the hold that John Haugvaldstad seemed to have on the industry and commerce of Stavanger. He pointed out that Haugvaldstad had also purchased a brick works outside town, where he could produce one hundred thousand bricks annually. But that was not enough: having gained proficiency in the trade of a dyer, he had also bought a building in the center of town, where he had started a dye-works, the only fairly large enterprise of this kind in the entire county. Kielland had found out that this business too showed a nice profit. On another piece of property, which he had purchased from Kielland himself, since the latter had been told that he would merely use it as a storage place for timbers suitable for ship's masts, he was now planning to build a woolen-goods factory.

Then Pastor Lunge asked whether the Haugeans, in spite of their numerous activities within the economic life of the town, nevertheless presented an even greater problem for the *church*. "I am told that there is supposed to be much abomination connected with their worldly activities," the minister said.

Mrs. Faust entered the conversation and told of an episode she herself had witnessed.

One day the neighbor's boy had been walking on stilts in the yard of her inn. John Haugvaldstad had passed by, and in a sad and mildly reproachful tone he had said, "Has your father given you permission to do this, my child? Just consider the fact that God has given you two strong and healthy legs to move around on. You might even call down His wrath on you by walking on wooden legs. There are in truth a great many who have to do so because they have lost their God-given legs."

The boy threw the stilts away and ran home, crying.

"Mrs. Faust's story makes me think of another," Kielland continued; "this, however, does not concern Haugvaldstad himself but one of his disciples. One day at our middle school, during recess the teacher in charge permitted the boys to put up posts for high jumping, and they were all trying to out-jump each other; some of the most athletic girls also took part, their skirts fluttering about their legs. One of the Haugeans passed by and witnessed the activities. Shaking from agitation he turned to the teacher and said, 'But don't you consider the fact that each one of these young boys has an immortal soul?' "

Everyone chuckled over this story and Kielland mixed another toddy. Those sitting at the table had a good view of the dancers, and so had I, from behind the drapes; it was principally the young people who were dancing. Just then they were dancing a minuet; all through the rooms could be heard the brittle music coming from the spinet.

"The Haugeans condemn all kinds of innocent games, including dancing, don't they?" said Pastor Lunge.

"That's true," Støren replied; "and in the same way all walking, riding, and driving for the sake of enjoyment."

"Well, in that case I don't think any of the Haugeans would think that the town's new minister was guilty of a sin by riding across Jæren to Stavanger, for that was in truth a doubtful pleasure!" Lunge said, laughing. "I have heard," he added when no one said anything, "that it is even considered to be idolatry if one picks a flower in the field and admires its beauty, since this should be considered nothing but pleasures for the eye and the flesh, and that even all singing of songs that cannot be classified as psalms, is looked upon as ungodly boasting."

Dean Støren said, "As far as dyer Haugvaldstad's behavior is concerned, I must admit that I find it to be unpleasant and repulsive. As their leader he sets a very bad example by literally letting his head hang to one side and by speaking in a pitiful, whimpering, and whining voice. Nor does his glance seem frank and open. All told, his appearance gives the impression of being put on and hypocritical."

"Isn't it so that he doesn't have the proper Christian matrimonial relations with his wife?" asked Alexander Lunge.

"They were both forced into matrimony, and there has, to be sure, never been any love between them," Mrs. Faust replied.

"In spite of the fact that they were married according to the ritual of the church," the Dean said. "But the situation is much worse in regard to the Quakers, who according to what I have heard, even intend to enter into matrimony in their own way and without the blessing of the Church. Just recently I received a report concerning a case in Christiania, in which one Knud Halvorsen, who was born somewhere in the district around Stavanger, is supposed to have committed such a sin, which surely is prohibited by the Seventh Commandment."

"But are the Quakers really so great in number that they represent a spiritual danger, as the Haugeans do?" asked Lunge.

"As far as our society as a whole is concerned, they are in a much weaker position," answered Støren, "for they don't possess the enterprise of the Haugeans. Most of the Quakers I know are poor fishermen."

"But as far as religious teachings are concerned?" asked Lunge.

Then Pastor Swensen Magnus spoke up, and he expressed himself in the most acrimonious terms. "Most certainly!" he said; "as far as religion is concerned, and also in regard to morals and politics, they will in future represent a great danger. Especially in my own parish there are already many who sympathize with them and show stubbornness toward their appointed shepherd and the organization of the Church. What they are working for — and you must believe me — is not only a new sectarian faith but also a new politics; wild, lawless republicanism and even anarchy. It is my firm opinion that in a crafty manner they use religion to mask their plans for a criminal plot against the current government. They appear at present to be rather insignificant, but what can we not expect in the future from these rotten apples from England, that lascivious land with its multifarious sects? Especially when Quakerism takes root among the people of this district, who more than any other province in the land can show examples of narrow-minded, selfish, and stubborn individuals. This is the bitter experience that I have had after I got to know them much better! And now they also want to get married in their own way? Well, let them do so, and I will in good time hold them responsible for their sinful life! Yes, I assure you that even if two dissenters came to me and asked me on their knees that I marry them — I would drive them out of the house; I would tell them, 'Away to hell with you, you who have the Devil as a father, and let him marry you! You will certainly have enough heat for your sinful love, both here and beyond!' "

"My dear pastor," Dean Støren objected; "it seems to me that you are a bit categorical in your expressions, but perhaps you have had more discouraging experiences than others?"

"I have among other things examples of those who sympathize with the Quakers refusing to attend the lessons preparing them for their confirmation," answered Swensen Magnus. "The fact that I have been deprived of a considerable source of income I take lightly compared to my not succeeding in giving them the true Christian religion. And then, when the day comes that they refuse to enter military service, when they reject all ecclesiastical organization so that their children are not baptized, and they demand to be buried without the singing of hymns and without prayers — going so far in order to have their will that they even take the step of having their dead ones buried in unconsecrated earth, what then — ?"

"Let us hope that God the Almighty will spare us witnessing such things," Dean Støren said.

"This can happen sooner than we think," Swensen Magnus replied.

I felt no sympathy for what the Pastor of Tysvær was saying, but I had an inkling that he was right that the day might be closer than the dean guessed.

Just then the conversation was interrupted. One of the young girls was standing in the open doorway. She curtsied and smiled and asked whether the ladies and gentlemen would enjoy the presentation of an amateur comedy.

This suggestion was received with much enthusiasm. The conversation had after a while taken on an irritable character, and it was, after all, a festive party.

The comedy was staged, and the evening continued with much mirth and laughter. At midnight we all went out into the garden. It was no longer raining; the sky was clear, and a pale silver moon could be seen through the yellow foliage of the linden trees. Colored lanterns were lit, but our stay out in the open became a brief one, for the air felt rather cool. When the fireworks had been set off, the guests reentered the house for a late snack.

It was just before dawn that the last carriages rolled out of the wide gate at Ledaal.

The Twenty-third Tale

I didn't go back to my lodgings after the party. Filled with thoughts of many kinds, I walked along lonely paths away from the city. It was just the time of morning when the light of the moon is replaced by the light of early dawn; the low hills toward the west were already silhouetted against a greenish-dark sky. The fields were fragrant, and the flight of the birds made the quiet dawn seem fully alive — there was not even the slightest breeze.

The path led into a swamp, across which there was a bridge of logs and flat rocks. The morning haze was still hovering over the wet terrain, and my head told me that I had drunk too much. The pale golden light of dawn slowly suffused the mountains to the east.

I had started out in a rather sad mood; but it yielded almost unnoticeably to a feeling of emptiness, and in the wake of emptiness came, suddenly and without warning, a great fear that made my blood run cold, as if I were face to face with the final horror. The sky crashed down around me like thunder, and the earth was a hollow chasm. I thought to myself, "That's the way insanity took hold of my father!"

Weak and powerless, I stumbled across the flat rocks on the swamp, and when I stood on firm ground again, I called aloud to God, "Send a human being my way!"

Then I noticed a horse lying sleeping on the ground. I walked over to it and lay down close to it and felt the warmth of its large body. Its even breathing and the smell of animal gradually spread a feeling of calm through me. It did not wake up, and I myself must have fallen asleep. I didn't recall anything until I looked into a large and bright eye in which my own face was reflected. I was so greatly moved by this, I couldn't tell why, that I was almost blinded by tears. I seemed to think that the horse's eye was huge and bottomless, and I embraced the horse and put my cheek against its muzzle.

Not even then did the animal move. My intense feeling abated after a while, and I must have fallen asleep once again. The sun was high in the sky when I awoke.

A man was standing looking down at me, but blinded by the light I could only make out green and dancing circles and did not recognize him until I heard his voice; he mentioned my name, it was Elias Tastad.

"Look at you, lying here so early in the morning," he said, and I understood that he was trying to make a joke out of it.

"I'm lying in hell," I answered him. "There's no mercy to be had for someone like me."

"Are you sure it's mercy you're looking for, Cleng, over and above all other things?" he asked.

"No!" I cried, "I'm not looking for mercy above all other things, but relief from the fire that burns within me."

"Isn't that the fire of sin that burns within all of us?" he said.

"I don't know, Elias!" I cried. "But this must come to an end, otherwise a person is going to die!"

"Come with me and get yourself some breakfast," said Elias.

Side by side we walked across the fields; he led the horse by the forelock. I was thinking about the party; everything about it seemed distant, as if it belonged to some time ages ago.

Elias tried to start up a conversation while we were eating, but I must have answered him sparingly and in a sullen manner, for he said at last, "You're not yourself today, Cleng."

"This is the first time that I really am myself," I answered. "You all know the happy-go-lucky Cleng who's as lively as a wave on the ocean. But have you ever met the Cleng who carries death on his back and Satan in his soul, Elias? Not even in the prison ship?"

Elias was silent.

"In that case he has hidden himself well," I replied, "but now he has to come out from under the ice and find a breathing hole, otherwise there's no saying what will happen."

Elias just looked at me. At last he said, "Today Guri Olsdatter's traveling chest arrives in Stavanger. Will you come and help me pick it up?''

Elias had become engaged to Guri Olsdatter from Telemark. I will now tell you how this had occurred.

Torbjørn Knudsen Svineli, a fellow from my home district, had been imprisoned at Chatham — on board a ship called the *Belliquer*. At that time he had been a Haugean, but during his imprisonment he had converted to the teachings of the Quakers.

About midsummer 1817 Elias Tastad and Lars Larsen went to Tysvær; they wanted to visit their brother in the faith, and they held silent meetings in the house together with people from Slogvig, Rossadal, and Hersdal. From that time on the flame of the Quaker faith began to flicker throughout Tysvær, but another flame was also lit: Guri Olsdatter attended the meeting, and Elias immediately became greatly infatuated with her and could not get her out of his mind. Before he left Tysvær he had proposed to her and she had said yes, but Guri also told him that she barely could be called a religious person, and she was even less prepared to become a Quaker. Elias, however, who otherwise was known for his sober mind and his good judgment, assured her that if she was only sincere of heart, her inner light would lead her to perfect insight and understanding. Then Guri cried from joy and said that if Elias promised to help her, she hoped that she could embrace the faith, for she was fervently longing for inner peace.

Guri was about eighteen years old at this time, with a beautiful face and figure, and Elias was a fine-looking man; he had regained his strength after the years of privation. Many people were delighted that he was now to have a woman at his side, but some wished that it could have been someone other than Guri Olsdatter. They said she was of a flighty and unstable disposition, cried and laughed easily and had bursts of anger, and that she couldn't taste liquor without getting intoxicated. Still, everyone had many good things to say about her.

Elias was past his first youth, and everyone who knew him was of the opinion that he was not greatly attracted to the female sex. But when love finally caught up with him it was sudden and impatient; he wanted to get married that very same summer.

It was about six months before this that Knud Halvorsen had gotten married in the Quaker fashion in Christiania, but *his* wife belonged to the Friends. It was otherwise with Elias and Guri; Elias for that reason gave in to her when she asked that they apply to the pastor at Skjold, request that the banns be read, and then be married in the church.

But Pastor Swensen Magnus had already been informed that Elias had held Quaker meetings in various places in the parish, and when he asked whether he had resigned from the State Church and actually adhered to this sect, Elias had to admit that he was a member of the Society of Friends.

"If such is the case, I cannot marry you for the sake of my conscience," Swensen Magnus said. "The children that might be the fruit of such a marriage, would be brought up in delusion, without obtaining a share in the blessings of baptism, in the divine grace of communion, or in the gift of confirmation. How could I bring myself to place my hand above your heads and thus contribute to a new generation gone astray contaminating my parish? Moreover," he added, "there are rumors that the Quakers in Christiania help themselves as far as marriage is concerned. And if you two in your obstinacy and thoughtlessness choose to live your lives under the sentence of God, then I don't want to help to have this sentence consummated."

And he waved them out of the room.

Elias had by now taken over his father's farm at Tastad, northwest of Stavanger, not far from the city limits; it is located in the parish of Our Lady.

He said to his betrothed, "The pastor at Our Lady will no doubt see things our way," and they immediately got ready and sailed to Stavanger.

But the minister in that parish asked why they had neglected to approach the pastor in the bride's home parish, as was the custom. When he was told the reason, he replied that he had to stand by his colleague and couldn't say yes in a case where his colleague had answered no. But he was a kindhearted man; he patted them both on the head and wished them better luck elsewhere.

Then they applied to the clergy in Stavanger, but in view of all that Elias had had to do with them before, he knew that he could not have high expectations. This happened the last year of Pastor Heyland's tenure, and when he heard what their errand was, he began to ridicule them, and then he urged them, just as Dean Støren previously had advised Elias, that they ought to go to England, where dissenters of all kinds were tolerated.

Then Guri Olsdatter lost her temper and spoke up to the minister, "It happens quite frequently that two young people in love cannot be joined in marriage because class and birth keep them apart. Then the reason is that parents, or family, or people who want to do them harm, intervene. But never before have I heard that the *pastor* was the only one to prevent them from sharing bed and board when they had sworn to be true to each other unto death."

Then Heyland smiled and replied, "I know the Quakers; they always know where to find other paths where the first one is barred; they know the art of helping themselves in matters where the law gives them no right to do so."

Guri asked, "And you will not object if that's what happens?"

Heyland replied, "That is no concern of mine."

From that moment on it was Guri who took the initiative. "When we came from Telemark, we lived a whole winter at Tjul," she said to Elias. "I wonder whether the pastor at Nedstrand wouldn't want to help us."

And as soon as they had got together some provisions, they set sail for Nedstrand. It was already autumn; they got a head wind and stormy weather, and the trip took them all of four days.

But they didn't fare any better after having had a talk with the pastor at Nedstrand. He asked them where they had stayed overnight along the way, and Elias answered, "In the boat underneath a sail, or in a boathouse."

"It's rather chilly to travel like that this time of year," said the minister; "and two people who are fond of each other, will no doubt want to keep warm underneath the same cover, I suppose?"

"Of course," answered Elias.

"Then one must be very strong not to have the desires of the flesh overpower one," the minister said.

"We've been that strong," Elias answered.

"Yes, we have," cut in Guri. "But how long time will it take before we can consider ourselves to be husband and wife, since we have pledged our troth before God, and it is only the pastor who prevents us from making the same promise before the cross and the altar?"

"That which my colleagues found to be the right thing to do, I also must concur in," said the pastor of Nedstrand. "Do you think it is possible that God might inform one of us that His will is such and such, and tell another that His will is just the opposite?"

He waved them out of his office, and they left.

Guri said to Elias, "The time I came with Talleiv and Uncle Sjugurd, we traveled through Suldal and Røldal. We'll go to the minister in that parish."

And even though Elias began to feel dejected, he did not make any objection. They rowed through the narrow fjords and then walked the rest of the way. Upon arriving at the Suldal parsonage, they immediately told the pastor of all that had happened and begged him from the bottom of their hearts to take pity on them.

When they had told him all, he said, "This is a matter that concerns the pastor in your home valley, Guri Olsdatter. He has both the right and the duty to let you be joined in marriage."

But Elias said, "Winter has already come to the mountains."

Then the minister replied, "Jacob served seven years for Rachel, and as a reward for his faithfulness he was given Leah for a bride. Couldn't you two wait until the end of winter? Go back where you came from, children. When spring comes, one can once again travel across the mountains; then you may set out for Telemark without fear or hesitation! The Lord be with you!"

Thereupon they traveled back to Stavanger. That winter Guri served as a maid in the house of skipper Johannes Stene; with his wife and children he had moved to the city from Kindingstad on the island of Finnøy.

During the month of March Elias and his betrothed made themselves ready for the long journey across the mountains. It took them five days to get from Stavanger to Hylen, for they had at times a strong head wind, and from there they walked the usual route up the mountain pass to Våge. Then they rowed across Suldal Lake all the way to Roaldkvam, which is the most distantly located village, lying nestled in the mountains. From there they went on skis, first as far as Bykle in the valley of Setesdal, and once again across mountains to Guri's birthplace in the province of Telemark. Elias was not a very good skier, but Guri had learned to ski as a child, and they completed their journey without any mishap.

When they crossed the mountains the snow was crusty and the sun was shining, but on the last day the weather suddenly turned very mild. They struggled on, sinking deep into the heavy slush. Dead tired they finally arrived at her home valley late in the evening and found shelter in a hay barn in the forest. The next morning they washed and dressed as well as they could and walked across the fields to the parsonage. The dog was the first one they encountered, and then the minister.

The minister didn't know much about Quakers, and the little he thought he knew, had nothing to do with reality. He believed — as some others did — that Quakerism had had its origin in Turkey and that its adherents secretly worked for violent rebellion the purpose of which was to have all Christian countries ruled by the Sultan and the Mohammedan infidels, and also that its members were in every way debauched and frivolous.

Guri did the talking. She told him who she was and what her errand was, for they still believed that their cause would be strengthened if they spoke the truth. But the pastor answered, "I am not a man to be fooled with! Yesterday a couple came to see me for the same purpose, and they had journeyed the same way across the mountains. They put on pious expressions and stressed the great love they had for each other; but I certainly didn't need that kind of assurance; the girl was already expecting a child. When I pressed them, they had to admit that they were half siblings. And that the father of one and the mother of the other had married after having been widowed, and the fact that the two young people had been born to their parents during their first marriages doesn't make much of a difference; I was obliged to look upon such a relationship as incest. But what you two are planning to do I consider to be much worse."

He looked sharply at Guri and said, "Your family has been like thistles in the meadow in this parish — I know it only too well — and you can hardly be any better. If I'm not very wrong, you seem to be pregnant and expect a child before the summer is over!"

This Guri denied. Then he said, "Do you really want me to believe that you have traveled across land and sea since last autumn, and this spring across the mountains, and every night slept in the same place and not come close to each other?"

Elias replied, "That's the way it has been, by the grace of God."

The minister laughed right in their faces: "I imagine there are people who are so constituted that they would not conceive even if the Angel Gabriel lent his assistance."

Guri burst into tears and repeated that she and Elias had promised to be true unto death. The pastor smiled again and mumbled something about that's the way every bitch yelps whenever she feels hot below the tail. "Such a marriage," he said, "contains its own punishment, and God cannot find it possible to bless such a union." Then Elias rose and hit the table so that ink splashed all over and the sand box fell to the floor: "There wasn't anything more between Joseph and the Virgin Mary than there's been between Guri Olsdatter and me! But we are very fond of each other. Is there no one who in the name of Jesus will make it right for us to share all joys and sorrows?"

"That would have to be the Devil himself!" the pastor answered. And he pointed to the door: "Get out of my house!"

The minister made a big outcry, and when people arrived he made them believe that Elias and Guri were wandering tramps who had threatened to kill him. The farmhand had the dog try to track them down and ran after them with a cudgel held high.

They felt they were not safe anywhere in the valley, and they therefore set out on the return journey across the mountains.

They walked all night; the weather was now colder, they could walk across the crust on the snow, and the moon was shining. Early the next day they came to a small mountain barn; they crawled in and lay down in the hay and fell asleep.

When they woke up, it was almost dawn. They heard voices outside; it was a man and a woman. The woman was weeping and wailing; the man tried to comfort her. They entered the barn, but Elias and Guri could not see them from where they were lying; but they could hear a part of the conversation, even though the roar from the waterfall nearby at times would drown out what they were saying. The noise from the waterfall was also aided and abetted by the wind which had been rising, and it was now snowing heavily.

Elias and Guri soon realized that these people were the same whom the pastor had turned away the previous day, before they had seen him themselves.

"If it's true what the pastor said, we can expect to end up in jail or on the gallows," they heard the woman say.

"I don't think it will turn out that bad," the man tried to console her.

"My grandmother has told me about two young people who were related and became fond of each other. They were not allowed to marry, and they had to live as outlaws in the mountains for the rest of their days," she said.

"But *we* are not related," he objected. "The pastor only wanted to scare us. Don't be afraid!"

"Oh yes," she said, "now I'm afraid. I think the only thing we can do is to go far away from here."

"But you know," he said, "that of movable goods I have nothing, but at home we will inherit both farm and fields."

"Yes," she sobbed, "we will inherit earth, all right! Six feet of it!"

"It was too hard on you to walk up those steep hills," he said. "Heavy going and not much sleep, that's when a person can't see any way out. Things will look better after we've had some sleep. Now we'll have a bite to eat; then we'll make ourselves comfortable in the hay."

"We could go to the city, live there, and hide so that no one would ever find us," she said.

"No one can hide," he said. "They'll find us in the end."

"Yes," she answered in a tone of despair.

They ate silently and then burrowed into the hay. But when everything had been quiet for a while and the man began to snore,

Elias and Guri heard another sound, as if the door hinges were creaking. They looked out through a knothole in the wall and saw the woman; it seemed as if she wanted to set out by herself in the driving snow storm, and she walked in the direction of the waterfall.

They didn't know what to believe, but both of them immediately left their hiding place and walked over to the man. They shook him, but he was in a deep sleep. They ran out and followed the tracks toward the waterfall.

The following evening the three of them found shelter in a stone cottage above the Bleskestad mountain farms. The man carried his dead sweetheart on his back: they had finally found her. While they were eating, Guri said to Elias, "I am a Quaker like you."

"When did you become one?" he asked.

"This morning," she replied, "then — if not before!"

"You need a stronger faith and conviction!" Elias said.

"A stronger conviction than the one I have now I will never have," she said. "And when we get back to Stavanger we will get married in the Quaker fashion, otherwise I will go and drown myself!"

The Twenty-fourth Tale

During the previous winter I had been living at Talgje part of the time, and also at home at Tysvær. Mother's health was not the best and she needed help on the farm. During Christmas I visited Cornelius and Kari at Hersdal. On the eleventh of December that year she had had her third child, a girl, and as the child was to be baptized on Christmas Day they asked me to be its godfather. But when I was to sign my name in the book, the minister asked, "Isn't your brother-in-law a dissenter?" Cornelius answered no. Swensen Magnus cleared his throat and very hesitantly entered my name in the protocol.

After Easter I went to Stavanger to live. At times I would get together with the Friends, but I was of two minds about their teachings; consequently, I also sought other company, and I had a weakness for being flattered.

Nevertheless, I would always come back and be with those with whom I had shared the misery of the prison ship, above all Elias Tastad. The day following the party given by Gabriel Kielland, Elias and I were working together in the fields, and when we had eaten the morning meal he asked me once again whether I wanted to go into town with him and fetch Guri's traveling chest, which had arrived from Tysvær.

"I can go with you and help you put it on the sleigh, if it's that heavy," I answered. "I am going down to the harbor in any case: I have to leave town."

"Are you going very far?" he asked.

"It suddenly came to me that there's a thing I have to discuss with Anne Cathrine," I answered.

He stood looking at me intently a little while; then he said, "You're not going to do anything you'll regret, Cleng?"

"That we won't know until later," I answered.

"Both Guri and I would very much like to have you as a guest at our wedding," he said.

That very same day I sailed to Finnøy. From the Kindingstad inlet I could see the smoke from the chimney on Anne Cathrine's house, but no one opened when I knocked on the door. I walked right in. She was sitting in a chair; two walking sticks were hanging by their hooks on the armrests.

"Oh, is it you?" she said. "It's been a long time. I didn't hear you enter; I must have been sleeping."

She looked much older and she had gotten quite a bit thinner. She had bags under her eyes as if she had been suffering from insomnia; her face and hands were covered with liver spots.

I asked her how she was, and she replied mockingly, "As you can see for yourself, husband mine; I am still alive and by and large in good shape. It's only my legs that can't keep up with me. But then again, you don't ask me to dance anymore."

"Well, that's the way things have turned out," I answered, and once again I screwed up my courage and asked her to agree to a divorce.

"I *know* that you have lusted after Sara Larsdatter," she replied, "and I really feel sorry for you if you haven't had more pleasure with her than with me."

"I don't ask for my freedom in order to gain anything, neither as far as Sara Larsdatter nor anyone else is concerned," I told her. "But I'm being torn apart the way things are with me now."

"So that's the way it is?" she answered. "But how about *me?* I'll tell you something that you've hardly known anything about, Cleng: When Anders Nord and I had been married two weeks, he was conscripted and served in the navy. He was a member of a gun crew, and once the gun backfired. Five men lost their lives, and Anders Nord lost what men take such pride in. I was never a cold fish, Cleng, but I stood it for ten years, and I never complained.

"It was about the time that we began to put up travelers who couldn't reach Stavanger, either because of stormy weather or no wind at all, or on other occasions, and many a fine fellow stayed in our house when Anders was home, as well as when he was away, which wasn't often. But fifteen years of that marriage of mine were to pass before I fell for temptation; when the sixteenth year had come and gone, I had a child in my arms. I had to be thankful that Anders didn't expose me and throw me out of the house. But he said: '*You* are welcome to the young fellows, but *I* want to have the children.'

"Anne Cathrine didn't have a good reputation during the years that followed. It was common talk that she made every man happy who stepped inside her house. But no one asked whether anyone made *her* happy. When my daughter had grown so big that I thought I would be able to feed us both without having to submit to any man who came around, I went to the pastor and told him my story from one end to the other, and I didn't paint an innocent picture of myself. But the minister was a good man; he said, 'You are entitled to a divorce.'

"Then Anders did something that I've never understood the reason for. He said, 'If you've gotten that much, you may have the rest also.' And he gave away all his personal property and all the securities that he owned in this part of the country — he was far from poor, Cleng — and then he went up north, to the country around the city of Trondheim, where we had been living originally, and made his home on a little farm that he owned, and there's where he died. I myself went to Stavanger and established the Admiral Cruys Bodega, and continued the kind of life that I had developed a taste for. I have nothing to be proud of, Cleng, but there's one thing that may make you remember me: I was kind to you when you were as lonesome as anyone can be on this earth. And for that you've hardly shown any gratitude."

"You lied to me and tricked me and said that you were suffering from an incurable disease," I answered.

"And you wouldn't have minded it at all if Anne Cathrine was actually suffering from a disease that would be the end of her!" she said, laughing shrilly. "Do you know what I've been wondering, Cleng; why people haven't yet found me choked to death with the marks of your fingers on my throat!"

"Shut up, you animal!" I cried, but she continued, "It will soon be twenty years since we got married, Cleng, and today I am closer to my last hour than I was then. But there are two things that you should know: first, that I didn't play sick for you at all. My mother had it the same way, and she died a few years later, as I told you that time. But whoever learns to hate intensely enough clings tenaciously to life. And this is what I decided to do: when I realized that you looked forward to the day that the worms and maggots would feast on my old body, then I decided to take out on you what I couldn't take out on Anders Nord. So I won't let you go, Cleng! I can live until I'm ninety, but hardly much longer, and then you'll still be a hale and hearty fellow. You can get married again just as soon as I'm dead — and there are sure to be many who'll want someone who's come into such affluence; as far as that goes, you may become Agent Kielland's successor and knight of the Order of Dannebrog! It's people of your kind who usually have honors bestowed on them."

"It's not honors that you've bestowed on me today, nor do you hold out any prospects for honors, Anne Cathrine," I interrupted her. "I think we've told each other all that we had on our mind."

With that I got up, and left without saying another word, and I sailed to the shipyard at Talgje. I had a keg of brandy standing in a room in the attic and I locked the door and began to drink.

I don't know how long I drank, but when my head finally cleared, I found that I had emptied the keg and my beard had grown so long that I estimated I had been on a bender for about fourteen days. What else I had consumed to keep alive I have no idea. I only remember that I woke one morning and was fully conscious. I looked out the window; the sea and the sky shimmered, the sun had just risen and the weather was beautiful. A mirror was hanging on the wall; I could hardly recognize my own face. The floor was covered with slime and was slippery from vomit and excrements. I crawled down the stairs with an effort. No one was in the shipyard, not a hammer blow to be heard, and I was wondering why the men had gone off.

Right across from the yard there was a cookhouse. A big kettle was hanging on a hook above the fireplace. I made a fire, and fetched some water from the well right outside. When the water boiled I poured it into a wooden tub and mixed it with the cold water; I undressed and got in, and when I at last was washed and scrubbed, I put on a clean shirt and suit.

I had also stored a keg of herring and a stack of flatbread in the attic. I downed the herrings whole, ate reams of flatbread, and drank a whole lot of water.

My six-oared boat was moored beside the main building. I shoved off, hoisted the foresail, and in fine weather sailed northward along the west coast of Finnøy. With no aim or purpose in mind, I just wanted to feel the wind blowing against my face.

When the boat rounded the northwestern point, I heard the bells at Hesby church and realized that it must be a Sunday. I also noticed that an unusually large number of people were on their way to church and I was wondering whether something special was about to happen. Suddenly the thought struck me: "Today is not a Sunday, but Anne Cathrine is dead; today they are going to bury her."

Driven by fear and curiosity I tied the boat at a landing and walked up a path toward the church. The weather was warm and summery; the haystacks made the air heavy with fragrance in the midday heat.

The last stragglers had already entered when I approached the church; and I was in great doubt as to whether I should continue or go back. Just then a man came riding along on a big reddish-dun horse; he was drunk and in a jovial mood. With one hand he was firing blanks from a pistol and with the other he reined in the horse so hard that it reared.

I didn't know him, and he didn't know me; he asked, "Who might you be, my good man?" I evaded answering him and asked instead, "Have people come here for a funeral?" Then he let out a big guffaw and fired the pistol once again so that the smoke drifted all around us. "Funeral?" he laughed. "Funeral? You must be the only one in the entire parish who doesn't know that we have a visitation by the bishop! His eminence Bishop Sørenssen is probably standing at the altar already!"

"Who are you, then?" I asked. And he continued laughing: "Do you want to know who I am? I am the bishop's assistant. I'm the one who shaves him at night, pulls his nightshirt on him when he retires and helps him on with his pants when he gets up in the morning! I'm the one who empties his night pot and looks up the Bible text for him! Last Sunday I received communion from his own hand, but today I've drunk the wine without having the bread. Come here, have a drink with me!"

He got out a hip flask; and if I hadn't known it before, I knew now that I was awfully thirsty, from all the brandy that I had consumed and all the herring that I had eaten. I accepted his invitation and drank from the flask; when I wanted to give it back to him, the man said, "You just keep it; you may need more."

Having said that, he rode away, his horse's hooves thundering on the hard ground.

But I entered the church.

The church was filled all the way up to the choir. I remained standing in the center aisle. Here too it was very warm, even though the brick walls helped to cool the air, and I was seized by a fear and thought I would be choked from the great mass of people that pushed forward and pressed in on me from all sides. During the psalm sung prior to the sermon I got out the hip flask, got down on my knees to hide what I was doing, and emptied it completely.

Then everything evil seemed to vanish, as if through a miracle; an elated feeling of bliss filled my soul. The mighty walls and the arches of the building, the sunlight, which slanted in a golden streak across stone and wood, the altar painting and the pulpit, which was finely carved — everything seemed indescribably beautiful, and I began to sob loudly. The bishop had already commenced his sermon, but since I was crying and could not stop myself, and the people around me were growing uneasy, he said, "Why is that man crying? If his soul is in agony, then I will let him open his heart to me in private, but not until our divine service is over."

Then I shouted, "No, I am not crying over myself; I cry because of the sin of Judas, as it says in Holy Writ! For truly: not a soul should come to this house and believe that, thereby, he maintains eternal life, but the church and everything about it we ought to shun like the Devil himself. And the Lord's Supper is hardly for any of you who sit and stand here, no more than the horned goat in the pulpit is worthy of passing round the body and the blood of Our Lord with his shaggy hands! I have talked with the man who pulls his nightshirt on, so I ought to know!"

"Is that man drunk or insane? Take him out!" commanded the bishop.

"I am not insane, nor am I drunk!" I roared. "But I have had the bright light of truth lit in my heart! Secretly I am an adherent of the teachings of the Quakers, but in the open I am a drunkard and a heathen, bringing shame on every creature on God's earth."

The bishop repeated his command, "Take that man out of here!" And some of those standing nearest me got ready to grab me, but I shouted once more, "I came in here voluntarily; I am leaving voluntarily, and never again will I put my foot in the forecourt of Hell!" Thereupon I broke a mighty wind; the sound was meant to reach the bishop's ear and it most certainly must have reached its goal; I turned on my heel and walked toward the door with the people giving way on both sides. I had a vague recollection that years ago I had guided Sara Larsdatter down the center aisle of a church filled to overflowing.

When I got down in the field, I lay down in a haystack and went to sleep. I didn't wake up until the sun was low in the northwestern sky. Feeling dizzy and confused, I strolled down to the landing, where my boat was tied up.

The following day I was hard at work; I drove the men to the limit and spared myself least of all. The boat standing on the slipway was ready at the time we had promised, and I sailed it myself to Stavanger.

It was then the end of August. I wasn't so dull that I didn't realize that people were talking about my visit to Hesby church; the shipyard workers more than once suddenly stopped talking when I unexpectedly appeared among them, but I heard enough to know what it was all about.

I had expected to be called in to the pastor, or even worse things: to explain my conduct to the bishop. But so far no message had been received, and I began to hope that Their Reverences perhaps would let the entire episode pass without reprimanding me. But whatever was going to happen, it didn't bother me very much. What did prey upon my mind was that I had disgraced my friends the Quakers by making believe that I was one of them. Judging by what had been said at Gabriel Kielland's party, it seemed that they would not have a very sweet cup to drain as far as they themselves were concerned, and it would hardly taste sweeter when Cleng Peerson's bile was to be mixed with it.

For that reason I had planned to make a very quick trip to the city; I didn't look forward to meeting people I knew. Thus, it could hardly turn out worse than it did: the fellow who grabbed the hawser was none but Lars Larsen of Jeilane. I had sailed into the harbor in the evening, just at the time that he was on his way home from his own shipyard.

"We had expected to see you with us when Elias and Guri were married," he said.

"Oh, did you?" I replied. "I thought I did you a favor by staying away."

"You're referring to your antics in Hesby church?" he said.

"That too," I answered.

"You hurt yourself the most," he said.

"If so, it was well deserved," I replied. "But there's no reason for you nor for me to fret over it. But I haven't had a peaceful hour since. You people will have enough trouble without being charged with my foolishness."

"When Our Lord has kneaded you long enough in His trough and put you over the fire, you may become a good loaf of bread, Cleng," Lars said.

"I'm afraid that I'll be burned on the outside and be raw on the inside all my living days," I answered.

"Do you know a man by the name of Stephen Grellet?" he asked.

"I certainly do," I answered; "we were the only ones that survived a shipwreck west of Tenerife many years ago."

"Stephen Grellet is in town," Lars said. "He would like to meet you very much. He has been here about a week together with Sir William Allen. Enoch Jacobsen sailed to England to fetch them, and they have had talks with all the authorities in the city discussing our case, and they have been met with goodwill everywhere. They have also managed to get us a building where we can meet."

"You are looking at things more optimistically now, Lars?" I asked.

"In spite of that I am not very optimistic, Cleng," he said. "From the various districts we get reports that the Friends, and all who sympathize with them, suffer all kinds of evil. And this is only the beginning. I'll tell you what I think, Cleng: the bigwigs in Stavanger bow and scrape for the English gentlemen because they are well known and come from a foreign country. But as soon as both of them are at a safe distance, we will be facing harsher conditions than ever before. Stephen Grellet is of the opinion that unless a whole lot of things improve, we ought to consider going to America. But William Allen encourages everyone to stand his ground here, no matter what happens."

"Where can I meet Stephen?" I asked.

"Do you see that vessel over there?" he said and pointed to a ship in the harbor. "They are all on board now and in bed. Tomorrow morning they will leave for Kristiansand."

"Stephen Grellet must not leave before I have a chance to see him!" I said.

Lars thought it over a while; then he asked, "Where are you going after delivering your boat?"

"Everywhere and nowhere," I replied. "It's of no concern to me where I end up. I would prefer to go to sea again. But whatever I do, it will end in disaster."

"Why don't you accompany them to Kristiansand?" he asked. "There are many things that Stephen Grellet would like to discuss with you."

"Just as soon to Kristiansand as to any spot on this earth," I answered. "No one will ask about me after I've gone; I don't have to account to anyone for my whereabouts; no one rejoices when I return."

"You're taking the dog watch on your own ship of life, Cleng," he said. "But there will be a new dawn following this. Now I'll row out to the ship and make arrangements with the skipper. In the meantime, you make delivery of your boat. I'll row you on board the ship later this evening. Then you can surprise Stephen Grellet when he gets up on deck early tomorrow morning! They weigh anchor as soon as the sun rises."

Then we parted. I got in touch with the owner and had the boat delivered to him. But when he wanted to treat me to a drink, as was the custom, I said, "I have promised myself that liquor is not going to pass my lips anymore."

He smiled: "I've heard rumors that you've been drunker than anyone since Noah took off his clothes, and still you delivered the boat on time, Cleng. For that I thank you! But I will advise you not to make promises that you cannot keep."

"We'll talk about that later," I said.

Lars rowed me out to the ship, and I boarded about midnight. The sky was clear; there was no moon. The hull of the ship was sharply silhouetted against the gleaming, phosphorescent surface of the water and the boathouses beyond, and through the masts and yardarms we could see the northern lights sweeping like a banner above the horizon to the east.

A ladder was dropped down to us; the watchman was on the alert.

It took some time before I could fall asleep. I was thinking of the next day. Little did I know then that my voyage was not to terminate in Kristiansand, but that I was to visit both Copenhagen and Gothenburg before I once again set foot in Norway.

I woke at the crack of dawn but nevertheless felt very refreshed, and I was up on deck before any of the other passengers.

I don't have to tell you, Anne, that Stephen and I were both overjoyed when we saw each other again. But now I must tell what had happened in Stavanger during Sir William Allen's and Stephen Grellet's visit. Enoch Jacobsen told me about it while we were on the way to Kristiansand and the weather was sunny and calm.

The Twenty-fifth Tale

Since Enoch Jacobsen had returned from prison he had time and again sent letters to William Allen asking that he come to the aid of his brothers in the faith in Norway. Each time Sir William had answered that as soon as he had done with other important tasks he would come and visit them. But he added that such a trip ought to be thoroughly prepared for, and he had in mind not only to meet the groups of Friends in Norway but at the same time to make a journey for humanitarian purposes throughout the European continent.

A letter containing good news arrived at midsummer 1818: he was finally ready to set out on his journey. An address had already been sent to King Carl Johan containing an urgent appeal to him not to sanction any law that would cause his own subjects to be punished for their religious practices.

Sir William asked at the same time whether Enoch could come to Newcastle and accompany him to Norway, since there were many tasks to be prepared for and thought about, and time was short. He also wrote that after having visited Stavanger, Christiania, and possibly other cities in Norway, it was his intention to call on the king of the two brother nations in Stockholm, having been granted an audience, and from there he was to go to St. Petersburg and Moscow in order to meet again his old friend Tsar Alexander; from there he was continuing to Constantinople to plead the case of the slaves; and finally to Verona, where he had been invited to attend a congress of the crowned heads of Europe. The last stage of his journey back to England was to take him through Northern Italy and France. His purpose on this trip, then, was thus not only to help his brothers in Norway but also in other places where a man's thoughts were not unfettered and where there was no freedom of conscience and belief; he also wanted to relieve and improve the lot of those who where persecuted and to speak up for the oppressed. In this work he was to be assisted by his brother in the faith and traveling companion, Stephen Grellet.

This is about what he said in his letters.

Enoch boarded the first ship from Christiania for England, and nothing untoward happened neither during the westward voyage nor on the return trip. Early one morning they caught sight of land south of the island of Eigerøy. There is probably no more barren area along the entire Norwegian coast south of Finnmark, and both traveling gentlemen were appalled when they could see nothing but bare rocks and cliffs; they asked where people could possibly live in a country that looked like that.

"Many cozy homes lie sheltered inland beyond those barren shores," Enoch explained; "yes, even a flourishing town."

"But there's not a tree or a green blade of grass to be seen," said Sir William.

Enoch said no more; he realized that they felt disappointed with the country to which they had come.

By lunchtime they had reached Tananger where the pilot came on board. He had his two sons with him as pilot apprentices, and Enoch began a conversation with them.

The pilot was a friendly and talkative man, and when Enoch told him that he was a Quaker, as were also the two foreigners who were with him, the pilot said that he also was yearning for the grace of God and felt attracted to the faith of the Haugeans. Both John Haugvaldstad and others had preached the gospel in Tananger, but he felt he greatly missed something in life since he didn't have the opportunity to read the Bible.

"If I could only buy a Bible," he said and confided to Enoch that among all the families that gathered for devotions and prayers in various homes, there was only one who owned Holy Scripture, and this volume had time and again almost become the object of conflict and disagreement, for everyone wanted to borrow it and keep it as long as possible. In the end they had to draw lots and let the Bible circulate among them. "But it has not yet come to my house," said the pilot.

Enoch was moved when he heard this, and he spoke in private with his two traveling companions and told them what the pilot had said. They decided to give him a Bible right then and there, and when they came over to him and placed the Bible in his hands he burst out crying.

His two sons were working somewhere else on the ship when this happened, and when they saw that their father had received a Bible, the oldest walked over to Enoch and his companions and fervently begged that he also be given one, for he was soon to get married. "I want to pay for it, I have enough money," he said.

Enoch replied, "We have only a few Bibles with us, but many New Testaments, and you shall have one of them, and when you have read it, you must get your neighbors together and read it aloud to them." The boy answered, "That's just what I had in mind." And when he had received the books, he hurried over to his father, and they compared the books, bindings, size, and print, and they both found Bible passages which they knew and became so absorbed in this that the skipper had to interrupt to ask the pilot whether they were on the right course.

The Bibles as well as the New Testaments were in the Danish language but had been printed in England, if I'm not greatly mistaken.

When the ship had rounded Tungenes, nature suddenly turned gentle and beautiful. Both William Allen and Stephen Grellet began to praise the natural beauty before their eyes and said that they would never have believed that such an oasis could be located so close to the desert-like coast they had just passed.

Enoch rejoiced at their words. To him the sight of Stavanger from the sea was an undiluted pleasure; he had not come sailing in from the seaward side since he had returned from prison. But it was indeed the most beautiful part of the year. The fields were turning green again following the haying, and the grain was taking on the first tinge of yellow. There was a certain tang in the air, for the wind blew out from shore, warm like a wind in more southerly regions; and along the shores swam ducks and eider ducks, and small children were bathing in the shallow inlets. The travelers grew even more enthusiastic — they called the country a paradisiacal idyll, and Enoch let himself be carried away and started to describe the marvelously beautiful places lying further away but not visible from the seaward approaches to Stavanger: fertile islands and majestic mountains.

The visitors were also impressed by Stavanger — the town does look its best from the seaward side — , and besides, it had indeed begun to flourish during the last few years. The period of prosperity had set its mark on Stavanger as it had on all the coastal towns in southern

Norway; new warehouses had been built, in addition to a great number of elegant private homes.

But they were most of all impressed with the cathedral. They said that it compared well with cathedrals in their own cities.

When the ship had cast anchor, the customs officers came on board, as did the son of Agent Kielland. When he heard that there was a Stavanger citizen on board in the company of two prominent Englishmen, he first turned to Enoch and bade him a hearty welcome, and then asked him who the two foreigners were and for what purpose they had come to Norway. Then he spoke to them in English and told them how happy he was to be able to welcome them to Norway. He had a near perfect command of their mother tongue; they were greatly astonished and asked whether every Norwegian was as well versed in foreign languages as in his own. This seemed very strange to them, they said jokingly, because they were not able to comprehend the least bit of the language of the Norwegians; to their ears it sounded like waves rolling against the shore and mountains caving in, and they thought it quite miraculous that a human tongue could be made to utter sounds like that.

Young Kielland looked upon all this as compliments, which actually had been the intention, and he spoke to the customs officers and asked them to speed up the examination of the two gentlemen's baggage. Then he walked straight up to Pharmacist Henrik Zetlitz, who also was the owner of an inn. Many people thought it to be even better than those run by Mrs. Faust and Thore Huusebøe. Young Kielland thought that the two English gentlemen would prefer the reserved and at the same time very friendly ways of the pharmacist to Mrs. Faust's bluffness and banter. He had taken note of the lean features of the two gentlemen, — the evidence of an abstemious life.

After having eaten at the pharmacist's sumptuous table and slept in the inn's soft beds, Allen and Grellet went for a walk in the city's environs. Enoch was waiting for them when they returned, and they continued to extol the beauty of the country. They said that to their surprise they had found that the air in these northern latitudes was just as mild and pleasant as that along the coasts of Cornwall.

This cheered Enoch up still more, and when they mentioned that they would like to pay the bailiff a visit the next day, if it was convenient to him, Enoch ran at once to the younger Kielland, who already had shown them so much courtesy, and asked him if he would be kind enough to arrange for an appointment. In the afternoon they received a note on which Bailiff Løwold assured them that he would be greatly honored if they were to come to his office the next morning at ten.

Bailiff Løwold was well acquainted with the Quakers' peculiar manner and dress, and he showed no surprise when his three guests stepped into the room without taking off their hats. He bid them welcome in a friendly and dignified manner, while letting them know how highly he thought of William Allen's energetic work in the cause of abolition of slavery, nor did he neglect to make a few laudatory remarks about the Swedish monarch and the Russian Tsar and his family.

Enoch served as an interpreter on this occasion and on all others when necessary; the bailiff did not know much English. Sir William asked among other things about whether there was capital punishment in Norway — and inserted in the way of complaint before the other was able to reply, that in England the judges were quick to pronounce a death sentence even for minor offences. Løwold replied that during his tenure in office — the last twenty-five years — not one person in Stavanger had had to atone with his life for a crime. He said that thefts did occur, but that this crime must be viewed more as a consequence of idleness than of hunger and need, and he added that people who had committed less serious misdemeanors were often put in custody in their own homes and had to give their word of honor that they would not try to escape. In Norway capital punishment was only imposed in cases of murder or high treason.

Sir William asked whether the bailiff looked upon it as an offense vis-à-vis the authorities whenever the Quakers in their religious practice had to heed the voice of their conscience, even if they found it necessary in the process to infringe on the letter of the civil or the ecclesiastical law, and whether he would consider that to be treason. Løwold answered with some vehemence, "Not at all, gentlemen, for it is below a man's dignity to make a compromise with his conscience, and I myself am opposed to all spiritual coercion. But in his work a government official will often have to make difficult decisions, and then the question is in truth to give to God that which is God's and to Caesar what is due him."

"But doesn't making that distinction bring you anguish sometimes?" asked Sir William. Bailiff Løwold cleared his throat twice and said, "Most certainly, my dear sir, most certainly."

They dropped the subject, and the bailiff, with a touch of reserve to his still friendly manner, said good-bye to them.

Thereupon they went together to Dean Støren, where the young pastor Alexander Lunge was present. The dean greeted them very cordially, and when they early in their conversation happened to mention the pilot from Tananger who had received a Bible with great eagerness and joy, Dean Støren had to admit that there was a great lack of Bibles in the entire district.

"In all of Stavanger there are only about fifty Bibles," he said, "and the city has today about five hundred families. Some time ago people were given the opportunity to order Bibles, and a great number of people signed up. Some people even paid cash when they ordered, but not one copy has so far arrived from the so-called Bible Society in Christiania."

Stephen Grellet told him that they were now on their way to the capital and that they intended to bring this question up. On hearing this, the old dean expressed great pleasure.

Pastor Lunge mentioned that he didn't own a copy of Holy Writ either but had to borrow the dean's Bible when he was going to give a sermon. Sir William promised to send him a copy from the ship.

The great warmth which the two ecclesiastics had shown cooled a bit, however, when Allen and Grellet began to speak about the conditions under which their brothers in the faith lived and worshiped in Stavanger. First the dean called attention to my censurable behavior in Hesby church; he had been told about it when Bishop Sørenssen had visited Stavanger. Enoch objected and pointed out that I did not belong to the Society of Friends, that in my spiritual agony I had sought the aid of Elias Tastad but had not up to now received the light of the Holy Spirit in a purified heart.

To this the dean replied, "I notice that these British gentlemen in every way behave according to their high estate and as befits god-fearing people, but it is not always so with regard to the Norwegian Quakers, and I never noticed any anguish of soul in Cleng Peerson when he a few months ago was a guest at the welcoming party arranged by Agent Kielland for our dear Pastor Lunge. As far as a virtuous and orderly life is concerned, we have a recently documented example which should serve as a warning to all pious and right-minded people; it concerns the leader and spiritual head of the dissenters, the man we just spoke of, Elias Tastad. He is living with a woman without having been legally wed, and that is an offense which in our country is deemed to be contrary to all propriety and decency. I will not deny that this man, as well as many others who join the congregation of the Quakers here in Stavanger, are confused in their beliefs and in their conscience, and not in that alone: also in their mind and in their will. Yes, I fear that some of them are even rather mad, being of the opinion that they can disregard every ecclesiastical or secular law just by saying: 'I am a Quaker! I do as I like!' It is true that we have freedom of opinion in this country — we have gained our national independence and all citizens possess their unabridged rights — but that doesn't mean that they have freedom to revolt, create confusion, and commit blasphemy! Both the church and the state must have the right to defend themselves against such conditions.''

The dean had worked himself up, and his face was flushed. He pulled out a handkerchief and wiped his perspiring forehead. Sir William did not seize the opportunity to reply, and the dean continued, in a more gentle vein:

"Nevertheless I am convinced that those who thus go astray will not feel encouraged anew to continue along the same errant path after you gentlemen have made them listen to reason. For I believe that they have only half understood the teachings they were exposed to in England, and with their penchant for what is new and different they have overlooked its noble and elevated principles.''

William Allen replied courteously that he would thoroughly investigate these circumstances and that he would provide guidance wherever there had been lapses or errors. "However, I will not fail to mention," he said, "that in England large and widely recognized dissenting churches have administered the Gospel and the sacraments according to their own rituals and thereupon have been satisfied with doing that, instead of, as would have been more correct, paying greater attention to the needs of human souls that are not fulfilled by pictures and signs. But that human being whose life is in accord with his God and his conscience, will not have any doubts as regards questions of faith and will be willing to sacrifice his life if that becomes necessary.''

Grellet and Allen discussed this matter in some detail and used as examples the lives and works of such men as George Fox, John Bunyan, and William Penn. Dean Støren said that he had read *The Pilgrim's Progress* and that the book had moved him deeply. The conversation continued in a friendly spirit, and they bade one another farewell with a sense of mutual understanding and sympathy.

The next few days the two Britons had several meetings with Friends and their sympathizers. First they visited Lars Larsen of Jeilane. Together with Lars and Sara and a fisherman who was lodging with them as well as a servant girl who worked for one of the wealthy families in town, they sat waiting for the Spirit to come to them, and they did not wait in vain.

From there they went to Enoch's sister who lived in another part of town, and together with her husband and their children they held another meeting, at which also the Spirit came to them and touched their hearts.

The following day there was still another meeting, this time in the home of Elias Tastad. Elias had spent most of the day telling people about the meeting. He had walked from door to door, and he had rowed out to the islands lying just outside Stavanger. When everybody had arrived, his house was completely filled.

The two Englishmen had requested that the pastors in Stavanger also be invited, but only Lunge showed up.

The Friends quietly waited for the arrival of the Spirit, and after a while first one, then another began to tremble, and they spoke with a fervor that made the listeners weep; only Pastor Lunge remained impassive and silent.

William Allen then spoke, and Stephen Grellet after him; and Lunge said later that he could not at all disapprove of their conduct; it was marked by thoughtfulness and dignity.

When the meeting was over Alexander Lunge said good-bye to them in a very friendly manner, and Enoch interpreted what he said; he had also served as interpreter for Lunge during the speeches of the two Englishmen, for the minister's knowledge of English was not very great.

Most of the people left when the meeting was over, but those who stayed behind were told that it would be useful to establish a regular society based on Quaker principles but to some extent adapted to local conditions.

It was from the time of this meeting that the Quakers in Stavanger emerged as a separate congregation.

Another important matter was also discussed. Both Grellet and Allen had learned about the troubles that the Friends had already had, and Grellet said that if things did not change for the better, he would recommend that they consider emigrating to a country where there was religious freedom, preferably North America.

William Allen did not share Grellet's views on this point: he was of the opinion that the Friends ought to stand fast and patiently put up with all insults and harassments. For neither one had been deceived by the gracious behavior of the ecclesiastical and other officials.

Elias Tastad, who had gone through the greatest trials, agreed with Sir William, while Lars Larsen of Jeilane, Johannes Stene, and Ole Franck were inclined to favor the idea of emigration.

It was also suggested that possibly someone might be sent ahead to

America to investigate conditions there. Some of the Friends had then mentioned my name, both because I had been faithful to them, they said, and also because I had traveled far and wide in the world and could make myself understood in several languages. But others were of the opinion that I was an unstable fellow and subject to whims and moods.

Allen and Grellet were also invited to dinner by Agent Kielland together with many of the city's notables. Being foreign visitors, the two gentlemen had the places of honor at the right and left side of Gabriel Kielland. His daughter acted as hostess, and the Englishmen were greatly impressed when they found out that the entire Kielland family knew English and spoke the language fluently.

In the course of the conversation Mr. Kielland let the guests of honor know that he had been acquainted for a long time with the religious principles of the Friends and had even attended one of their meetings in London. This came as a surprise to many of the guests, since his many risqué stories had given them the impression that he preferred other kinds of company when he was abroad.

The question of the lack of Bibles was also discussed at the party, and Dean Støren said that even if he had a thousand Bibles he was quite certain that he could sell them within a very short time, and at the full price. They discussed this further and agreed that the Bible Society in Christiania be asked to send them as many Bibles and New Testaments as possible. The Society was also to be asked that one-third of these were to be sent free of charge, for the use of the poor, one-third at half price, and one-third at the ordinary sales price.

On this occasion, too, Pastor Lunge received the Bible that he had been promised; similarly, Sir William turned over to the dean a few Bibles and New Testaments to be given out to the poor and pious members of his congregation.

But when all this had been taken care of, Agent Kielland, as so often before, proved to have a surprise up his sleeve. He showed the guests an ancient and very beautiful edition of Holy Scripture, which was a part of his private library, a translation into Danish in several volumes. Everyone leafed through it and admired it. Thereupon Agent Kielland made a very courteous request of the two Britons that they take it with them and present it to the Bible Society in Christiania as a token of gratitude.

A sigh was heard from the entire assemblage; the two ministers sighed most audibly.

But other topics were also discussed in Kielland's home that evening.

Stephen Grellet said that in England one would rarely see fields of oats as luxuriant as those in Norway; but he was surprised that they raised such a small quantity of potatoes. To that Kielland replied that he had encouraged the cultivation of this new vegetable, but the common people were unfortunately full of prejudices and not willing to learn. Still, he was certain that there would be a change for the better within some years.

The Englishmen asked him to continue to exert his great influence for good, since they, like him, believed it would bring results in years to come.

Apart from that, they did a lot of things that attracted favorable attention during the week or so they stayed in the city. Accompanied by Enoch Jacobsen they visited schools as well as the prison. In the schools, William Allen told the children about his own fatherland beyond the North Sea, and Grellet spoke about North America with its cities and wide plains and its many wild animals. They comforted the prisoners in the jail and they admonished them to conduct themselves well and look forward to the termination of their stay and then become children of God. They told the city officials that they found the schools to be good and the prison conditions less harsh than in England.

While they were staying in Stavanger the news of their presence spread throughout the city and the surrounding districts, and when they, on a Sunday evening, held their last meeting in a large hall rented for the purpose, hundreds of people showed up and filled the room and also the vestibule and the stairway. On this occasion, guided by the Spirit, Stephen Grellet made a powerful speech, and when he had finished talking, many people pressed forward to shake the hands of the two foreign visitors.

All this had happened just before I arrived, and the same evening that I had sailed the new boat from the Talgje shipyard into the harbor at Stavanger, a crowd of people had accompanied the two Englishmen through the city and down to their ship.

It was during the voyage to Kristiansand that Enoch Jacobsen told me most of what I have just written down. But I also talked with my friend Stephen Grellet, and he asked whether I might consider making a trip to America, as had already been suggested among the Friends. Even though I didn't know about the objections that had been raised, I answered that the Friends would certainly regard me as unfit, and rightfully so.

Then Stephen asked, "Where are you going now, Cleng?"

I answered, "I'm on the run, like Jonah of old; I have rebelled against the Lord."

In a mixture of seriousness and jesting he said, "Where are you planning to go? Not to Nineveh, I hope?"

"I'm traveling about as if I am blind," I replied. "But my intention was to debark in Kristiansand. That's as good a place as any."

Then he said, "You go ahead and do as you've planned: leave the ship in Kristiansand. But there you can easily get a ship to take you to Gothenburg or to Copenhagen or Hamburg. From these cities there are frequent sailings to America. You will do the right thing, and a smart thing too, if you investigate conditions over there and go back to the Friends in Stavanger and give them the information they need. For neither Sir William nor I have much confidence in the glib tongues of the government officials; we fear that our brothers in the faith are going to suffer new and even greater harassments. Some day they may even be driven out of the country by force, and then they will surely thank you if you show them a place where they can go."

We parted in Kristiansand, and only two days later I was on a ship bound for Copenhagen.

There is not much to tell about this voyage. I will only mention that all knowledgeable people in Denmark's capital pointed out that Gothenburg would be the most convenient port of embarkation for Norwegian emigrants. For that reason I continued on to Gothenburg, and in this flourishing Swedish seaport I spoke with several shipowners who had ships calling at American ports. Some of them thought they could accommodate as many as fifty passengers, and I answered that would be sufficient under any circumstances.

Some time later I journeyed back to Stavanger, and even though not everything that I could report was very promising, the Quakers began to discuss in private the possibility of emigration. Other circumstances helped to keep the issue alive: in 1819 Ole Franck got married after the Quaker fashion, as Elias Tastad had done, and he too was called before the dean and reprimanded, but he replied that Elias and Guri had been turned away when they had gone to see the clergy in Stavanger and had asked to be married in church.

Støren became very angry when he heard that and said that they had not been in touch with him. But Old Franck, counting on his fingers, gave the names of ministers that they had begged and implored and was about to start on the fingers of his other hand, when the dean rose, red in his face, and pointed to the door.

This occurrence, as well as many others, made the thought of leaving ripen in our minds. But it was one specific event that became decisive, and I will soon tell you about it, Anne.

The Twenty-sixth Tale

Shortly after my return from Gothenburg I visited Elias and Guri for
the first time since they had got married. Elias was working in the field
when I came, but she called him in right away.

In high spirits she said, "Now we'll both put on our very finest attire,
Elias, so that Uncle Cleng can see how we looked on our big day — so
that you can see what a fine fellow I have for a husband," she said,
smiling and gently stroking his hair.

They went into their little bedroom and came back in the way they
had been dressed for their wedding. Her cheeks and neck were flushed,
having the tinge of a rose petal. She took both my hands in hers and
said, "Come on into the parlor, Uncle Cleng," — she was the first one
to call me "uncle," Anne — "and look at all that we have been given
and how beautiful it is." She showed me their wedding gifts, and she
pointed at the chest of drawers and a table on which there were white
napkins and flower vases.

"I would never have believed that I would ever have things as nice as
this," she said, and her face was shining like a light toward me. "The
house I grew up in had the chopping block in the kitchen, and we
shoveled the dirt off the floor every Christmas and Easter."

When we had been sitting talking a little while, she went into the
kitchen, and she shortly returned with a plate with newly baked white

bread and a little wooden tray with three cups of steaming tea; but just as she placed it before me she burst out crying.

I tried to pass it off as a joke and said to her, "Guri, dear, are you crying because I'm going to drink all your tea?"

"Oh no, Uncle Cleng," she sobbed; "I'm only thinking of how everything has changed since the time my brother and I came to this part of the country. When we were living in the houseboat at Nedstrand I knew what Aunt Sara had gone through for our sake, and I was the unhappiest child on God's green earth. And before that we had been wandering from door to door, with no money and no one to look after us. But you helped us, Uncle Cleng; not even a real father would have taken better care of us than you did."

Feeling a deep sense of shame, I thought of the reason why I had crawled on board the houseboat that night, drunk and reckless. I said to her, "I have never taken as good care of you as you deserved, Guri." But she replied, "Without you I would probably still have been a good-for-nothing, and I wouldn't have met Elias either. No, I'll never be able to thank you enough!" She smiled through her tears, "And now you're sitting here with me, and I can have the great pleasure of treating you to food and drink. How good God must be, who held His hand over poor Guri from Telemark!"

About a year after the wedding Elias and Guri were richly blessed in their marriage. They had twins, two beautiful girls, and they named them Siri and Petra, but they didn't have them baptized. Elias expected to be reprimanded by the authorities, but when nothing happened both he and the other Friends hoped for a while that conditions had improved.

They were to be bitterly disappointed. Their real ordeal, however, did not start until the pioneers had emigrated, but all this will be dealt with later in our story.

What happened to Elias and Guri during the summer of 1821, which I shall relate now, was only a foretaste of the many evil things that later were to befall the little Quaker congregation.

During July and August that year there was a measles epidemic in Stavanger and the surrounding countryside. The disease was usually accompanied by an inflammation that went from the ears to the brain and in most cases led to death. It ravaged the town to such an extent that on the average every tenth family lost a child; more than fifty children died. This happened during the late summer when the harvest was brought in; the grain fields gave such a yield that year that few

people could recollect anything like it. But wherever the farmer worked
with his sickle, the Grim Reaper used his scythe; and the church bells
pealed more often than the dinner bell.

Elias's and Guri's two daughters also caught the disease. Their
parents watched over them six nights, but it happened in their case as
in so many others that the sickness attacked the brain. The town physician knew no remedy for it, and a wise woman whom they asked for advice was also unable to help them.

When the children had been dressed in linen and had been laid out,
Elias went to see Dean Støren and asked that they be buried in the city
cemetery, but without any interment ceremonies and singing of
hymns.

"If they are to rest in the church plot, they must rest there according
to church regulations," Dean Støren replied.

But since he knew that Elias had had a bad year in many ways — two
of his cows had suddenly died and he had lost his boat and fishing gear
in a storm — he thought to himself, "Perhaps he finds it hard to pay
the stipulated fee," and he said, "This won't cost you anything, Elias
Tastad, I shall forget all about the price involved."

But this made Elias angry. He answered, "You must have buried
many corpses during the last few weeks and you must look forward to
taking care of many more since you can be so magnanimous toward
me. But if I thought it was right to give my children the kind of funeral
you recommend, then I would take the shirt off my back and the shoes
off my feet in order to give the dean his due. Don't you understand yet
that I consider the sprinkling of earth and the singing of hymns and the
reading of a ritual to be empty gestures and that it is merely for the
sake of my conscience that I reject your offer?"

The dean liked Elias's audacity; he was not used to being talked to
like that by the common people. But at the same time he felt very indignant because of Elias's reproaches, and he replied, "If you presume
to act contrary to the regulations of the church, we will have a talk
about that later, Elias Tastad."

"That I shall do with a light heart," Elias answered, and he mentioned an old law to the effect that persons belonging to other persuasions than the Lutheran faith had the right to be buried without any
ritual or ceremony.

The dean stood up and said, "Are you going to teach me
ecclesiastical law, Elias Tastad?"

"Yes," Elias replied, "since the dean doesn't seem to know it."

Having said that, he turned, left the room, and went home. Then he and Guri got the house ready for the first burial in Stavanger to take place outside the walls of the cemetery, as far as anyone knew. It was true that suicides and those who had committed major crimes had been denied consecrated ground, but customarily they had been buried very quietly. Elias, on the other hand, intended to arrange a burial that everyone would remember.

That is what did happen, but in another way than anyone could have imagined.

When Elias told Guri what the dean had said, she was beside herself and begged him to accept the dean's offer for her sake. But Elias answered, "No, not even if an angel from Heaven came down and asked me to change my mind." Guri asked, "Where, then, do you intend to have our children buried, Elias?" And he said, "You know I have a small piece of property at Våland. That is the spot I have selected for their graves. Our little ones won't be alone for very long."

Then he assembled some planks and nailed together a coffin that was large enough for both girls, and he placed them side by side, just as they previously had shared the same bed.

Before they had become ill, they had been lovely children — they resembled their mother — but now they had gray splotches all over their faces, just as everyone did who died that summer. People had begun to murmur about epidemics and plagues.

But wherever fear takes hold and terror strikes, as so often when the rod of the Almighty punishes mankind, people do not bow down in repentance but rather take to all kinds of wild behavior. During those warm and sunny days, when sorrow was a visitor in so many homes, there was as much drinking and carousing in Stavanger as during the merriest of fairs.

Then the rumor spread that Elias Tastad was going to bury his children in his own field, without any service, and the day and the hour were made known.

Superstitious people said that the epidemic ravaging the town was a punishment that the Almighty had sent because of the Quakers, since they had revolted against the customs of the Church and the secular laws. The day that the two little ones were to be buried, a multitude of people, including some of the town's worst riffraff, gathered outside Elias Tastad's house. They shouted that he was responsible for the calamity that had descended on the town.

Guri clung to him and wailed, "Do you hear what they're shouting, Elias? But it is not your fault; it is mine! I should never have married you, for I have never fully shared the faith that is yours."

"This is not the time to talk about these things," Elias replied; he felt intensely sorry for her, but she didn't realize it.

In her despair she walked down into the cellar and emptied a bottle of brandy and immediately became greatly intoxicated. Not until the time that the Friends who had gathered upstairs were to accompany the parents and the relatives to the burial spot, did she emerge, and she could hardly stand on her feet. She embraced one after the other, and she laughed and cried and used blasphemous language about God and men.

She and Elias had decided that they were to carry the coffin themselves, but Lars Larsen and Ole Franck decided to take over. Right behind them walked Elias; he was supporting his inebriated wife. Then came all the Friends who had come to attend, about twenty people in all.

Some of the rabble that were following behind started to sing an indecent song, and many others joined in. Guri, too, chimed in, and she unbuttoned the front of her dress, got out a hip flask, and toasted everyone, laughing, yelling, and gesticulating. Some of the mob spat at her, put out their tongues, and shouted, "There you can see what kind of people the Quakers are!" While Guri was reeling about she stumbled and fell, but Elias pulled her gently to her feet; he dusted off her clothes and put her hair in place; once again he put his arm in hers and supported her on the way to the burial place.

Some of the onlookers also recognized me, and one of them shouted, "There's the fellow who desecrated the Hesby church!" — while others roared with laughter, "No, he is Mrs. Sælinger's gelding!"

The mob followed us all the way, and when the people in the houses along the road saw the procession, they too ran out and joined it.

When the two children had been interred, Guri regained her senses and realized what was happening. She asked Elias to accompany her over to the edge of the grave, and when she saw the coffin she sobbed and wailed.

But some of the people set off firecrackers, others shouted hurrah and were dancing; an accidental onlooker would indeed have thought that a merry festival was going on.

We were supposed to come together in Elias's and Guri's home afterwards, but most of those who had been invited probably thought that due to her condition it was best to take their leave now. When Elias got wind of that he unobtrusively let those Friends who were there know that he would very much like to see them at his house in the evening. This was about three o'clock in the afternoon.

Many of those who were to travel with the *Restauration* across the ocean were there that evening, and they talked more seriously than ever before of pulling up stakes and settling in America. Still, it is small wonder that we didn't do much talking that night; our sorrow had bereft us of all joy and gaiety.

Lars Larsen of Jeilane was the one who up to now had been most eager to go to America. And now he had special reason that no one knew about; he had fallen in love with a girl by the name of Martha Georgiana Pedersdatter. After having witnessed all the evil that had happened in connection with the funeral, he decided that she was not to live under such conditions in the future, that is, if she would accept his proposal.

It was Lars who once again turned the conversation to the topic of emigration. He said to Elias, "Now that you have seen what can happen here, would you now consider coming along to America?"

"Here I'll stay even if the Evil One himself makes his home in the town," Elias Tastad replied.

"That he's already done," said Lars.

"In that case I would rather stand at the threshold of Hell during my earthly life than cross it in the afterlife," Elias answered. "But it is far from me to reproach anyone who is thinking of leaving, and I will help all I can to get each and every one on board ship when the time comes."

Lars reverted to the subject he had mentioned previously: "We ought to send a man ahead to investigate the country and find out what it can offer us. I maintain that no one we know is better suited for that task than Cleng."

Several agreed with him, while others remained silent.

I said, "The Lord chose men like Moses and Aaron to lead the people of Israel through the desert to the Promised Land. I am the only one among you who is unworthy."

I got up to leave; but they all asked me to stay, and when Lars took me by the arm, I sat down on a stool by the stove, turned my back on them, and hid my face in my hands.

"It must be you," he emphasized.

"There's only one thing I ask," I said; "that you can forgive the shame that I've brought on the Friends. Then I will leave the country and never come back."

Lars was unyielding: "Suppose you get a good man to accompany you to America?" he said, and turned to the assembled mourners: "Is anyone interested in going with Cleng to America?"

"Well, *I* am," was heard from one of those present; his name was Knud Eide.

Knud Eide was a carpenter in town. We had only met a few times but I liked him from the beginning. He was a calm and thoughtful fellow, possessing characteristics that I greatly lacked. Therefore I said, "You would be the right man for the task, Knud." But he answered, "Only together with you, Cleng, would I consider going. You have traveled farther than anyone we know, and you know the language."

Once again the others concurred, but I gave them no promise. All the same, I thought to myself, "If I just once could show the Friends that I was worthy of their trust."

Other matters were also discussed that evening. It was getting late, and most of the people went home, but a few stayed behind. Then Lars Larsen felt an inner urge that we must conclude the day with a silent meeting.

We all sat silent, for a half hour or perhaps longer. Guri Olsdatter was the first to speak; her voice shook when she said, "The Spirit commands me."

Everyone knew that she had a hangover, and I felt ill at ease for her sake; from my own experience I know only too well what one might think of doing in such a state. But Elias said calmly, "Speak up, Guri."

She rose to her feet and said, "Forgive me for opening my mouth, for I have brought shame on you all and not least on you, Elias; I am the most lowly of all of God's little Friends." And she burst into tears, but Elias got up and held her close, and she calmed down.

Then he asked, "What is the Spirit saying, Guri?"

She replied, "This is the Spirit's voice in me: that I shall invoke the Lord's blessing on Cleng Peerson."

And Lars said, "And I heard it say the same."

But I got up to leave: "I am not the kind of man who deserves to be blessed."

Then Elias said, "A blessing is not given for merit, but through God's mercy."

Lars asked again, "Are you willing to go to America, Cleng?"

And I answered, "Before, I have always gone wherever I fancied without giving a thought to whether I was being blessed or cursed."

I was going to say more but couldn't utter another word.

"Then you will enter into the service of the Lord, Cleng?" asked Lars.

I replied, "In Holy Writ I have read about the Persian King Cyrus that he was called the servant of the Lord, even though he was a heathen in the view of Israel. And if the Lord practices the custom of selecting those who are unworthy, then His will must be done one more time."

Then Guri Olsdatter stepped up and placed her hands on my head. I fell to my knees, and everyone present formed a ring around me. Guri invoked the Blessing of Aaron over me and added these words from the Prophet Isaiah, "When thou passest through the waters, I will be with thee; and through the rivers, they shall not overflow thee: when thou walkest through the fire, thou shalt not be burned; for I am the Lord thy God, the Holy One of Israel, thy Saviour: I gave Egypt for thy ransom, Ethiopia and Seba for thee."

But when I looked up again, I saw Sara Larsdatter standing near me, and our eyes met. She too had placed her hands on my head, and in her face shone the same brightness I had seen that morning when the fog lifted from the boat, when we had set out on our journey to Røldal church.

Summer has come to Bosque County. Today is the Fourth of July and people are celebrating, but I myself have not been much out of the house; I can't stand the heat as well as I used to.

I have also gotten to be a slow writer; perspiration drips from my hand onto the paper, and the ink makes splotches. It is about time that I stop writing. But if Providence grants me renewed strength this fall and winter, then I will take up my pen again. For most of the story still remains to be told.

Forgive me, Anne, if perhaps you think that you have encountered too many people and names in my story, and some of them you have hardly learned to know. But we shall meet them again, many of them in fact. Some of them, however, will gradually leave the story, among them Elias Tastad.

You ask how he fared later in life?

Already on the day of the burial that I have just told about, he was ordered to come before the dean. After Støren had reprimanded him severely, Elias, without having been asked to do so, reported to the civilian authorities. He was immediately indicted, but the matter had not yet come before the court when the news spread that Ole Franck had died. Elias buried his friend in the same spot where he had given his twins their final resting place. This time, too, he had at once refused any offer of hymn singing without charge and the sprinkling of earth on the coffin. This happened in 1822; by then Knud Eide and I had been across the ocean for quite some time.

The case was argued in the lower court, which acquitted Elias; the court affirmed that the law not only gives dissenters the *right* to bury their dead without any ceremonies, but it even prescribed that that's the way it should be. But the judgment was appealed to the appellate court, where a new verdict was delivered, and it went something like this: "Elias Tastad is ordered within a certain date to exhume from the unconsecrated earth the bodies of his dead children so that they can be buried in the proper place and with the ceremonies fixed by statute. If he still hesitates and does not carry out what he has been enjoined to do, within the period determined, he is ordered to pay a fine of five dalers for each day that this task is left unperformed."

But Elias refused to dig up the earthly remains of his children. When the sentence was passed, it was almost two years since they had died.

Elias had had many setbacks during this time. He had stood surety for a friend of his who later went bankrupt. Thus, he lost the farm at Tastad; he and his family moved to a little cabin at Våland, close by the piece of property that served as a burial ground.

Men from the county governor and the bailiff came to his cabin for the purpose of obtaining some of his property in lieu of the unpaid fine. Elias opened the door wide and told them, "Here is my house and my possessions; take what you think is worth the trouble to carry away."

The fines by that time had run into a sizable sum; the men looked around in the parlor and then walked away without executing the sentence, for the house was gray with poverty and there was nothing to take.

When it had been decided that Knud Eide and I were to make a trip to America via Gothenburg in September, 1821, I went back to Tysvær to say good-bye to my mother.

"Such a long journey you have never made before, Cleng," she said. "It's a lucky man who can set out on a voyage. You might not know it, but my father, the pastor, wanted me to get married to a skipper. He was a fine-looking young man, and if I hadn't already met your father, I might have taken the other one — even though I didn't love him — just in order to hear news from the wide world every time he came home!"

She had been walking back and forth, between the kitchen and the parlor, preparing our meal. She sat down on the bench facing me: "But at times it has seemed to me, Cleng, that when I married your father I set out on a more hazardous journey. Many people have been of the opinion that I received little benefit from joining my life to a man who was sick and in straitened circumstances. But I tried to sustain a dream within him and keep alive a yearning, and at times I think that is the reason he was able to look forward to a great freedom before he died. If that is so, I wouldn't exchange the house here at Hesthammer with the proudest ship and the longest voyage. But even so, I'm still dreaming about taut sails and the wide open ocean, even at my age."

I embraced her, and she pressed her face against my shoulder. Our eyes met again, and I noticed that her glance was bright and clear. Age had woven its pattern of lines in her face, but there were none of the furrows that are caused by bitterness and sorrow.

I said to her, "That yearning for a great freedom you implanted in me, too, Mother."

"I shall never forget," she resumed her musings, "the time you set out on your first journey and wanted to get to the place where the sun was rising, without oars and without sail. Or the time you left on your pilgrimage with Sara Larsdatter. And later on, every time you left home, I thought to myself: I can walk with him as far as the bridge that separates the Hesthammer property from Falkeid's, or I can accompany him to Kårstø and watch him set sail. He is just like the rapids in the river; they seek the ocean and become one with the infinite that touches the shores all over the world. But I — I am the wind that fills his sail; it will take him as far as my longing can go. And it can go far, Cleng! Good luck on your voyage! It may be that God will let us live until we see each other again. And if I should be gone by the time you come back, then sit down by the graveside and tell me what you have seen and heard. There's never been a great distance between us, Cleng, not even when you were on the other side of the earth. And it is my belief that the distance between heaven and earth may very well be shorter than anyone can imagine."

She walked into the kitchen to carry in bread and milk, and through the open door she shouted, "Oh yes, Lars, your brother, asked me to give you his best regards. Take a look in the storeroom: there you'll see a traveling chest and a sealskin bag; you could keep the one that would be of most use to you, he said."

I walked into the storeroom and saw the two things she had mentioned. The chest was beautifully decorated, and the bag had been sewn together with the skill for which Lars was renowned.

"The chest will be heavy to carry," I said; "but the sealskin bag is just as if it was ordered for me."

I have had it ever since. It was in that bag that we carried our provisions when we walked from Milwaukee to Fox River, Anne.

Mother and I ate our meal together. We felt at peace with ourselves and with the world.

The next morning she was standing on the promontory waving good-bye. First I sailed to Finnøy; I also had to say farewell to Anne Cathrine.

She was sitting in the chair by the window as usual; the walking sticks had been supplanted by crutches.

The news of my coming had preceded me; she knew why I had come, and she greeted me with a toothless smile: "Now at last will Cleng Peerson get his freedom!"

"If that is so," I answered, "then most people would think it was not too soon."

She scrutinized me; her brown eyes were still sharp and sparkling.

"You've not been home very much, Cleng," she said; "and you've not had much scolding from me for traveling far and wide. If you hadn't been backed by Anne Cathrine's money, it might just have happened that you too would have had to work hard for a living. But you have frolicked like a frisky calf over hill and dale, and I think it's probable that you will do just as much frolicking in the future."

"Even though the tether was long, there's never been any doubt where the stake was standing," I answered; "and as far as that goes there will be no change."

"But don't you ever think of the day when I'll be on my deathbed, Cleng?" she cackled.

"There were times when I felt like doing you in," I said. "But now I don't care anymore."

"What you just said may be useful for me to recall when I sit down to write my will," she replied.

"Yes, don't you ever forget it!" I said. "If the day ever comes that I sit with all your papers and valuables in my hands, I would certainly know what to do with them! I would tear them into a thousand pieces and throw them in the fire."

"Couldn't you do with some money, now that you're going to travel so far?" she asked. "Your friends the Quakers are not among the most affluent people in town."

"They certainly are not," I answered; "but now they have collected enough money, and they are going to invest it in a trading company in which you don't have a single share, Anne Cathrine."

"If there are any firms in which I don't have any share, it's because I don't think it's under good management," she replied.

"With or without money, I think I'll be able to get along for a year or so," I answered.

"A year or so!" she laughed. "You'll never come back, Cleng. You would be a fool if you did!"

"I am going to finish the task that has been entrusted to me," I replied, "and I'll be back. Farewell, Anne Cathrine," and I offered her my hand. I hardly expected that she would take it, but she did, and she squeezed it hard; she still possessed some of her old strength.

"Farewell, Cleng," she said; "you'll always have your own way in this world. You're just like a cat — you'll always land on your feet."

She cleared her throat and sat up straight in her chair: "Our marriage didn't start off right, Cleng, and the end is hardly much better. We never got to know each other well, we two. Now and then I've sort of felt that the Devil himself gnashes his teeth as he sits in Hell with those who are damned. But Cleng Peerson would never understand that. That's why he never had any need of compassion and had no compassion to give."

I was going to answer her, but I couldn't utter a word. I gently withdrew my hand; hers fell down into her lap like the wing of a dead bird.

I walked down to the harbor. It was foggy but there was no wind. Once on board the boat I could hardly make out Anne Cathrine's house.

I had to row since the weather remained calm. But I held to my course in spite of the fog. I found my way by rowing from island to island and from one shore to another.

We sailed from Stavanger in the bark *The Doughty Farmer;* it was on a day in September in the year of Our Lord 1821. The news had spread all over town and not only the Friends but many more had come down to the harbor. I walked from one to the other, shook their hands and said good-bye. Some people cried, and others laughed, but I had never before taken with me so many good wishes when setting out on a voyage.

Sara Larsdatter was there too. When I went to shake her hand in farewell she handed me a conch shell. It suddenly came to me that I too had a small gift that I wanted her to have; it was on board the ship. I ran back across the gangway and got hold of it; it was a music box made of porcelain, one I had purchased in Amsterdam during my sailing days. One winds it up, and the cover rotates; and on it a boy and a girl are dancing, they dance round and round, stretch their arms out and reach for each other, but neither manages to grasp the hand of the other.

I wound it up, and she accepted it, and when we cast off she held it up so that I and everyone could see it. A melancholy tune came from the little box — the boy and girl were dancing round and round.

I was not to see her again for a very long time, and that image of her lived on in my memory. Later on, when the wind filled the sails and the ship made a foaming wake, I would hear the song of the conch shell, and not that alone, but also the tune from the music box, and I thought to myself, "She is close to me still. And it is for her sake that I'm going away."

We were towed out through the shipping lane, for there was not a ripple on the ocean. Knud and I sat next to each other on the deck; we didn't talk very much. We saw the land stretch out before us, with yellowing grain fields and flowering heather. Everyone could live and enjoy a good life here, I thought, if freedom and justice were not only words that were printed in a constitution but were also written on everyone's heart.

When *The Doughty Farmer* had rounded Tungenes, we set sail. A favorable wind came in from the ocean and filled our sails. The moon was up, and the shadows of the sails moved about as if something intangible were about to take on material form. All that lay behind me seemed to be present, and everything that lay ahead did not seem distant. We had land on our port side: on our starboard side the ocean spread out before us as far as the horizon and beyond.

The Twenty-seventh Tale

My story will now deal with the sloop and those who were on board. But I consider I need first to give a detailed account of the circumstances that brought about the voyage.

I am not going to repeat to you, Anne, what I have told you before. Let me just mention that, inspired by ideas of the time, which had come from such various sources as the French Revolution and the struggles for religious liberty, the poor and common people of many countries attempted to rise to a higher level of human dignity by improving their earthly lot as well as demanding the right to worship God according to the voice of their own conscience.

Thus, in Norway for the sake of their own future and that of their children a few at first and later many more began to entertain thoughts of going to America. To the common people's way of thinking that continent was as far away as the moon, but to those who had been to sea it was not totally unknown; some even knew that persecuted and liberty-loving people from Holland and England had gone there centuries ago.

Thus it happened that they sent me to America in the fall of 1821, my companion being Knud Eide, a relative of Martha Georgiana, Lars Larsen's wife. Our task was to investigate whether emigration was possible and what we could look forward to. We sailed via Gothenburg and reached our destination safe and sound.

As originally planned, we were to stay in America for about a year, but due to certain circumstances I did not return until 1824. And now I will tell you why.

It was arranged that the Society of Friends in Stavanger should invest money in merchant Simon Lima's establishment, and funds were to be transferred to Knud and me through another firm in New York, and thus we would receive the necessary means to carry out our task. But it so happened that after we had arrived on American shores — we had just received our first payment and had come to the office to receive the next one — we were told that Simon Lima's business had gone bankrupt and that there was no chance of our getting any further assistance from Stavanger.

Knud and I debated what we were going to do. We agreed at once that we ought to get paid work somewhere and thus earn what was necessary for food and lodging as well as the return trip. There were plenty of well-paid jobs to be had, and we had no complaints either about the Friends or on our own behalf; our being compelled to stay longer than planned would give us greater knowledge of conditions in the New World.

But this was not the only reason why my stay in America was to last almost three years.

Knud Eide was several years younger than I, but he had much earlier in life put behind him the wanton playfulness of youth. A victim of trials and tribulations, he had become a pious man, one whom I should have tried to imitate, but I have always been slow in following a good example.

At one time we had been working in the forests in the area west of Albany, the capital of New York State. The construction of the Erie Canal had begun, and an enormous amount of timber was needed for the locks and dams.

There and everywhere else throughout the land there lived many more Indians than is the case today. One afternoon when Knud and I were walking home — it was the month of September and the weather was warm — we passed a thicket below a precipice close to a river. We suddenly heard moans and wails, and when we walked in the direction of the sound we found a young Indian girl lying on the ground. She had been injured, and when we tried to lift her up, she screamed from pain; we found that her right leg had been broken.

I had earlier become acquainted with several Indians in her tribe, and I understood a little of their language; she knew a few English words. She told us that she had left her camp and had ridden into the woods on an untamed horse; a large bird had suddenly flown right in front of them, the horse had shied and galloped terror-stricken downhill. She had fallen to the ground and had remained lying there, and the horse had disappeared.

This had occurred quite a distance from the camp, and she had been lying there for two days, without any other food than the berries she had been able to reach.

I comforted her and told her that I knew the location of the camp. Knud and I made a stretcher of branches and withies and carried her back to the camp. We got there by midnight; a red and waning half-moon rose above the treetops.

As we approached we were challenged by one of the sentries, and they all rejoiced as they surrounded the stretcher and recognized the youngest daughter of the chief, his favorite child. He himself and some of his men were out looking for her for the second day in a row. Two horsemen were immediately dispatched to search for him and tell him the good news.

In the meantime, Knud and I were royally treated and thereupon shown into an empty tent where we immediately lay down and went to sleep.

The next morning the chief returned. By words and gestures he expressed his joy and gratitude, and ordered a celebration to be held that very day because the Great Spirit had shown him such great favor, and the white brothers were to be guests of honor.

A freshly killed deer was roasted on a spit over the fire, and the strong Indian beer was served in large sacks made from hides; and several clay jars with strong coffee were boiled and mixed with honey and sugar. Both men and women were busy getting everything ready. In the evening before an open fire the men of the tribe, dressed in colorful garb and with splendid feather headdresses, presented dances whose secret meaning was only understood by the initiates. Everyone was eating and drinking; Knud Eide and I were seated next to the chief, right outside his own tent.

Then he suddenly produced a small bell and made it jingle. All the dancers disappeared at once — all of them being men, as I just mentioned — and in their place two young women stepped forth in the open space in front of the fire. They too wore splendid garments, and they danced a soft and rhythmical dance, always getting closer to the spot where we were sitting, next to the chief. When they got very close, they bent down and were lying flat on the ground with their faces next to our feet; and the chief made us understand that they represented his gift and thanks for the good deed that we had done: he wanted to let us have his two oldest daughters for our pleasure as long as we wished to stay in his camp. Two tents had been made ready, one for each of us.

I was not unfamiliar with this custom among the Indians, and I had on several occasions accepted what they had given out of the goodness of their hearts, for they look upon things differently when it comes to customs and what is immoral.

Nevertheless, each person ought to act according to his own conscience, and Knud declined the offer, even though he was unmarried; but a girl to whom he had given a pledge in Norway made him steadfast. As for myself, I thought I was excused by the fact that I was married to the ancient and shrewd Anne Cathrine Sælinger.

It so happened that the chief was greatly displeased when Knud declined his offer, even though one could hardly tell from his appearance; but he handed me a piece of the deer's kidneys and heart, and I ate it and drained the bowl and he once again filled it with beer. Knud then stood up without touching his own bowl, and in a very courtly manner asked the chief for permission to leave. "I'm going back to my cabin," he said; we were then living in a log cabin a few miles distant.

As for myself, I was already feeling a bit intoxicated. I did not refuse when the chief once again filled my bowl, and I ate the remaining portion of the deer's kidneys and heart. The Indians believe that this will arouse one's passion, but I had no need of having my passions aroused. And I stayed with the chief's daughter all night.

Toward morning it so happened that a mighty wind arose and swept through the forest. Like a shot the storm broke. It tore up trees by the roots, and the lightning split branches and set the dry grass on fire — until the rains came with the force of a deluge. By that time many of the tent poles had been wrenched from the ground, among them the one from the tent in which I was staying with the chief's daughter.

The wind calmed down after a while, and the sky cleared — the air had unexpectedly turned much colder —; then the elements again went on a rampage, with thunder and a terrible hail storm. At dawn the ground was white and the trees were bare.

The camp was a scene of confusion; people were running hither and yon, some in order to tether the frightened horses, others in order to bring into safekeeping the tents and belongings that had been swept away.

I had a hangover and was in a bad mood; quietly I slunk away.

For a while I walked about aimlessly, half stunned, but when it cleared up and the day dawned, I knew in which direction to go and it didn't take me long to get back to our cabin. The puddles outside the wall were covered with ice; never since have I seen anything like it here in America.

But when I found out that Knud was not in the cabin, I set out to search for him, and I shouted his name at regular intervals.

A network of paths ran through the forest, trod by animals and occasional wanderers; some of them ran in the direction of the Indian camp. I chose one of them and it proved to be a lucky choice: I almost stumbled over Knud, but he was lying there unconscious and looked half dead; his face was ashen and filthy as if he had been kneaded in clay.

Here is what had happened to him: feeling very tired he had only walked a short distance away from the Indian camp before he had sat down with his back to an oak and fallen asleep. He didn't wake up until the storm had hit, and a bolt of lightning that had struck the top of the tree and had gone into the ground via the trunk had paralyzed his left foot and burned him severely. The skin below his knee was blue and brown.

He was unable to get up on his feet nor was he able to seek shelter from the huge hailstones that were hitting him on the head. Wet and cold, he crept on all fours a stone's throw in the direction of the cabin, but the distance was about two miles.

I had put on a dry sweater; this I placed around him, and hoisted him onto my back, and carried him home.

Inside the cabin I took off his pants and shirt, put him to bed, and tucked him in well. His breath was even, but it sounded as if he were sleeping. I immediately made a fire, and within minutes the room felt snug and warm. Outside the wet leaves of maples and oaks were glittering in the sun — they were still green — and the sun had risen; but the grass north of the cabin was all white from all the hail.

I walked over to the brook to get water; in the meantime Knud regained consciousness. I boiled the water and mixed it with rum and made a hot and refreshing drink.

It seemed as if he was recovering; he could explain what had happened, and he complained about a pain in his foot. I had an ointment made up of animal fat, honey, and camphor. I rubbed it into his foot and put a clean linen cloth around it.

He finally fell asleep. I stayed at home the next day, since he not only needed someone to watch over him but I myself was tired and in a melancholy mood.

He remained quiet most of the night, and I also got some rest, but I didn't doze off until early morning. When I woke up and spoke to him, he did not answer — he merely tossed in his bed and moaned.

I immediately made a fire, and in the light from the fireplace his face looked feverish and his eyes shone. When I bent over him he did not recognize me, but he began to speak deliriously.

I mixed him a toddy, made up of honey, brandy, and hot water. He was not capable of drinking it, but I moistened his lips and then let him rest. Now and then he moaned and groaned and mumbled words that I couldn't make out. He took a decided turn for the worse.

It was a whole day's walk to the nearest physician; he was hardly to be called a physician, however. He was a drunken sailor by the name of Hawkins; but he tried to make people believe that he could cure their ills. Besides that he was useful when a corpse had to be shaved and tended to and when horses were to be gelded; moreover, he owned a tavern and conducted a liquor business. I had heard that he knew how to deal with many kinds of ills, provided he was sober, but that was not very often.

I did know, however, that he set stiff prices. I emptied my own purse and also counted Knud's money and found that we altogether had three dollars and five cents.

I made myself ready to go that same evening, and I walked all night. On the forenoon of the next day I reached the city of Schenectady and entered the tavern of Hawkins the physician. He was standing at the counter, his eyes red and bleary, his hair and beard thick and shaggy. Across his huge belly he had fastened an apron which at one time must have been white; now it was full of spots from grease and blood. With rolled-up sleeves he was cutting pieces of beef, frying them while now and then taking a swig from a mug filled with beer. His arms were like clubs and were so hairy that one could hardly see the skin. Steam from the grease and water rose around him like sputtering clouds.

He was well able to take care of his business although he was intoxicated. When I asked to speak with him alone, he tossed his head indicating where we were to go, and I followed him through the door behind the counter. A half-covered corpse was lying on a stretcher; he was only half-finished shaving it.

I told him what had happened to my friend and that he needed speedy help, and Hawkins asked immediately how much I was able to pay. I put my modest amount of money on the table.

"Is that all?" he pooh-poohed. "For such a small amount of money I couldn't even get drunk on my cheapest kind of brandy. It is easier to

285

take care of the dead than the living," — and he nudged the corpse with the tip of his shoe — "and there's more profit in it. Come back when your friend has croaked; I'll shave him at a reasonable price and make sure that he'll safely get into the claws of Satan."

I got up and walked out of the room. The tavern smelled from burned meat. Hawkins followed me: he swore and threw the charred piece of beef to a skinny dog that was lying under the table, whining for food.

I knew of no one else to approach, and when I asked someone in the street, I was told that the nearest fairly good physician was located in Albany.

And without further ado I set out on the road to Albany.

Without my noticing him a man had overtaken me; I started when I suddenly heard a strange voice; "You look so sad, dear sir; has anything evil happened to you?"

From his heavy accent I realized that he too must be a foreigner. His voice was friendly and so was the expression in his face, and I told him immediately what had happened.

"My name is Frederick Rapp," the man said. "I am of German descent and I can hear that you too are a European." I replied that that was so and told him briefly about my mission in America.

"I'm afraid that no physician in Albany either will go with you that far from his own district," he said. "But if you will agree to let me help you, I can say that I'm not entirely ignorant when it comes to that profession. I shall be glad to keep watch at your friend's bedside and will take as good care of him as I know how. In the meantime, you yourself can get some sleep, which you must be greatly in need of."

Whereupon we walked down the road together. When we reached the log cabin, everything was as when I had left; Knud had kicked off his bedcovers and he was delirious. I put the cover over him, and Frederick Rapp made me go to bed. I didn't wake up until twenty-four hours later.

Knud's condition had not improved; his breathing was uneven, and Frederick Rapp said that he had not eaten at all. Rapp had from time to time moistened his lips with a wet cloth; otherwise there was not much he could do for him.

I relieved him at the bedside, and as I sat there watching my friend approach death because of my frivolity, a feeling of shame and remorse welled up within me, and I beseeched God to forgive me and I gave Him my promise that I would become a Quaker; for among those who invoked the name of the Lord, the Quakers, it seemed to me, were the most sincere in obeying His commandments. While I was praying thus, sorrow and weariness descended on me and once again I fell asleep.

I woke up at last when I felt someone touch me. Knud had gotten out of bed and was standing over me; he was naked and his body was shiny and clammy from perspiration. I thought that his mind was not yet quite clear, but when he spoke to me he sounded quite calm and collected; he said, "You have always been my faithful friend, Cleng."

"I have been faithless toward you, Knud," I replied; "and it is because of that that you are now suffering. But I have prayed to God that He take mercy on you and your body and on me and my soul, for this is what you and I need the most."

"Everything will be all right," Knud said. "I'll soon be well again."

He supported himself on me and I lifted him and carried him back to bed. But as I laid him down, his entire body started to tremble. I put my hand above his heart — it had stopped beating. I took a stick of wood from the fireplace and held it above his face: his eyes were unseeing and his mouth looked wizened.

I woke up Frederick Rapp, and together we washed Knud's body and prepared it for the funeral.

"Which minister shall we get in touch with?" Rapp asked. I answered, "He was no friend of the clergy and belonged to the Society of Friends. I think he would have been most happy if he were buried quietly, but someone ought to read what the Bible says about resurrection. Could you do it?"

"You are the one closest to him; therefore you yourself ought to read from the Scriptures," he said.

Then I could no longer hide the truth, and I confessed to him that it had been through my frivolous deed that Knud had died.

Frederick Rapp reprimanded me, but not in the way I had expected: "Do you know so little of the heart of the Lord that you think He punishes your sins by taking your friend out of this world? Do you think He strikes the innocent in order to chastise the guilty? In truth, His wisdom and His love are greater than that! For it is not because of our piety that we are kept alive or because of our trespasses that our days are limited in number."

"Are you perhaps a minister, my dear sir?" I asked.

"Alas, no," he replied; "far from it. I'm a member of a little flock that was persecuted by both the laymen and the learned in my country. Almost twenty years ago my father, together with his relatives and his close friends, had to leave Germany because they believed that also in our day the Lord will look with pleasure on a social order in which reigns that community of spirit and material things that characterized the first Christian congregation. People call us Rappites. We live in a fraternal community in which we pray and work and have all our property in common in mutual tolerance and in modest circumstances, but no one among us is in need."

"We have attempted to realize these views in our settlement called Harmony in the state of Indiana," he continued. "Perhaps you will find an opportunity to visit us? Or, if you don't want to travel so far inland, perhaps instead you might see what we have accomplished in Energy, Pennsylvania, or you might want to join us in planning a new colony in that state? We have already initiated preparatory work and investigations. It is to be called Economy."

His account aroused my interest and sympathy, and I questioned him further about the principles underlying the Rappites' faith.

I marveled as I listened to him, and I said, "Indeed, before I go back to Norway I will pay a visit to one of your colonies."

"But where shall we bury your friend?" he asked.

"I would like to bury him by the tree that was struck by lightning," I replied; "for I am bound to pass by here quite often whenever I return to this place. It won't be difficult for me to take care of the grave; he was always a good friend to me."

We prepared the body, carried it out of the cabin, and dug his grave as close to the oak tree as we could on account of its roots; when it was sufficiently deep we lowered the body down and covered it over. There were no flowers to place on his grave because of the frost and the storm; but from the branches of the maples yellow leaves fell down, resembling hearts and open palms. This was on a mild day in November; there was a southerly breeze and warmer weather had followed the frost.

I read some passages from the New Testament that Knud had brought with him. For a while we stood there bareheaded; then we walked back to the log cabin.

Frederick Rapp stayed with me overnight, and when he left early the next morning, I accompanied him. On the previous evening he had told me about the purpose for his coming to the state of New York. A bit southeast of Albany, near the Massachusetts border, a group who called themselves Shakers, had founded a settlement known as New Lebanon.

In those days this settlement had gained wide renown both for its peculiar customs and methods and the impressive results that had been achieved; hardly anyone traveling through that district failed to pay it a visit if there was an opportunity to do so.

This was what Frederick Rapp told me the evening before when we had been sitting by the fire in the log cabin.

The sect known as Shakers had been founded by a woman by the name of Anna Lee, and it had already been in existence for nearly a hundred years. A distinguishing feature of its adherents was the fact that married as well as unmarried members practiced sexual abstinence. When great spiritual agitation seized Anna Lee, she would start shaking all over; from that the sect had gotten its name. It taught that when Christ returned to the earth, He would come in the form of a woman, and after a while Miss Lee was herself venerated as the returned Messiah. Each one of their small settlements, which were not so few in number, might resemble Paradise before the Fall. They were laid out as beautiful gardens, and the conduct of all members was characterized by innocence and self-sacrifice.

After having left the log cabin, we first called on my employer, a man by the name of Zenk. He represented the firm that was constructing the Erie Canal. Just at that time they had started to speed up the work of excavation, having been instructed to do so by Governor Clinton of the state of New York, who was desirous of having his name linked with the completion of it. For that reason the canal became popularly known as "Clinton's Big Ditch."

Mr. Zenk had his headquarters not far from Schenectady. When I told him that I should like to be released from my contract, he said he was sorry to hear it; he was in great need of men. But I told him, as indeed was the truth, that I might wish to return later on if he could use me. "You're welcome any time," Mr. Zenk said; he was a man of good will.

Thereupon, Frederick Rapp and I continued our journey. We crossed the Hudson River, and walked along one of the many roads in that area all the way to New Lebanon, where we were received in a very friendly manner.

What I heard and saw there exceeded even what Mr. Rapp had told me, and I received a powerful stimulus to adopt many of the methods of the Shakers in regard to agriculture and gardening as well as their principles of owning everything in common and living in peace and harmony.

Apart from this, not much is to be told about the journey made by Frederick Rapp and myself; we reached without any trouble his colony in Pennsylvania. There, too, I found industry and order everywhere. Every morning both women and men, all those who were not engaged in work inside the house, went out in the fields. It was the time of sowing the winter wheat; people were preparing for the winter and a new spring. No one said "This is mine — " about a piece of land, or, "That is yours." Children of school age attended a school that the colony had established, and none of the old or the sick were neglected. Every day began and ended with Mr. Rapp or one of his deputies reading from the Bible and leading the people in prayer.

As had been the case during my visit to New Lebanon, I was greatly attracted to most of what I saw and heard, and I was more strongly confirmed in my intent to establish a similar colony, when and if my friends would arrive from Norway.

I mentioned this in a letter to Lars Larsen in Stavanger, and when his reply finally arrived, he said that he to some extent shared my view. Nevertheless, he advised me to show reserve in my letters both in regard to decisions and to expressing my opinions on this particular point.

He wrote, "Even though I know that among those who plan to emigrate there are found some who would gladly join a colony of the kind you describe, you must realize that this does not at all appeal to everyone. In the thousand-year history of our country, a man who did not own land has always striven harder to become a landowner than anything else. And I find it even more difficult to believe that people who already own a farm, and have to leave it, will be satisfied being tenants of some kind on a community farm. Most of those who intend to come with us across the sea, the poor as well as the affluent, not only look forward to the blessing that is represented by freedom of conscience, but also harbor the hope of gaining prosperity in the New World."

I had been in touch with the Quaker Joseph Fellows, my friend from the years in the prison ship, on several occasions. He had at first been living in New York City and then in the town of Geneva on Lake Seneca. He was a representative of the big land-selling firm of The Pultney Estate, and following his directions I traveled around and looked at many of the areas the company had for sale. I especially made note of a piece of land in the far north of New York State, on the shores of Lake Ontario.

It was a level area gently sloping down toward the lake, largely covered with forest, and through the property flowed a brook which, as

I was told, never ran dry. It ran toward the north, but with numerous bends, in such a fashion that many of the future farms might border on it. People called the brook Bald Eagle Creek.

In its entire length the section faced on Lake Ontario. The lake is like an ocean and provides a wide view. It was for that very reason that I selected a piece of this area for myself; big ships would frequently sail past.

It was on a day in December that I saw the place for the first time. It had been very cold during the night, and wherever Bald Eagle Creek ran slowly and widened into pools it was covered with a thin film of ice. But Lake Ontario was not ice-covered; it lay there completely placid and blue. I thought that this was the very best that America had to offer: forests and fertile farmland, and fresh water — infinite, like the ocean right outside the door.

In another letter to Lars Larsen I emphasized the advantages of the spot but did not neglect to mention that the forest consisted of very large trees and that this might possibly slow up the clearing and the cultivation of the land. Joseph Fellows too had called this to my attention.

But Lars didn't seem to mind that; in the last letter I received from him he wrote that at least one wouldn't have any worries about where to obtain firewood!

I myself was later on to hear much abuse because I had secured for them an area which was so hard to till, and they thought that it was due to cunning and laziness that I had selected for myself the property facing directly on the lake, where the landscape was more open and the forest more sparse.

The Twenty-eighth Tale

But before I tell you about my journey from America back to Norway, I have something to confide to you, Anne.

Following my visits to New Lebanon and Energy, I roamed about quite a bit and took casual jobs here and there, since it was my intention to get to know more about the country and the living conditions, but it was also because I could find no peace. Night and day I could see Knud before me, but I drowned my sorrow in drinking and wenching, and the promises that I had given my Creator I did not keep.

Once again I took a job at the canal — this time between the cities of Syracuse and Utica — far away from civilization, in a district where people feared neither God nor the law. We were living in barracks put up along the river; each group of workers got together to hire a cook to prepare the meals.

A Canadian woman of French descent was in charge of the cooking for my crew; she had come from the north, from Quebec, with her daughter after her husband had been killed in a fire which had burned down their house, too. The woman's name was Jeanette; she was about fifty years old, and her daughter Yvonne was sixteen.

During the fire the mother had saved her daughter from certain death, and her face and arms had been horribly burned. But the daughter had not sustained any visible damage; I have seldom seen a more beautiful girl: her hair was like a river in the night, her eyes were so dark that one couldn't see the rim of the pupils, and her skin was like milk and roses; her figure, even at this early age, reminded one of Shulamit, who was praised by Solomon for her exceptional beauty.

Don't think evil of her mother when I tell you that she had let the men she was cooking for have their way with her. Having been thrown ashore on the beach of Sodom by an unkind fate, she had to yield or keep on wandering. And where could she go, where could she hope for better conditions? But she watched over Yvonne like a hawk.

One day, when I had been working on the canal in this district for about two weeks, it so happened that Jeanette had to go to the nearest town in order to buy food for the household; but her daughter could not accompany her. She was indisposed and had gone to bed in the room that she shared with her mother. Her mother had advised her to bolt the door. But when evening came and many of the men were drunk, about a dozen of them broke into her room, beat her, and raped her.

It was about the time of day that I returned to the camp. I had put up traps in the forest, and after work hours I had gone into the woods to inspect them. When I found Yvonne lying prostrate and learned that some of the men who had committed the outrage, were still inside the barracks, I seized some of the movable goods lying about — frying pans, ladles, and carving boards — and hit the men over their heads and did not stop until they had all been kicked out of the house; some of them were lying in a dead faint, others fled into the forest or were staggering about, while others spat out loose teeth and rubbed the blood out of their eyes.

Then I turned to Yvonne, the poor child, and I tended to her to the best of my ability until her mother came back from town. Throughout that first day she just lay there completely impassive, but later she clung to me as if I were the only one from whom she could expect security.

After that day, her mother, too, looked to me for protection, and the three of us discussed what we should do; for there was no sign that the men had bettered their ways; on the contrary, they had sworn to avenge themselves on me and only to leave Jeanette and Yvonne in peace when they felt like it.

In that situation I happened to think what the kind Mr. Zenk had told me about a year before, when I had left the construction job near Schenectady. In view of the current speeding-up of the construction job I feared that perhaps there would be no more work in those parts and that Mr. Zenk and his crew had perhaps been moved or disbanded.

But one must never be afraid to make an attempt, and as soon as I mentioned my plan to the women they were eager to leave. We got ready very quietly, and one night, when the others were asleep, we left the camp and set out in an eastward direction, along the road that leads toward Schenectady and Albany.

Sometimes we slept in the open, but usually we were able to get a roof over our heads, in a tavern or an inn. We had agreed that we should pass Jeanette off as my wife and Yvonne as our daughter, so that they would never be left alone, either by day or by night; otherwise they would have been less safe than Sara in Egypt.

We encountered that good man Zenk where I had bid him farewell the last time, and he offered all of us work; he was even in special need of a few women to do the cooking and keep the canal workers' clothes in order. The latter work was given to Yvonne who was handy with needle and thread.

As before, Jeanette at certain times had to go to town to purchase food for the household; that was her responsibility. She traveled by horse and wagon. Once, while she was on the way back, she was overtaken by the winter's first violent storm, a heavy snowfall followed by rain without end, and when she finally reached the camp, exhausted and numb with cold, she had contracted a fever. For a whole week she was delirious and ate nothing at all.

But one morning, just before I was leaving for work, Yvonne came to me and told me that her mother was much better and had asked for me to come to her.

I went with the girl, and the two of us sat down by her bed. When Jeanette began to speak and brought forth her request, I could hardly believe my own ears.

"Yvonne will soon be without a mother, as she has long been without a father," she said. "But I am very happy that I know one man who can be both mother and father to her and even more than that. Yvonne and I both ask you to take her as your wife. She very much wants to be that; she is very fond of you. Don't you too feel attracted to Yvonne?"

I had seldom been as bewildered as I was then. Finally I answered, something like this: "It is true that I feel greatly attracted to your daughter, her being so beautiful and nice in every way. But I have reached the age of forty and she is only sixteen. I could be her father — let me rather be that! — for she will soon find a husband of suitable age. Besides, back in Norway I was united to a woman who for all I know is still living, even though she is now past eighty: but she has never done me any good, and it's not because of her that I'm going back. I was given an assignment to do here in America, and the time for my departure is drawing near."

"But I must ask you to promise me one thing before I die," Jeanette said; "that you don't leave her alone one single night or let her stay alone in her room. For I couldn't rest in my grave if it should happen that my child once again is befouled by malicious and cruel men. I would so much rather see her under your protection! — For I have learned that you are an honorable and noble person."

Her words made me burn with shame, but I was also deeply touched by the way both of them relied on me, and I said, "I don't know how to decide what is right and wrong in this case; but if you do soon leave us, then I promise to protect your child as long as I possibly can."

Jeanette died the very next day, and when she had been buried, in as becoming a manner as we could arrange, I moved, according to her request, into the room that she and Yvonne had shared; I slept in the empty bed along one wall, and the girl lay in her bed along the opposite wall. I never entered the room until she had gone to bed, and in the morning I got up before she was out of bed.

Thus passed more than a month.

As the time for farewell approached, Yvonne became ever more downcast and silent.

When I entered our room the last evening we were together, I found her in my bed. I went over and sat down on the edge of the bed; she made no sound and seemed to be asleep. Then she suddenly sat up and, weeping uncontrollably, she embraced me, covered my entire face with kisses and tears, and said, "My dearest friend, you who have never done me anything but good, how can I show you my gratitude?" I bent my head down toward her breast so that she couldn't see my face; I had lost control of my will and my desire. I sat down by her side, and I drew her near with great tenderness and gentleness so that she was not to feel any pain or fear, so that the pleasure we had in each other would be complete.

Much is forgotten during a long life, but that hour I shall remember in my dying moments; it was itself like death and resurrection.

The next day, I was ready to leave for Albany and from there go by the steamer *William Penn* down the Hudson River to New York. When I returned early from work in the forest to say good-bye to her, she was nowhere to be found. I shouted and searched and finally heard that some people had seen her walk in the direction of the canal. When I reached it, others told me that she had asked to borrow a rowboat. She had an errand over on the other side, she had said.

Just at that spot the Erie Canal flows quietly in the old riverbed, but down below there were some rapids where locks were soon to be built. There was no boat to be had, and I ran along the river bank as fast as I could. When I reached the place where the crew was working, I asked whether they had seen the boat and the girl. They replied that they had seen her, and that she had passed the first rapids without any mishap.

"But what was she trying to do?" they said. "It looked as if she was trying to commit suicide! And if she doesn't manage to get the boat over to the bank before she reaches the next rapids, she must have as steady a hand and be as quick-witted as a redskin in his canoe."

"And you did nothing to stop her!" I shouted.

"We didn't have a boat, and we didn't know what her errand was," they said; "but we shouted to her and got no answer."

I ran further down along the river and soon found a rowboat; I jumped into it, shoved from shore, and rowed with the current as hard as I could until I approached the rapids.

I didn't see any boat lying above the falls, and since I thought it would be the work of a madman to try to negotiate the rapids, I beached the rowboat and continued running along the river bank; the churning waters sounded like thunder ahead, and the spray felt like rain against my face.

Right below the rapids I could see a rowboat drifting bottoms up, but there was no sign of Yvonne. I shouted her name, but the masses of whirling water drowned me out completely — there had recently been a heavy rainfall in the area; it was past New Year's before cold weather set in that year. I searched both banks of the river and got a crew to come along to help me, but all in vain.

A few days later I left and traveled to New York according to plan. I had learned that a ship destined for Denmark, would soon be ready to sail. On it I crossed the ocean and from Denmark I continued on to Kristiansand and Egersund.

The Twenty-ninth Tale

From Skagen in Denmark to Egersund in Norway I secured passage on a sloop whose home port was the town of our destination. The vessel proved to be a splendid sailer; it made good speed, and it lay particularly well in the water. Across the Skagerak we had a fresh breeze turning into a gale from the southwest.

With a certain purpose in mind, I started to query the owner about the sloop. He told me that it originally had come from Hardanger; it had been built there in 1801. Its owner had given it the name *Emanuel*, after his first-born son who had just died from smallpox at an early age. When the following year he had been blessed with another son, he had given the sloop a new name and called it *Haabet* (The Hope).

Like so many other Hardanger boats it sailed regularly to Gothenburg with herring and brought back grain from Denmark. Its present owner had bought it five years earlier; he had rebuilt it and extended and equipped it with a sloop's rigging. At the same time it had been given its third name: *Haabet* was changed to *Restauration*.

Now you know which vessel I was on board, Anne, and you will not wonder at the fact that I still know all the ship's dimensions: after the rebuilding its tonnage had been increased from a little over twelve to slightly more than 37 register tons; the vessel was 54 ft. long, 16 ft.

wide, and it drew 7 1/2 ft. below the waterline when in ballast. Its name was painted with neat silver letters on a black plate.

The owner was now close to seventy and suffered so much from rheumatism that he could only handle the ship with great difficulty, and he mentioned to me that he intended to sell it and retire for good.

"If that is so, I think I might be able to get you a substantial buyer," I said.

I shall tell you later about the actual purchase and how the *Restauration* was equipped for the voyage across the ocean. However, I will here and now record a strange event which is not at all unconnected with our story.

Not far from Egersund, there is a river flowing into the sea. It so happened that after a brief stay in the town I had set out on the road to Stavanger and had reached the river some distance from where it ran into the sea. There I saw a young girl standing up to her waist in the rushing icy water. It was just at the time of the spring thaw; masses of blue and wet ice were hanging from the tops of the steep mountainsides and the snow was still lying in grayish-white patches wherever the mountains cast a shadow.

A group of people were standing on the steep river bank; among them I especially noticed a powerfully built fellow with a straggling, bristly beard, dressed in tatters. Even at a distance I got the impression that he was an evil and violent man, and when I got closer and heard his hoarse voice and caught the glance in his small ferret's eyes lying under a low and slanting forehead, my first impression was intensified.

He shouted to the young girl and made a threatening gesture with his fists, "Go out till it reaches up to your neck! Then the sheriff will spare me. Otherwise, it'll be chains for me!"

Later on that day I heard what had happened before I had arrived.

The girl's name was Elen and she belonged somewhere up north. Besides that the passersby didn't know much about her. But they knew much more about the man who had shouted to her. He was known as Spinningwheel-Jørgen and had committed more than one evil deed. For that reason he had spent some time in the jail in the Egersund town hall.

Then it had happened that the girl Elen arrived in town, and the first thing she had inquired about was whether there were any sick or lonely people, or if anyone was in jail. Thereupon she had visited those who needed assistance and had helped them to the best of her ability. She cleaned the rooms and made the beds, washed them or went errands for them, or helped them in other ways.

Then she had come to the gate of the town hall, and at first the guard would not let her in, since many people thought that Spinningwheel-Jørgen was a dangerous man when he got angry. But finally she was allowed in.

As soon as Spinningwheel-Jørgen found out who she was and what she wanted, he began to weep and to bless her, and he told her that he was the father of thirteen starving children and that his wife had been suffering from consumption for five years. He had been stealing fish out of other people's nets and lobster from their pots solely in order to save his family from destitution, he had said. But he repented bitterly, and he had no other wish than to atone for his evil deeds and then begin a new life.

Elen had believed him; she had no way of knowing that he had neither wife nor children, although with regard to the latter there might be some doubt. Just because she was greatly touched by the thought that it was because of concern for his loved ones that he had perpetrated the wrong of appropriating other people's goods, she had promised that she would get him what he needed: a file, a knife, and a few fistfuls of hemp. "For one goes plumb crazy from sitting here with nothing to do," he said; "and making ropes is a useful activity."

She had hid in her dress all that he had asked for and had brought it to him the next time she visited the jail; he had thanked her and blessed her and had called her an angelic emissary of God.

Then one Sunday morning the rope was all finished, the knife and the file had been used for other purposes than those intended by Elen, and he had broken out of the town hall and run off. But a man who knew that Spinningwheel-Jørgen belonged behind bars had recognized him not far from town and had given the alarm.

Just at that time Jørgen had reached the river, and it also so happened that on that very morning Elen had come to the same place in order to see whether the first spring flowers were in bud; she wanted to pick some for a sick person whom she visited regularly.

When Spinningwheel-Jørgen saw her, he shouted to her and said that he was being pursued, that they wanted to kill both him and his dear ones. "But if you for my sake would wade into the water until it reaches your neck and threaten to drown yourself if they try to catch me, then we'll both be saved," he said. She had hesitated, but he forced her into the water.

In the meantime a number of spectators had gathered on a crag above the river, mostly women and children; some of the men had already set out to get the sheriff. Spinningwheel-Jørgen was standing on a point of land, making threatening gestures with his knife at the people pressing behind him so that his retreat would be secure. And with wails and shouts he implored Elen to wade further into the water; and so she risked her own life to gain his freedom.

The water reached her waist; she reeled in the current and was about to lose her footing. But he made her remain in that position for about a half hour. It was just then that I arrived, and a moment later the sheriff rode up. He had a pistol in his belt and seemed willing to use it, but Jørgen was still able to keep full control of the situation: "If you touch me, that innocent girl will drown herself!" he shouted. "And if you try any tricks, I'll jump into the river myself! No one will catch me alive!"

"Is there no boat around?" I asked the sheriff. "If anything's to be done, it has to be done in a hurry."

"There should be a rowboat just below that promontory," he answered, "and if you can get someone to help you, it will be fine to use it."

A young boy standing next to us immediately said he was willing to come along; we ran down to the river bank and found the rowboat where the sheriff had indicated.

But during the few minutes we were away, what everyone had feared happened: Spinningwheel-Jørgen had made the girl go farther out. Suddenly she lost her footing and went under, and just then our boat rounded the promontory. We rowed as fast as we could and set our course for the spot where we thought she would emerge. I let the boy do the rowing and got ready with the best boat hook.

At that spot the river widens into a pool, and the current was exceptionally strong. When the girl reappeared, she was quite close to us. I put the boat hook aside and tried to grab her with my hands.

I made it, and soon I was able to pull her into the boat. Her teeth were chattering and she was soaked through; but she was fully conscious, and I was no little surprised when she addressed me by my name, "Is that you, Cleng Peerson? Have you returned from America?"

"How in the world do you know who I am?" I asked.

Then she told me that she was the oldest daughter of Daniel Stensen Rossadal in Tysvær, my old neighbor and friend. I should perhaps have recognized her, but the last time I had seen her she was only a child.

"What's wrong with you, risking your life like this?" I asked angrily, although I pitied her at the same time.

She didn't answer me at all. I had wrapped my jacket around her. She was chilled through and through; her face and hands were blue from the cold.

"I'm on my way north to Stavanger and Tysvær," I said. "Perhaps you'll come with me, provided you don't end up sick in bed?"

"Yes, I'd like to come," she said, "but first I have to find out what's going to happen to Spinningwheel-Jørgen."

"Let Spinningwheel-Jørgen go to blazes!" I snorted. "He doesn't deserve your worrying about him!"

"But he's got a sick wife and thirteen children," she said.

"If he's got thirteen wives and one child, it would be closer to the truth!" the boy said laughing.

We had placed the boy's jacket too around her, and as soon as the boat touched land we got her into the nearest house and into bed. Hot drinks and a long sleep did wonders, and the next morning she wanted to get up. The only thing that seemed to bother her was some stiffness in arms and legs.

"Stay in bed another day, and then you'll probably be as good as new," I said. And she did not contract any of the illnesses that we had feared, such as pneumonia or others that ravage the lungs and the chest, but the next day her limbs were even stiffer than before.

"I think it's best that I get out of bed," she said. And sure enough, as soon as she tried to move her arms and legs, her condition improved. At once she started to help with the housework, and I noticed that she had a way with everything she did. She seemed to be a kind and well-behaved girl; neither was she as simpleminded as I had thought at first.

She had still not told me very much about the reasons for her being there and about the cause of her strange behavior that morning; but I learned a bit more from the sheriff. He was of the opinion that she was afflicted by a kind of pious confusion of the mind and believed herself to be called to preach the word of God to anyone who would listen.

On the morning of the fourth day Elen said, "Now we'll try to set out; you're not going to wait any longer for my sake. I am now convinced that I can stay with my family until the time I leave for America."

I had by then learned to know a little of this remarkable person; but I just couldn't help staring open-mouthed when I heard her say that.

Not until we talked together en route did I find out the reason for the statement she had made.

We started out about three in the afternoon; it was toward the end of March, with long days and a full moon, besides, if I remember right.

Elen was around seventeen years old at that time, tall and a bit coarse-limbed, but nevertheless her figure appeared slim and delicate. It was her face that made her seem beautiful; she had large, bright eyes, and her cheeks and chin were soft and rounded. Her smoothly combed hair was parted in the middle and made a gentle frame for her face.

We were both riding on hired horses.

I always like to carry on a conversation when I travel with others, and I began to tell her in some detail about my stay in America. Many times she interrupted me with questions to clarify a matter or she voiced her own opinion, and from everything she said I gathered that she had a keen mind. And now that I gained her confidence, she began without any pressure from me to tell me about herself.

"Ever since I was a little girl," she said, "things others never worried about affected me greatly. I would often lie awake at night, and thoughts would drift through my mind. Sometimes I wept and sometimes I laughed, so that Father and Mother woke up and asked me what was the matter, but I couldn't give them an answer. As I grew older, it got worse, and I knew that they were afraid I was losing my mind. At last I confided in them and told them that I had become convinced that I could hear a voice bidding me go out among the people and make prophecies. But I saw from their expressions that they both were worried, and they warned me against going off and said it would be best if I stayed home. But during the night I would still hear cries as if from a long way away, and the cries gave me the feeling that someone had been abandoned to fear and terror or weighed down with pain and that I was the only one who could help that person. Then I couldn't sleep; but I mourned for all living things. The cows in the byre and the lambs and all the domestic animals I regarded as my own brothers and sisters, and I felt that I was related to every creature, so that even trees and flowers and the clouds in the sky seemed to be limbs of my own body. Yes, the clouds that rise out of the sea were just like the tears of many good people, but I still felt joy at seeing them, and I would often walk alone in the rain, and the sound of the falling drops and of the wind was as dear to me as the sound of my father's footsteps in the hallway in the evening.

"There is no one that I love more than my father, and the last thing I'd do is to hurt him or do something he disapproves of; but he didn't understand the cry that called me in the middle of the night. And in spite of the fact that he was the one that I could most easily have confided in, I never again mentioned a word to him about it, nor that it felt as if my body was growing and growing from the inside and grew larger than a parish or an entire country and as if my arms and my limbs and my heart would burst; that was the reason why I had to get up and walk about during the night. I didn't want to frighten them, and I often felt

302

great pain and bit my lips till they bled, but in my suffering there was also blessedness.

"Then I left home; I could do nothing else. I asked my father whether I could borrow his knapsack, and he got it for me; I noticed the grief in his face and was not able to console him, but I embraced him and wept. And when I got together some of my clothes and made a bundle and asked my mother if I could take some food with me, she also clasped me tight and wailed, 'My child, what's going to happen to you?' And I answered her, 'I don't know, Mother.' She asked, 'Where are you going?' I replied, 'Out into the countryside, or perhaps in a boat, and when I come to a house where I want to stop, I'll know it beforehand.' And she asked me, 'What do you want to do?' 'I'm going to console people.' 'Not everyone needs to be consoled,' said Mother. 'Everyone needs to be consoled,' I replied, for I had many times seen a cup running over, and in the cup was the lot of man, namely pain; but that I didn't dare tell my mother or my father either.

" 'Take care of yourself,' Mother said. 'You're almost grown up now. Not everyone will want to treat you well.' But I said to her, 'No one can do evil unto me.'

"They accompanied me as far as the gate in the outlying fields, and when I had walked up to the top of the nearest hill and looked back, they were still standing there. I waved to them, and they waved back.

"I walked that entire day, and I wondered why I didn't receive a sign to stop at some of the houses that were visible from the road; something urged me on.

"This was in early spring, in March, just like now. In the shade the ice formed sharp needles on the surface of stagnant ponds; the fields had not yet gotten their tinge of green, the hills of heather were brown. It is the most miserable month of the year. But everything I saw filled me with joy, the way I always feel when the trees are turning green or when the summer smells of newly mown hay. And I thought: 'And it will get even more beautiful here,' and it was as if so much beauty awaited me that I must die.

"Some time in the afternoon I reached a small cabin, and there I heard the voice of God telling me to enter. In the doorway I met an old woman, and she said, 'Who are you, stranger? Go away! I'm poor enough, I have nothing to share with you.'

" 'But I have something to share with you,' I answered, and we sat down to eat together; she was staring at me round-eyed, but she said nothing.

"I had noticed that she walked with a limp and asked whether she would like me to fetch water from the well and carry in wood for the fireplace.

"'Do as you wish,' she replied, 'but I haven't asked you to do so, and you must not expect to get paid for it.'

"I wondered why she talked like that, but I told her that I didn't desire any pay. She asked once again, 'Who are you really?'

"'I am a prophetess,' I replied.

"She guffawed so loudly that her mouth was twisted, but she immediately turned serious and asked, 'What do you prophesy?'

"I felt shamefaced and said to her, 'I'd better go.'

"'Perhaps it is best that way,' she replied; 'do you have friends to stay with overnight?'

"'Is there a house a little further on along the road?' I asked.

"'Not only one but many,' she answered. 'But don't you have anything to prophesy?'

"And she smiled, but I didn't know whether it was a kind or an evil smile. 'No, nothing,' I replied.

"I said good-bye and left; she followed me out of the house and said, 'You must be very careful and watch out!'

"It was already dusk, and once again I rejoiced in seeing the colorful clouds high above and a thin web of darkness woven in with the air; but the tree crowns were still sharply silhouetted against the sky. I finally reached a fence and a gate; to my right there was a house. I knew that that was the house I must enter. I knocked on the door, and a man opened it. He had a bushier beard than my father and his clothes were not as tidy as his, but the two might be of the same age.

"'May I stay overnight here?' I asked.

"'Yes, of course,' he said. 'Step inside.'

"A young boy was sitting in the room; he was no doubt the son in the family. They offered me food, and I ate, but I was used to better food in my own house.

"They swept the crumbs off the table with the palms of their hands and threw them on the floor; a dog emerged from under the bed. They got hold of a bottle of brandy and a pair of dice and began to throw, and at the same time they stole furtive glances at me and one of them asked, 'You're not afraid?' 'No, I'm not afraid,' I replied.

"The one who had gotten a six three times in a row, got up from the table and bolted the door, and he said to me, 'Go up in the loft and lie down on the bed.' I did as he told me. The one who had spoken then came up to the loft and began to force his attentions on me, but he didn't manage to do me any harm, since my inner being was filled with prayer. He suddenly started to cry; he stroked my hair and said, 'God bless you, my child!' Then he climbed down from the loft.

"It was very late in the evening, and I immediately fell asleep.

"The sun was shining when I opened my eyes. Through the stair opening I could look down into the parlor; the two men and the dog were lying on the floor, fast asleep. I stole downstairs, lit the fire, and got together a meal from what was in the house and my own food, and I swept the floor and washed the bowls and plates and set the table, and when they still had not awakened, I bent over them and woke them up.

"We sat down to table together. But we had hardly begun to eat, when the sheriff of the district was standing in the doorway. 'Where do you have the stolen goods?' he asked. They didn't answer, and he then wanted to know who I was.

"The sheriff's clerk was waiting outside; he was called in and told to put handcuffs on the men; I was only asked to come along with them; thereupon we were all ordered to mount the horses. They had four horses altogether, and I was told to sit behind the sheriff on his horse.

"The two men and I were locked into a detention room; when we had been sitting there a while and gotten used to the darkness, they asked me who I was. And I answered, 'I am a prophetess.' Then the youngest one began to guffaw and made fun of me; but I felt very sorry for both of them and went down on my knees and prayed for them, and while praying, words came to me that exceeded my understanding and were unknown to me. The young one continued to mock me, but the bearded man rebuked him, 'It's true what she says; she's a prophetess.'

"The sheriff released me the next day, and he said to me, 'You'd better return to your home; you don't know how to keep out of trouble.' He pointed in the direction from which I had come, but I replied, 'Someone is calling me ahead.' He shook his head and let me go.

"Thus I kept on going; I walked on and finally reached a busy place where there was an inn and a fair. There I noticed someone leading a blind boy onto a seesaw made from a long wooden plank on which he was made to walk back and forth. The ground all around was covered with pieces of broken bottles, and his hands were gashed every time he fell, which happened often.

"Then I went over to the man who amused people in this manner and asked if I could be allowed to take the boy's place. He at once gave me permission. The spectators had shouted with joy every time the boy fell into the broken glass and hurt himself, and they exulted no less when I balanced on the plank without falling down and walked many times from one end to the other. But when the spectators finally began to get bored and demanded that the blind boy be put back up, I deliberately plunged down to the ground, and the result was that I cut my wrist; yet the cut did not bleed even though it was quite deep.

"The man asked me, 'Who are you?' I answered him the way I had the others. And he asked me, 'What do you prophesy?' 'I prophesy that because you are evil you will die before nightfall,' I replied, and the spectators began to talk all at the same time. Some of them threatened me, while others asked me to protect them from any evil that might befall him.

"I was dismayed at what I had said, and I wanted to steal away from them. Since it was already dark, I walked around the farm buildings and found a barn in which I lay down to sleep. But no sooner was I back on the road the next morning than I was stopped by a man who asked whether I was the one who had been balancing on the plank. 'Yes, I was the one,' I answered. 'Then you are guilty of a man's death,' he said. 'Did he die?' I asked, but the man retorted, 'Don't try to play innocent.'

"Thereupon I was interrogated by the sheriff. When he had asked me all kinds of questions and I had answered him, he said, 'Be careful, child, go back to your parents! Go back voluntarily, otherwise I will have to pay for your transportation.'

"But when I was released I asked my way until I found the boy, and I took him along with me, and we wandered on and arrived at many unknown places. We worked for our meals on a number of farms; our longest stay was at a parsonage. On weekdays I helped out in the house, and the boy, who was unable to do very much, sang songs to entertain us; he had a beautiful voice.

"On Sundays we went to church; I led him by the hand. But on weekday nights the pastor would gather together all the people of the household and would explain passages from the Bible, and he then questioned us on the articles of faith and read aloud from a mission periodical; it was sent him from some people calling themselves Herrnhuters. One Sunday when I had been listening to his sermon in church many kinds of thoughts had been awakened in me and I felt an intense longing for Christ; I was once again greatly moved at the evening service, and I stood up and asked whether I could speak out about how I felt. The pastor gave his permission, and I began to speak about God's great love which permeates everything even unto the tiniest creature, yes, even lifeless nature, and thus in a way casts a reflection into our visible world. And I said that inside our very being there is a bright and shining dwelling in which the Saviour resides, and that the soul may speak to him friend to friend. And in the heart there is a sanctuary, I said, that is like a garden, in which the soul and the Saviour walk side by side, while He explains to the soul the nature of eternal bliss. Eternal bliss is a state in which the soul and the Saviour are united in such a way that no one can say, 'This is he,' or 'This is I!' but they are one, and wherever they go red flowers will blossom all around. And I added, 'All this I have seen and experienced, and I now see it once again.' And because I really saw it, I began to weep from joy. The pastor said that my confession had been most heartfelt and sincere although somewhat obscure.

"From that time on I began to talk about these things. Many people and groups did not care to hear me, but the Quakers accepted me, and I found that they were no strangers to the truth about the inner light that I knew so well.

"Just as in other places, the authorities in that town too ordered me to return where I came from; if I didn't, they would lock me up. Then I got a strong urge to go down to the harbor that night and ask to go along with any boat that was preparing to sail, no matter where it was heading.

"I followed my urge, and I boarded a boat whose home port was near Egersund.

"While we were sailing along the barren coast, a storm arose. Giant waves buffeted us, and there was no harbor where we could find safety. It was late autumn and the boat filled with snow.

"When the storm finally abated, we were closer to our destination; but my feet were frostbitten and I could hardly walk. And in a few days I had the same pain in every limb.

"But it also happened that the feeling of joy that I felt on seeing beauty everywhere, mostly in the faces and the character of human beings, was greatly increased, as was my joy in beholding the Saviour in the abode of my soul and the flowers that sprung up wherever He trod. At night, when my body ached and I couldn't sleep, I saw it all as a bright image framed by the darkness all around me.

"While I was lying like this in the same manner, I had visions of what I should say if I found someone willing to listen, and I very often would use just those words; but it also happened that nothing was left of the visions, as when water disappears in the sand.

"Once I had been walking across hills and mountains; I was freezing, but I finally found the road leading down to a valley where I had never been before. Then I lost the use of my limbs and couldn't reach any house or dwelling; I lay down to rest in the open. Early the next morning a man stumbled over me; he was on his way to the forest to cut logs

— it had just been snowing —, and he carried me to his house and called the sheriff. But the sheriff knew who I was, for rumors of my coming had preceded me, and he said, 'This is insane behavior, I'll have to force you to go back to your home." I replied, 'If I have to, I'm willing to do that. But I didn't go out into the world because I lacked kindness from my family.' He asked me, 'What do you think you can accomplish for the Lord by wandering around like this?' I answered, 'I don't know.'

"Nevertheless, he let me go."

This was the end of her story.

"What do you want to do now?" I asked. She said, "I want to go home and stay with my father and mother until the sails are set."

"Are you so certain that there will be a ship going to America and that you'll be along?" I asked. And she replied, "Last night, while I was lying awake, it was just as if the wall receded and behind it I saw the sky and the ocean and a ship, and I was on board, and also Mother and Father and all my brothers and sisters, and other people I know."

"You know where I've just come from, Elen?" I asked.

"Yes, you've been to America," she laughed.

"But did you know what I was doing there, before you dreamed about me?" I asked, and she replied, "Oh, yes —! People say that you've never been able to sit still, and that you travel across the oceans and the continents and do just what comes to your mind!"

"Then you and I are pretty much alike," I said, and we both laughed.

Thereupon I explained to her in greater detail about my assignment. And now I have told you, Anne, the story of Elen; you too will get to know her among the group of pilgrims who traveled on the *Restauration*. But I will also soon tell you more about some of the others.

The following day we reached Stavanger. Through the bare tree crowns we could make out the green-crusted towers of the cathedral, and smoke rose from many chimneys into the mild moist evening air and settled low over Breiavatnet Lake. The air was still, and the sound of the beating of the wings of many birds melded with the ringing of the bells.

The Thirtieth Tale

A funeral was taking place the day we arrived in Stavanger. At the intersection where the road led up to Lars Larsen's house at Jeilane, we had to rein in the horses and make way for the funeral procession. I noticed that many of the prominent men of the town were present, the business community being especially well represented. The coffin seemed to be of the expensive type, while the number of people attending was smaller than usual.

I asked a man standing nearby which one of Stavanger's citizens was being buried, and he answered, "Don't you know that? In that case you must have come from a long way away! It is Madame Sælinger; she was one of the town's biggest shipowners; during the last few years she even came close to rivaling Agent Gabriel Kielland."

"Yes, I think I've heard the name," I replied, happy over the fact that he had not recognized me.

And I added, "Wasn't she pretty mean, as well as being rich?"

"Many people thought so," he said. "It's easy to get mean if you think that you've been deprived of some of life's blessings. Madame Sælinger was married three times and never achieved happiness."

"What you say is food for thought, for sure," I replied. "Perhaps you are a master of arts?" I asked — even though I didn't believe it; his clothing was rather shabby and worn, and I had already noticed that he blew his nose with his fingers.

"I'm a shoemaker," he replied, "and from the way people take care of their footwear it is possible for me to tell their character. Madame Sælinger, too, had her shoes made and repaired in my shop, and believe me, I deserve to be called a fool if she wasn't better than her reputation! *And* I was proven right — even though she had to die first. For she has willed her whole fortune to the town — on condition that the money is to be used to build a charitable institution for aged women of quality, both widows and maiden ladies." — "Is her third husband dead, too, since he was not remembered in her will?" I asked.

"He left for America many years ago," the shoemaker answered; "and besides, he was always a wild and dissolute fellow, according to what people say. There's probably little chance that he'll ever return."

"You can't tell," I replied. "But thanks for the information, my dear sir, and good luck to you." And I backed my horse into an adjacent courtyard so that no one in the procession could see me.

When the procession had passed, Elen and I rode up to Lars Larsen. That very same evening he called together the people who had sent me abroad, as well as others —, in fact, as many as his rooms could hold.

As I have already told you, Anne, I had sent many letters from America to Lars Larsen, and everyone present knew their contents, except the letter in which I had indicated that we ought to establish our colony after the fashion of the Rappites. Nor did I mention it on this occasion, but otherwise I made a much more detailed report than I had in my letters.

I had brought with me a map of the northeastern part of the United States, including both New York City and the state of New York. After pointing out to them where Kendall was situated and describing the vegetation and the soil and the prices at which land could be bought, I described the easiest route to get there: along the Hudson River to Albany, and on from there via canal barges, provided Clinton's Big Ditch would be completed before our arrival.

My account was received with a great deal of enthusiasm. The Friends were also happy over the fact that I had gotten in touch with Joseph Fellows and other Quakers and that they thus would not be isolated from other fellow believers and others who could help them when they arrived in the New World.

I also mentioned that I had taken note of the sloop *Restauration* of Egersund as a well-suited vessel in which we could cross the ocean, and Johannes Stene, the most knowledgeable man in regard to ships, said that he would like to take a closer look at the boat as soon as an opportunity presented itself.

Having given them all the news, I soon learned that among the Friends a lot had happened which until then had been unknown to me.

In regard to the question of emigration to America, the Friends continued to be of different opinions. Elias Tastad in spite of all he had been through, wanted to remain in Norway, and he was not the only one. Most of them, however, were of the opinion that in view of the prospects that I had held out to them and all the troubles they feared they would experience in their native land, they wanted to leave and to do so as soon as possible. In Norway the situation was now so bad that no one could take safety and freedom for granted, they said. They mentioned several instances, such as the case of the brothers Knud and Jacob Slogvig from Tysvær, who were kept in custody at the Stavanger town hall, one of them because he had refused to serve in the army and the other because he did not want to be confirmed.

I knew both of them very well and decided to look them up the following day and ask them to tell me themselves about their situation. They more than anyone else would have need of good news from America.

It had so happened that much commotion and disagreement had arisen among the clergy and the common people in my home district of Tysvær. This was most especially true of the people on the farm of Slogvig; in the words of Pastor Swensen Magnus, the farm "was the worst hornet's nest of Quakers found anywhere," and that was said in spite of the fact that no one on the farm had formally become a member of the Society of Friends. But it was undeniable that Anders Slogvig, the father of Knud and Jacob, on several occasions had praised the French Revolution. In addition, Knud had been credited with saying that a republican form of government would be more just than a monarchy; similarly, other statements of his had seemed to indicate that he harbored revolutionary views.

As for myself, I am not able to say whether the pastor in his heart of hearts really believed that the Quakers wanted to overthrow the monarchy and establish a republic and what he described as "conditions like those one finds in Turkey."

But no matter — I visited them in jail the following day. There they were enduring a hard life indeed, for the ceiling was so low that they couldn't stand upright, and the cell was so tiny that they could hardly stretch out their legs when lying on their bunks; they were, however, allowed to remain in a sitting position.

And this is what they told me:

When Jacob — who was in his seventeenth year — was to register for confirmation, he had refused to do so unless the pastor on the basis of Holy Writ could prove that confirmation was truly an ordinance instituted by God.

The pastor tried to persuade him, first with mild words, then more severely, and when all was to no avail he acted summarily: he demanded that the boy be committed to the penitentiary so that he could be instructed there and later be confirmed, or he would have to move from the parish and stay away forever.

This sentence may seem unjust to you, Anne, and you may think that it was an exceptional case. But that was not so at all; for it did use to happen throughout the Norwegian realm that slow and retarded children were put in jail for weeks and months until the main points of the doctrines of faith had been hammered into their heads with the aid of harsh treatment and severe discipline. Pastor Swensen Magnus had once said to one of the slow learners, "I am confirming you not because of your learning, nor for your piety, but solely because of your advanced age and your long beard."

As far as Jacob was concerned, his case was taken to court, and the court supported the pastor.

Jacob and his parents consulted together, and agreed that he was to go to sea and stay out of the country an appropriate length of time; it might happen that the pastor in time would modify his demands.

The day of departure came, and Jacob and his father were to travel together to the city of Stavanger. The other members of the family accompanied him to the boathouse. When he wanted to shake his mother's hand in farewell, she held him close and cried; and he said, "I would rather spend a year in prison and then be able to stay with you, Mother."

Thus nothing came of the plans for a trip to town and hire on a ship, and Jacob waited at home until his case had twice come before the Supreme Court. The verdict was sustained, and once again his family accompanied him to the boathouse; this time he was going to travel in the sheriff's boat.

His mother asked, "You are quite certain that you know everything?" And he answered, "I am certain."

As soon as the boat touched the jetty in Stavanger, he was taken to the town hall and put in a locked room. The pastor turned up and examined him first in regard to the basic truths, as to Who was his Creator, his Redeemer, and his Comforter in Heaven; to that he replied fully, reciting the Articles of Faith, and without hesitation quoted the interpretations of Luther and Pontoppidan. Then the pastor asked questions based on all of Pontoppidan's Explanation of the Catechism, and Jacob gave the answers without any mistakes from the first question to the last.

Then the pastor asked him, "Do you *believe* all this, then?" But Jacob said, "I am being called to account for what I know, not for what I believe."

"Also for what you believe, you obstinate fellow!" exclaimed the pastor angrily. "For it is a pledge of faith that you are going to make before the altar and the countenance of the Lord."

"Yes," Jacob answered, "the pastor is right. For *no other* reason will I be placed behind bars, than that I can be administered the only saving faith and later confess it — under the same kind of constraint."

Jacob had also said other things to provoke the pastor. Swensen Magnus asked him whether he had any opinion as to the Beast in the Book of Revelation and who it really might be. "Well — if it isn't the pastor," Jacob said, "it can hardly be the pastor's wife?" The pastor turned red with anger, but he clenched his teeth and did not open his mouth in reply. His wife was so ugly that it was spoken of far and wide.

Jacob laughed when he told me this. I asked him when he expected to be released.

"I've almost finished my entire sentence, four months," he said, "and I have been ordered to stand at the end of the line in Skjold church next time there's confirmation. But I shall be very careful not to answer a single word during the catechization. Afterwards I'll stay on the farm until everything is ready to ship out; then I'll join you on your trip overseas."

About his brother Knud I can tell the following. When he had reached the age for military service, he was called up by the navy. He told them that he regarded it as sinful for a man to kill his fellow human beings and, furthermore, that he was unable to swear allegiance to the king, as was required.

He was summoned before the magistrate's court and told to swear allegiance or to pay one speciedaler for each day exceeding the stipulated time. He also submitted a writ of defense that he had authored himself, in which he thought he could prove that the New Testament fully supported his views.

This case, too, was appealed all the way to the Supreme Court, and the verdict was to the effect that he was obliged to take the prescribed oath of allegiance. However, the judges were of the opinion that he could apply to the king for dispensation, saying that he was willing instead to make a solemn promise, just as the Herrnhuters had been allowed to do. However, when an approach was made to the Ministry of Justice in this respect, it was maintained that under no circumstances could Knud be exempted from taking the oath. He was, on the other hand, advised to seek the counsel of a minister, so that he would possibly be influenced to change his mind.

A letter was sent from the Ministry of Justice to the Ministry of the Navy, and another from the Ministry of the Navy to the Ministry of Ecclesiastical Affairs, and from the Ministry of Ecclesiastical Affairs to the bishop of the diocese, who asked one of the pastors in the city of Stavanger to convey to Knud the proper understanding of what the Bible says about oaths and military service. By this time *he* too had been put in jail.

The minister visited him in jail and said, "I come to you as the shepherd of your soul." Knud replied, "I don't know of any shepherd of my soul except the Saviour."

When the minister began to admonish him according to Holy Writ, the way *he* understood it and in line with the Augsburg Confession, Knud turned his back on him and put his fingers in his ears; then, still being able to hear the voice of the minister as a low buzzing sound, he began to hum and in that way completely drowned out the other.

Thereupon the pastor gave up and walked away — and Knud expected that his penalty would be increased. But just the opposite occurred: three days later he was released — although he was ordered to appear at the next session of the court.

So he did, and he still refused to swear allegiance. Some time later the officials showed up at Slogvig in order to levy execution on his property. A traveling chest and fifteen lobster pots were all that they could seize as mortgage, and that was not sufficient.

Then he was again summoned to appear in court, and he was required to do the same as before, namely, to swear allegiance and to serve in the military, an obligation imposed on all the male citizens of the realm provided they are of good physical and mental health.

But Knud rejected all demands on the same grounds as before, and was once again put in jail. This happened about a month before I returned to Stavanger; this is how it happened that I found both brothers in prison when I arrived.

I asked Knud, "What are you going to do now?"

"As you know," he said, "they usually sentence malefactors like me to leave the country, and I hope it will happen about the time that you have your ship ready to sail for America. Even if no one else goes with you, I will! And when you get back to Tysvær, tell my entire family that I would like to take them along."

Less than a week later I was once again with my own family, following a four-year absence. It was a great joy to see my mother again; she was still in good health, and so was my sister Kari, the wife of Cornelius Nilsen Hersdal, and my brother Lars.

Now it remains to tell of the many preparations that were made before the voyage could begin; but first I have to tell you something in confidence, Anne.

On the day I watched Anne Cathrine's funeral I felt a cry resounding within me: "You are free, Cleng! You are free!"

And that very same evening, after the get-together at Lars Larsen of Jeilane, I walked over to the cemetery and found the fresh grave containing the coffin of my wife Anne Cathrine. And in a kind of frenzy I began to jump and dance on the soft earth. I didn't come to my senses until I saw a young couple leaping across the graves and over the wall.

The cemetery is a hallowed spot for the living as well as the dead.

But when I had fled in the opposite direction and again was all alone, my melancholy thoughts turned to Yvonne who was no longer among the living.

But it so happened the following Sunday, when I attended a silent meeting of the Society of Friends, that I noticed in the assembly a young woman whose appearance pleased me so much that I immediately was filled with a blissful hope that she might be my intended one. She was young, hardly over twenty, with a clear and steady glance, and her mouth was at the same time both soft and firm. Her curly hair was blond and arranged in a bun at the back. She was beautiful and had a fine body and behaved in many ways as a lady of quality, but her clothes revealed that her circumstances were modest. She spoke a few times during the meeting, and although she always expressed herself in a quiet and unobtrusive manner, what she said seemed to be both straightforward and authoritative.

While walking home in the company of Elias Tastad, I asked who the girl might be, and he answered, "She is Martha Georgiana Jørgensdatter; she is engaged to Lars Larsen, and they are going to be married next Christmas."

The Thirty-first Tale

Among the members of the Quaker congregation in Stavanger there were also a number living outside the city, but in the county. For that reason it was customary for the congregation to hold one of its bimonthly meetings once a year some place or other in the district, preferably on a Sunday in the fall — when the hay had been put in the barn, but before the grain had been cut — and not too far from town. Many of those who could be expected to attend were employed by others and were only free on Sundays.

That particular year it was decided that a bimonthly meeting was to take place at Fogn, one of the large islands in the fjord. This was the home of my late fellow traveler Knud Eide; Martha Georgiana too was born and bred here, as was also the case with her half-brother Ole Johnsen Eide. Many people on the island were sympathetic to the Quaker cause.

The weather had been generally fair and sunny; the meadows had produced a second crop of hay, and the barley was ripening. Toward the east we could see one mountain peak behind another, all of them sharply silhouetted in the clean, crisp air.

The fjord was full of sailing vessels, and as we approached the island of Fogn, whenever people recognized one another, they shouted loud greetings, many sailing up close to other boats and beginning a conversation even before they had got into the harbor.

The meeting was to be held on the Eide farm, and the crowds were flocking there, group upon group, — hundreds of people in all. Only a few of them were Quakers; many of the others joining us were relatives or friends. But we knew that some of our opponents would also show up, since we had heard a rumor that anything might happen that day.

It had been announced that after the business part of the meeting had been attended to, I was to tell about my stay in the United States. Indeed, the entire town and county had heard about my return to Norway.

When the time came for me to speak, I stepped up on a big rock and asked in a loud voice if everyone could hear me. Both those nearby and those furthest away replied in the affirmative.

I began my speech by bringing to them a greeting, his last, from Knud Eide. Choosing my words carefully, I depicted his courage and his perseverance and the gentle way he endured his sickness and faced death, and I conveyed to them a wish that he had expressed toward the end — although it was not the complete truth, I thought it would touch many a heart — that an apple tree from his home district be planted on his grave. "In this assembly," I said, "there must indeed be many who will follow in his footsteps, and I promise that I shall lead you to the spot and show you where the seed will sprout."

As I had figured, everyone was touched by these words; I was indeed moved myself and also felt great satisfaction when people round about began to sob loudly.

Since I knew very well that everyone hadn't come to be swayed by fair words, I was not taken aback when an angry voice shouted, "You sold Knud into slavery among the Turks! Any fool knows that! But that's to be expected of Cleng Peerson — once upon a time he sold himself, hook, line, and sinker, to Madame Sælinger's moneybags!"

I cleared my throat and said, "My good man, you're right. It's true that I've never put a very high price on my own honor, and I will immediately step down and never open my mouth again. But I don't think anyone here believes that I would have dared come to you here if I were guilty of the evil deed of selling your friend and mine, my very brother!"

And I stepped down and mixed with the people. But then was heard a shout that drowned out every one else: "Let Cleng Peerson speak!"

And when several men lifted me up and carried me back to the spot where I had been standing, I forgot all about regret and shame; I had been roused to action by what had happened, and I continued in a loud voice: "But *I* know where slavery flourishes and where the Turk ravages the land, and I shall now give you an example of it!"

I bent down and held out my hand to Jacob Andersen Slogvig, who was sitting right below me; I pulled him up on the stone, introduced him to the assemblage, and told them about all that he had suffered: "But when he didn't think it was right for him to be confirmed according to the teachings of the Church, the secular authorities, with the blessings of the pastor, sentenced him to four months in prison. During that time he was to be instructed in how to be saved, even though it became evident that he already was as brimful of biblical knowledge as any ecclesiastic and could not be stumped on a single point in Christian doctrine. That's right, isn't it?" and Jacob replied, "Yes, that's right."

In the same manner I spoke about his brother Knud; I said, "This is his brother, and he has suffered many kinds of harassment for several years and even been in jail because he didn't want to swear allegiance to the King or serve in the military, even though Holy Writ says: 'Thou shalt not swear!' — as well as: 'He who takes the sword, shall perish by the sword.'"

I also called Elias Slogvig up, and I asked him, "You didn't want to have your youngest child baptized, did you?" And he replied, "No, I didn't, because I believe that baptism was a preparatory and precedential act in the Christian congregation. But now we have received complete enlightenment through the Holy Spirit, baptism is an unnecessary thing, yes, it may even lead to the ruination of the soul if anyone sits back and thinks that baptism is enough instead of seeking true conversion." I asked him, "What happened when you didn't allow your child to be baptized?" He replied, "First I received several requests from the pastor to bring it to church; but when I still did not obey, he dispatched the sheriff, who seized the child with force, and it was baptized under duress."

Then the pastor of the parish unexpectedly stepped forth and asked, "But has your child been harmed in any way by being blessed through holy baptism?"

Elias burst into tears in front of the entire assemblage, and he replied, "My child is as dear to me now as before."

The pastor spoke again, "Why are you so stiff-necked? Does it not say in Holy Scripture that the authorities do not carry a sword in vain? And why do you have contempt for the shepherds of your souls? Have you not read that the Lord placed some to be shepherds and teachers among you, and that you ought to honor and respect them? Well I know that often we can make mistakes and do people injustice, but you are preaching revolt against the existing order, and it is not spiritual freedom that you are aiming at, but republicanism and other godlessness, inspired, as you are, by the ideas of the French Revolution, without, however, having understood them correctly or digested them. For I know you, I know that many of you are a little mad and have weak natures, and you reveal an unequaled obstinacy and foolhardiness! You take delight in the new and the peculiar, you have a desire for distinction and a kind of freedom and independence that it is impossible to achieve without overthrowing society. Yes, I have even noticed that the Quakers generally come from the lower classes and that they do not possess that spirit of enterprise and the ability to become affluent that characterize the Haugeans or the Herrnhuters. But instead of using your ability and talents in order to earn your daily bread in Norway, you believe that as soon as you are ashore in America, ripe fruits will fall from the trees and still your hunger." Lars Larsen got up and answered him, "It is true that most of us are lowly and humble people, but I would remind the pastor that among the English Quakers there are many who associate with kings and princes. Still, they look upon that as nothing compared to how they please their God. And bear in mind that the reason that so many of us are still without means is that we were confined to the prison ships and were not until recently able to take advantage of the increasing prosperity that is beginning to be evident in town and country. But so that we should not starve and suffer, the English Quakers have arranged it so that a system of poor relief has been established among us, according to which those of us who have more than is strictly needed, share with those who have less. In the same way it is our hope that we will improve our circumstances and enjoy greater spiritual freedom if we emigrate to America. But I had hoped that our friend Cleng, instead of getting into an argument that profits us little, instead would inform the people here assembled about what North America can offer its inhabitants."

I did not feel that his gentle reproof was unjustified, and without getting into further altercations I began to describe the country to them: that already far out at sea one could smell the fragrance of forests and fields as if they were a garden in full bloom.

"And it offers much more," I said, "than it promises from afar. The air is clean and the climate mild, with a clear sky most of the year; but in winter the cold may in some areas be more severe than in this country. There is plenty of food for everyone who will take the trouble to go out and get it. The sea abounds in lobsters and crabs, and in the forests there are turkeys and wild fowl, geese, and pheasants, as well as many other birds good for eating, in addition to game animals such as elks and deer. Fruits and various kinds of nuts and berries are growing wild everywhere, and the people grow some vegetables that are unknown in this country: pumpkins, squash, and tomatoes, as well as corn, which we call maize. I have eaten all these fruits and vegetables myself and find them to be excellent. And there are fish not only in the ocean but also in the rivers. These rivers are among the longest in the world and are connected by lakes that reach thousands of miles into the very heart of the continent; they are so big that if you are out in the middle of a lake you cannot see the shores in any direction, and many are navigable even for steamers."

"Now you're lying again! You're known to be a braggart and a loud-mouth!" someone shouted.

"Then it may indeed be true as the rumor has it," the pastor inter-jected in a mocking tone, "that America only a few years ago had a large population, but a plague like the Black Death laid the land waste — so that they who emigrate will find farms with cleared and fertile fields, with buildings, clothes, and furniture all ready for them, exactly the way they looked when their former owners departed this life. That is the belief of many a man in this assemblage."

"No," I replied; "most of the country is still uninhabited and has no doubt been that way down through the ages, and everyone has to work to make a living. But one has more gain from one's toil than here in Norway. I have often heard the rumor that the pastor mentioned, but it has not been spread by me; why does the pastor bring it up here? Perhaps he wants to set up a smoke screen and spread the idea that I am telling lies?"

"Cleng Peerson is known for many things, including his inclination to paint a gray landscape in lively colors," the pastor replied. "It is my intention solely to urge you all to be thoughtful and to deliberate and —"

"And be humble and servile?" I interjected and cut the minister off for good; I lifted up Elias Slogvig's child who was toddling around the stone on which I was standing — the child that he had been forced to have baptized —, I lifted it high above my head and shouted, "Look, this is Elias Slogvig's child, the one I just mentioned! When it grows up, will it then have to crawl before any tyrant who has the power to place his boot on its neck, and kiss his shoes, and thereupon suffer beatings and kicks in addition? Or is it to possess the freedom to act according to its own conscience without fear of judge or pastor? From the moment we leave Norway behind we shall not be forced to slave for the rich the way our ancestors have done; in North America everyone can in truth be the architect of his own fortune — not only his own but also that of his children. Therefore, any one of you who loves freedom, shake the dust of Norway off your feet and leave this Babylon! The land of Canaan lies beyond the sea! Over there a fisherman can be elected senator and a crofter become president!"

With this the bimonthy assembly came to an end. On the way to the dock I stopped at a farm and asked for a drink of water; my throat was as dry as a flour bin.

A girl came out, and I immediately recognized her; she was Martha Georgiana, Lars Larsen's fiancée.

"Nice to see you again," I said. "Weren't you at the meeting?" — for I had not seen her there.

"Yes, I was there," she answered.

"And what about you —," I asked, "are *you* going to America?"

"Yes," she replied; "when Lars leaves, I'll go along."

"But first I suppose you'll celebrate your wedding?" I asked and made my voice sound indifferent. And she answered, "At Christmastime."

All at once our eyes met, and neither one of us looked away.

"I must say you're very good with words, Cleng Peerson," she added.

I remained silent; then I said, "Thanks for the drink, Martha Georgiana."

Once again she looked me straight in the eye, and I was at a loss to know whether her glance revealed distrust or kindness. She slowly closed the door when I turned to leave.

Not long after the bimonthly assembly at Fogn I traveled with Johannes Jacobsen Stene to Egersund to inspect the sloop the *Restauration*. We bought it for a price of 1,800 speciedalers. Johannes Jacobsen sold his own vessel for 1,200 dalers and thus became the owner of the sloop, both in name and in fact. Some of the other emigrants contributed various amounts to cover the balance of the purchase price.

This happened, however, after I myself had left Norway once again.

As a traveling companion this time I had a man by the name of Andreas Stangeland, a modest and friendly fellow of twenty-five.

This time, too, we traveled via Gothenburg, but our ship had to call at Falmouth in England before setting out across the Atlantic.

The very day after Andreas Stangeland and I had embarked at Gothenburg, I began to feel unwell, and I became very ill, feeling worse than I could remember ever having done before. The skipper thought it was pneumonia, basing his opinion on my symptoms and what he could find out from *A Medical Manual for Seafarers*. But when we approached Falmouth, I forced myself to go up on deck; even though the fever had left me, I felt very weak indeed.

It was only with an effort that I managed to stay up on deck in fair weather, which was then the case; but suddenly and quite unexpectedly I was thrown against the ship's rail by the oncoming waves; they were so strong that I broke my left leg. It was a bad oblique fracture.

After that, the captain refused to take me with him across the Atlantic. He maintained that the voyage would be the death of me, or I would at best remain a cripple for the rest of my life. A physician from a local hospital came on board and voiced the same opinion.

Still, it was very much against my will that I was carried ashore and brought to the city hospital. My leg was put in traction, and I was also treated for what remained of my pneumonia.

My health returned slowly, but the assignment entrusted to us by the Friends suddenly looked very precarious indeed.

In the meantime the Swedish schooner had crossed the ocean. But before it had left Falmouth harbor Andreas Stangeland and I had thoroughly discussed how we best could handle the matter. At first we weighed the pros and cons: he could immediately return home or stay with me until the spring; or he could continue with the ship to New York. One difficulty was that he didn't understand the English language; but the skipper came to our aid as far as that was concerned. He offered to introduce Andreas to a Norwegian he knew in the city, and he assured us that this man would help him in every way.

I myself wrote a letter that he was to give to my friend the land agent Joseph Fellows. In it I asked Joseph to see that Andreas would get the necessary guidance so that he could do the most pressing of his duties before the arrival of the sloop. Its departure had, as far as we knew, been set at somewhere around midsummer the following year.

We also discussed in detail whether we should let our friends know what had happened. We decided that it would be best to keep my condition a secret, and that Andreas was not to send any communications direct from America to Norway. As the preparations over there made progress, he was to dispatch his reports to me, and I would send them on under my own name.

I found it necessary to proceed in this manner for several reasons, and I will mention them to you in all frankness. You should know that some of those who at first had been very eager to leave Norway had become less enthusiastic, and anxiety had superseded confidence; they had begun to give thought to all that is entailed in leaving one's family, friends, and dear ones forever, in parting with farms and lands, leaving behind all one's belongings, and commending oneself to the capricious ocean and a strange new world. Several of the women were greatly concerned — mostly because of their small children; some of them had even pleaded with their husbands to stay home.

I feared that if these people were to find out that the man who was to precede them and arrange everything was now lying sick in England, this might be the last straw. And my dream, which like a growing tree, had been striking ever firmer roots, would be shattered. This dream was that I — helped by concealment and cunning if that were necessary — would gather all the emigrant Norwegians into a communitarian society on the pattern of the Rappites, with everything being molded the way I thought would be most useful and serviceable, and with me in a way serving as their president. Still in all, I would not seize any external or undeserved power, I thought, but would rather be the one who would help everyone in the spirit of kindness and humility. Alas, how little I still knew myself, Anne, — and I was over forty! How did I dare compare myself with Frederick Rapp! I did not possess his faith and piety, nor did I have his ability to build a community. But I was under the delusion that a man who can find the place were a city might be founded, is also able to govern it and serve as its mayor. Behind the mask of false meekness I was hiding these delusions of grandeur both from myself and from others.

Nevertheless, I must tell you that at the time that Andreas Stangeland left me and throughout that winter, it was my hope to get to America ahead of the Sloopers. But I remained ill and weak — even though I was well enough and callous enough to change the reports that I received from him — as if I myself had reached my destination and was also the one who was arranging everything. Still, my conscience did bother me day and night, and I formulated plans about returning to Norway instead, before the departure of the *Restauration* — and then I would either pretend that I had come from America or gradually prepare my friends for the truth.

But even as late as May I was still feeling weak and unwell. Consequently — since I could not postpone it any longer — I sent a letter to Lars Larsen, telling him that I was staying in the city of Porthleven in the south of England and asking him to arrange that the sloop would call at that port and pick me up. Since I didn't say any more, he and the other Friends would believe that for some reason or another I had left America and arrived in England; I added some veiled expression to the effect that I intended to look up some Quaker friends of mine in the district.

I regained my strength with the return of summer, and I remained at Porthleven waiting to be reunited with the emigrants.

But I was constantly turning over in my mind whether I should continue to lie to them or tell the truth when the time came.

The Thirty-second Tale

Iver Halvorsen Reveim was the name of one of the Quakers living in the vicinity of Stavanger. He had been introduced to the Quaker faith by his brother Knud, who, as you know, had been a prisoner in England. Iver Halvorsen was, as far as I know, the only one of the Quakers who was sentenced by a court of law to leave the country.

Already before Iver had joined the Society of Friends he had displayed his rebelliousness by refusing to pay the tithe to the clergy. When the tithe after some time came to a large amount, an execution against his property was held, and bedding and other belongings were taken; they even went so far as to remove the stove from his sitting room and sold it to pay his debt.

He thereupon refused to have his two youngest children baptized, and he was once again taken to court. The sentence was to the effect that he had to pay twenty speciedalers for every week after a certain deadline if he continued to refuse to have them baptized.

Since he did nothing to carry out the sentence, the fines in time amounted to a considerable sum, and following another execution against his property most of his livestock was expropriated: a horse, seven cows, two rams, thirteen sheep, and two lambs. He was allowed to keep one calf.

But in spite of all this Iver was still a prosperous man — he owned his own boat and gear and was part owner of several other vessels, and in addition he had a lot of money — and partly through neighbors and friends and partly through wise purchases at the autumn market at Stavanger he was fully able to replace all his livestock.

In another court case which also concerned his attitude toward the authorities and his being a Quaker, he was banished from the country, being told to leave within eight weeks. He appealed the verdict, however, and the Apellate Court upheld him.

When the question of buying the *Restauration* came up and he was asked to become part owner and to join the emigrant party, he answered, "Since I have fought so bitterly for the right to remain in the land of my fathers, should I now sell out and forget about it!"

Nevertheless, he made a Jephta's sacrifice. Late one evening there was a knock on the door of Lars Larsen of Jeilane; Iver was standing outside. He was pale and drawn when Lars let him in, and his hands were trembling as if he was suffering from a fever.

Lars let him rest and quiet down a bit and did not ask him what was the matter. But Iver said, "I have decided that Halvor is to leave the country and go with you to America, provided he himself is not opposed to it."

"Have you mentioned it to him?" asked Lars.

"No, I'll do that tomorrow," Iver replied. And he added, "As far as I'm concerned, he can take with him any of my belongings."

Halvor was his eldest son; he was fifteen years old.

Lars countered, "God will surely not demand such a sacrifice of you. Let him stay at home!"

But Iver replied, "You know what I have suffered, and I can probably bear what the future must bring. But I am an old tree bent by the wind, and I would not be sorry to see Halvor have the chance to grow straight and stand tall."

Thereupon Iver rode home. He talked to his son about it, and the latter said yes. Halvor Iversen Reveim was the youngest of the emigrants to cross the sea at his own risk.

In the case of each individual emigrant one could dwell on very special reasons and circumstances that led to his leaving: Ole Hetletvedt had been jilted by a girl; Gudmund Haugaas had had a quarrel with the landlord he was working for; Endre Dahl had been crushed by poverty. But I cannot discuss all this in greater detail because more significant events have to be included in my story. However, I think you ought to learn how it happened that my sister Kari and her husband, Cornelius Nilsen Hersdal, with their four children finally decided to emigrate.

When Kari and Cornelius had met each other for the first time, it had happened like this: on a very foggy day she had been working far out in the fields of the farmer in the neighboring district; it was late in the summer. The farmer was cutting down birch trees, and Kari was putting together bundles of leafy branches.

The farmer went home in the early evening, but she continued working until dark; thus, when she came to return to the farmhouse she was not able to find her way. Hours went by, and the people on the farm began to worry about her. The farmer went outside and began to ring the bell on the storehouse roof so that she could be guided by the sound.

Kari rejoiced when she heard the bell; actually she was not very far away, since her sense of direction was better than she thought.

She followed the sound; but she was not the only one to do so. Cornelius Hersdal — who lived in another part of the district and who hadn't seen Kari for years — was just then in the vicinity; he was looking for a runaway bullock. When the mist descended on everything, being a stranger in the area, he was completely lost. Then the bell sounded, and at the storehouse corner he and Kari bumped into each other and clasped each other in order not to fall.

Cornelius stayed the night on the farm, but he slept very little. The reason was that when he and Kari had bumped into each other and he had seen her face in the light of the lantern that the farmer had placed on the storehouse steps, he had thought to himself, "She's going to be mine."

Kari served on the farm a whole year after this, and both the farmer and his wife were very satisfied with her. When she was leaving them, the farmer said, "You've been a good and faithful worker, Kari, and I'd very much like to give you something besides your wages. What would you like?"

She blushed, and did not answer. He said, "I know what you're thinking of. You'd like to have the storehouse bell, but you think it's too much to ask. Right?"

And Kari's face turned even deeper red; between tears and laughter, she said, "How did you know that?"

"I knew it," he said, "because we men sometimes are smarter than you women like to think! Ask my wife, she knows me!"

And the farmer's wife laughed and said, "He's read me like a book for twenty-five years; you've got to watch out for him!"

The farmer went out at once, got hold of a ladder, took down the storehouse bell, and gave it to Kari. Later on it became the ship's bell on the *Restauration,* and she brought it with her to Kendall. There it turned out to be a good thing to have. About that I will tell you later.

During the time they were engaged, Cornelius, together with the other men of the district, was called up by the military to fight against the Swedes. They all returned about the time they were expected — with two exceptions. One of them had been killed by a Swedish bullet, and no one knew anything about Cornelius; he had disappeared during a skirmish. Whether he was dead or wounded or taken prisoner no one knew.

But Kari walked every day to the top of the nearest hill. From there she could look out over the ocean, and every sail and every approaching horseman that she noticed rekindled her hope that perhaps it was her fiancé coming home.

One day while she was standing there as usual, someone put his arms around her from behind and covered her eyes; she resisted with all her power when one hand clasped her breast and the stranger tried to kiss her. Then she knew who it was; she cried in joy, "It's you, Cornelius!"

He had been a prisoner of war, but he had not suffered any mistreatment — and he had later crossed over the border and had walked right across the entire country.

Right after that they celebrated their wedding. They were always very happy together and were deeply fond of each other.

But Cornelius also loved his land as if it were a human being; he lived at Hersdal, a farm which is located higher up than Hesthammer and in a northeasterly direction.

Cornelius was considered to be one of the Friends almost from the beginning, even though he had not sent in a written application for membership in the society. But every time he came to Stavanger he participated in the silent meetings.

I visited him and Kari the very first Sunday after I had returned from America in the spring of 1824. Kari would later often remind me about my visit to Tysvær: "You lay on the bed and knitted," she said; "of course I remember it! You even took the stocking I was knitting away from me; you claimed that it was impossible for you to tell us your story unless you were doing something with your hands. And lying there, you seemed to be describing a magnificent picture for me, of a land where the trees were swaying from all the fruit on their branches and where the soil yielded the richest of crops. And I thought of our own unproductive soil and all our sloping fields. But it seemed to me that even you were completely fascinated by your own account; you got up and began to pace the floor, your eyes were shining, your entire face lit up, and suddenly you threw away your knitting and began to wave your hands about to show us what a marvelous country America was."

It's possible that I did just that. It was my intention to make them both come along, and I knew that it would not be easy to persuade Cornelius.

When I left their farm the following day, he accompanied me across the yard, and I spoke as follows, "Wouldn't you consider taking Kari and the children and coming along with me if other people, maybe, from this district also decide to leave?"

"Never," he answered.

Kari had overheard us; she was going over to the cookhouse. She stuck her head out through the door and said, "Oh yes, we must leave, Cornelius!"

"Never," he repeated. "I know what it is to be away from the land where your roots are. I won't move from Hersdal even if I have to stay behind all by myself!"

It was shortly after this that with many others we all traveled to the bimonthly assembly at Fogn, the meeting that I have already told you about. But Cornelius remained adamant.

During the fall of that year he was summoned to the pastor, and Swensen Magnus demanded that he answer for his sectarian sympathies. A law then in force could be interpreted to the effect that Quakers could be forced to leave their homes and settle at the nearest place of refuge, where the authorities had granted the Quakers the right to hold their meetings. Stavanger had not as yet been designated such a place of refuge, but the pastor said or at least made believe that the town was actually an official refuge for Quakers, and he indicated to Cornelius that he might have to move away from the parish.

When Cornelius returned home and told her what had happened, Kari said, "If we're going to be driven away from Hersdal, we might as well go to America as to Stavanger. It amounts to the same thing."

"Not quite," Cornelius replied; "for I could always sit on a hill top the way you did when you where waiting for me to come back from Sweden. But in America it'll be difficult to know even which direction Tysvær is in."

"But when I was standing there, you came from behind and put your arms round me," Kari answered. "If you lived in Stavanger, I'm afraid that the farm here would get to be like a sweetheart who'd be out of your reach, forever. I'm sure it would be much better for us if we traveled far enough so that you wouldn't get a chance to fret and grieve over what you've lost; and that way, you wouldn't see your sweetheart in the arms of another. Besides, you might give some thought to me and the children! The kind of future in store for them here will probably not be much to look forward to."

Cornelius remained silent for a while; then he said, "If the truth is to be told, if I were sure of obtaining my own land, I would rather go to America than stay in Stavanger and just walk on cobblestones until the end of my days. But I'm afraid that if the day ever comes that I sow and reap in a strange land, I'd feel as if all my ancestors had risen from their graves and followed every step I made and blamed me for not tilling the land of my forefathers."

They spoke no more of it until Christmas. But during a get-together at Rossadal it so happened that Cornelius met most of the others from that parish who later sailed to America on the *Restauration*. The fact that Knud and Jacob Slogvig had weighty reasons for leaving and spoke accordingly did not seem to change his thinking. He was quite impressed, however, by the fact that such a sober-minded man as Daniel Stensen Rossadal had practically made a final decision. Daniel was not so much leaving for his own sake, but rather for that of his daughter Elen. She had traveled around, preaching and calling herself a prophetess, and people had often complained about her. Besides, she had had a vision of a small ship in the middle of the ocean and had interpreted the vision as being the ship that was to take them to America. I don't know if Daniel believed all this, but he was greatly worried about his daughter and believed me when I told him that in the New World no one would threaten or frighten a person who lived according to his convictions in matters of faith.

When Kari and Cornelius were on their way home from the party, he suddenly said to her, "We'd better leave after all."

"In that case, I've got good news for you," Kari answered. "Your brother will go too."

"Nils?" Cornelius exclaimed, so sharply that she gave a start.

"Yes," she said. "Aren't you happy about that?"

"I'm far from happy about that," he replied. "Here I've gone about easing my conscience with the idea that Nils might take over Hersdal. I was going to practically make him a gift of it."

Once again he was filled with an feeling of anguish and indecision, but Kari did all she could to persuade him.

Then one day the following spring he heard that Daniel Rossadal had had a message from the city: those persons in Tysvær who had indicated that they might leave had to give him a speedy and firm promise that they were actually leaving, provided they still intended to do so; Daniel came to Hersdal, and when he had told them why he had come, Cornelius just sat by the stove chewing on a wood splinter. He chewed so long that it became pulp.

Kari was almost crying: "Don't you *want* to, Cornelius?"

He spat the remains of the splinter into his palm and sat there rubbing it; at last he answered, "Some people leave because they would like to, others because they have to. As for myself, I'll be leaving like a blind man, who is taken by the hand by someone and who doesn't know where the next step will lead him. But the animals are to stay on the farm. They are not to be sold one by one and spread like chaff before the wind. It should be enough that *people* leave and lose their homes."

That spring, auctions were held both at Hersdal and Rossadal. Few of the things sold fetched a good price; but the money was nevertheless sufficient to enable both families to equip themselves with what was necessary and have enough left over to pay for the voyage and buy land in America.

They kept their bedclothes and regular clothing, and both households took with them as much dried and smoked meat as was available, as well as plenty of flatbread. All their kitchen utensils were also to be taken along, but they sold off most of their farm tools and implements, in accordance with the directions I had given before I had left, since I knew that they could buy better farm implements over here and that the prices were moderate. But my sister Kari took along with her her griddle for baking and the storehouse bell; Cornelius brought along his anvil and his finest ax.

It remains for me to tell that Cornelius, in spite of the decision that had been made, began to feel increasingly restless as they got closer to the time of departure. One morning he was not in bed when Kari woke up early in the morning. It was right before midsummer, and she wondered why he had not returned — she thought he had stepped outside at the call of nature — since most of the farm work that was to be done prior to their departure had already been taken care of.

Having lain awake waiting for about a half hour, she put on her clothes and went out, and from the doorway she saw him mowing the meadow right below the house.

Nothing specific had been agreed with the new owner, but Kari had had the understanding that all the hay would be his, and it was very unusual in Norway to start haying in June. But the spring had been quite warm and wet that year, and all the vegetation was well advanced.

When Kari came back in, she noticed that his food was still untouched; he had not eaten anything. Then she prepared a meal of flat-bread and butter and sour milk, as well as herring and cold potatoes, and she brought it out to him. "Have you begun mowing?" she said. But he continued working as if he didn't want anything to do with her. About the food she had brought, all he said was: "Just leave it there." She put it on a flat stone and remained standing there, watching him intently. Since he behaved as if his own wife were a stranger to him, she felt greatly hurt and also a bit worried, and she finally walked back to the house.

When it was time for the late morning meal, she once again brought him some food. The food she had brought earlier was still there, untouched, and he did not reply to her when she spoke to him. The sinews in his neck stood out like taut ropes as he wielded the scythe. The veins swelled in his forehead, which was covered with a film of perspiration; it ran into his eyes, falling like tears down his cheeks. The grass yielded to his powerful strokes; he swung the scythe like a man out of his mind.

Then she walked over and stood right in front of him: "What is wrong with you, Cornelius?" But he didn't even ask her to move away; she had to jump out of the way of the flashing scythe.

Thus the entire day passed. In the afternoon she once again walked down to him. He was so tired that his arms and legs were trembling, and he lay down on the grass; he put a jar of sour milk to his lips and emptied it in one draft. Then he threw himself on the grass and lay there as if he were dead, with his arms and legs stretched out and his eyes closed. Kari sat down next to him, dried his forehead with a handful of grass, and once more she said, "What is wrong with you, Cornelius?" "Don't ask me, Kari!" he wailed, and he turned away and hid his face.

He immediately seized the scythe and began to mow, keeping it up until the sun set. Then he ate the rest of the food that had been left for him out in the field; he returned to the house, went to bed, and fell asleep at once. And Kari has told me that when she lay down at his side, she noticed that the skin of his palms was cut to shreds.

She could not sleep for a long while, and she woke up early the next morning. Finding herself alone in the bed, she walked out to him in the meadow, where a large section had already been mowed.

He kept it up that entire day also; by then most of the haying was all done. When she spoke to him, his answers were as short as before. He came back to the houses late in the evening, grabbed an armful of half-dried hay, carried it into an empty stall, and lay down to sleep.

The third night she stayed awake until dawn. Then she slept an hour or two. She got up and stole into the cowbarn. He had left the empty stall and crept over to one of the cows — she had put them inside for the night since it looked like thunder. He was sound asleep, his head resting against the animal's muzzle, and he had his arm around its neck.

Walking alone across the fields in the early morning hours she saw in a new light all that owning this land meant to him. She went back to the house and got out a scythe, and out of love for her husband she began to mow where he had left off the night before.

Cornelius came out not long after, and for the first time he spoke to her without her first having addressed him; with harsh words he reproached her for not leaving him in peace.

She had not expected such a reaction from him, but she dropped the scythe and hurried back to the house. She woke her eldest daughter and asked her to take care of the other children, and then she went to see her brother-in-law Nils, who had hired out on another farm in the district, and asked him to come with her immediately.

Kari and Nils came to Hersdal toward evening. Cornelius had by that time almost finished mowing the last piece of pasture; he had only a small strip to go, and Nils held her back, saying, "Let's not go down to him now."

The sun, nearing the horizon, cast a red light across the fields; as Cornelius, dead tired, was wielding the scythe, his shadow ran before him like a ghost.

Having cut the last blade, he fell to the ground and lay there — it looked as if a big tree had been torn up by the roots in a storm — and when Nils and Kari ran over to him, he was weeping and shaking all over. Then he lifted his raw hands toward heaven and shouted, "O God, can you forgive me? God, can you forgive me?"

But that night he slept under the same roof as the others, and they spoke with each other. He said to Kari, "For hundreds of years, generation after generation, there has been a man of my family tilling the soil of Hersdal to get food for himself and his family. Their hands were sore and worn, but they got their harvest, and, except when the crop failed, it gave everyone what he needed. It's always been that way in our time, Kari, and there's no reason why it shouldn't have gone on that way. I didn't think I could possibly leave it until I had trodden it step by step, just like they used to every spring and fall, as long as my family's lived here."

Very soon after that the emigrants from Tysvær left their homes, all in one group. The Slogvigs' boat was to take them to Stavanger. Thus

Knud and Jacob Anderssøn became the first ones to embark on the long voyage. Their parents were going to accompany them to Stavanger, and as they locked the door, their father said, "Much can happen in a little place like this. First one of you had to serve in the penitentiary, and later on both of you did. But now you're on the road to freedom. The Lord be with you! Fight for your salvation and for the republic!"

Then the vessel lay to at the Hervig boathouse, and those who were to leave from there went on board. Finally, they called at the harbor of Kårstø. The people from Rossadal and Hersdal were all gathered here; among the latter were also Cornelius's brother Nils and his wife, Brita Christophersdatter, and also two young men by the name of Gudmund Haugaas and Georg Hesja.

Among those who saw them off I must first mention my mother; it was the last time she saw her daughter. Kari has told me herself what Mother told her when she said farewell: "If I possibly could, I wouldn't have hesitated a minute to come along with you. As long as I can remember I have had a dream that is always coming back: I see a ship at full speed, its sails billowing, and then I am wandering through an unknown land, and I know no hunger or fatigue, but I am filled with a feeling of melancholy joy. But here at home cows and cats, as well as people, are waiting to be looked after. God bless you all," — and she embraced Kari and each one of her children and took Cornelius's hand in both of hers. As long as they could see her, she was standing on the dock, waving; her white hair had worked loose and looked like wing-beats in the wind.

Most of the grown men among the Sloopers were used to boats and sailing, but no one thought himself capable of being in command on a long voyage of the kind that lay ahead. For that reason they got in touch with a young skipper who lived in Thomas Madland's house; he had had to stay on shore for about a year due to an injury to his foot. His name was Lars Olsen Helland, and he hailed from Bergen. For the past year he had had a job in Simon Lima's shipchandler store; he had at the same time taken an interest in the teachings of the Quakers, as well as in one of Thomas Madland's daughters. Now he was fit, and he said he was willing to captain the *Restauration* across the Atlantic.

He was authorized by the Friends to hire Peder Eriksen Meland as chief mate; this man also came from Bergen. On May 9, 1825, Peder Meland sailed the sloop from Egersund to Stavanger.

Much discussion took place as to the best course to be taken across the ocean. The shortest line drawn between Stavanger and New York would take them north of Scotland and then toward the southern point of Newfoundland, continuing along the coast of the United States to their destination.

The less experienced among them thought that this would be the best route. But Lars Helland was not of that opinion, and he was supported by both Lars Larsen and Johannes Stene, the ones who besides himself had the main responsibility for the success of the voyage and were also the most knowledgeable.

Skipper Helland explained the problem like this: "You know that southwesterly winds prevail along the coast of Norway in the summertime. We must figure that that will also be the case over large parts of the North Atlantic. In other words: we'll have the wind against us, and then soon enough the shortest route could become the longest. If on the other hand we lay our course so far south that we get into the area of the trade winds, we can hope to have a favorable wind all the time — here the winds usually blow from the northeast. And we also avoid the greatest danger known to seafarers sailing to America: all the icebergs that drift down along the coast of Labrador and Newfoundland this time of the year. And you must consider," he added, "how tightly packed you'll be, with so many people in such a small ship; it would be a very good thing if as many as possible could stay up on deck as long as possible. So I propose that we set our course for Madeira — where we can obtain water and provisions for the last time — and that we then sail due west until we reach the Bahamas. Then we sail in a northerly direction, straight for Cape Hatteras and then to New York. We must reckon that the crossing will take us about three months."

Everyone knew by that time that I was in England after — as they believed — having spent the winter in America, where everything had been made ready for them to the best of my ability. It was therefore decided that the *Restauration* was to call at Porthleven and take me on board.

The skipper also maintained that it would be useful if we could take on fresh water in England, since the ship's tanks were rather small and we could on no account hope to get across the Atlantic safe and sound without strict rationing.

Lars Helland also proposed that since space was limited it would be a good thing if the emigrants would arrange to do their cooking in common. As for provisions, he recommended salt and smoked meat, in addition to Lübecker sausages, which are a good remedy against seasickness, as well as dried fish, flatbread, and ship's biscuits, in addition to other kinds of food that would keep over a long period of time. He finally advised them to bring along plenty of sour milk in addition to beer, but each family was to take with them a minimum of kitchen utensils and tools. They complied with this suggestion, but some did it very reluctantly, since they had brought from their homes many objects that were dear to them and that they were very unwilling to relinquish. But Helland informed them that the total space put at their disposal on the lower deck amounted to about 480 square feet, or less than ten square feet for each person. And of this about 250 square feet had to be given over to sleeping quarters.

Lars Larsen nailed the bunks together; it was so arranged that a married couple were assigned a double bunk, while two children were to share a single bunk. Adults and unmarried girls were to stay far forward, and the unmarried young fellows were to be astern; they all were to be on the same deck and there were to be no partitions except large pieces of canvas that were hung so that each family could to some extent be all by itself. The skipper and the mate had a cabin together, far astern.

The bunks were put up on the wooden deck that had been constructed over the cargo of rod iron which they had taken on on my advice. Based on my experience in New York, I was of the opinion that they would be able to sell this cargo at a handsome profit. The iron weighed no less than 6,300 pounds in all; it had been purchased from three different dealers.

Lars Larsen also constructed a galley on the deck, and next to it a small storeroom for the firewood for the cooking; some of the firewood, about two cords, was also stored below deck. A chopping block was brought on board by Ole Olsen Hetletvedt; it had been cut from an oak tree that he had felled on his own farm.

The ship's hull was black, and its name, as I have mentioned before, had been painted in silver on the stern. Besides foresail and boomsail it had a jib and a staysail, a topgallant sail and a trysail. Two small dinghies were kept on deck; apart from that the ship's life-saving equipment was rather modest. However, it must be said that the vessel, under the guidance of the skipper, was readied in a painstaking manner, at least as far as all essentials were concerned. One thing, however, he neglected to do: to take out insurance against attacks by Spanish and Moroccan pirates by obtaining the so-called Latin and Algerian Papers.

Lars Larsen had had the thoughtfulness to obtain a letter of recommendation from the leader of the Quakers in Stavanger, Elias

Tastad. Long before their departure the letter was sent to the land agent Joseph Fellows. When the recommendation was to be formulated, Elias Tastad had gone for the first and last time in his life to Gabriel Schanche Kielland to ask his help. Although both he and other Friends knew how to speak English, because of their stay in the prison ship and also because of visits to Great Britain, they were less knowledgeable when it came to writing.

This is the letter of recommendation that Agent Kielland drew up following Elias Tastad's dictation; it was sent to Joseph Fellows and was later given to me, and I have taken care of it until this very day:

"As this our friend and member Lars Larsen Geilen with family think proper to leave us to spend the rest of his days in the United States of America, we can give him no farther help than to recommend them to their friends in that country, who no doubt will give him the best advice. In other respects we must recommend him to the help of his Maker.

Stavanger the 30th Day of the 10th Month, 1824.
Elias Eliassen Tastad."

Skipper Helland mustered his crew on June 27, whereupon the sloop *Restauration* was declared ready to sail.

All the pilgrims then embarked — singly or together with relatives, and in his farewell speech on the pier Elias Tastad used an illustration from Holy Writ, comparing them to Noah and his sons Shem, Ham, and Japhet when they with their wives entered into the Ark and the Lord Himself closed the door after them.

"Would that the breath of the Lord be the wind that fills your sails," he said, "and that God's promises be the dove which, with an olive leaf in its mouth, will meet you on the other shore."

Guri Olsdatter, Elias Tastad's wife, began to sob loudly at these words, and she shouted, "It's for my sake you're staying behind in Norway, Elias!"

As you know, it was because of her weakness for intoxicating liquor that Elias had barred her from the Quaker congregation, and he had done it in spite of the fact that he loved her dearly. He said, "Don't take on, Guri! It's my own conviction that makes me stay home. I have to look after a poor and oppressed flock; they would indeed be panic stricken and scattered by wolves if their shepherd were to leave them." And he turned toward his wife: "You too, my dear wife, will also someday be counted among the sheep of our Lord." She threw herself into his arms, and he held her in a close embrace until her weeping abated.

Many of the emigrants have left behind testimony to the effect that their leave-taking caused them much pain and sorrow but also that they were full of hope for the future. The notes that Lars Larsen made at this time have been preserved, and at the moment the ship shoves off we will listen to him as he speaks for the entire party:

"After that I sold everything I owned, and I embarked together with my wife Martha Georgiana, who is very precious to me. She was pregnant and was soon to bear a child, our first one. For that reason I was at times filled with anxious thoughts; but Siri Madland, the wife of the blacksmith Thomas Madland, who was herself the mother of six children and an experienced and considerate woman, told us to be of good cheer and feel confident about the future.

"My pious foster sister Sara was also one of the emigrants. She had for a long time been unable to make use of her voice, and she remained mute until the day of her death.

"When our departure was drawing nigh, we commended ourselves, the entire flock, to the mercy of God; thereupon we immediately left the safety of dry land and the comfort of the harbor and set out on the precarious ocean where we knew that horrors would ever menace us. Still, we did not forget that which is written, namely that Our Lord and Master Himself is the one that stills the tempest, and that He some time during the fourth watch of the night walked on the sea when His disciples were afraid and in great danger."

The Thirty-third Tale

The sloop *Restauration*, of about 38 register tons, sailed from Stavanger early in the afternoon of July 4, 1825, which was a Monday. The embarkation of the passengers had already been postponed about a week because of several obstacles; two of them deserve to be mentioned here.

Skipper Johannes Jacobsen Stene, who had paid out 1,200 of the 1,800 dalers that the sloop had cost, and who consequently is listed correctly in the documents as its owner, failed to get his sixteen-year-old son Svend to join him on the ship.

This is the way it happened: Svend had looked forward to the voyage to America with fear and great misgivings and had been hoping for the longest time that nothing would come of it. He believed untrustworthy rumors about conditions in this distant and strange land, for instance, that the Turks were ravaging the land, and that they captured young people and cut off their ears and sold them as slaves.

One night toward the end of June Svend took one of his father's rowboats and rowed from Stavanger to the island of Finnøy, a distance of about fifteen miles; that was the place where his mother's family came from and where he himself was born. His uncle and his grandfather were still living there, on the farm called Kindingstad, one of the biggest in the parish.

When the young boy arrived early in the morning and beseeched his grandfather to keep him hidden until the sloop was far out to sea, the old man readily agreed. He looked upon the projected voyage across the ocean to be both an ungodly and a reckless act.

This was the first day of haymaking; every able-bodied person had gotten up early, as had also the grandfather, Old Svend. He was past seventy and had given over the management of the farm to his son, but always kept a watchful eye on the work and the activities. Crofters and hired hands were already hard at work in the fields, and the grandfather was just whetting his own scythe.

It was then that Little Svend appeared, unannounced and unexpected, and his grandfather found him a hiding place.

But that same afternoon his father and two other men landed at the Kindingstad inlet.

As soon as the father discovered that both boy and boat were gone, he made certain assumptions which proved to be correct. They finally found the boat in a dense alder thicket, even though Old Svend had thought it was safely hidden. But the boy had been hidden better. The father pleaded with and threatened the others to tell him of the boy's whereabouts, but without result, and when he and his two companions had listened long enough to various rumors which prevailed, they searched every boathouse and barn and even every wooded area, all in vain, and eventually returned to Stavanger without the boy.

With that Little Svend leaves our story. He never saw his parents again, and they never saw him.

But if Svend's flight hadn't delayed the departure, another circumstance would have done so: one of the emigrants, the merchant in Stavanger known as Simon Pedersen Lima, had had difficulties in getting his emigration papers ready in time. The reason for this will be explained later, but as late as the forenoon of the very day of departure he was being interrogated by the city court in Stavanger. He finally had his papers stamped and was given a valid passport. He and his wife and three children were the last to board the ship. The very next moment a rope was thrown over to the tow-boat and the hawser cast ashore.

A large crowd had gathered, for the news about the flock of pilgrims who intended to seek a new Canaan had spread far and wide, and that morning it was known all over town and the surrounding district that the hour of departure was at hand.

Some of the spectators mocked them, but most felt friendly toward the emigrants, even though they couldn't understand that intelligent people would expose themselves to the many dangers and horrors that they were sure awaited these foolhardy people. Several had one or more of their close family on board the ship. Tears were shed on both sides of the ship's rail, hands were squeezed and promises made.

Twenty-two-year-old Jens Thomassen Madland received a note with greetings from a girl he secretly loved; he hadn't dared reveal to her his feelings for her. He read the note and shouted, "I want to go ashore!" But the hawser had already been cast off, and there was water between the sloop and the pier. Then he suddenly saw her in the mass of people, and he shouted, "I'm coming back!" But his voice didn't carry in all the noise.

Another emigrant, Ole Johnsen Eide, had the previous evening made a promise to Malinda Asbjørnsdatter, who had been a widow for three years, following the death of the late shoemaker and skipper Ole Franck. Malinda was 27 years old, lovely looking and pious natured, and none of those characteristics nor her other good points had been lost on Ole Eide.

They had been secretly engaged for some time, and it had originally been decided that the wedding was to take place at midsummer, so that they could travel across the ocean as husband and wife; but because of her little son Peter's delicate health Malinda decided to abstain from the happiness that she had so long been yearning for, since she was afraid that a strenuous sea voyage might imperil the life of the boy. But Ole Eide had made this promise: with the help of God he would come back to Norway the very next summer, or at least in two years, and then he would not leave the country unless he could bring her back with him as his bride.

That promise he kept.

But since they had poured out their agony to each other beforehand, they were both calm and talked as if they were facing no more than a brief separation. She held her son in her left arm, and as the sloop began to move slowly away from the pier they clasped hands for the last time, and Ole Eide stroked Peter's cheek.

The leader of the Quakers in Stavanger, Elias Eliassen Tastad, was among those who stayed behind; he didn't want to leave his flock without a shepherd. Before the sloop left the pier he had said a hearty good-bye to each and everyone, admonishing them to vigilantly and cheerfully walk always in that Light of Truth that had been lit in their hearts, even through the greatest troubles and death itself. When he at last came to Martha Georgiana Jørgensdatter they looked each other firmly in the eye, but her lips trembled and she said, "You, too, walk vigilantly and cheerfully, Elias, until the Light of Truth shall completely permeate us in Heaven."

Martha was happily married to the leader of the expedition, Lars Larsen of Jeilane, and was at that time eight months pregnant with their first child. She and her husband were the only members of the Quaker congregation among the emigrants, but most of them did belong in their hearts to the Society of Friends, and later on others joined local congregations here in America.

The ship's cook was Endre Salvesen Dahl from Sokndal in the district of Dalane; he left behind him a wife and seven children. None of the seven were grown up yet. His wife was in the last month of pregnancy with their eighth child; she was feeling quite weak, and therefore it had been decided that she stay behind. The oldest children, standing there on the pier, were pale and tight-lipped. The younger ones laughed or whimpered according to their age and how much they understood of it all, and the smallest one, sitting on its mother's arm, looked around with big eyes; the child had never before seen a ship that close nor so many people gathered in one place.

Endre Dahl was the only one who embraced his wife in front of everybody, and they burst into tears and buried their faces in each other's shoulder. They were never to see each other again. His wife died not long after, and Endre later remarried over here. He was converted to Mormonism and in his old age became the leader of about two score Norwegians who left our Norwegian settlement near the Mormon center of Nauvoo on the Mississippi and followed in the footsteps of the prophet Brigham Young to the New Jerusalem he had founded in Salt Lake Valley.

Many close and distant relatives as well as friends and acquaintances had come to Stavanger to say good-bye to the emigrants. As long as they could still be heard, the people on board and those on shore exchanged comforting words, reminding each other that just as the Lord had saved Noah and his family in the Ark during the Flood so He would once again take pity on His chosen ones in a small ship on the endless ocean.

The city said farewell with flags flying on every pole, and the *Restauration* ran up its big new flag; it snapped and crackled in the wind. The weather was not too pleasant: there was a strong wind from the southwest, and low-lying clouds were rushing across the sky, but they brought no rain with them. The pilgrims were favored with a fair wind as far as Tungenes, a distance of about seven miles.

But there they encountered the open ocean and heavy seas.

One of the emigrants, Nils Nilsen Hersdal, later called Big Nels, was twenty-five years old on the day of departure, and his wife, Brita —

they had just gotten married — had bought a white kerchief which she wanted to give him as a birthday present. She was holding it in her hand when the fort at the Kalhammer promontory fired all its cannon as a farewell greeting just as the sloop was sailing past. She got such a shock from the booming guns that she forgot what she had planned to do, and after that it wasn't very long before she and many others got something else to think about: seasickness became prevalent just as soon as the ship had rounded the Tungenes promontory.

Among the most miserable sufferers was the above-mentioned Jens Thomassen Madland. When he was unable to stand up on his feet, partly because of the ship's rolling — and his unwillingness to go below as long as land was still in sight — he crawled on all fours from the windward side to the leeward side of the ship and slipped his arm through the loop of a rope that was attached to the mast. The waves were already coming in over the ship's rail, and the lower parts of the sails were soaked black with water.

Jens had his parents and five sisters with him. His father was standing by the wheel, his mother by the steps leading to the deck below, clasping the two youngest of her daughters. Then a huge breaker swept in, taking all three of them with it. Both children were thrown against the mast; one of them sprained her arm and the other was hit in the temple, but none was seriously injured.

Jens grabbed them and held them steady, and when they came to after their fright, one daughter started to shout, "I want to go home!" and then the other: "Take me home!" — and they kept it up. But Jens remained silent.

Their father, the smith Thomas Madland, had witnessed the entire scene. He turned deathly pale; his lips were like gray stripes in his face, and the knuckles of his sooty hands turned white. "In the name of Our Lord!" he said, and swung the rudder around, setting a course back to the harbor.

Lars Larsen of Jeilane immediately ran over to him, and so did the skipper, Lars Olsen Helland, as well as the owner, Johannes Jacobsen Stene. "You're not going back!" they exclaimed. "That's exactly what I'm doing," he replied.

But they all regarded one another as brothers and as equals, and no one tried to take the rudder out of his hand.

When they once again were close to shore and in calm waters, he let Lars Helland take the rudder, and walked over to his three children standing by the mast and told them outright what he had decided. "I saw you get that note just as we cast off from the pier in Stavanger," he said to Jens.

It was evening by the time they anchored in a bay that is called Dusavig — about three miles north of Stavanger. The wind abated, and a silent rain began to fall in the twilight, but the sky had cleared by midnight; there was not a cloud to be seen when the sun rose at half past three in the morning.

Everyone stayed on board; most of the passengers had slept a few hours. When they woke up they experienced the most beautiful morning they had ever seen. The air had once again become summery and warm, and the surface of the sea was completely calm. Small codfish and red wrasses scurried to and fro below the sloop's keel and were silhouetted against the white sandy bottom. The early fishermen had arrived at the beach; they boarded their boats in order to pull up their fish traps or nets, and when they saw the vessel with all the people on board they set their course in its direction and entered into conversation with them before they rowed on to the fishing grounds.

Thus, everything that was homelike and familiar once again surrounded the pilgrims: smoke began to rise from all the chimneys round about, haymakers gathered in the farmyards and were later seen in the meadows with rakes and scythes. The cattle were waiting by the gates leading to the outer fields, and the milkmaids came carrying churns in their hands or a wooden yoke across their shoulders.

All this they saw, and because it had been given to them another time and so unexpectedly, they appreciated it more than ever before, and the loss of it overwhelmed them — as when in a dream one has just about attained the greatest bliss and then suddenly is torn out of the arms of Morpheus. Houses and fields seemed to them to be shimmering, just as the ocean deep seemed to the children to be flickering and fluttering, as they were hanging over the railing watching the play of the fishes.

After everyone had eaten breakfast together, they all gathered around the three who of their own free will and with their parents' consent were going to leave the ship. In parting, teacher Ole Olsen Hetletvedt, the Haugean, read this text from the Bible, from Paul's epistle to Philemon: "For perhaps he therefore departed for a season, that thou shouldest receive him forever." Their father placed his hands on their heads and blessed each one of them; they all cried at their mother's breast, the two small daughters and Jens, the grown son. His father said to him, "From now on you are going to take my place." "I'll do as well as I can," Jens replied.

Their parents did not accompany them ashore, but Lars Larsen lowered a small rowboat and brought them to the nearest boathouse. Then something unexpected happened: the girl who had sent the note to Jens was standing on the jetty; she was the one who took the rope end and made the half hitch around the pole.

The fact that she was there had happened in this manner: as soon as the sloop was out of sight upon leaving Stavanger harbor, she had set out on foot and walked the seven miles out to the Tungenes promontory. There she sat on the outermost naze even before the sun rose. She kept peering out to sea; boats were to be seen both far and near — but not the sloop. Thereupon she turned back and got as far as Dusavig. Then she caught sight of it but thought at first it was a mirage, caused by her feeling of loss and by the long sleepless night.

But when she even heard voices and saw people she thought she recognized, she immediately left the main road and walked along a path leading down to the beach. She came around the corner of the boathouse and walked onto the jetty the very moment the boat came alongside; seeing Jens step ashore she put out her hand and wished him welcome; no other words were uttered.

But the boat immediately pushed off, and the four remained standing on a hillock right above the boathouse. The sloop set sail; it looked like a bird spreading its wings in flight. The first early breeze of morning began to waft the ship along. Once more they were waving from shore, and on board everyone waved back.

This was the last time Jens and his sisters saw their parents. The very same day he walked into his father's smithy, where the embers were still aglow in the forge.

Jens became a highly respected blacksmith in Stavanger. He was very happy in his marriage, and he had many children. His two sisters also became happily married, and Thomas Madland's kin increased greatly in Norway also. But here they all make their exit from our story.

Even before they weighed anchor that morning, the Haugean, Ole Olsen Hetletvedt, took out his hymn book and read the "Prayer for Seafarers at the Time of Departure"; he stood in the bow of the ship and in his loud and clear voice sang two verses of the hymn for seafarers so that those who had left the ship and were walking up from the boathouse, stopped and listened too.

It turned out to be a beautiful day, their first on the ocean, with the sun shining from morning to night, and with a changing breeze that seldom made the sails bulge. The distance covered that day was therefore rather modest; not until evening did they get out of sight of land.

Everyone was busy with his own tasks, and despite the pain of departure all the pilgrims seemed to be in a light and happy mood. Quite frequently though, one, then another, would stand by the railing and stare at the low, receding coastline.

There were many children on board: five boys and fifteen girls in all, most of them of school age; on the first day of sailing they were given their first lesson. Teacher Ole Hetletvedt gathered them on the hatch cover midships, and they read the Fourth Commandment about honoring one's father and mother so that one's days may be long in the land. And when Ole asked which land was meant as far as they were concerned, one child answered, "Norway!" — while another said, "America!"

Their teacher then told them how it should be interpreted, retelling the account in the Bible about the patriarch Abraham who departed from Ur in Chaldea and after distant wanderings beheld the land of Canaan and heard the promise of the Lord: "This land I will give you and your sons!"

Then one of the smallest girls asked, "Is that America?" — and she pointed toward the horizon where blue and golden clouds towered up like distant and beautiful landscapes against the evening sky.

"It is farther than that," Ole Hetletvedt replied; he himself was facing toward the east, where the twilight hovered. He remained silent for a while and then gave them a lesson in Norwegian history. He told them that where they could still make out a narrow coastline once lived a man by the name of Erik the Red. His son was Leif Eriksson, who discovered America. "From here people have been traveling toward the west long before us," Ole said.

Brita Hersdal once again got out from among her keepsakes the neckerchief that she had forgotten to give her young husband the day before because she had been frightened by the cannon. Behind the mainsail she tied it around his neck and pressed a light kiss on his cheek. But when he tried to grab her in order to make a more thorough job of it, she wriggled free.

Later on they all gathered in a circle, and they had a silent meeting with worship and contemplation of the Deity, as is the custom of the Quakers.

And the sun sank into the ocean, behind billowing clouds, and the first day of the voyage of the pilgrims had come to an end.

Here I have put down the names of those who were on board, as far as I can recall; for most of them I have also added their ages, as well as the family relationships that existed between many of them. I must ask you,

Anne, to read this list very carefully, and later on go back to it as often as you find it necessary, so that you won't be confused by the great number of names you will later have to keep track of, especially because so many of them are quite similar. Even though you may look upon much of this account as being deficient and unclear, — and no doubt rightfully so — I am not to be blamed for the fact that you will encounter so many men by the name of Nils and Lars and Ole and women who are called Bertha or Brita or Martha or Sara! And in the same way, when they arrive in America and come to baptize their children, those who were born over here may in one family call their daughter Susan Ann, in another the same, and in a third Sarah Ann — for this I am not at fault, Anne. Here follows the list of the "Sloopers":

Carpenter Lars Larsen of Jeilane from Stavanger, who was the leader of the party, and his wife, Martha Georgiana Jørgensdatter. Their oldest child, Margaret Allen, was born on September 2, 1825, when the *Restauration* had crossed most of the Atlantic and was in the vicinity of the Bahama Islands. At the time of departure Lars Larsen was 39 years old and his wife was 22. With them was also Sara, Lars's sister, the mute girl. I had been in love with her, but the passion I had felt for her for many years was no more.

Among the pilgrims there were also the farmer Cornelius Nilsen Hersdal, 47 years of age, his wife Kari, age 36, who was my sister, and their children: Anne, Nils, Inger, and Martha, their ages being 11, 9, 6, and one year.

The owner of the sloop, Johannes Jacobsen Stene, and his wife Martha Svendsdatter, both 39 years old, and their daughter Martha Helene, age 4. Their son Svend, 16 years old, fled into the woods and did not come along. About this I have already told you.

Aanen Thoresen Brastad, 29 years old, his wife Bertha Karine Aadnesdatter, age 35, and with them their three daughters, seven-year-old Sara, six-year-old Anne Marie Kristine, and the newborn Bertha Karine. — Aanen died the following year, and not long after his widow married his brother Nils, who was also on board the sloop and was about 21 years old.

Farmer Daniel Stensen Rossadal, age 46, his wife Britha Johanne Ovesdatter, 39 years old, together with their children Elen, Ove, Lars, John, and Hulda, who were 18, 16, 13, and 4 years old respectively (the last-mentioned was a newborn baby).

Blacksmith Thomas Jensen Madland, 45 years old, his wife Siri Iversdatter, age 55, their daughters Rachel, Guri, and Serena, who were 18, 15, and 11 years old. As mentioned before, their son Jens, who was

22, and his two small sisters left the ship at Dusavig and continued to live in Stavanger. Thomas Madland, however, died the following year.

Merchant Simon Pedersen Lima, his wife Marie Karine Størchersdatter, both 43 years old, and their children Greta Birgithe, 11 years old, Severine Marie, 8, and Simon, 3.

Nils Nilsen Hersdal, the brother of my brother-in-law Cornelius, age 25, with his wife Brita Christophersdatter, 20 years old.

Ole Johnsen Eide, a half-brother of Martha Georgiana, Lars Larsen's wife. He was 31 years old at the time of the departure and, as previously mentioned, engaged to Malinda, the widow of his late friend Ole Franck. She, however, did not go along.

Cook Endre Salvesen Dahl, 41 years old, who had left behind his pregnant wife and their seven children.

The brothers Knud and Jacob Anderssøn Slogvig, 28 and 18 years old respectively. Some people have maintained that the former crossed the ocean on a later occasion, but he was indeed one of the Sloopers.

Servant Gudmund Danielsen Haugaas, 26 years old.

Mail driver Thorstein Olsen Bjaadland, age 30.

Georg Johnsen Hesja, 16 years old.

Halvor Iversen Reveim, about 15 years old.

Teacher Ole Olsen Hetletvedt, who was in the prime of life.

Then there was the skipper, Lars Olsen Helland, in addition to the mate, Peder Eriksen Meland.

The Thirty-fourth Tale

The first night at sea had come to an end, and the first dawn was breaking. They awoke to find fluttering sails above their heads and no anchorage to be found anywhere. They saw the sun rise from a horizon unbroken by any silhouettes of islands or mountains.

Those who are experienced sailors know what a beautiful and at the same time strange feeling this imparts — perhaps more so in quiet weather; the clear surface intensifies the feeling of infinity. It is as if our very nature is opened up and in fleeting moments perceives a breath of the true content of existence; even the old Magis obtained wisdom by studying the depth of the heavens and the orbits of the stars.

All was completely still that entire first day; at dawn there was not a ripple on the surface of the ocean, and there was no afternoon breeze; there was hardly a wave to rock the little vessel. The sails were hanging limp, seagulls were streaking past the masthead, a clump of seaweed on the starboard side lay there for hours, and a tarred floorboard was drifting slowly by on the port side; blue and yellow jellyfish made their way slowly past the ship on both sides. And Ole Hetletvedt, who was an experienced fisherman, thought he could see schools of mackerel ahead. He let out a line and bait, but he caught nothing.

Thus, everything felt as if it were strange and familiar at the same time — as if this were the sea that each and every one had seen from the shore of his childhood and, at the same time, was a distant ocean: invisible coasts passed by; wind and storms were waiting perhaps with destruction or with favorable winds along the way. They had made their decision and were subject to the same whims of fate as the Israelites of old, when that people departed from slavery in the land of Egypt; they were surrounded by deserts and vast emptiness, still far away from the hallowed spot in which the Lord God was to reveal Himself; and beyond the last obstacle there was a Promised Land.

Yes, Anne, their decision was final: they, like that people of yore, were conscious of being pilgrims on the way to their Canaan, and their daring was greater, no less, for they had no songs or prophecies inherited from great and holy men. No, they relied on the word of Cleng Peerson only, God save my soul; had I really spoken the truth when I had described to them the new world beyond the ocean?

Later they would have good reason to reproach me.

My sister Kari has told me that she slept very little that first night at sea. The previous day had been exceptionally warm — they were rarely to experience anything similar, even in tropical climes.

The ship itself and everything on board had absorbed the heat of the sun and threw it out like a huge oven throughout the long hours between midnight and morning.

Cornelius had finally fallen asleep. She knew that he had brought along a box filled with earth from the Hersdal farm — it was standing at the foot of his bunk — and he had said to her, "If we are lucky enough to reach our destination, this earth is to be mixed with the soil that is to be mine over there. And if it happens that I die on the ocean, then I want to be lowered into the sea together with the box."

Lying awake, Kari recalled his words. The sound of snoring penetrated through from the outside, worry consumed her on the inside; everything conspired to keep her awake.

But she was not the only one who could not sleep. Some of the oldest girls were still whispering to one another; once in a while they would giggle at a secret joke and an angry voice would tell them to be quiet. She had been unable not to notice their great embarrassment when they had to undress in the presence of strangers; some of them had only loosened their skirts and bodices. Now that each one had retired under her own cover in the darkness, they felt protected and well hidden.

A child began to cry, and she heard the mother's comforting voice. It was Bertha Karine Brastad's little daughter, who was between three and four months old; she had been sickly ever since she was born. Both she and her father were to be lowered into their graves the next year.

Bertha Karine was that very night lying with Death both to the right and left of her, and she did not know it.

Soon after another child woke up, then several others, among them Kari's youngest child, who at that time was a year old. It had been put in the next bunk; it crawled across the board over to its mother, groped for her face in the dark, slipped down at her side, and fell asleep. She moved closer to her husband, and between his body — heavy with sleep and sweaty from the heat — and the child's tiny limbs she felt hard pressed, as if there were no room for her.

She could hear Britha Rossadal lull her five-month-old Hulda to sleep, heard the sound of hungry lips that closed around the mother's nipple and a blissful sigh — the milk had begun to flow. With a feeling of great tenderness she pressed her own child closer to her; it was sleeping with softly bent fingers and with moisture on its forehead.

The ship was heaving gently on the faint groundswell; it was as if everyone and everything were resting at a sleeping breast. The gurgle of the waves gliding alongside made her for a time less tense. Above them could be heard the intermittent steps of the watch on deck or a low shout; but she could not make out the words although the voice seemed to be quite near.

Astern, one of the big boys woke up. Half asleep, he crawled out of his bunk, rolled over the fellow next to him, and walked out to the primitive toilet to relieve himself. It seemed to her that the air suddenly felt more stuffy than before, filled as it was by the smells and exhalations of many bodies; she felt as if she were in a coffin and the lid had been put in place, and for a brief moment she felt almost terror-stricken: "I'm being choked, I must go up on deck!" — until she quieted down with a meager consolation: many nights would be just like this one. The further south they got, the more would they be tormented by the heat.

No, their ordeal up to now was as nothing: there were no sick people that first night, no stench from vomiting; they had fair weather and no battened-down hatches; she could get up and stand upright without being thrown to the deck, and she could walk about without danger to life and limb.

After a while the sound of the ship and the sea and the people pressed less hard on her consciousness and she was just about dozing off when she awoke with a start: somewhere in the darkness she heard the heavy breathing of a passionate union. Her face reddening, she pulled the bedcover over her head and thought that during the nights to come others would be listening and that she would be the one being watched.

A girl or a young fellow filled with yearning and with fire in his blood, but who had no one to embrace, would by lying like her, all aquiver or hiding his head under the cover. Three months on the ocean were in store for them all.

Once again she reemerged into reality, again she heard someone, half asleep, crawl out of his bunk, someone turned a spigot and drank, someone fumbled in the half-dark across the planks searching for the spot that had been set aside as a privy; the sound of a stream that went astray, and hit the deck made her painfully wide awake. A cross voice began to bawl out the boy; he hurriedly ran back to his bunk.

Once again all was quiet and remained so for a long time. At last she heard a sigh and someone said loudly, "O Lord! Help us, O Lord!" From another side of the room could be heard muffled sobbing.

All this my sister Kari later told me in confidence, and on the basis of what she said I can now describe to you, Anne, — as if one looks in a broken mirror — the pilgrims' first night on the ocean.

Yes, I call them pilgrims and that's what they were; but even in the case of the most pious among them it was a fact that they were encumbered with bodies and bodily needs and with the numerous weaknesses of human nature. They could be driven to impatience and their anger easily kindled, and it happened at times that they would forget the welfare of their neighbors in favor of their own. In spite of that, their consciousness of being pilgrims was plain in many ways, and when night was waning and they had their first meal together with prayer and thanksgiving and later spent the day up on deck with various chores, their conduct and behavior were marked by that faith for whose sake they were on their way, not only by each one showing Christian kindness to his neighbor but also by practicing their religion in the way with which each one of them was familiar.

Thus it happened that Ole Olsen Hetletvedt, who was a Haugean, as was his custom took out his Bible, and when asked he read aloud from Psalm 65: "By terrible things in righteousness wilt Thou answer us, O God of our salvation; Who art the confidence of all the ends of the earth, and of them that are afar off upon the sea: Which by His strength setteth fast the mountains; being girded with power: Which stilleth the noise of the seas, the noise of their waves, and the tumult of the people. They also that dwell in the uttermost parts are afraid at Thy tokens: Thou makest the outgoings of the morning and evening to rejoice."

Daniel Stensen Rossadal, who was greatly influenced by the Quakers, also opened his Bible, but he read quietly to himself.

They also held silent meetings on board after the fashion of the

Quakers. They sat silently on deck, gazing at the inner light of the soul which is the revelation of God's Nature, and they awaited the coming of the Spirit, and everyone who received its admonition conveyed a greeting or a message.

Already on that first day most of them felt like members of one big family. The few among them who had not known one another before they embarked in Stavanger, got acquainted, and some of them became fast friends. But you must also keep in mind, Anne, that the deck of the sloop was hardly larger than a sizable living room.

When the weather was pleasant, as it was during that first day, men and women kept busy almost the same way as they would have at home: mothers were nursing their babies; the men got hold of knives and other tools and began to repair various kinds of equipment, or making different useful things and objects; and the children were playing. Thus, Ole Johnsen Eide got out a piece of calf's leather that he had brought along and made the billfold that he was to carry during all his years here in America.

The older children spent their time with pranks and games until Ole Hetletvedt, being the schoolmaster, gathered them for a lesson in reading and Bible study. He was a gentle and pious man, not like so many other Haugeans who are hostile to young people taking joy in life. Still, he found it necessary to warn them, pointing out to them what a dangerous playground such a small deck can be. And everything went well that first day as did the entire voyage, although an accident could very well have occurred that very day: Guri Madland, the second oldest daughter of Thomas Madland, grabbed Gudmund Haugaas's razor just as he had put it down for a moment on the hatch after having finished shaving. As a prank she threatened to throw it overboard, and he ran after her in order to wrest it from her. The razor was folded, but when she suddenly stumbled it suddenly opened, and she got a deep cut in her hand. Fortunately, the wound proved not to be dangerous, but it was bleeding profusely; appalled, Gudmund placed her hand against his mouth and he thought her blood tasted very sweet. Two years later, when she was seventeen and he twenty-seven, he made her his wife, but happiness would prove allusive during those years that Fate allotted them to be together, about twenty.

Next to Martha Georgiana, he was considered to have the brightest head of anyone on board the sloop; but he had a fickle nature and many queer ideas which became more so when he got to know the teachings of the Mormons; he even maintained that he could recall the days of the patriarch Abraham. It also happened that he was seized with attacks and spoke in foreign tongues; for that reason he was highly respected by the Friends, even though he never joined them but went his own way. He was a good-looking man, hot-headed and tender-hearted at the same time.

This first day at sea turned out to be one of the best of the entire voyage. The feeling of loss in regard to friends and relatives left behind was in the case of most of them subdued by the fact that they had some loved ones with them. But there was one who could not shake off his melancholy: Endre Salvesen Dahl, the cook, who had said good-bye to his pregnant wife and seven children. He had burnt the porridge and scorched the bacon, but no one blamed him for that.

The fact that everything on board was new to them also served to divert them. Ahead of them waited boredom, the worst enemy of the seafarer. One day is just like another, and one is bored even in the company of one's best friend.

But the opposite also becomes evident during such a voyage, for friendship is tested in a time of trouble. I shall later tell you about what the pilgrims did, both good and evil, and about the events that occurred under way. Here I will merely mention the weather and the sailing conditions prior to their calling at the English port. It is all quoted from the ship's journal or based on the accounts that the emigrants have told me numerous times.

This first very calm day was followed by others with a fair breeze; the sky was clear and the air was mild. The departure with its tribulations, the grief caused by saying farewell, heavy seas and seasickness, all now seemed like a distant dream, and the least experienced among them believed that the farther south they got, the greater assurance they would have that the voyage would continue in such a pleasant way. The heat and the filthy air below deck were still hard to take for most of them, although habit had already begun to have some effect.

Among the small troublesome situations that came their way during this first leg on their voyage, I will mention the following: while the ship was just north of Dover, where the English Channel is at its narrowest, a heavy fog suddenly enshrouded them. Just before, they had been able to make out land far to starboard, and they knew that they were quite close to the Goodwin Sands, which many say is the biggest ships' cemetery in the northern hemisphere. From the sloop they could see distinctly one hull after another half buried in the mud, their masts looking like gaunt trees of the forest. Captain Meland, however, knew full well that this was not the only place where such dangers threatened; on both sides of the shipping lane there are sand banks, among them the Downs, and the channel which ships can negotiate safely is in certain places very narrow. The ships not only had to pass through but in addition had to stay clear of the banks and also of one another, by day as well as by night.

The fog did not appear to close in from any special direction. It seemed indeed to be rising out of the very water, and before they knew it they were completely surrounded by it. There had been a westerly breeze, filling the sails; then suddenly side winds and waves hit them from both starboard and port.

The color of the fog changed from golden to flowing red to blue; because in some places it was very dense and in other places much less impenetrable, it seemed as if flames were leaping up, then being smothered in smoke, and again rising up when the haze drifted up toward the setting sun. Just as suddenly it cleared around the ship and they sailed into what seemed to be a pool in which the surface of the water looked like melted copper. They caught a glimpse of the sun, which now looked dark green and whirled round and round like a mighty wheel as it drowned and disappeared — for the last time — right above the horizon.

On a ship there are instruments to determine its course and its position; one makes observations of the sun's altitude during the day and can set one's course according to the moon and the stars at night. It may also have lanterns to illuminate its way; but no source of light — no matter how powerful — can pierce the fog. Similarly, neither the ship's bell nor its horn can be relied on to the same extent as previously — it may even seem as if the sound reverberates from walls that are soft and resilient. And even if the sound does reach the listener, it may be a source of terror rather than of help. On board the men of the watch are listening: did the sound come from our starboard side or from port? Is it nearer or more distant than the last time we heard it? This hidden and unknown vessel — is it holding to a steady course, or has it perhaps shifted its helm?

A ship in such a situation can reef its sails, it may even abandon its sea anchor if thought advisable, but it cannot lay by; it must be prepared to get along in an emergency situation — oh, I know it so well, Anne, and I could fully understand the fears of my sister Kari, when she told me about the events of that night. But she had derived comfort from a letter that I had had someone write: on the basis of Andreas Stangeland's reports I had informed my friends in Norway about conditions over here the way he looked at them. The letter had been sent to Lars Larsen of Jeilane, who in turn had let Thomas Madland make copies of it so that many more could read it. I have myself saved the copy given to my sister; in it one may read these words:

"I hereby inform you that I have safely arrived in America. After a voyage of six weeks we came to New York where I found my friends, all of them in good health, and they received me with sincere affection.

"I feel greatly troubled in my mind in regard to your coming to America. When I think of my sister and my other friends — oh how I wish that that time had passed, and how I would rejoice at hearing that they will come to New York, and I can embrace you all there.

"Above all, treat one another in a brotherly fashion; don't owe anyone anything except the love you have for one another; let us look upon one another as the men that we really are, in our wretchedness and powerlessness; then we will also realize that we need help and salvation from the hand of the Almighty, and we will obey His calls and His admonitions."

I had, moreover, given them good advice regarding the forthcoming journey and had told about Andreas Stangeland's deeds in such a way that they would think that I had had a share in them and had even made them appear as my own. Thus I described, based on his own account, the trip by steamer from New York to Albany, and how in Farmington I had bought a cow for ten dollars in addition to some sheep, and also how I had built a loghouse twenty-four feet long and twenty feet wide and I had obtained a good oven from Rochester for the price of twenty dollars.

But this as well as many other things were solely the results of the efforts of Andreas Stangeland; throughout the state of New York he had had good help from friends of his among the Quakers; nevertheless, later on it was to be shown that the picture he had drawn for the emigrants was more optimistic than was the actual situation.

My sister Kari had read this letter, and she believed every word of it, and it proved to be a comfort when evening came and the wind was increasing in strength and the fog remained as impenetrable as ever. On shore the fog is usually swept away by a strong wind, but at sea there may be both fog and storm at the very same time, as if mists were welling forth from an inexhaustible abyss.

Finally, the women and children went to bed, but they kept their clothes on throughout the night. All the men remained on deck.

Several times they heard the sirens of passing vessels; but the other ships were never so close that the danger of collision seemed imminent. But toward midnight a signal was heard, first to starboard and immediately after another to port, and it was clear that the two ships were drawing closer.

Captain Helland held a steady course. There was a full moon; the air was milky white, being somewhat luminous without their being able to see anything in any direction. The sirens sounded ever more petulant and sharp, as if the strange vessel, instead of giving way, set its course for the narrow channel in which the sloop was slowly gliding forward with only a few sails set.

At the very moment that Skipper Helland was to give the order to reef the sails and brace aback, the silhouette of the ship on our starboard side emerged from out of the fog; the sails could be seen before the hull became visible. It was gliding slowly across the bow of the *Restauration*. The sloop's helm was immediately put hard over; the two ships were so close that their sides scraped against each other, but rather gently, not enough to even awaken those who were below deck and had fallen asleep.

After a while the other ship also moved away, and they did not experience any similar danger that night or the next twenty-four hours, even though the fog did not lift.

The weather didn't clear up until the third day. Then they had the open sea to port, but to starboard they could see the faint outline of the English coast: white bluffs, being cliffs of chalk, bright in the sunlight, and above the cliffs they could see waving green fields disappearing into the bluish haze in the distance. Forests could also be seen; the tree trunks formed a dark wall and the green crowns were waving in the wind. They could make out a city at the head of a wide bay; fishing boats were leaving the harbor for the open sea. Later, not far from the Isle of Wight and close to the entrance to Southampton harbor, the Sloopers for the first time saw a steamship. Filled with wonder, they gathered on deck in order to get a good look at this curious vessel which moved steadily ahead at a fast pace but without sails, with a huge cloud of smoke ascending from a tall funnel.

After the fog cleared, a fresh fair wind returned, and with the most favorable conditions that anyone could wish for they sailed along the entire south coast of England until they had passed Lizard Point. They kept close to land on the western side of the peninsula and finally entered the harbor of the little town of Porthleven.

The town faces the Atlantic, and even in fair weather the waves roll heavily against the shore. The entrance to the harbor is rather narrow and the undertow is very strong; but the pilot guided them safely past the breakwater and into a wide and smooth harbor. There they cast anchor and made ready to receive a new supply of food and water.

A new passenger was also waiting on shore; it was with both joy and dread that he was looking forward to meeting the emigrants again.

The Thirty-fifth Tale

The arrival of the pilgrims at Porthleven created quite a stir among the local population. The people looked at the strangers' peculiar clothes and listened to their unintelligible speech with wonder and interest. Soon a huge flock of people were gathered at the dock where the sloop was tied up.

There were many tasks to be performed during the short time they were to lie in harbor. In the case of the women, this first day was devoted to washing clothes. But when the next morning brought beautiful weather, some of them agreed that they ought to take a walk into the countryside, for it had been decided that the *Restauration* would under no circumstances leave until late afternoon. A large group — mostly women and some of the bigger children — took along lunch baskets and started out. They walked through the cobblestoned streets of Porthleven and then set out on the highway.

They had been at sea for over a week, and now, when they once again saw lovely fields and meadows, they sensed a yearning sated and a joy derived from the presence of earth, grass, and trees and the many aromas that are part of nature.

Cornelius Hersdal was one of the few men who came along.

After having passed through the environs of Porthleven, they set out toward the north, in the direction of the city of Helston. Kari told me many times how the beauty of the country had delighted her: the fields

were green once again following the haying; cows and sheep were grazing; they were indeed finer-looking animals than those she had had in
Norway.

The landscape was grandiose, and soft and friendly all at the same
time, billowing as if an ocean had been stilled; beech and oak groves
spread out like islands; vines wound around old, knotty tree trunks.

At last they stopped not far from Helston, at a place where there were
even a few palm trees to be seen. The palm trees growing in the south
of England are not indigenous; nevertheless, the ones that have been
specially planted in this area seem to be thriving. The sight of them
gave the emigrants a feeling of being in a world far distant from the
meager Northland, and they looked upon it as a promise of all the good
things that were in store for them.

Many kinds of flowers grew at the side of the road; the children
scurried about and picked as many as they could hold. They still felt as
if they had a swaying ship's deck underfoot, as if the ground was rising
and sinking, but the sea had been transformed into fields of grain waving in the wind.

Among the few women who stayed behind in Porthleven was Siri
Madland. Together with her daughter she was in charge of the common
housekeeping that week, and they went shopping in order to obtain a
new supply of milk and bread, in addition to some of the year's produce
being offered in the town's marketplace: potatoes, turnips, cabbage,
carrots, and peas in the pod.

You probably expected, Anne, that I would have been standing on the
pier wishing the pilgrims welcome to England; but, actually, I hadn't
even been told of the day of their departure from Stavanger.
Nevertheless, I did expect that they would arrive around that time.

But the very day prior to their arrival I had gone to Helston in order
to settle an important matter. Thus it happened that I quite unexpectedly ran into the group of Sloopers who were on an outing, just
when they were eating by the roadside near the town. There was
general rejoicing, and Kari and I were especially happy to meet again.
The strange country at once seemed completely transformed — as if we
through magic had been spirited back to our homeland; since I immediately began to question them about their trip and their departure
from Norway, none of them touched on what I was so reluctant to dwell
on: what I had been doing during the winter just past.

Neither was this mentioned when we all of us arrived in Porthleven
and met the rest of the Sloopers, nor when we the next night had to

leave and set sail — more quickly than any one had imagined and under quite novel circumstances. You will probably understand this somewhat better, Anne, when you hear what I now have to relate.

Both Captain Helland and others had noticed that Simon Lima became unusually fidgety when the time neared for the sloop to enter the harbor. In contrast to all the others, he had said he didn't care to go ashore. He was therefore assigned the job of watchman, and the sloop was thus entrusted to his sole charge for several hours that day, since he was the only one on board. His wife and three children all joined the group that set out for Helston; together with Johannes Stene and Lars Larsen the captain was to take care of a few things in Porthleven, one of them being to get a supply of fresh water.

You haven't heard about Simon Lima before, Anne, but I have included his own confession in my story later on — at a place where it seems more proper to deal with it. It was his fear of the consequences of an evil deed he had committed that had made him leave Norway, and he thought that fate perhaps would overtake him in the very first port abroad. For that reason he was beside himself with fear, and as soon as the others were out of sight he opened a cask of brandy and treated himself generously to it.

He became intoxicated immediately, and in this condition he began to complain of what a wretched person he was; but the Englishmen who had gathered by the sloop didn't understand what he was saying. Then he suddenly made a complete turnabout and began to sing a vulgar song that he had heard sung by the seamen in Stavanger. Many of the listeners knew the song; partly because of its contents, but also because of Simon Lima's faulty knowledge of English it was sort of distorted in his mouth and did not at all sound any better. The risqué words somehow seemed disguised and only half recognizable, and its coarse contents became comical in an unintentional manner. After the first few stanzas his listeners egged him on to continue, but he didn't know any more stanzas and remained standing there with an empty expression in his face.

Although Simon didn't realize what they wanted him to do, he was roused to action and suddenly shouted to them in Norwegian, "Buy brandy?"

Through their connection with Norwegian sailors, the people standing there knew a few words of Norwegian, one of them being the Norwegian word for brandy, and they replied enthusiastically, "Yes, sailor! Brandy! Buy brandy! Sell brandy!" They fetched coins out of their pockets and offered them to him. Simon held out the mug that he had been drinking from, and when the nearest person had given him a coin, he gave him the mug, and the man filled it from the cask and emptied it. Thereupon, the mug went from man to man, and because by turns it would end up in Simon's hand, he would toast each and every one.

He had probably never thought of charging money for the drinks, but since the townspeople had started to pay, they continued handing over money. It had been intended more as a game than as buying and selling; but Simon's pockets were filled with copper coins.

Finally Siri Madland and her two daughters returned from market. Since they had purchased a great many things, one of the market women had come along to help them carry. When the drunken men saw the women, there was a great commotion and they thronged around them; it was all done in a spirit of fun, but Simon, who was much more befogged than the others, thought the Englishmen had an evil purpose in mind, and just as he charged forward in order to protect Siri, he pushed one of the men so that he fell off the pier and into the water. One of the Madland sisters immediately pulled her dress off and jumped into the water — she was both quick-witted and able to swim — and even though the fellow had cooled off a little, he gesticulated wildly, but she caught hold of him and pulled him on board a rowboat that had been pushed out from shore.

Because of all the commotion the harbor police turned up and when they heard that one of the ship's crew had sold drinks to the local population, they demanded that Simon Lima, according to the law, be surrendered to them. And since they didn't have much to do in a peaceful spot like Porthleven, they enforced the law with so much greater zeal. They also demanded that the ship be impounded until everything had been fully investigated and all fines paid.

During these tumultuous goings-on the women and children returned from their outing, and I was along with them. When the police saw us, they may have thought that it was our intention to come to the aid of the drunken Simon, for they spurred on their horses and blocked the road. Some of the children became frightened and began to cry. The police then left us alone and once again tried to get the drunken Simon back to his senses — they probably thought that he was the captain of the ship — and demanded to see the ship's papers; they also asked the reason why we had put into harbor just there.

But they couldn't get an intelligent word out of Simon Lima. I was about to give him the help he sorely needed and the policemen any explanation they were entitled to, when the situation again changed: the real captain returned with Lars Larsen and Johannes Stene; they had been somewhere to obtain a new supply of water, three large barrels which they were hauling in three handcarts. The street was steep, they had difficulty in braking and shouted, "Out of the way! Out of the way!" — and tried to get through the crowd. But the police thought that they were bringing on board a new supply of liquor and seemed to want to take the barrels away from them. The three men were determined to defend themselves, and everything got even worse when the children, scared out of their wits, began to run along the piers; they shouted and cried, and some of them jumped on board and hid under the tarpaulins.

At that moment I stepped forth from the crowd, stood directly in front of the policemen, and addressed them in English; since they heard that I had a command of their own language, they listened and at once seemed to be a bit more well-disposed toward us. But I didn't know anything about what Simon Lima had done, and when they pointed out that he had sold brandy and had to be indicted according to law, I voiced my regret and asked whether this offense might not be settled in an amicable manner.

In this we might possibly have succeeded if Simon at that very moment hadn't given a start when he saw me. If he had been sober, he would have remembered that I was going to join them in Porthleven, but being so intoxicated he must have thought he was seeing a ghost in broad daylight, and evidently quite delirious and in an uncontrollable rage, he gave out a loud shout and made as if to jump overboard. Once again the police intervened and threatened him with a stay in the town's jail.

Again I stepped in, saying that we would be responsible for Simon and would put him below deck immediately. When the police demanded that the following day, when he would have sobered up, we show up at the jail and give an explanation, I agreed even without conferring with the captain or anyone else.

The policemen rode away, but I didn't tell the pilgrims about the promise I had made. However, I took Captain Helland aside and told him it would be a smart thing to leave as soon as possible and without anyone noticing us; for based on earlier experience I knew that anyone who had run-ins with the authorities in circumstances like these would have to reckon with several weeks before he could get permission to sail. And since I also knew too well how the autumn storms act up along the east coast of North America, I thought it absolutely necessary that we arrive in New York before the middle of October.

It was evening; it was getting dark, and gradually all the townspeople had left the harbor area. All the pilgrims were now on board ship; most of them had gone to bed. I was up on deck together with the captain and the crew as well as Lars Larsen and Johannes Stene; they were all privy to my plans to make an escape.

Very quietly a small light rowboat was lowered — it was about two A.M. and pitch dark. Silently we cast off, and with woolen rags wound around the oarlocks we began to tow the *Restauration* out toward the sea. Without meeting obstructions of any kind we succeeded in pulling the ship past the breakwater, and before daybreak the sloop was once again in Atlantic waters.

The first few days we were to have no complaints about lack of wind.

When we had got back from Helston, the women and children had felt tired and flustered — not only because they had had little opportunity to move about during the past week, but the air had become much more sultry and oppressive. I myself noticed how the flies became aggressive and that the swallows were swooping much lower than usual.

Some time before sunset the horizon grew dim with a grayish-yellow haze, and gradually billowing clouds appeared. In the evening sporadic and distant heat lightning lit up the sky, and finally we could hear the thunder. Just when the sloop left the outer harbor and once again was on the mighty ocean, the first bolt of lightning pierced the heavy cloud cover and tore it like a knife cutting into a heavy curtain. The thunder mingled with the sound of the wind and the waves.

The sloop could indeed take this and much more, but for the first time during the voyage the waves inundated the ship; the heavy seas swallowed it up and then spewed it out again. We kept well clear of the rocky coast looming up to starboard.

As soon as we had passed Lizard Point, the storm set in in full fury, and the *Restauration* could test its strength with the elements. The day had been a rough one, but the night was to be much worse. The thunderstorm continued, flashes of lightning like giant windmill vanes covered the heavens, the wind shifted from one direction to the other, the breakers grew ever larger. I was at the helm. In flashes of greenish-blue phosphorus, the ship was silhouetted against the sea and the sky: the mast, the sails, the seething deck — until it once again drifted into darkness. The crew and every free hand did all they could to keep the ship against the wind, to fasten anything that might be loose, and do whatever else was necessary.

The women looked after themselves and the youngsters below deck.

The hatches were battened down; each and every one were in their bunks and tried to stay put. Most of them suffered from seasickness and were quite indifferent to their surroundings. Some of them had gotten hold of some German sausages, since they were known to be a good remedy against seasickness; but they threw up the pieces of meat with the bile.

Brackish water, which had collected in the ship's bottom, moved from side to side; old smells mingled with new ones and made the room seem like the inside of a rotting belly. Frightened children clung to beams and planks; some had their arms around their mother's neck, holding on for dear life. An oil lamp had for some time provided a flickering light; it suddenly died out. Kari told me later it was as if a human being had passed away.

Planks and beams bent, every nail and every joint were put to the test. Higher and higher the sloop rode the crests of the waves, ever deeper she sank down in the troughs and rose again, until the rhythm was broken without warning and the ship quivered and remained still for a number of seconds.

The galley was swept overboard together with pots and pans. But Endre Dahl grabbed hold of the stove and managed to save it. A piece of the bulwark was torn off, an iron bar got loose and plowed across the deck, cutting into the planks like a hot knife in butter.

But the sloop managed to survive that night of terror also.

Simon Lima had been sleeping it off when we had left Porthleven and he was in a stupor for the first twenty-four hours. But he was finally awakened by the storm; he crawled up on deck, and staggered over toward me by the helm, and said, "So it *was* you after all?" "Yes, as you can see," I answered. "I'm the one that's responsible for all this," he said. "What are you guilty of?" I asked. "I am fleeing from the countenance of the Lord," he said; "just like Jonah." I didn't reply, but when he resumed his wailing, I tried to pacify him, "The storm didn't come because of you, Simon," I said; "we are all in the same boat."

There was a break in the clouds, the moon was shining, the sea was frighteningly white. And I thought to myself, "Who is the Jonah on this ship if it isn't Cleng Peerson? Who has been overtaken, if it isn't me?"

I had been overtaken in the sense too that I had met Martha Georgiana again, and what I had feared and hoped throughout a long winter in a foreign land, could no longer be avoided.

She was in her eighth month of pregnancy, but she seemed even more beautiful than before she had married. Her body and her bearing had gained greater dignity; her face bore witness to her feeling a great peacefulness.

As long as the storm was raging she had stayed below deck, but Kari told me that she had shown no sign of being seasick. On the contrary, she was well enough to be able to take care of the others.

The storm quieted down at last, and there was little damage to the ship and the sails. A fair wind was blowing, and every watch brought us farther toward the south. The air had felt cool following the thunderstorm, but now it was again quite warm, and the sun was high in the sky.

Martha Georgiana had brought materials with her up on deck, and when I passed her one day and in jest asked her whether she was writing to her sweetheart, she looked at me without smiling and said, "I am writing to Elias Tastad. I promised to give him a full account of our voyage." Bending down over the paper, she resumed writing, and I thought she didn't want to converse with me any further. But as I was walking away she said, "If it's a boy, Lars and I have decided that he is to be named after Elias."

I hesitated before asking her, "Will you have the baby before we can expect to get to New York?"

"Yes," she replied.

"Then we could have selected a better time," I said; "a better time for our voyage."

"It was not up to us to decide the time for the voyage that *we* had to set out on," she answered, and I dimly perceived a double meaning in her words, just as she most certainly must have perceived a similar one in mine. "Endre Dahl's wife chose to stay home," she added; "*I* chose to come along. I was afraid that I would never see Lars again if I stayed behind!"

"Your marriage is a happy one, Martha Georgiana," I said.

"I don't give much thought to that," she replied; "but it's true enough."

I walked away without answering her. I sat staring at the deck, when a hand was laid on my shoulder. I looked up; it was Captain Helland with Lars Larsen and Johannes Stene.

"We would like to speak with you, Cleng," Helland said.

I got up, and we walked down to the lower deck, entered his cabin, and closed the door behind us.

Captain Helland asked, "You saw the water barrels on the pier in Porthleven, didn't you?"

"Yes, of course, you brought them down to the harbor yourselves when the excitement was at its worst."

"Right," Helland said; "but did you notice whether they were brought on board?"

"No, but I suppose they were?" — and I heard my own voice as if it belonged to someone else; I had had the experience of being at sea without water. And we had women and children along, women nursing their young ones; Martha Georgiana was on board.

"We had two full barrels from before," Captain Helland said. "We have been using them up to now. The others can't be found anywhere. I'm afraid that we've just left them on shore in all the hullabaloo."

None of us said a word; then Lars asked, "How many days will it take us to get to Madeira?"

"With the fair wind we've got now it shouldn't take more than a week," I replied; "but how much water do we have?"

"Enough for about two days, at our regular rate of consumption," Helland replied.

"Then it's high time that we start rationing," I said.

"It's high time," Helland repeated. "And there's no beer left, but luckily we have some sour milk."

"Then we ought to be able to make it," I said; "and when we reach the area of the trade winds, we can be sure of making good headway."

We parted, and the skipper told the pilgrims about the situation. Not one opened his mouth in complaint, not one blamed those who deserved to be blamed; each and every one was calm and in good spirits.

But the wind and the weather did not come up to our expectations.

By the time we were supposed to have entered the area of the trade winds, the wind quieted down almost completely; for several days we had only a moderate breeze coming from different directions. A number of signs told us that we were slowly approaching land. Birds were flying above the ship much more frequently, and we noticed seaweed drifting in the water. Several ships passed us at a distance. Both the Canary Islands and Madeira are frequently used as provisioning ports, since they are situated at the crossroads of the sea routes between the continents.

At last, on the afternoon of July 29 we observed a ship approaching us at fairly close range. It held to a steady course right toward us. We welcomed the sight, especially since our water supply was just about to give out, and the heat had gotten steadily worse. During the day the ship's hull and deck became very hot and did not cool off until the next morning, at which time the boiling sun again rose in the sky.

But now we could look forward to a change for the better, and the pilgrims all thronged up on deck. They saw yet another ship rise above the horizon, and they felt even more confident of being saved from their predicament.

We followed the ships' movements in our binoculars: one of them seemed to be turning a bit to starboard and the other one to port, but in the slight breeze we closed in on one another very slowly.

Both of the strange ships were larger than our sloop and and were also much faster. We were hoping that they might be Swedish or Norwegian ships, and when we thought we were at the proper distance, Captain Helland hoisted the distress signal which the Swedish foreign ministry had instructed Norwegian shipowners to use whenever they encountered a Swedish ship in African waters.

Great was his consternation when through his binoculars he saw both ships hoist a pirate flag. He immediately told Lars Larsen, Johannes Stene, and me.

We all realized that there was no possibility of flight; neither were we able to offer any resistance.

It was then the practice — and I suppose the arrangement is still in force — that a shipowner or a skipper whose ship was destined for Mediterranean or South Atlantic waters, prior to departure could take out insurance against being harassed by pirates. They are the so-called Latin or Algerian papers. I can't go into detail about how they were obtained, but I will only underline the fact that the men who were responsible for the voyage — Lars Larsen, Johannes Stene, and last but not least Captain Helland — had neglected to take care of this important matter.

It is true that it had been their intention to set their course so far from Europe and Africa that they thought they were running no risk of meeting up with pirates, and it was perhaps true that these particular pirates were based on out-of-the-way ports on the desolate north coast of Madeira; in that case we would not have gotten very far with any insurance policies even if we had had any. What to do now? It seemed that we could look forward to a great deal but not to fresh drinking water.

I suddenly got an idea — ideas have come to me like that from the time I was a youngster and far into my old age. As soon as I thought of it, the idea seemed as comical as it was foolish; but I just had to mention it to the others, and since no one had any better suggestions and we had to act in a hurry, they all agreed to my proposal.

At Captain Helland's request, I ordered all the pilgrims to go below. I had already asked him to provide a bucket of tar and also a bucket of red lead; then I instructed them all in how to make up their faces and hands with red and black spots, making them look as if they were suffering from the bubonic plague or some other horrible disease. Thereupon they were all ordered to go back up on deck. When the pirate ship got close enough they were all to stretch out their hands together and shout for help and mercy as loudly as they could.

This was all done according to plan.

One of the pirate vessels fired a warning shot. I told the pilgrims that if there were more they shouldn't bat an eyelid. Captain Helland stood at the helm. Men, women, and children gathered along the ship's railing on both sides of the ship and did as they had been instructed; they wailed and shouted, and their red and black spotted hands and faces were indeed a horrible sight.

What the brave pirates thought, they only know, if any of them are still alive, but they showed no sign of pity or sympathy. Both ships turned sharply, and they sailed away from the pilgrims, who once again were left to their own devices. It was not a very hopeful situation, but at least much to be preferred to the one the pirates had had in mind for them.

First they had to rid themselves of all the tar and red lead that they had on their hands and faces. They rubbed themselves with rags and pieces of cloth and then made energetic attempts with Doorbridge's salt-water soap; but the result was not a very happy one. They looked more like mulattoes and Indians than white people.

What sort of welcome this kind of emigrant party would have received upon arrival on the North American continent — about that I have no opinion, Anne. But another port was closer at hand — the large island of Madeira.

With their arrival in Madeira their great need of drinking water was alleviated; but we should immediately note that their stay in many ways was unworthy of pilgrims.

About that I will deal in my next tale.

The Thirty-sixth Tale

At dawn a few days later we saw land rise above the horizon — it was Madeira's jagged peaks. Like floating clouds, looking almost transparent, they were silhouetted against the blue haze.

The sloop was lying motionless in the water; not until evening did we manage to tow the ship close to the eastern promontory, São Lorenço Point. We had planned to seek a port in order, if at all possible, to take in a new water supply immediately. But the coast seemed wild and desolate; in spite of the nice weather huge waves were crashing against the shore. We were afraid that we would not be able to get safely through the breakers, and when it got dark we set a course away from land.

The next morning every one was on deck very early. A gentle breeze came from the northeast, the haze had lifted, and the landscape in front of us emerged sharp and distinct.

The pilgrims rejoiced at the beauty of it all, for Madeira resembled in many ways the scenery that they were familiar with. The tallest peaks were shrouded in mist, but otherwise the sky was clear. The sun rose, its rays gilding the waves and the entire ocean.

Knud Slogvig kept watch at the prow; as he stood there looking at some dolphins playing on the surface, his attention was caught by an object bobbing up and down in the water; it seemed to be drifting along. He gave a signal to the man at the helm and at the same time called to Lars Larsen.

Lars was busy hauling in a fish. He had put out a line and had already made such a good catch that there was enough for dinner for all of us.

It was difficult to determine from the deck what kind of object it was, but when Lars had looked at it through his binoculars, he gave orders to lower a boat; he and four others, Ole Eide, Halvor Reveim, Gudmund Haugaas, and Georg Hesja, took their places by the oars.

The sloop lowered its sails and laid by, and the rowboat was soon next to the floating object, which turned out to be a barrel or cask of some kind. It was heavy and was covered with shells. It was almost black; it most probably had been floating in the water a very long time.

Lars had a rope ready. He threw off his jacket and rolled up his shirt sleeves; he then bent over the gunwale and attempted to place the rope around the barrel. It proved to be a difficult job, for the cask was larger than anyone had first thought; in addition it was bobbing up and down in the waves. Lars had to stretch the upper part of his body far over the gunwale, while two of the others lay down in the boat on the other side so that it would not take in water.

As Lars was busy with this and had no eye for anything else, Ole Eide suddenly shouted, "Watch out for the shark!" Lars at once pulled back; a white belly made a lightning arc up toward the keel, the shark's saw toothed mouth agape. In the very second that Lars pulled back the shark snapped its jaws together; it was so close that its head knocked against the barrel and made the water splash all over.

But with a valiant effort Lars had gotten hold of the rope. They didn't see the shark anymore, and having gotten over their fright, they tightened the rope and tried to pull the barrel over the gunwale.

It proved, however, to be much too heavy; therefore they towed it all the way back to the sloop, where they put more rope around it. Two of the crew manned the windlass, and soon the barrel was up on deck.

Judging from the sound, it would contain some kind of liquid. The people were all excited: they thought that it might be water, turned it this way and that, and scraped off the masses of seashells and looked for a bunghole.

Finally they found what they were looking for.

We knocked the stopper out with a hammer. A sweet, strong smell rose from the barrel. I recognized it immediately, since I had encountered it in many foreign ports: it was indeed Madeira in the literal sense of the word.

No one had tasted a drop of water since the morning of the previous day; the little water left at the bottom of the tanks smelled bad and tasted worse. And the last of the sour milk had been consumed at the evening meal. Many of us, especially among the children, had begun to suffer from upset stomachs.

But since we were fairly close to land and had good prospects of soon quenching our thirst with fresh water, the captain decided after consulting with the three of us whom he often turned to when in doubt, that each and every one who so desired should be allowed to drink with moderation and accept this gift that the ocean so unexpectedly had presented us with.

They all came with cups or mugs or tankards, whatever they had available, and they slaked their burning thirst.

We who had given permission did the same, and every one agreed that a more delightful drink we had never tasted: it burned with a fire and was at the same time refreshing and slaked our thirst while it simultaneously called forth a desire to quench it in full measure.

We felt its pleasant effects through emptying one cup only, and Captain Helland agreed to my suggestion that anyone who so desired might have a second cup. He set a good example by being the first to help himself a second time.

But after every one had emptied his cup a second time and the captain a third time, he decided that all rationing was to come to an end. To this no one had any objection.

Thus it happened that the pilgrims within a short time found themselves in a state of euphoria, a state which most of them had previously had only hazy notions about. I showed no more moderation than most of the others; but I had a bit of experience in this regard and also perhaps greater powers of resistance. At any rate, I can still remember some of what they said and did. I tell you this, Anne, without giving any thought as to whether it might reflect honor or dishonor on them. But you will see that because most of them were in truth pilgrims, even under the influence of alcohol they were still pure of heart, and I believe that none of them abandoned themselves to censurable conduct — even though they did speak with less inhibition than was their custom.

First I must note that Thorstein Bjaadland seemed to be of the opinion that he had returned to his profession of being a driver for the royal Norwegian postal service, since he had placed himself astride a coil of rope and shouted, "Giddap, giddap!" while putting the empty mug to his mouth and making believe he was blowing his posthorn. I remember it very clearly and also that I thought it to be very amusing.

Captain Helland, who showed that he couldn't take much alcohol, walked over to Siri Madland, the oldest of the women on board, embraced her, and proclaimed that he was very fond of her daughter Rachel, who he thought resembled her mother! Thereupon he asked for her blessing for the reason that he intended to ask for her daughter's hand. Siri Madland took another swallow from her cup and replied generously, "I would be happy if you took all three of them; then I would know that they would be in good hands."

Simon Lima leaned against the mast and wept while he was counting on his fingers and said, "This I have escaped, and this, and this," — and he continued in this way —; "oh, God, when the perils are safely behind me and I have no more fingers to count with, what do I do then?" "Then you must start counting with your toes," I said and turned my back on him. Without any warning my chest felt just as if it were going to burst, and through the flickering light I saw Martha Georgiana's face; she was sitting on the center hatch. I bent over her and repeated time and again this assurance, "I'll be a good boy, Martha Georgiana, I'll be a good boy." But she stared at me uncomprehendingly and asked, "Where did you leave Lars?"

At that moment Lars came staggering over, and that man of peace threatened me with his fist and shouted, "You stay away from her! I've seen how you crawl up to her like a gray cat!"

I seem to remember that I gave him my hand and said, "Forgive me, Lars."

But the peaceable Elen Rossadal also walked over to me and bawled me out, calling me a liar and a cheat, and saying that I had deceived them all. At that I got very angry; I stepped closer and hit her, and she started to bleed from her mouth.

Nils Hersdal came running over; he was the biggest and strongest man on board ship — I have already told you that he later was called Big Nels — and he grabbed me by the neck and lifted me up and shook me as if I were a sheepskin blanket. When he dropped me, I was still conscious and I could see the deck and the people as if in a red haze. One of the last things I can remember was Sara Larsdatter bending over me, loosening the kerchief she was wearing around her neck, and wiping the blood off my hands; that done, she walked away silently. Ole Hetletvedt sat with a quiet, blissful smile, humming a religious melody. But Simon Lima had given himself over to inconsolable weeping. He walked from one to the other and stopped at last in front of me and asked us all for forgiveness because he, like another Jonah, had mingled with the just: "Ten fingers on two hands," he said; "and against ten of God's commandments I have offended. It was because of me that the storm came, and it is my fault that the sharks surround us. I beseech and implore you, Cleng: do not throw me into the sea! Wait till we get to a port on Madeira; then I will report to the authorities."

But I didn't understand what he meant, and I don't think anyone else did either. Johannes Stene said, "Take care, Simon, or the sharks will get you without any help from us. You almost toppled into the sea a minute ago."

Johannes filled another cup, I clinked with him, dried my face, and got blood on my hands. After that I can hardly remember anything, only that I felt sorry for the small children, who also were drunk and were crawling around in a daze.

At last a great silence must have descended on the ship. Everyone fell asleep, some up on deck, others in their bunks below or wherever they happened to be — and what I can relate about subsequent events I have either guessed at or I know that it must have happened that way, or I was later told about it by people who had seen us from shore.

The *Restauration* had been lying still with sails reefed already before we had lowered the boat in order to get hold of the drifting barrel; after it had been hauled on board, no one had bothered to do anything in regard to the steering of the ship.

But in the afternoon the wind freshened; it blew from northeast, and the sloop was moving in a southeasterly direction a few cablelengths from shore. One after another the towering promontories were left behind and the ship finally approached — after having passed Cape Garajau — the south coast of the island. At the head of a wide bay lies the capital, Funchal.

The guards on the city's fortress observed the little vessel drifting by, with no one at the helm and no flag flying from the yardarm. In fact, at first glance it seemed as if there were no one on board.

The current took the *Restauration* into the harbor of Funchal. In the meantime the ship had been reported to the commandant of the fortress. Since he thought it all very strange, he ordered a warning shot to be fired from one of the guns of the fortress. So was done, but aboard ship nothing happened.

Another report was given the commandant. With a fierce expression he walked from his residence and ascended the observation tower; his siesta had been spoiled.

Looking more closely at the sloop through his binoculars, he found to his consternation that there were many people lying about on deck, their arms and legs stretched out as if they were dead.

His hunch was converted into certainty: this was a plague-stricken ship and everyone on board had died. Such things do happen; indeed cases are known of ships having experienced such a calamity, having drifted about for years until the sails crumbled away and only white bones were left of the miserable crews.

Uncertain of what to do, the commandant ordered one more warning shot to be fired. When the smoke drifted away and there was still no sign of life on the ship — which was still drifting toward the harbor — he decided to have the guns aimed at the vessel and to use real cannon-balls in order to sink the vessel. If a plague ship were to drift ashore, it would be disastrous for the entire population of Madeira.

When well-disposed, even Fate may at times have a trump card up its sleeve. It so happened on this occasion that out in the roads there was a merchant ship from Bremen. The men on board had also had their attention drawn to the *Restauration*. When the skipper of the German ship first looked through his binoculars toward the fortress and realized what they intended to do, and then looked at the sloop, where he saw three or four small children crawling about among the many motionless people, he knew that he had to act at once. He signaled to the fortress to make the men realize the consequences of their decision, and at the same time he ordered his chief officer to shout through a megaphone to the sloop, "Show your colors! Show your colors!"

This was done, and in all the tumult a few of the pilgrims, I being one of them, woke up. Bewildered at the discovery that we were so close to populated areas, a big, beautiful city climbing the steep slopes surrounding the bay, I did not at once realize where we were. But when I heard the warning shouts from the German merchant ship and saw the gunsmoke wafting away, I immediately realized that something serious was afoot. If I remember right, I got Captain Helland out of bed; but at this point he was still in a pitiful condition and was hardly able to stand up.

Nevertheless, our flag was hoisted; neither I nor anyone else seems to know for sure how this was done; but you may possibly get an idea about the condition we were all in when I tell you that this chapter in our story has later on been retold in three different versions. My sister Kari, who was considered by all to be a level-headed woman, one who never bragged or exaggerated, insisted that she was the one who hoisted the flag, without the help of a living soul, while Thorstein Bjaadland has maintained that he was the one who was responsible for the deed. I believe, however, that he is wrong, since I seem to remember that even after we had dropped anchor he was lying there asleep with his head resting on the coil of rope he earlier had thought was a mail coach.

The third version has it that some of the bigger children found the flag hidden among some barrels on deck, and that they attached it to a boat hook which they then held up in the air.

But there is one thing that is certain: when young Brita Christophersdatter woke up, she was lying next to her husband in the the middle of the deck, holding his hand, and when she realized that they were in great danger, she rushed forward, lifting up her long, flowered calico skirt and waved with it as if it were a signal flag.

The danger had subsided, the sails were hoisted, and Captain Helland took the helm; while everyone slowly returned to the everyday world, the sloop made its way toward the inner harbor.

Port officials as well as representatives of the civil and military authorities were among the crowd gathered on shore. An immigration officer and the town physician were also there.

The Portuguese customs officers were the first to board the ship. The captain, who now could make himself understood in English, reported on the voyage, and they found everything to be in order.

The other officials raised certain questions in regard to the extraordinary conditions that had seemed to prevail on board when the sloop had come into sight. Since these gentlemen understood very little English and I on the other hand was not totally ignorant of the Portuguese language, I attempted to serve as interpreter. I conveyed the question to the captain, who said, "Tell them the unvarnished truth, and also that we are on our way to America!"

As soon as I made it clear to the officials that we all had become roaring drunk after having taken on board the barrel that a kind fate had provided us with, there was much merriment among them and also among the people gathered around. Thereupon we were provided with fresh water so that we could quench our thirst.

Later on large oxen were driven down to the harbor; they were harnessed to magnificent sleds with colorful canopies and covered with multicolored pieces of cloth and beautiful flowers.

By signs and friendly gestures the people made the pilgrims understand that these vehicles had been brought down to the harbor in their honor. We all got ready, and since the ship was moored and the watch was on board, all the passengers and the entire crew, who had put on their best clothes, were driven through the narrow steep streets up to the residence of the American consul.

The name of the consul was John H. March.

The Thirty-seventh Tale

Consul March had also heard the shots, but he had not paid any special attention to them since they often had gunnery practice at the fortress. When he later on spied the large crowd approaching his residence, he may have thought that they were taking part in one of the local festivals that were arranged from time to time by the townspeople — usually in connection with a memorial day for some saint or other. As for himself, the consul was a liberal Presbyterian. He resumed reading the documents on his desk until he was disturbed by joyous shouts, followed by a continuous ringing of his door bell. When a servant finally opened the door, one of Funchal's leading men asked him to inform the consul that guests from far away requested the honor of meeting with him.

I have been told that even before the consul had received the message, he came down the stairs and walked over to the main entrance. He caught some words of a language that he had never heard before and saw a group of people dressed a bit like New England Puritans. Curious — and at the same time a little brusque, as seems proper for a consul — he asked what kind of commotion this was and whether we had any wishes to convey to him.

The city's prefect of police stepped forward — Consul March had not noticed him until then — and, using the most grandiloquent civilities of Portuguese etiquette, he first asked that the people be excused for disturbing the consul in his highly important activities and then briefly told him the story about the landing of the Sloopers, leaving out none of the comical and dramatic aspects of the story.

Soon the muscles in the consul's cheeks began to twitch, and before the prefect had ended his story, his face was purple from keeping back the laughter.

When he had wiped his spectacles and his nose and stroked his well-cared-for beard to make sure it had retained its elegant symmetry, he went out on the front steps and asked whether there was anyone among the emigrants who could act as his interpreter. He wanted very much to convey his greetings to them.

I volunteered, and repeated sentence for sentence the consul's message.

On behalf of the United States of America he first wished the emigrants good luck on their dangerous voyage across the ocean; at the same time he encouraged us by saying that it was his firm conviction that it would be a very pleasant trip. Then he informed us in well-chosen words of the sincere gratitude of his nation for our intention to cultivate new areas of virgin and fertile land beyond the seas. In this connection, he called the pilgrims a new and fresh pulse beat in the body of America, and expressed the hope that they would also be able to take part in the governing of the country and exert an influence in the highest circles. I felt a flash of joy when one of his phrases, somewhat freely translated, could be rendered in the same words that I had used during the bimonthly assembly at Fogn: "Over there a fisherman can become a senator and a crofter president!" — and I did not let the chance pass me by.

The consul continued, "As the local population already know, the consulate's annual garden party is to be held tomorrow. It is a pleasure for me to express my sincere wish to see all the emigrants as guests of honor on that occasion. And together with the notables of the city I also take this opportunity to invite the entire population of Funchal."

Jubilation crested like a wave higher and higher; the people laughed, embraced one another, and clapped their hands, and some of them seized the nearest pilgrim by the arm to join in a ring dance; but the Sloopers held back.

When the noise finally abated, the consul continued, "And if the emigrants find it possible to stay another few days, I ask them to do me the honor of joining me in a drive by ox-drawn sleds to the environs of the capital and up into the mountains, so that they can get a good impression of this island of ours."

I thanked him on behalf of the Sloopers for all his kindness, said that we would be very happy to accept his invitation, and also informed him that the things we had to do would in any case extend our stay at Madeira to almost a week.

I myself was well accustomed to the changes and vicissitudes of this world of ours, but to the emigrants this event was more of a surprise since they could not help thinking of the circumstances under which they had left England and how they had been in danger of their lives both during their encounter with the pirates and when the sloop had been drifting into Funchal's harbor with no one at the helm. Encouraged by these new and promising events, they voiced the hope that perhaps people in America would prove to be just as friendly as the republic's consul in Madeira, and of this I assured them, once again rejecting all the unreliable rumors that were rampant in Norway.

During the rest of the day we took care of some urgent business. Captain Helland, for example, saw to it that we were provided with a new and ample supply of water, and he also ordered various kinds of provisions that they were running short of. But those among the Sloopers who had not been given special tasks to do, went for a walk through the streets of the town, where they especially noticed the luxuriant vegetation and the wealth of flowers. Even the river which runs through the town was completely covered with what amounted to a veritable roof of violet bougainvilleas.

In spite of the bountiful nature, a large part of the population showed signs of poverty and there were numerous beggars. The pilgrims did not have much to give away, but when Elen Rossadal saw a crippled girl of her own age sitting at the corner in something that looked like a wheelbarrow and reaching out her hand to passersby, Elen gave her a flowery kerchief which due to the heat she was holding in her hand, and the girl grasped her hand and kissed it. Elen then discovered that the girl had sores both on her mouth and her hands and she gently stroked her cheek and shared an orange with her. It was the first orange that Elen Rossadal had ever tasted; I had just bought it and given it to her, and I saw what happened.

Later on everybody boarded the ship and got a good night's sleep. They had eaten well, they had quenched their thirst, and they were quite overwhelmed by the many impressions of a world that to them seemed thrilling and exotic.

The next morning they all washed from head to toe below deck — first all the men and boys, then all the women and girls — and put on, just like the previous day, their best clothes before going ashore.

That far south it gets dark pretty early at the end of July. Lanterns, of many shapes and giving off lights in many colors, hung in the trees in the consul's garden. It seemed like a fairy-tale forest, and rippling brooks and an artificial pool gleamed and sparkled; the garden sloped steeply down toward the shore.

Consul March had asked a group of young people to perform the old dances, while singing to the accompaniment of tambourines and castagnettes. He thought the emigrants would enjoy it, but to his great surprise they paid little heed to the exhibition. When he asked me whether it wasn't so that they also had folk dances in Norway, I explained that these people had a puritanical outlook on life and looked upon dancing as a frivolous pleasure.

"But for myself, I am not that strict in my worship," I told him, "and if the consul gives permission, I would like to demonstrate how Norwegians dance when they are having a good time."

It so happens, Anne, that during the years of my roaming youth, I had learned to dance the Halling. I therefore asked that a cap be put at the tip of a long pole, and Consul March asked one of the young girls from the city to step forward, and said, "This is the most beautiful girl in town; she is to hold the cap." I then performed all the leaps and bounds that are part of the dance and finally kicked the cap off the pole. As soon as the girl realized that I had actually done so, she ran over to me and gave me a kiss. Many of the pilgrims also received kisses by the people next to them; they were a bit taken aback, since we Northerners do not relish giving vent to our emotions. They wiped their lips and looked embarrassed.

There was an abundance of fine wines, and the consul asked first one, then another, to have a drink with him, but everyone bowed and withdrew without tasting the wine. This surprised the consul a bit, for even though it had been explained to him that they were devout puritans, he could not help recalling in what condition they had arrived the previous day.

Thus it happened that as the festivities proceeded, everything became exactly the opposite of what had occurred when the *Restauration* had arrived: when it got close to midnight the pilgrims were the only ones who were still sober. The townspeople were completely unmindful of the sorrows of this world — and the consul was almost in a similar condition.

But he was sober enough to give some thought as to whether he had offended them, and he asked me why the guests from the North were not enjoying the party. I did not want to take it upon myself to answer for all of them but turned to Lars Larsen, and he spoke to the consul along these lines: he regretted that on his own behalf and on that of the others that the pilgrims had arrived in the city in such a condition that they had exposed themselves to great danger and had thereby been a disgrace to their Creator. But they hoped that the consul in spite of this transgression would still be convinced that they were true pilgrims on the way to North America, where they expected to find their Canaan.

Consul March expressed his pleasure at the sincerity they showed vis-à-vis the Divine, and he assured them that the North American republic was exactly the kind of refuge that people of all persuasions longed for. He congratulated his country for receiving such pious immigrants and repeated his offer to take us on a trip in ox-drawn sleds. Lars Larsen thanked him quietly and withdrew.

I then wandered by myself around in the garden and quite involuntarily witnessed the following: I was sitting on a rock right behind one of the many garden pavilions. I heard someone speak Norwegian and I saw Captain Helland and Rachel Madland approaching. They noticed the arbor, saw that no one was inside, and entered. After they had conversed about different things, Helland began to tell her about his future plans; he said he would like to settle down in New York, and he asked Rachel what she intended to do over there. "I suppose I have to stay with Father and Mother," she answered. Captain Helland sat silently a while and then asked her, "Perhaps you would consider coming along with me?" When she didn't answer, he said quietly, "Well, don't be angry with me, Rachel, I didn't mean any harm. Let's make believe I never said anything."

But then she blurted out, "But you must know very well that I would rather be with you than with anyone else in the world!" The captain said, "God bless you, my wonderful girl!" and he embraced her.

Later in life Rachel became the very model of fidelity, and when her two daughters were grown up, she told them about this proposal and that she had never been kissed by anyone but her husband, neither before nor after — this in the way of admonition, since she thought her daughters were becoming inclined to adopt the frivolous ways of the cosmopolitan city.

She and her husband remained in New York and were very seldom in contact with the other emigrants who arrived on the *Restauration*. All the more reason for engraving this event in our memory; our stay at Madeira was also to contribute to the blessings that have come the way of the pilgrims and their descendants.

As for myself, I walked away from the arbor and sat down at the outermost point overlooking the ocean; I sat there looking at the breakers far below at the foot of the mountain; a full moon illuminated the scene. I recalled events of long ago: how I had lured Sara Larsdatter to come with me and we had traveled across land and sea all the way from Tysvær to Røldal, just for her to touch the wonder-working crucifix in the church and be cured of her muteness. I thought of the hopes and the longing I had harbored for us both through youth and manhood and how strangely everything can turn out: now that I was free I did not feel any love for her but was helplessly attracted to Martha Georgiana.

By this time she had become much bigger — she was now in her eighth month — but this merely served to increase the tender feelings I had for her. I looked forward to the time that we were to reach land and I could get away from her, for I knew that only by fleeing would I be able to conquer the temptation that consumed me. Lars had indicated that he did not think of becoming a farmer; rather he planned to settle in some town or other and continue as a boatbuilder or carpenter, a work with which he was already familiar.

But don't let me dwell on these things; at that time they brought me only pain but now they seem indifferent to me — but not completely so. I would rather tell you how the following day I was put to an unexpected test.

Everyone without a single exception took part in the trip that the consul had arranged for us. For quite a long ways we were taken by the same kind of magnificent ox-drawn sleds that had received us on our arrival — as far as the cobblestone roads led. The stones had been brought up from the beach; they were all round and polished by the waves; that is why the runners of the sleds were gliding along so easily.

We continued on muleback, past a town by the name of Canara de Lobos, and over to a lookout right by the sea, Cabo Girão; it is situated at an altitude of almost two thousand feet, and the cliffs plunge almost vertically into the sea. The surroundings were exceptionally beautiful: on the slopes of the valley there were luxuriant vineyards; the grapes were just then harvested and transported to the presses in bags of goat skins. Consul March, who had joined us on the trip, purchased on his own behalf one bunch after another of heavy, lush grapevines, and the pilgrims helped themselves, inordinately praising this delicious fruit which they had never tasted before. Still, they were not at all surprised that it surpassed any other fruit, since they knew that grapes are mentioned and praised several times in Holy Writ.

At the highest point of Cabo Girão one can see the city lying below and the coastline with the black volcanic columns silhouetted against the blue ocean — and small boats with sails that reminded us of shark's fins were gliding back and forth. At this sight Elen Rossadal burst out in a loud prayer of thanks to the Lord for having allowed such a wonderful landscape to rise out of the ocean. But on the way down she did not forget to bring with her the biggest cluster of grapes to give to Lars Larsen and Martha Georgiana, both of whom had halted near the lookout where the road came to an end.

When the rest of the party, following a brief rest, decided to walk back to town, Martha expressed the wish to wait there a while since she didn't feel well. I stopped and stayed with them; I said something about their possibly needing a little help. The real reason, however, was the fact that I just wanted to be near her.

While we were sitting there, she noticed a tree down below on the steep slope; it was leaning over the escarpment. It was a wild apple tree. She said, "How fertile and luxuriant everything is here!" Lars asked, "Shall I get you an apple?" "No, don't, you'd almost be risking your life," she said, laughing, half frightened; she didn't think he was serious. But I said, "Then you must let *me* get you an apple, Martha Georgiana!" "I should say not!" she poo-poohed; but when I got up and they both realized that I intended to do what I had said I would do, Lars became indignant. "Absolutely not! If anyone goes, I'll go!" "Then we can go together," I answered, and without saying more we set out downhill, he in the lead and I right behind: but I could feel that he was a bit angry with me. Martha Georgiana called once more and asked us to return, but we made out as if we didn't hear her.

As I've mentioned, the apple tree was standing at the edge of a precipice; its bare branches stood out like the fingers of an open hand against the horizon and the sea below, its apples looking like blood-red pearls.

I hadn't intended to take away from Lars his right to pick the fruit for his own wife, but I followed him solely because I had already started and would have felt ashamed if I had to turn back. Thus I let him lead the way; he got to the tree first, and as he reached out over the precipice in order to pick an apple, he lost his footing and plunged into the abyss.

When the next moment I stood where he had been standing, I saw him hanging far below. He had been caught by the branches of a small and stunted oak tree; its branches seemed like claws as they rose against the sky. Motionless, Lars was lying in its grip, as if resting, with his arms spread out as if he were nailed to a cross.

I shouted, but he did not answer.

Whether he was dead or alive no one could know. Nor would anyone have doubts about what would happen if he revived: his very first movement would cause him to slip and continue his downward plunge. Jagged rocks of lava and the thundering surf could be seen directly below him.

My common sense told me that it would be impossible to reach Lars by foot. Nevertheless, I started to walk down. Like a sleepwalker I first placed my foot under a small root, then on a rocky outcropping, on a loose stone that almost tipped over but stayed in place, all the while grabbing a hold of tufts of grass, and then on a withered bush which nevertheless must have had a sufficient grip in the soil or the rock.

As I advanced downward, all kinds of strange apparitions rose before my mind's eye. I suddenly recalled a dream that I had had repeatedly the previous summer: Lars was dead, and it seemed as if streams of water were flowing all around him. Just now I saw him like that in real life: he was lying motionless on the knotty branches, and the surf far below seemed to be running like a current in among its branches.

That is what I was thinking about, and also this: if Lars falls down before you reach him, Cleng, then you may get the opportunity to win Martha Georgiana. The one who hadn't hesitated to risk his life to save her husband — could she do anything but love him? A mere movement might be sufficient when you are down by the tree — just a slight movement of your hand and he will begin to slide, and you will desperately try to grasp him, but in vain.

At last I was by his side. Lars still lay motionless, as if he were tied by invisible ropes. I called him by name, but he did not respond. Very carefully I crawled out on the trunk and out among the branches; below me was nothing but the air and the sea. He had a cut in his scalp, but when I finally grasped his wrist I could feel his pulse beating.

How it all happened I can't remember, and I have never since been able to call to mind a clear picture of what transpired. But I must have heaved him onto my shoulder; I tied his hands with his belt in such a way that they held firm around my neck. The ascent began, and finally I was back by the apple tree.

Martha Georgiana was standing there. She said, "I saw what you did, everything."

I lowered Lars to the ground; from a brook close by I fetched some water and moistened his forehead. Slowly he regained consciousness;

but neither that day nor the next was he able to recall anything about the accident or about what had happened immediately preceding it.

When our ship was ready to depart and we had taken on board all kinds of food supplies, always keeping in mind what was needed and also what space and money were available, we received a gift from Consul John H. March in the form of baskets of fruit, oranges, bananas, and grapes. Everyone was allowed to help himself to his heart's content as long as the supply lasted. We now know that everything that is green and grows is a good remedy against scurvy, which all seafarers dread, and I have since thought of the consul many times with the deepest gratitude.

On the whole it may be said that our entire voyage was free from many kinds of misery that have plagued emigrants ever since, even as late as the present time. It has indeed happened that the number of passengers has been decimated before the ship reached land. In our case, it was just the opposite: Martha Georgiana gave birth to a bouncing baby girl. It happened on September 2; by that time we had crossed most of the Atlantic Ocean. We were in the waters off the northern Bahamas.

What I wish to tell you above all, Anne, is the fact that after I had saved Lars's life, Martha Georgiana evinced both confidence and trust in her relationship with me. She acted as a sister does toward a brother. This is how I remember that she once told me how it had happened that she and Lars had become engaged.

"I was determined when it came to Lars," she said. "He would hardly have been able to get the words out without me to help him get started! Often, before she finds the one she chooses, a young girl will think a lot about what her husband ought to be like. I had imagined a tall, powerful-looking fellow with dark, wavy hair, someone not much older than myself. Then it turned out to be Lars, whose hair is graying and is almost twice my age. Since I met him I've begun to think that gray hair is attractive — yours is, Cleng!"

"Then maybe I can get sufficiently gray to suit you?" I asked jokingly.

She smiled slightly and continued, "He was more determined when he thought of our leaving for America. He did not know much about *my* doubts and *my* anguish, for I didn't say much about it, but he always stuck to his decision: 'Cleng has said so, and we can trust in him' was the constant refrain. I can confess to you, Cleng, that unlike *him*, I haven't always had complete faith in you. People said that you had a big mouth and one couldn't believe what you said, and the big words you came out with during the bimonthly assembly at Fogn I thought just backed up what people said. But today I know that I did you an injustice."

She grasped my hand and squeezed it. Immediately I got up and left; I ran down below and wanted to be alone. It was a beautiful day and everyone was up on deck. Lying on my own bunk, I buried my face in the pillow and was no longer able to hold back my tears.

When the pain had subsided and I looked up, I noticed that I was not alone. Sara Larsdatter was sitting on the chest; she had been witness to my commotion. She came over to me and stroked my hair; it was if she once again was wiping blood off my head. I remembered the first time I had seen her hand; then it was still a child's hand. Now it was beginning to age; the skin was no longer soft and smooth but was rougher than before, knuckles and veins showing clearly. I didn't know what I should say or do; but because I couldn't forget everything that had been between us and now I felt attracted to another, I bent forward and touched her hair with my lips.

For weeks we kept a steady course somewhere between the thirtieth parallel and the Tropic of Cancer, and the wind and the weather continued to be as pleasant as one could wish. Most of the time we ran before the wind and made good speed. The days were warm but not uncomfortable and the nights were so agreeably pleasant that everyone who so wished could sleep up on deck.

With the exception of a few showers, often accompanied by thunder, there was no rain during the entire time; the sky was almost always without a cloud from dawn to dusk, but at times large billowing clouds would gather in the western sky at sunset.

Once in a while we enjoyed the company of dolphins; they are supposed to be the most intelligent of all animals and are even said to be able to understand human speech and can learn to speak themselves; it also happened that flying fishes made sparkling arcs above the waves; at times they would land on the deck of the *Restauration.*

Yes, I could say much about the joys that fill the heart of a seafarer when sailing before a favorable wind toward a distant horizon; but I do not want to dwell on this any longer. It is time to call to mind the day that Martha Georgiana gave birth to her child.

It was not an easy birth. When she had not given birth following two days of pain and struggle, I realized that even Siri Madland, who was acting as midwife since she was especially knowledgeable and was the oldest woman on board, began to worry. She was of the opinion that it would be a breech birth, and even a man can understand that such a delivery is unusually difficult.

It so happened that Lars Larsen just at that time became seriously ill; it was a result of the blow he had sustained on the head when he fell over the precipice on Madeira.

The entire first day of her labor he sat by his wife's bunk, even though Siri Madland brusquely gave him to understand that she wanted him to leave. Then he suddenly — on the morning of the second day — fell forward and lost consciousness. After a while he came to, and asked where he was, and then collapsed a second time.

I took charge of him and placed him in my own bunk. Children and young people and all those who had no business there had been chased up on deck long before, and that did them no harm, for the weather continued to be pleasant: sunshine all day, and cool nights with stars in the sky.

Lars regained consciousness after a while, but he was so dizzy that he couldn't stand on his feet. Martha Georgiana's pains had temporarily subsided but now her labor recommenced with full force and she had little strength left. Being almost delirious, she asked about Lars, and Siri Madland told her that he was sleeping.

"Then let Cleng come sit by me," Martha asked.

"Now you don't know what you're saying, child," Siri said.

"Yes, I do, Siri," she said. "I need a firm hand, and Cleng has that."

I could hardly believe what she was saying, and I thought of hiding some place or starting a piece of work that would be impossible for me to leave.

I was already about to leave when Siri called, "You've heard what she's saying. You'd better go to her no matter what."

I sat down next to Martha; I took a piece of cloth and wiped the perspiration off her forehead, and I let her grasp my hands and squeeze them hard in order to gain some strength. For a while I forgot that it wasn't my child she struggled to bring into this world, and even though both before and many a time since, I have shunned pain, the thought has now and then occurred to me that I would gladly have endured much if only once in this life, I could have been a woman and given birth to a child.

But when the actual birth was drawing near, Siri Madland said, "Now you'll have to leave, Cleng, we've no use for you any longer." I wiped the perspiration off Martha Georgiana's forehead for the last time and noticed that she was almost unconscious. But even before I rose to leave she cried out again. It sounded like the cry of an animal in the forest.

An hour later, when the child had been washed and placed in her arms and both were sleeping, Lars regained consciousness, and I sat down on the edge of his bunk.

"It's all over, Lars," I said. "You're the father of a daughter."

An almost childlike smile spread over his face, and he said, "I must go and see her." He got up but immediately had to sit down again; he turned pale, and asked me, "You must let me lean on you, Cleng." I held him by the arm, and together we walked over to the bunk in which Martha Georgiana was lying with the little one in her arms.

Martha Georgiana opened her eyes at that very moment, and Lars kneeled down and placed his head on her breast.

Martha Georgiana soon regained her strength, and so did Lars. Everyone on board shared their joy. Endre Dahl — who had left his wife when she was in her eighth month and often thought of her for that reason — drowned his sorrows among his bubbling pans and kettles, preparing the best food that the ship's galley was capable of. A week following the birth, when the young mother was on her feet again, we arranged a celebration which boasted the tastiest food I had eaten since many years previously I had been invited to a party by Consul Gabriel Schanche Kielland in the city of Stavanger.

It was on the day of the party that for the first time in a long while we noticed seaweed floating in the sea and seagulls flying above the mast. We looked upon that as a good omen, for the newborn child as well as for the rest of the voyage. And it was not long before we sighted one of the Bahama Islands.

By then the child had been given a name. It was her father's wish that she should be named Margaret Allen, after the pious and distinguished lady in London. Lars had worked for her for about a year after he had been released from the British prison ship, as I have told you before, Anne.

The Thirty-eighth Tale

Thus two months and even more passed for the pilgrims on board the *Restauration*. After a while they felt as if they were members of one big family; they shared all joys and sorrows, and they were resigned to the monotony of each day. Ole Hetletvedt gave lessons to the children, chiefly in religion and arithmetic; in addition, he made them memorize and sing a number of hymns.

Among the few but precious books that they had brought along there was also an almanac, and based upon that he explained to them about the wind and the weather and the seasons, about the church holidays, about high and low tide, about the eclipses of the moon and the sun, and where the most brilliant stars are to be found in the sky. And when it got dark they would watch the sky and could make out the constellations they had read about, and Ole explained that all this represented not only the beauty and grandeur of an inanimate nature but also proved the majesty of a merciful God. From the writings of modern astronomers he knew that the stars are distant from the earth and also incredibly immense and that they move in orbits assigned to them by the Lord Himself.

I did not remain inactive either. Martha Georgiana began to study English under my guidance, "for that language will be the one that my child will speak," she said. But when she first realized how difficult it is to learn a foreign language, she laughed and said that when they came

to America she would remain as mute as her sister-in-law Sara. But I
asked her to take heart, and with good reason, since she was both intelligent and eager to learn. I could not help letting my glance dwell on
her lovely mouth — especially when with a mixture of boldness and
timidity she made an effort to make her lips and tongue produce the
sounds of the English language.

At the stipulated time our instruction period would come to an end,
and she would go below to feed her child. But in my inner being stirred
thoughts of many kinds, most of them sad and wistful.

One day she was sitting with the child in her arms, and Lars, as was
his wont, walked over to them. His angular face took on an air of
softness and warmth, and when he saw the little one swaddled in some
pieces of cloth, he said, "You didn't even get a cradle to lie in!" But I
answered, "The entire ship is her cradle, and the ocean is the rocker on
which the foot of God is treading." Martha Georgiana turned toward
me, and in her face I thought I saw what I secretly had wished for, for I
felt at the same time both happy and depressed. She said, "In your
mouth all words come out sounding different, Cleng." But I got up and
walked away from them.

For almost an entire week we had been hoping to see land, and some of
the passengers became impatient, among them Cornelius Hersdal. "If I
only had land underfoot soon!" he said; he could be standing for a very
long time by the ship's rail breathing deeply like a dog: "But I smell
only salt and seaweed, salt and seaweed!" But one morning he
brightened considerably: "Smell the breeze," he said; "earth and sand,
trees and animals! You can smell it too, can't you?" "No, I can't smell
anything like that," I replied, "unless it's the bacon" — for Endre Dahl
was just preparing breakfast in the galley. Cornelius said, "I'll wager
that we see land before the sun goes down." And very excitedly he
began to pace the deck. "Wasn't it you who took along two pecks of dirt
from Hersdal?" I asked. "Can't you go down and bury your fingers in
that for a while?"

But that very evening we sighted land, just as he had predicted. A
low coastline with white sand and palm trees was silhouetted against
the setting sun.

At first there was great excitement on board, and everyone expressed
joy at the longed-for sight; then a great quiet descended on the group
of pilgrims. But Lars Larsen lifted up his two-week-old Margaret; he
pointed to the coastline and shouted, "Margaret, Margaret, look! There
you see the world!"

The Atlantic Ocean was now behind us. At midnight we dropped anchor, and at dawn we lowered a dinghy and rowed toward the shore. There didn't seem to be any natural harbor, and we didn't know exactly where we were, but figured that it was one of the northernmost of the Bahama Islands.

That proved correct; the name of the island was Wattling. Columbus, too, is supposed to have made his landfall here, long ago.

The captain, Johannes Stene, Lars Larsen, Cornelius Hersdal, and I were the first party to go ashore. A large crowd had gathered on the shore, most of them Negroes. They were very friendly toward us, and all of them spoke English — which was quite natural, since Wattling has been a British possession for over two hundred years.

They showed us where there was a good anchorage; the pilgrims stayed there for three days. Wattling is a low coral island as are also the other islands in that archipelago. The climate is called subtropical and is very pleasant, and the soil is very fertile. Tropical fruits of various kinds as well as tomatoes grew there, and among the animals that could be caught and eaten I must mention giant turtles first of all. The natives prepared splendid meals for us, made of such ingredients, and Endre Dahl picked up a trick or two from them so that after our departure we could enjoy meals that were different from and tastier than those we were used to.

We also replenished our water and food supply; then we weighed anchor and set sail. We set our course due north, since we planned to reach land around Cape Hatteras; it was my intention to travel overland from there to New York.

I must tell you, Anne, that I still hadn't revealed the truth. When the question once in a while had come up, whether everything was fairly well prepared for them in America, I would reply by alluding to those statements in Andreas Stangeland's letter that we all knew, or I made out as if anything new that I told them from my first trip in America referred to the last one, or as if the preparations that I had planned had already been taken care of. For it was my hope that Andreas Stangeland had been able to do all this, and I knew that he would get all possible help from Joseph Fellows. But I was still tormented by dark misgivings, and it seemed increasingly urgent for me to get there ahead of the others and make the necessary investigations and make up for whatever was undone. I also would plead with Andreas that he would back me up and help me cover up the lies I had told the pilgrims, at least until I could make certain that they were satisfied with all that had been done and that they might possibly agree with my plans to establish that Christian and communitarian Eden I had been dreaming of.

During the first few days after our departure from Wattling we continued to have pleasant weather with a southwesterly breeze. We all reckoned that the short distance we still had to cover would not bring us any troubles.

But things were to turn out otherwise!

One night before dawn we noticed that the sea got rougher, and when I stepped up on deck I saw a cloudy sky and a dark sea, the waves running with white crests. We were sailing on a starboard tack, the sloop was pitching, and within an hour water was churning over the deck. Then something strange and sinister happened; we couldn't help looking upon it as a bad omen. A wave that poured across the deck brought with it something that was whiter than the foam, and when the breaker receded it had left a skeleton behind on deck; it lay bent around the mast, as if it were clinging to it. I won't be surprised if this sounds quite unbelievable, Anne. Still, I once read in an old ship's log that something similar once happened south of the Azores; the ship and the skipper were both Norwegian. I can't give you a good explanation for it, but if you recall what I've said before about plague ships, just imagine a dead man remaining on the deck of such an unmanned ship. Then the flesh will disintegrate and be washed away and only the naked carcass remains. It will be parched by the sun and the wind and the bones will be filled with air, and for a time the tendons will keep the bones together.

Should a wave wash the whole thing overboard, it will at least for a while float on the surface. But it is also possible that such a skeleton was swept away from a desolate beach.

In any case, the sight made us shudder, and some of the men wanted to throw the skeleton overboard. But Thomas Madland suggested that it be placed in a piece of canvas which thereupon was stitched together and a stone placed inside it so that it would sink to the bottom. We all agreed with him, and Cornelius Hersdal said, "If three shovels of earth are supposed to go with it, I'll be glad to give some of the soil I've brought from my own farm."

This surprised me a bit; for I knew that those who lean toward the Quaker views are opposed to rituals of any kind. Ole Hetletvedt read from the hymn book those Bible passages that are prescribed for burials. When he thereupon had sung a hymn about resting in the womb of the earth and the resurrection of the flesh, the skeleton was lowered into the sea on our lee side.

Thus it happened that a funeral was also held on board the *Restauration,* even though the pilgrims had not lost any of their own.

Still, that might very well have happened, since now one then another would take sick, so that the storm — it lasted for weeks with alternating force — was not the only hardship we had to endure.

The one who was stricken the hardest was Thomas Madland, and he never fully recovered. I am afraid that when he became the first Slooper to die the following year, it was caused by the illness he had contracted on board ship. It so happened that Thomas couldn't stand any kind of fruits and wouldn't eat any of the good things that we had brought on board at Madeira and Wattling. He did, however, have a fondness for peas and cabbage.

But it was very probable that he and others among us had been infected by some disease at Wattling; we suffered from diarrhea. But Thomas also began to vomit blood. We tried all kinds of remedies, but it was all in vain. We tried wormwood brandy as well as other medicines whose effect we surmised might be proportional to their power to burn our throats. Finally, Endre Dahl thought of crushing a piece of brick into a powder, and he mixed the powder into Madland's pea soup. After that there seemed to be some improvement.

But none of us were spared, and, as weak as we were, we used our last ounce of energy to get the sloop through the storm.

I must also mention still another vexation, which if it had taken place under different circumstances might not have caused such great inconvenience as it did. While we lay in port at Wattling, the children had been playing with the Negro children and had even visited them in their huts. Because of this they brought with them lice on board ship.

There were other uninvited guests on board, equally unwelcome — although one is loath to see them leave the ship. When the storm had been raging for about a week and we were exhausted and almost helpless, a big rat appeared one morning on deck. It ran back and forth and we tried to catch it. Finally, it did a balancing act on the bulwark, and with a leap that would do credit to a deer, it jumped overboard.

This would not have upset us but for the fact that right after that another one staged the very same scene, and then they came — at times two at a time, even three and four, and they ran wildly from stem to stern until some of them voluntarily sought death by drowning or were washed overboard by the waves. At last, an ancient beast, so big that it reminded one of a raccoon, yellow and tattered and without a tail, as if it had been injured in some way, dragged itself along the deck until it reached the rail on the lee side, where it in vain tried to jump up on the bulwark. I seized a wooden pail and threw it after the rat. Just then another breaker crashed down on the deck, and our last glimpse of the rat showed it riding astride the pail on the way to a watery grave.

This seemed the more ominous and sinister since we knew the proverb about rats always leaving a sinking ship. True, so far the storm had not been too violent, but when it turned much worse the following night, none of us were in a happy mood.

Martha Georgiana's little girl was suffering greatly from seasickness and the milk she was able to get down was constantly vomited up. Like many of the others, she in addition suffered from diarrhea, and for each day that passed she became more emaciated and gray.

"Is it far to the real America?" Martha Georgiana asked me. "Now it's not too far," I replied. "Do you think we might ask the first woman we meet in America to give Margaret some of her milk, for my milk is poisoned," she complained. "Your milk is not poisoned, Martha Georgiana," I told her; "but if you wish, I'll be able to get your child a wet nurse until you have regained your strength."

Then came the storm, the real storm. We were directly south of Cape Hatteras; with a fair wind we would have reached Norfolk, Virginia, in about twenty-four hours; that was the port where I had decided to go ashore.

But Fate had decided that I was to share even the final time of troubles with my shipmates.

During the entire wearying journey along the American coast we had had an unfavorable wind; first it blew constantly from the northwest, and then it suddenly started to blow from the northeast. As an additional danger, the ship was now forced in toward land. The coastal waters are shallow and a row of islands, even sandbanks, form an extended arch parallel to the shores of the continent. Hardly any other area along the eastern coast of the United States is as greatly feared, because this is the home of violent storms; this is where they originate, and this is where they return in a perpetual circular course. Many a ship's hull has been ground to pieces, many a mast has snapped, and many a soul has perished in the shipping lanes outside Cape Hatteras.

This holds true for the bigger ships. Imagine then our little vessel, so crowded with passengers that it made you think of the churchyard on a Sunday after the service.

Everyone had to go below deck, except the few who had a job to do. When we were children we had made bark boats and sent them on their way to sea; and we had never seen them again. In this terrible weather the *Restauration* was nothing but a chip of wood; the deck lay practically as often under water as did the keel. When the ship eventually lifted itself up on the crest of a wave, the bowsprit and the stem would point to the sky; it was as if the low-flying clouds were driving a wedge between the sky and the keel and set us on the course taken by the Flying Dutchman. It was hard to tell the ocean and the sky apart; we were standing in the churning spray, among flapping sails, with the breakers looming above us like curved knife blades, ripping and slashing us like an assailant who rips open a belly, and then letting us descend into the depths as when the gravedigger lifts his spade.

All movables on deck and everything that could be torn loose had long ago been swept overboard. The galley, the stove, all cooking utensils and dishes — they were all gone. The sailor at the helm had secured himself with ropes. With most of our sails trimmed we kept away from the shore; through the spray we could see the torn banners of our sails above us; and even though the sloop was a defiant standard bearer, it was now locked in a struggle against an enemy who has never shown mercy. Black from moisture, torn to pieces by the wind, the foresail was hanging like a plaintive missive addressed to the Almighty.

But every heart on board, including mine, also represented such a missive. Still, I continued to hold my own in the face of the accusations of my conscience; but aside from that, I did my duty, and perhaps more.

Below deck, most of the pilgrims lay almost unconscious, suffering from seasickness and exhaustion. Like driftwood, indifferent to life and death, they were tossed from one end of the deck to the other; no one knew any longer where his bunk was located, no one knew what was fore and aft. Chests and clothing — all their belongings — had been thrown helter-skelter; even the latrine had been knocked down, and the stench mixed with that of the vomit and all kinds of repulsive smells.

Many had been thrown against the ship's ribs or beams; they lay there with bloody faces; their eyes closed, their mouths twisted, and their lips pale. Some of them were still groping for a hand to hold on to. But in this wretchedness Martha Georgiana was still holding her child close to her; nor did I see any other mother who was so weak that she wasn't able to take care of her children.

The only ones, who in these circumstances, appeared least troubled were, strangely enough the two whose infirmities were evident to all: Elen Rossadal and Sara Larsdatter. Wherever possible they gave aid and succor: slaking someone's thirst; giving someone a blanket against the cold; bringing a child back to its parents.

Everyone was freezing, for our course was set toward the north, and autumn was approaching. It seemed as if the storm had come from the North Pole itself. If anyone still had strength enough to feel any anxiety or dread, they would have been even worse off than they were. The lethargy caused by the terrible storm thus turned out to be a boon, a gift of grace.

There is still another experience I have to tell you about, Anne. What I said before about the sail being like a missive spread out before the face of God is not something that I have invented after all these years. It was actually so; from where I was standing, tied with ropes to the helm and holding the ship to the wind, I felt it was just like that. Tired unto death, but still wide awake, I thought I saw a revelation: that the mast was like a growing tree rooted in the ship's bottom, its top finally reaching above the storm and the drifting clouds, into a clear and placid sky. And in just the same way that in my youth I had climbed up the shrouds on a ship, I rose up — even though I was still tied to the helm — to greater heights, and foam and spray shimmered under me; but then I suddenly saw a summery and sunny coast close by, mirrored in a sea without a ripple, and beyond it were white dunes and apple trees heavy with fruit and yellow corn fields. I recognized the beautiful New England landscape.

And when there was a break in the clouds — at dawn the following day — I once again set our course toward land, but encountered nothing but giant waves breaking against a flat and desolate shore. Once again I changed our course, holding the ship close-hauled against the wind.

Then Simon Lima, who had not been very sick, at least physically, although he was among the most anxious, cried as if beside himself, "We are corpses in a coffin, and this is the death of us all!"

Elen Rossadal answered him, also speaking as if she had had a revelation, "The breath of God is filling our sails, and angels are at the helm. The harbor lies ahead, and we will soon be saved!"

Seldom have words of comfort been spoken to hearts that had greater need of them. This was at midnight on a Friday. When Saturday dawned, the air was clear and the storm was abating. We took our bearings and judged by the coastline we could make out from our port side, that we were north of Virginia Beach, not far from the well-known Cape Henry, a point on the shipping lanes which lead in toward Norfolk.

Our calculations proved to be correct.

As for the other events of that day, I must mention that the wind steadily slackened — even though the waves still were quite huge — and the temperature was rising. As we once again appeared to approach safety and the people on board were filled with new hope, some of them gave themselves over to uncontrollable hilarity while others were overcome by the danger that they had passed through, so much so that to my ears it sounded as if they were raving. This was especially true of two of the smartest men on board; they were both peculiar in that they were easily influenced by all kinds of novel impulses; the two were Endre Dahl and Gudmund Haugaas. They both had become convinced that since the Lord had protected them against destruction, it had happened because He had selected us from among His entire creation. The pilgrims were indeed the kin of holy men; we belonged to the lost remnant of the ten tribes of Israel, and just as God in days of yore had led the Israelites across the Jordan, He would now lead a small remnant into the Canaan of the New Covenant, which was the United States of North America.

As we were nearing shore, Dahl and Haugaas seemed transfigured, holding each other by the hand, tears streaming down their cheeks. Gudmund Haugaas said, "Yes verily, I can recall the time of the patriarch Abraham! I can see the tribes, one generation following another, a thousand years of chastisement and of mercy!" And Endre Dahl added, "I too am one of the lost sheep that the Lord has found and led to Zion!" They embraced and then fell to their knees and praised the Lord Whom they called the God of Abraham, Isaac, and Jacob.

All this made a strange impression on me and probably on most of the others, and we feared that they had lost their minds. But they remained sensible in all other things; right after that Endre started to prepare the first meal in several days, and Gudmund helped him.

But these two were not the only ones who thanked the Lord. When our vessel early on a Sunday morning lay securely anchored in Norfolk harbor, we all gathered up on deck; the sea around was as blue as the sky above, with only tiny ripples in the surface of the water. As so often before, Ole Hetletvedt read from the Bible, this time about the Master Who was sleeping in His disciples' vessel on Lake Genesareth, and how He was awakened by them and that He had rebuked the wind and the waves — a comforting scene to seafarers down through the centuries.

It was suggested that we dispose of the ship and the cargo in Norfolk and that we all proceed by land to New York. But I advised strongly against it. And when the weather two days in a row remained pleasant with no wind, the captain, after consulting with the mate, decided that the voyage was to continue. They were of the opinion that the shipping lane would from now on be much safer and also that we now could much more easily reach harbor if new storms were to descend on us.

At any rate, the stage coach was the swiftest means of communication, and the whole flock agreed with me that it would be very useful if I went ahead by coach to prepare for their arrival as best I could.

We parted company, and the *Restauration* weighed anchor once again.

The Thirty-ninth Tale

There is nothing of importance to tell about my own journey by land; upon my arrival in New York I put up with some friends of mine,

The ship took several more days on this last part of the voyage than had been estimated, not because of bad weather, but because the aftermath of the storm brought with it a complete calm. While the ship held to its northward course they were seldom so far away from the coast that they couldn't see land on their port side, and since they spent a week and a half on the voyage they got a good impression of what this new land was like.

Most of the time they could see nothing but a flat shore, since they were now passing the long row of beaches which lie like a breakwater along much of the east coast of North America. The weather being so beautiful, they also maneuvered the sloop through one of the several inlets and proceeded across the bays that dented the coastline. In many places the scenery was so beautiful and the country seemed so fertile that they were overwhelmed by the sight. Small fishing villages alternated with cultivated land with orchards filled with fruits and berries, and fat cattle were grazing in the green meadows.

Wherever the pilgrims approached the native population they were met with great friendliness. When they passed a place called Beach Haven Inlet and dropped anchor in a nearby harbor — I think it was Little Egg Harbor or Parker's Cove — a man walked over to them and asked who they were. Lars Larsen tried to tell him, and when he finally understood that they had sailed from Europe in that little vessel — for he couldn't believe his own ears — he embraced those standing near him and told them that he was a direct descendant of one of the pioneers on the *Mayflower*. He immediately invited them to his house, and without further ado arranged a celebration, which was also attended by several of the neighboring families. The pilgrims were offered freshly baked bread and they could pick what they wanted from the fruit trees in the garden.

When they left the next day, the kind gentleman sent on board a good supply of milk, which they had sorely missed during the voyage, in addition to bread, apples, and pears. Since he knew the ship channel very well and had some business up north, he steered his own boat ahead of them and thus showed them the way through the narrow channel, inside the long narrow island known as Long Beach.

The air was warm, just like on a fine summery day in Norway; the leaves of the trees had been green where they had made their first land-fall, but as they sailed northward along the coasts of New Jersey the woods began to assume the red and golden colors of the fall, brighter and more glowing than the colors they were used to from their homeland. Reality did indeed match in every way the picture that I had drawn at the bimonthly assembly at Fogn. Filled with ever rising ex-pectations, they sailed up Lower Bay and could make out Long Island on their starboard side. They were approaching New York City.

The day was a Sunday, October 9th, and while the sun filtered its light through the crowns of the oak trees on Staten Island and a great peace descended on the surroundings, they continued up Lower Bay. They dropped anchor near The Narrows just when darkness set in. They went to sleep believing that all worries were past and had no inkl-ing of the troubles that were in store for them.

Before we dwell on these things, let me briefly mention a circumstance that I have just alluded to before, namely the fact that Cupid had not been inactive on board the *Restauration*. Thomas and Siri Madland's daughters were especially afflicted. It had finally become evident to all that Captain Helland had proposed to the oldest girl, Rachel, who was eighteen years old. But the fifteen-year-old Guri had not escaped either. When the sloop entered calm waters following the storm off Cape Hatteras, Gudmund Haugaas, in spite of his conviction that he was able to recall happenings as far back as Abraham, had become in-terested in more mundane things. The last night before the arrival in

New York he confided his feelings to Guri, and in spite of her tender age she too had been kissed before leaving shipboard. They were married less than nine months later. About the youngest one, Serena, who was only eleven years old, I can tell you that she later on became engaged to and married Jacob Andersen Slogvig.

I shall say no more about Cupid's doings, since the pilgrims soon had other things to think about.

Their first contact with American authorities took place at the quarantine station. I had prepared them for this, and on the last day at sea — north of Sandy Hook — they all washed thoroughly from head to foot. Then each and every one put on his Sunday best, and when the captain, on Monday morning the 10th of October, appeared with the entire group at the quarantine station, they were received in a very friendly manner. The officials were used to quite different conditions when people arrived from across the sea: not only would the newcomers be unkempt as a result of the long voyage, but they would also be very sick and emaciated.

But since the Sloopers, in contrast to most immigrants, had been sailing along the coast for some time and thus had been able to obtain food from shore, they were all more or less in good health. The public health officers complimented them on their appearance when they gave each one his prescribed bill of health.

But since they arrived on a day of rest, quite a lot of dirty laundry had been piling up. This was found by the health officers when they inspected the ship from top to bottom, and the pilgrims were then sent to a big floating jetty where they could wash their clothes. The women were busy at it until evening, and since a fresh breeze came up during the night, all the clothes were dry by the next morning; they were fluttering from the lines that had been tied between the ship's yard-arms.

They had already started to worry about their faithful Cleng Peerson not having shown up. But as you know, they were still outside the actual harbor area, and New York was even at that time a large city of 15,000 inhabitants, and the docks were spread throughout the city, even though the area around Battery Park on Manhattan was at that time, as it is today, the usual point of disembarkation. Incidentally, they were towed up to the Battery the following day. But they were to miss me even more when the customs and immigration officers came on board.

Certain circumstances connected with the ship made both its owners and the captain violators of American law, since they had infringed on a highly important paragraph of the navigation laws. According to this law, no ship arriving in the United States of America was allowed to carry more than two passengers for each five tons deadweight. Since the sloop was merely of 38 tons, it was only permitted to carry sixteen passengers at the most. Even though the crew was not counted, the number of passengers was no less than forty-five, three times the legal limit.

The law prescribed a 150-dollar fine for every passenger in excess of the limit, and if strictly calculated, it would add up to the considerable sum of 4,500 dollars. Bear in mind now, Anne, that the sloop itself had not cost them more than 1,800 dollars. And now the situation was such that if they were able to sell the ship for the same price that they had paid for it, and in addition all the bar iron — and they had planned to use this money to pay for their journey to Kendall and the new farmland — even if they were able to make a moderately favorable deal, they would nevertheless have incurred a huge debt and have nothing to pay for future expenses.

The customs officers did not have the authority to disregard the law, but since they were very kindly disposed toward our friends in distress, they stretched a point as far as they could. The chief customs officer very generously set the ship's tonnage at sixty tons and omitted to include Margaret Allen Larsdatter in the list of passengers. But even so, the fine would amount to much more than 3,000 dollars.

In the eyes of the law we were all guilty and could even have gone to jail. The captain was the one who would be held chiefly responsible, but the men who had been put down as co-owners of the ship also shared responsibility.

That night a meeting was held on board ship; people's hopefulness on approaching their destination had changed to worry, and no one could come forward with a workable solution; their only hope was that their faithful Cleng would soon show up. This was the first time that the captain and Johannes Stene uttered harsh words about him, and no one contradicted them.

Then came the worst of the evil days they were to experience in New York, October 12th. On that day an attorney by the name of Robert Tillotson, on behalf of the state of New York and all the other states, presented them with a document impounding the *Restauration* with its cargo and everything else that might be on board. He also asked that Captain Lars Olsen Helland be placed under arrest, and his request was immediately acted upon. I must here respectfully state that our

American authorities on this occasion showed themselves to be bigger boors than they usually are, something that I myself can testify to; for I arrived at the very moment that things looked most difficult for them.

But if they had any hopes that I knew how to straighten out this tangle, then they overestimated me. I must confess that I had not expected anything like this; that this time too everything turned out better than one might expect was partly due to luck and partly to the fact that in this strange country we had numerous friends. They came to our aid, and I was fortunate to be able to act as the intermediary.

But at the time I was told about these troubles, I had no idea how I should tackle the problem. So I spoke to them in the most cheerful way I could and told them not to worry about anything, prompted also by the fact that my pangs of conscience had not all abated during my stay in New York. Then Rachel Madland embraced me and called me her "wonderful Uncle Cleng"; she had been close to despair when her fiancé, Captain Helland, had been put in jail.

"Before the sun sets tomorrow night, Rachel, he will be a free man," I said. And as far as the 3,000-dollar fine was concerned, I assured them that the entire sum would be in the hands of the authorities in a very short time, and also that the confiscation of the *Restauration* with cargo and equipment would be rescinded within a few days.

This I promised without having any idea of how the matter was to be approached, but everything had a happy ending. And it happened in this way:

My good friend, the real estate agent Joseph Fellows, was visiting New York on business just at that time. He had been looking forward to meeting the pilgrims, since he knew about their expected arrival.

I looked him up, and when he heard about the pilgrims' straits, he immediately got in touch with one of the most affluent Quakers in the city, Mr. Francis Thompson, the founder of the well-known Black Ball Steamship Line. Mr. Thompson immediately produced a temporary payment of 600 dollars. This had the effect of releasing Captain Helland from jail at once. Joseph Fellows and I were present when he got out, and we drove in one of the city's most elegant horse-drawn carriages back to Battery Park where the sloop lay at anchor.

In the early evening, on Thursday the 13th of October, we boarded the *Restauration*. It had been a windy and cold day, with rain and hail. Just then the sun broke through the clouds, and it seemed as if the sky was on fire; its red glow also lent a reddish tinge to the deck and the many worried faces.

Although 600 dollars were obtained through Mr. Thompson, the sloop was still impounded, and the city authorities had told the pilgrims that they had to be off the ship by midnight. Thus, in spite of their joy at their captain being free, they were still in a very difficult situation; but I told them once again that they shouldn't worry: "Midnight is still six hours away, and before the clock in the church tower strikes twelve you will have places to stay overnight." Thereupon I began to ponder how I could possibly keep my promise.

I was convinced that my Quaker friends in the city would do their utmost to get the Sloopers roofs over their heads. But whether they would be able to receive such a large group without any forewarning was another matter. I also knew about a pretty good hotel for immigrants; it was located on Broad Street, but was usually packed with people.

We acted quickly. Joseph Fellows and I went to see the owner of the hotel; it was named after a Dutch pioneer, Edward Van Voorhis, who once had owned an inn located in that spot, during the time the city was still in the possession of the Dutch and was known as Nieuw Amsterdam. Edward Van Voorhis's son had built the hotel, a brick building, just as ugly as it was large, and now in a state of decay after many years of heavy use and the ravages of time.

When Joseph and I had figured out how many could be accommodated in the hotel, we then looked up some of the most wealthy among our Quaker friends and told them about the situation in which their fellow believers from a distant land found themselves. In brief: it took us exactly two hours to obtain lodgings for each and every one. We returned to the sloop with this good news before the clock had struck ten. The Friends were gathered on deck for a silent meeting during which they silently prayed to God Who had guided them across the sea. The Haugean Ole Hetletvedt was standing in the stem, apart from the others, praying loudly; the erect figure and the full beard reminded me of that servant of the Lord, Moses, as Holy Writ depicts him standing on the shore of the Red Sea. Both he and all the others were so transported by their devotions that they did not notice our arrival, nor were they aware of the large group of spectators who had gathered at the dockside; they all seemed to listen with evident astonishment to the strange language in which the prayers were made.

But, I, of course, understood every word, and it gave me a strange feeling to stand there carrying the answer to their prayers with me. Even before Ole Hetletvedt had finished his prayer, I shouted so that everyone could hear, "Friends, we were present here while you were praying! Before the Almighty stirred your hearts to ask Him for help, He was on the way Himself in order to fulfill your prayers."

The pilgrims had already made themselves ready to leave the ship, like the Israelites in days of yore; they had on their traveling attire, and they had brought chests and other belongings up on deck. And when I asked Ole Hetletvedt about that, he replied, "Since we didn't know what to do, we acted according to the command of the Lord, that when you pray for something, then believe that it already has been granted you."

I immediately got hold of four wagons, each drawn by two horses, and we loaded all the pilgrims' belongings on the wagons. The wagons drove off, and we all followed in a long line.

But as the pilgrims walked from Battery Park to Broad Street, they did not go unnoticed by the people in the street; crowds gathered on several street corners. For even though New York at that time was one of the important gateways for immigrants, it seldom happened that such a large flock of strangers passed through the streets of the city.

But the pilgrims themselves were not much aware of the attention they attracted; they were all filled with fervent joy and at the same time were fascinated by the life of the city: the bustling traffic, the magnificent buildings, the elegant ladies and gentlemen out for an evening stroll. Underneath their coats and shawls the ladies wore dresses that did not reach below the ankle, and underneath one could make out the sheen of white silk stockings. They wore tiny, light shoes fastened around the ankle with black ribbons — according to the fashion of the day — and they all carried silk parasols with thick handles. Most of the women wore so-called bonnets, while the gentlemen's hats were tall, black, and trimmed with fur, and the men themselves were dressed in black from head to foot with the exception of their neckwear, which consisted of stiff collars and satin neckerchiefs. Their coats were short but had long tails; their trousers hugged the legs and they were kept in place by straps underneath the high-heeled boots which were narrow and pointed. Many of the younger men were also twirling a black stick, and they all wore black goatskin gloves.

If one in addition considers the fact that the wide streets were brightly lit and that many of the buildings were several stories high, that bay windows and spires were seen everywhere, and through the open doors of boardinghouses and also more exclusive eating places one could hear gay music and laughter that mingled with the chiming of the bells from a church steeple, then it seemed to the pilgrims as if they had landed in a city that combined the wantonness of Sodom and the splendor of the New Jerusalem.

I myself walked at the head of the long line of immigrants, and whenever any of the spectators shouted some question at us, we all stopped and I answered so loudly that I could be heard on both sides of the street and even farther: "We are pioneers who have come from a country beyond the sea, and our intention is to seek happiness and prosperity over here and make your glorious country even more glorious! We will till the earth and build canals and steer the steamboats on the big rivers, and we will dig for copper and precious metals in the mountains of America!"

The crowd responded with great enthusiasm; they shouted back at us, "Good luck to you, brothers and sisters from a distant country! We wish you a warm welcome!" When I translated this for the pilgrims, some of them cried for joy.

Without anyone of us knowing it, Captain Helland had brought along a Norwegian flag; he lifted it up high, and it waved in the wind; and in the light from the numerous windows, open doors, and gas lights along the street its colors could be clearly seen. The spectators shouted, "What a beautiful flag! Perhaps our country could adopt it as its own now that its citizens come to live with us!" Another one said, "Perhaps your country would like to join our union and place a new star in our own flag?" I answered them, "Yes, we want to be a star both in your flag and in your nation!"

Thus it happened that as we approached Van Voorhis's hotel, a large crowd had joined us, so that the police were watching us attentively, although they had not interfered in any way.

As soon as we had spoken to the hotel owner, he spread an issue of *The New York Daily Advertiser* before us and said, "Are you the people who are mentioned in such a favorable manner in this newspaper?" And he showed me an article with the heading "A Novel Sight."

I shook my head since I didn't know that the New York press had been aware of the arrival of the pilgrims; but both Lars Larsen and the captain as well as Cornelius and Nils Hersdal and many others informed me that on October 10th a man calling himself a journalist and correspondent had visited the ship. They did not know the meaning of these words, but since they believed he had been sent by the authorities, Lars Larsen had acted as interpreter and had answered all his questions, and most of what he had learned was now printed in the city's newspaper.

Despite the fact that it was late evening and most of the pilgrims were tired following the many unexpected events of the day — great troubles and even greater joys — they asked me to be so kind as to translate for them what was printed in the newspaper. Since I have saved this issue all these years I can here put down the entire text for you, Anne, so that you also may derive pleasure from it and note the goodwill the pilgrims were met with in the New World:

"A vessel has arrived at this port with emigrants from Norway. The vessel is very small, measuring as we understand only about 360 Norwegian lasts or forty-five American tons, and brought forty-six passengers, male and female, all bound to Ontario county, where an agent, who came over some time since, purchased a tract of land. The appearance of such a party of strangers, coming from so distant a country and in a vessel of a size apparently ill calculated for a voyage across the Atlantic, could not but excite an unusual degree of interest. They have had a voyage of fourteen weeks and are all in good health and spirits. An enterprise like this argues a good deal of boldness in the master of the vessel as well as an adventurous spirit in the passengers, most of whom belong to families from the vicinity of a little town at the southwestern extremity of Norway, near Cape Stavanger. Those who came from the farms are dressed in coarse cloths of domestic manufacture, of a fashion different from the American, but those who inhabited the town wear calicos, ginghams and gay shawls, imported, we presume, from England. The vessel is built on the model common to fishing boats on that coast, with a single mast and topsail, sloop-rigged. She passed through the English channel and as far south as Madeira, where she stopped three or four days and then steered directly for New York, where she arrived with the addition of one passenger born on the way.

"It is the captain's intention to remain in this country, to sell his vessel and prepare himself to navigate our waters by entering the American Merchant Service and to learn the language."

Who were put up at the hotel, and who stayed overnight in private houses may be of little importance in this context; I do want to mention, though, that Martha Georgiana and Lars Larsen were guests in the house of the prosperous and pious Quakers Goddard and Lydia Glazer, and they later named one of their children after Mrs. Glazer.

The next morning I took most of the men along with me to Wall Street where all their Norwegian money was exchanged into American currency; it added up to merely a modest amount.

The most important task was yet to be taken care of. The ship had to be released from confiscation, since our future in the United States at that moment was dependent on one thing only: the sale of the ship and the cargo which was supposed to yield enough money for us to be able to establish ourselves as farmers in our new homeland.

408

The following day, October 14th, the case involving the *Restauration* came before the court for the first time. A judge by the name of William O. Van Ness presided. Mr. Francis Thompson and Joseph Fellows had written a petition on behalf of Captain Helland and the owners of the sloop, and it was presented to the court. The petition cited briefly my own connection with the case. Also included was the itinerary of the sloop, the circumstances that had led to the confiscation, and the fines that had been stipulated. It was also stated that the person on whose behalf the petition had been written had come to the United States in order to establish a settlement in one of the uncultivated areas within the borders of the state of New York, and it was very important for them to be able to resume their journey toward their final destination before the rivers were covered with ice and all traffic on the waterways would be impossible.

It had from the very beginning been our intention to go by steamer up the Hudson River to the capital, Albany, or to Troy, and to continue from there along the Erie Canal, which had just been completed but not yet officially opened.

In conclusion, the document stated that the only reason that the pilgrims had been fined was their complete ignorance of the laws of the United States. On that basis they asked that the ship be released and also that the fines that had been demanded and partly paid be waived.

The petition was passed on to higher officials and finally came to the attention of President John Quincy Adams in Washington. The document of acquittal was signed by the President himself and the Secretary of State, the date being November 15th, 1825, in the fiftieth year of the independence of the United States.

Until all this had been arranged, Lars Larsen, Johannes Stene, and Captain Helland, together with Rachel Madland, had to stay behind in New York. The latter two had decided to get married as early as possible.

All the others left New York, the day of departure being October 21st. On that day we boarded a Hudson River steamboat for Albany. Its speed was about six miles per hour, and this first part of our journey was estimated to take about twenty-four hours.

Epilogue

Next I shall tell about our departure from the big city and our journey to our final destination. However, I must add right here, Anne, that although the *Restauration* was released — as I have just told you — there were still many tasks facing the Sloopers. Neither the ship nor the cargo had been disposed of; and if our friends in New York hadn't supplied us with money and helped us generously in many other ways, we would have been in a very bad fix. It is possible that the pilgrims would have had to stay on in New York and would have had to live humbly on the charity of others until the end of winter.